# The Mysteries of Nuorg

Vincen headed directly for the Great Forest. How much time had elapsed since the last adventure started? Were things in the Great Forest just as they were before they left? Bubba had only noticed Mystic's missing Staff. Indeed, there were a lot of questions to be asked and answered, but time for that was not available. He flew to an area surrounding the once majestic dwelling in the center of the Great Forest. It sat just a little to the north of the main path. He noticed everything, other than the absence of his three fellow adventurers, was normal.

MessyHouse Publishing
Franklin, TN
2011

# The Mysteries of Nuorg

**Chris McCollum**

**This book is dedicated to**

*My indescribable wife,*
*Jeanne*

*And the two other greatest things*
*That ever happened to me,*

*Christopher and Madilynn*

*Who have put up with the*
*perpetual husband and father*
*in training...*

# 1

"Well Keeper, what do you think of that?" The old Eagle perched on a tall chair in the Keeper's enormous gathering room. As he awaited an answer, he quietly contemplated his feelings about the whole matter.

Hugoth smiled a great Bear smile before answering. He continued ambling to and fro, doing his best to tidy up the room after the exodus of the previous visitors. "I think it went fine, considering."

"I'll give you that. We were very fortunate to rid Nuorg of a major problem."

"Yes sir. That didn't happen a bit too soon. Although, his exit could have been painless for me had I removed him earlier. I'm afraid this shoulder pain will linger thanks to his attempt on my life."

"Tell me Hugoth, did that actually surprise you? Did you not think somewhere in that massive head of yours that he would very likely try to kill one or more of us? Pardon me for saying this, but I am glad it was you and not a weaker creature."

A small voice piped in from the window ledge where a marvelous little Hawk perched and listened. She was patiently waiting for her brother to return from a short errand. She tried to avoid interrupting the conversation, but could not help jumping in. "Excuse me, sir? Did you say kill one or more of us? And when were either of you going to let the rest of us in on this dangerous little secret?" She asked or rather demanded and she was more than a little bit agitated.

"Karri, before you get your red tail feathers in a snit, we don't think that he knew of your involvement in the entire scheme of things." The Eagle was not sure how the Hawk would reply to his reasoning. He was soon to find out.

Her lovely large eyes flared with the intensity of an exploding volcano. Her every feather stood angrily on end. "How dare you? You were not sure if he knew? You were not sure?" Each short question was bitterly spat from her delicate beak as if they were poison. Her small body angrily quivered. Immediately she closed the distance from her perch to a chair directly across from the elder Eagle with less than a flutter of her wings.

Again, she asked. "You were not sure? What then are you sure of?"

The Eagle was taken aback by the intensity of her tone. "Karri, Karri, please calm down. There is no need for that attitude right now!"

"If not now, then when? I sat back and observed like a gentle little lady just as you requested of me. Now, I don't think that persona is warranted any longer. Where is my brother? He needs to get here fast. I have a few revelations to make of my own!"

Hugoth could not remain silent any longer, "Karri, I personally guaranteed you and your brother's protection and I never had any intention of anything to the contrary happening. Now," his voice was becoming very intimidating, "Calm down at once. I will not have any of our group doubting any of our plans. Do you understand?"

The Eagle followed each of the participants with wide-eyed interest. He was not about to interrupt these two, not now.

Karri did not answer, nor did she calm down. She rudely turned away from Hugoth, ruffling her feathers and digging her talons deeper and deeper into the high back of the well-worn chair. "Ugh", she spat towards the wall, "What is it with you opposites?" Clearly, she was not calming down.

"Karri," Hugoth called. "Did you hear me?"

Nothing.

"Karri, Karri! Enough!" Hugoth nearly roared. "If I sensed that you were in any danger, I would have taken care of Charlie immediately. My feeling was that he was after me. I had our Eagle friend here occupy his time or else I would have dispatched him myself...way too early. Mystic did an excellent job of extending Charlie's stay until the Staff returned to fulfill its own brand of judgment. I do not need you flying off with that heated temper of yours. You kept it well hidden and I intend for you to continue doing the same until you really need it to power you to explode, understand?" No answer, "Karri Booth-Hewitt, do you understand me?" Hugoth had moved to within an eyelash of the Hawk. The moisture from his snout wetted Karri's feathers and, with each of his forceful breaths, he nearly blew the sky-traveler off of her perch.

Mystic looked on with a new appreciation for the leadership abilities of this huge Bear, not only was his size imposing, he also knew how to handle each individual on an intellectual level.

"Okay, fine, I have heard you, Hugoth. Now back away from me so I can see your eyes or, I promise I will bring a bleeding pain to your humongous snout you won't soon forget."

Hugoth backed away until he was staring a hole completely through the Hawk's beautifully feathered head. "That's more like it," he whispered.

The huge Bear turned toward the old Eagle, "I don't know if using these young ones is worth it Mystic. Why can't they just do what they are told and be done with it? They all have new ideas, new ways of doing things that have been done just fine for more years than I can count. Plus, they want to be involved in all the decision making as well. Is this how it will be in the days to come? Oh please tell me it won't be. Things are about to get bad out there. Will it really be necessary to involve them in every strategic detail?"

The Eagle smiled as well as sky-travelers can, "Yes Hugoth. Yes to everything."

Karri had finally heard enough. She jumped off the chair, landed on Hugoth's massive snout, jabbed her sharp beak at his tender nose and brought forth a steady trickle of blood. "Did you hear him Hugoth? He said yes to everything! Opposites, ugh."

Mystic the Eagle chuckled at the humorous sight before him.

"Well I certainly didn't expect that kind of an adventure. When Vincen called us together I was thinking maybe a nice little picnic, what about you?" Lightning, the irregular Badger was asking the question to a much smaller four-legger, his friend Bubanche, the Cheetah.

"I'll have to say, it caught me by surprise too, Lightning." The Cheetah turned to a large grey Wolf standing close by. "How about you Mystic? Did you have any idea while you were dipping your nose in that puddle of water that we would be summoned to save our lands from some terrible threat that only a few of us even know about?"

"Bubba, I have to agree with you. I had no idea. Not even a tiny inkling of the idea. I was just entranced and maybe too curious."

"Well you know what they say Mystic, curiosity kills the Cat, maybe not the Wolf." Lightning cheerfully elbowed the little Cheetah to the ground. "Oh, sorry about that, Bubba."

The Cheetah just rolled his big eyes at Lightning and then stared off into the distance.

A very rare sight, to say the least, was heading back with the band of four-leggers. Two-leggers had not been welcome in the Great Forest for as long as any of these three could remember. But sure enough, not only was one about to enter the Great Forest, he was also becoming a close friend. Frederick Mounte had proven his worth during the Nuorg adventure and was sent back with the others to the Great Forest. He was instructed to continue lending his support and accumulated wisdom to any upcoming adventures. He was not necessarily the bossy type, so he politely brought the others back to reality. "Sorry to break up this little rest session of yours, but we have a lot of work to do. Where is the Great Forest and how far to your dwellings?"

"Oh sorry Frederick", answered Mystic, "I guess you're right. We need to get moving."

Bubba quizzed the others, "Does anyone have any idea how long we've been gone from here?"

Mystic shook his head, "I certainly don't. We won't know until we get back home. Once there, we'll ask around. The answer may surprise us...who knows?" He nodded to Lightning. "Lead the way."

"With pleasure Prince Mystic."

"You know," mused Mystic, "I kind of like the sound of that."

Lightning picked up his large ax-pike, Bubba handed his rapier to Frederick and Mystic gripped the Staff between his strong jaws. Frederick slid the rapier into his bag. He placed it beside maps, notes and everything else he brought with him. The leggers looked none the worse for wear; still, they were a rag-tag looking bunch of characters. They set off in the direction they believed would get them back where they belong. The Great Forest was not that far away and the sooner they got there, the better they would feel.

Frederick was the first to ask, "Where is Vincen?"

Bubba answered matter-of-factly, "Oh, I am sure he is watching us. There's no need worry Frederick. He will get wherever we are going before we do. He just has that way about him."

***

From his perch, Vincen had been watching. He was watching the small group heading for the Great Forest and he was watching over the mountain trying to comprehend what was about to happen. He figured whatever trouble was coming would have to come from over the mountain. He couldn't see it any other way. He correctly surmised that worrying would not help anything right now, so he took wing for the dwelling places. With age, his emotions were becoming more visible. He wanted the tears to stop before the others saw him and he certainly needed rest before they arrived. Furthermore, what was coming was not to be toyed with and his young friends may be in completely over their heads.

***

As the leggers continued their walk to the edge of the thicket which eventually led to the Great Forest, a steady rain began to fall.

Menacingly dark clouds gathered above them. Whether a foreboding sign of the future or just a seasonal shower, to each of the leggers these particular rain drops felt unusually cold and discomforting. The group walked in silence with enormous burdens beginning to weigh heavily on each pair of strong shoulders. The rain fell harder.

Frederick gathered his long, curly hair tightly behind his head and wrapped a string around it. He pulled up the warm hood of his long black coat, tucked his bag full of information inside the somewhat weather-proof garment before firmly wrapping his arms around his chest. His eyes stared straight ahead as Lightning continued to lead the way. As the unforgiving rain dripped off the front of his hood, a circling wind blew the stray drops back into his face. The more he thought about their predicament, the colder each drop felt. He muttered to himself, "I know there is good in this world and I hope that the one in charge of it sees fit to lend us all of the help we are going to need."

Bubba was walking tucked up to Frederick's side and overheard his plea. The young Cheetah cocked his head up, squinted his top eye to divert the streaming rain and replied to the two-legger, "Frederick, I do too."

Mystic walked alone at the rear of the group. He held the Staff firmly in his jaws. He could not afford any accident with it from now on. No creature he had ever known possessed so much power for good or evil as he did right now. The Staff was amazingly powerful and he correctly guessed they had just barely tapped its potential. He was not going to voluntarily release it to any creature who had not been in the cave under the Forever Trees when it showed itself the last time. He followed behind the others as the rain completely drenched his shiny, grey coat of fur. At least the globe was not glowing. As of now, everything seemed to be getting back to normal. The Wolf was glad of that.

"Mystic," called the deep, strong voice of the irregular Badger as he turned his large frame around to summon the Wolf, "Come up here and tell me if there is a better way through this painful thicket than the one Bubba and I took getting in here!"

Mystic broke into a trot. He arrived at Lightning's side as the larger four-legger pulled to a stop in front of a treacherous looking wall of thorny, spiny scrubs and hideously mangled trees with low mal-formed branches that almost scraped the ground. The wall dared any creature to try and pass through its thick maze of tangles. "Is this where you two broke through?"

"Well, I'm not sure. We were in such a hurry to get to you that I can't remember what course we actually took. Bubba, do you?"

"No, I'm sorry. I can't remember the exact spot either...especially in this downpour." Bubba shook the rain from his face, "All I know is we were in a very big hurry. We could have come through this mess anywhere along this tree line. What I do know is that it was not a very comfortable passage."

"Agreed. Where is Vincen? He could at least give us a sky-traveler's opinion whether there is an easier entrance or not."

Frederick stared blankly at the thick under growth. Not having an opinion on the matter, he just wanted to get somewhere dry. The collection of information regarding the Staff and its ever increasing number of secrets needed his attention more than the thicket did. He felt a twinge as the hairs on his neck stood on end. He jerked his head up, even through the drenching rain he could make out a large flying object. Was it Vincen? "Hey, what is that?" Frederick got the others' attention and anxiously pointed toward the object in the sky. "Well, who or what is that?"

Lightning was the first to respond, "It's not Vincen. That winger is flying much too high. I have never known an Eagle to fly that high before."

Mystic chimed in, "Lightning is correct. That is not Vincen, but I hope he might know who it is!"

Bubba did not seem too concerned about the sky-traveler. He was now staring directly at the globe on the Staff and much to his relief, it was not glowing. "Look, look at the Staff. It's not glowing. If it were glowing, I would be on the other side of this impenetrable wall here, but it is not, so I am still here with all of you."

"I'll have to agree with you, little Cat." Frederick was also staring at the globe.

The oversized Badger was not as easily calmed. "Well, I can see the Staff is not glowing, but I still want to know who that is and why is he here. I will make that my job to find out. Okay, as long as he's up there we can't worry. Let's spread out...we need to get through here. Each of us needs to look for an easier entrance into this thing. When you find an opening that is more, well...open, call the rest of us. We have work to do."

7

The branchy wall was so thick that discovering an opening, even a small one, was a daunting task. Each four-legger looked for openings that would accommodate their particular stature. It was quickly decided amongst them to just find any opening, large or small. They would cut their way through if necessary.

Lightning found a gap between two decaying willow trees he could possibly squeeze through. He felt good about it and called to the others. "I think I've found a way through. Let's go."

The group quickly gathered near Lightning as the rain became even more of a deluge. The Badger was pointing his ax-pike at the gap between the willow trees. "We go through there. Me first." Lightning took a deep breath and exhaled completely. His intention was to make himself thinner in order to stuff his body through the smallish opening. Before he had to inhale another breath, Lightning again pointed the ax-pike toward his target. With a thunderous rush, he charged toward the two helpless willows. Just as he approached the opening, he turned his body sideways and lunged through the opening. He almost succeeded. He bumped hard against the right tree, which left him gasping for breath. He involuntarily gulped down an enormous breath of air that re-inflated his torso. Now he was too big to fit. Before he became completely stuck, he pushed back on both trees with all of his strength and barely managed an escape back to the others. "Hmmph," he shrugged. "One more time then." This time he took a deeper breath and blew the air out of his lungs until he almost fainted. Again pointing his ax-pike where he wanted to go, he reaffirmed his intent to all. "Here we go!"

Again he charged. This time he was able to stuff his immense girth completely into the opening and was pleased when he popped through to the other side, only to find himself looking at more of the same thicket. This was not going to work. Mystic crawled through with no problem, followed by Frederick and Bubba. Now they were all inside the front wall of the thicket with nowhere to go. "Excuse me please. I have to get back out of here -- quickly." Lightning took another deep breath and blew it out to the fullest extent possible. After closing his eyes and wishing himself the best, he aimed his ax-pike just as before and literally burst back through the opening to the other side. Thankful to be back out in the open clearing he breathed a loud sigh of relief.

"Whew!" Again he was followed by the other three.

Bubba hurriedly scanned their new position while circling the group. "I got bad news," Bubba called out with rain water streaming down his snout. "We are not where we were before we went through those willow trees."

"Uh uh, are you trying to humor me at a most inconvenient time," answered the not so sure Badger. "We have to be exactly where we were because all we did was (and he swung his ax-pike for demonstrative reasons) squeeze through there, wait a partial click, then squeeze back through there!" Lightning immediately took on a confused look. Again, he pointed his ax-pike in the same directions trying to convince himself of what he thought was so. "There and there."

"Uh," Mystic dropped the Staff from his mouth. "I don't think we are either, Lightning." Mystic was just as puzzled by the new surroundings as the Cheetah.

Frederick glanced around with a completely confounded look of his own. With a twinkle in his eyes, he chimed, "I don't know what it is with you creatures, but we need to talk..."

Bubba could not help himself, "Okay, so you pointed your ax-pike in the same direction two times? Back to back. You didn't turn around or use your other arm. Right? So, we may actually be twice as deep into the thicket or not in the thicket at all."

"What?" Mystic asked with a look that could not be explained on his face.

"Well, I'm just saying that we may have traveled in the same direction twice rather that turning around and coming back to where we were."

Lightning was still replaying the paths taken with even more demonstrative waving of his ax-pike for no creature's benefit but his own.

Frederick dropped his chin and rubbed the sides of his head with the heels of his hands. He couldn't help but chuckle. "Yes, we have to talk, but now we have to get out of this rain."

"And where might we do that two-legger?" asked Mystic with one large paw securing the Staff to the ground.

Frederick raised a hand to his left and pointed, "There."

The rain had let up for the moment, giving Frederick time to scan their position. A hooded outcrop of trees about 50 two-legger strides away beckoned to them. The tree's top branches had leaves that grew so intertwined that water gave up trying to seep through them and took a more lazy approach, flowing down across the curvature of branches and off the low side. The high side faced them, mimicking the look of an open sky-travelers beak. Frederick led the way this time and made quick work of getting beneath the overhang. Their new shelter was large enough to easily welcome a group of 30 or more creatures of various sizes. From the current state of the area, they could tell no creature had frequented there for some time. At this point, that did not matter. Water was not pouring through, it was spacious and, for the time being, it was dry. Those points were reasons enough to relax and give each of them sufficient time to dry out. Frederick welcomed each in with a polite wave of his hand. "Welcome wet travelers. May I suggest that each of you four-leggers shake the water out of your fur on the far sides of this shelter? Once you have shaken dry, only then will I attempt to remove my coat."

Mystic granted the two-legger's request. The great Wolf placed the Staff in Frederick's open hand before heading to the left side to shake himself off. Bubba followed and finally Lightning, still swinging his ax-pike in an apparent attempt to reverse the last few directions they had taken. Water was violently hurled in every direction as each four-legger shook every hair on their body vigorously until their fur was only slightly damp. They paraded back to Frederick like three puffed up, creature shaped clouds. The two-legger laughed a long, necessary laugh. He handed the Staff back to Mystic and stated, "You creatures may well be my friends, still, you all look hilarious and reek of wet Dogs!" He pulled back his hood, shook out his hair, unfastened his coat and hung it on a tree limb to dry. The bag full of Staff secrets was dry and safe.

No one knew how long they had been awake. The last time they slept was in Nuorg and that was some time ago. The return back to their homeland and subsequent journey had left them all visibly drained. Frederick sat near a small tree in the rear of the shelter with the bag in his lap. Bubba positioned himself at the foot of Frederick. Mystic lay to the side of Bubba with both front paws and his head on top of the Staff. When Lightning eventually set his ax-pike down, he placed himself next to Frederick and blocked the three smaller creatures from the open side of the make-shift dwelling. They talked no more that night. Each went to sleep with several thoughts racing through their head. The sun would rise soon enough; now, they needed rest.

***

Frederick was the first to awake. The rain had stopped during the night, leaving a fresh crease in the air. Those at his side, not smelling so fresh, were completely lost in deep sleep, their thick fur still drying from their trek in the deluge. Their previous adventure had taken a physical toll on their bodies that was only now showing itself. Frederick had not experienced their entire adventure, since they came to him and not vice-versa. He rubbed the sleep from his eyes then exhaled a large morning breath. He stretched his arms wide as he pushed himself into a standing position with the help of Lightning's extra large mass of muscle, flesh and fur. As soon as he stood, he noticed something wasn't right. He tried to keep silent and step around the sleeping Cheetah at his feet, but something happened. His feet were hopelessly fastened together. He went spinning and sprawling over Bubba. He momentarily righted himself, but soon continued hopelessly hopping across the ground. He eventually lost his balance for good, let out a gasp and hit the earth hard. Wheezing a loud moan, he glared at his feet to see what was binding them. A shiny, long rapier blade was sticking completely through both of his ankles to the hilt, the thin blade catching glimmers of sunlight. His mind was telling him he should be writhing in pain. He was not. Surprisingly, he felt no pain what so ever. Frederick pulled his knees up, bringing the rapier's handle within reach of his hands. Grimacing from the unknown, he delicately tugged on the rapier. The blade slid painlessly from his ankles. This was peculiar. He shoved himself off the ground with his good arm, wincing as the pain in his swollen elbow reminded him it was there and worse for wear. Frederick took the rapier in his hand and raised it high. He asked of it, "What other secrets do you hide within your slender shiny self, little sword?"

Frederick strolled under the canopy holding the rapier aloft as if asking it to guide him. Suddenly, he turned the rapier on himself and jabbed it through his thigh. No pain. No blood. No sensation that anything out of the ordinary had happened. He pulled it out of his thigh and stuck it through his side, again nothing. He raced over to the sleeping hulk that was Lightning and fiercely jabbed the sharp blade into one of the massive tree trunk legs of the four-legger. Not

11

even a whimper escaped the sleeping beast. He tried the same stunt on Mystic, right through his front paw. Again...nothing. Frederick smiled to himself, "I may as well have a little fun with the Cat." He quietly stepped to the front of Bubba. He gently slid the rapier through the little four-legger's paw and into the ground as deeply as he could without waking the Cheetah. "This is truly an amazing weapon," he whispered to himself. The two-legger picked up his bag, walked to the edge of the shelter, sat down and jotted some new notes. Soon the others would be awake and he could share this new bit of information with them. He smiled and got back to his business.

\*\*\*

*An amazing morning yesterday. My stay in the land of Nuorg temporarily ended when my new friends and I were sent back up on a mission to repel the harbingers that threaten a return of the "Terrible Years". As I have written here before, the last several years have been lonely. I have spent much of my time soul-searching, longing for forgiveness for my unintentional involvement in the killing of the Great Wolf's kind. Had I known on that day what I know of things now past, obviously there would have been a very different timeline. Here I sit, sharing a short respite of solitude with my thoughts and writings. Some day, I hope to return to the pages written since my chance meeting with the Cheetah, just to relive the partially unexplainable coincidences once again. Amazing. Such an odd lot of characters. I just now experimented with the Cheetah. It will be interesting to see what happens when he awakes. It seems the rapier this young Cat has carried around for years is akin to the "Staff of Hewitt" in that it seems to have its own personality as well as hidden secrets. This very morning I awoke to find it stuck entirely through both of my ankles, yet I experienced no pain or sensation of its being there. Odd? Yes, one would think so. I removed it with ease then proceeded to poke it through my other limbs with the same effect. No feeling or sensation of its penetration through flesh, muscle, or bones. I slid in through my cohorts' limbs as easily as my own. Not even a slight gasp escaped their snouts. It is now pinning the Cat's paws to the ground. When he wakes from a much-needed, good night's sleep, there should be quite a ruckus, I suppose. Hah! I forgot how much I enjoy company, albeit company of the animal kind or as they describe themselves; four-leggers. Talkers, I have come to notice, are the only humans these creatures will trust. It was uncomforting to meet the Talker in Nuorg who turned out to be very bad indeed. Where did he come from? Where did he get the ability to "Talk" to the four-leggers and sky-travelers, another description taken from their vocabulary. Was it a trick of some kind? What separates the good Talkers from the bad? That may prove a downfall of the blessing. Back to the Cheetah's rapier, can an inanimate object go through a purification process as did the living creatures? It had just been used in an attempt to kill one of our group, very nearly succeeding, just before the ancient Eagle demanded for the Wolf to roll the globe. Our group emerged unscathed, but "Charlie", the other Talker, was entrapped inside the thing. The rapier survived to lie glistening on the floor. Was it, as I said, also purified or did it pass the purified test? In doing so was it bestowed with its own power? I have so many questions. Even the strange ax-pike carried around by our largest friend seems to have been bestowed some kind of energy or power. The ax-pike, much to the chagrin of Lightning, has taken us to a place none of us are familiar with. We were looking for a gate to get back to the Great Forest. We thought we had found one. We passed through only to find ourselves in a tight spot with no way out except for the same opening through which we entered. Lightning pointed the ax-pike back toward the opening, we crawled through it and here we are. Not in the clearing from whence we came, but in a clearing somewhat different. Well if it all be known, it is much different. The mountains that we were facing are not here. I can not find them anymore. Mountains just do not disappear. Do they? The four-leggers have not noticed the mountains' absence yet. When they awake, we will need to discuss it. This land where we are now is not menacing, just not where I was expecting us to be. This is not the Great Forest. I can't help but wonder, if the strange tool of Lightning's does take us to different places, does it take us where we want to go or does it take us where we need to go? I must wake the others. 'Til next time...*

***

Mystic was the first four-legger to wake. The first thing he noticed was Frederick's absence. The second thing he noticed was the rapier pinning Bubba's paw to the ground. He was instantly on his feet and heading for the blade's handle. Just as he was preparing to wrest the blade from his dear friend's ankles, a realization hit him. How could Bubba continue to sleep through this impalement unless he was feeling no pain? Instead of rescuing the Cat, Mystic did his best to rouse Lightning from his sound slumber. If Lightning would wake in time, the show would be much more enjoyable.

Frederick returned as Mystic was prodding and poking the Badger. "So you discovered the trick of the rapier, eh?"

"How did you find out about that?" Mystic asked.

"Oh it wasn't difficult really. When I woke up this morning, it was binding my feet. They was no blood, no pain...no discomfort of any kind, so I experimented on the three of you. I was a swordsman run amok. I pierced your legs, back, neck, chest, and nothing! It was as if I never wielded a weapon at all. I pinned Bubba's paws to the ground to see what kind of reaction we would get from him. At times, what he says makes me wonder if he is the youngest after all. Then, there are times when it's obvious he is."

"You really ran that blade through us all? I never felt anything."

"Yes, I really did. I hope you will forgive me, but I had to know. Once Bubba wakes, we will discuss this and a few other things that I think are very important."

"So be it two-legger. If you would be so kind, will you help me wake this sleeping giant?"

"Absolutely, Prince Mystic."

"Thank you." Mystic laughed at himself, "Prince Mystic...that rolls off the tongue nicely, does it not?"

Frederick agreed, "That it does my friend. It certainly does."

"Wake up you slumbering creature. It's a new day. Let's move!"

"Ahhhhhhhhhh!"

Mystic cut his eyes at Frederick then they both shot glances at Bubba. The Cat was in a fit of turmoil.

"What have you done? Why me? Why did you stab me with my own sword?" Bubba was beside himself.

Mystic gave up trying to wake Lightning. He turned his full attention to Bubba. The Cheetah was madly hopping around as if he was experiencing great pain. "What have you done? What did I do to deserve this?" The ranting questions went on and on.

Frederick reached out to Bubba. "Calm down. Do you feel any pain in your legs? Do you see any blood? Are you dying? Think about it. I want you to stop hopping around before you hurt yourself or one of us!"

Bubba could not concentrate. "What are you talking about? One of you three stabbed me!"

Bubba, bordering on mild insanity, stumbled on a large rock and crashed to the ground. Before he could raise himself again, Frederick raced to his side and effortlessly removed the rapier. "Can you settle down now?"

"Oh. That was it?" Bubba was mystified.

"Yes my friend...that was it."

"Hmmm...interesting. Now explain it please."

Frederick sat down near the still-sleeping Lightning and, in clear sight of both Mystic and Bubba, pushed the rapier blade completely through his leg. To the pair he added, "This phenomenon is very strange, is it not?"

"I have never seen anything like this. Never in my short life have I even heard of such a thing. The world of two-leggers is a very strange world. How many more secrets do you have?" Bubba was not only curious, he was becoming angry. "Why couldn't the two worlds just stay separated? I don't think I want any part of this anymore. This goes against everything I know." Bubba grimaced and let out a long, disgruntled breath. He stared at Mystic, then Frederick before turning away and leaving them. "I am going to have to reevaluate my role in this adventure. Staffs that purge people into evil balls of light, axes that take us places we don't want to be, blades that cut at one time-don't cut the next time, hidden wells that spring from nowhere, water that won't drown you...what is next? I would rather just go home."

"Bubba certainly brings up some interesting facts, Frederick." It was now Mystic's turn to speak. "What could all of this mean? Who is doing this and what kind of minds were at work when all of this began? What did he mean when he said axes that take us where we don't want to be? Wait...where we don't want to be? Where are we now?"

Bubba spoke from the other side of the shelter. "When we went through the gap in the trees the second time, we ended up here. Surely, Mystic...surely you can surmise that we are not in the Great Forest! We have obviously been transported somewhere else by some purified object where we can't feel safe again. Frederick, any guesses?" Bubba was angry and frustrated yet he still had a keen sense of everything going on about him--even if he never mentioned it to anyone. "Did neither of you think about it? If the Staff can do strange things, why can't our other inanimate objects? They witnessed the same purification process we did. Can they now be living lifeless lives? I think Frederick's bag may have a crucial part in our adventures from now on. Will we reach a point where these enlivened objects take on adventures of their own? A time when we can just sit around in a cozy little circle eating bark kakes while our tools go fight our battles? Someone, anyone, please...speak up."

Mystic and Frederick simply looked at each other in surprise. Where had that come from? What was Bubba trying to rationalize now? They sat alone together to ponder Bubba's statements. Lightning rolled over and began to snore.

## 3

Vincen headed directly for the Great Forest. How much time had elapsed since the last adventure started? Were things in the Great Forest just as they were before they left? Bubba had only noticed Mystic's missing Staff. Indeed, there were a lot of questions to be asked and answered, but time for that was not available. He flew to an area surrounding the once majestic dwelling in the center of the Great Forest. It sat just a little to the north of the main path. He noticed everything, other than the absence of his three fellow adventurers, was normal.

He lit on a low hanging branch overlooking a small garden tended to by a group of smallish but determined furry four-leggers. Each had a white stripe running down the entire lengths of their dark-brown, furry bodies with thicker stripes on each side of pointed noses. Uncharacteristically large front paws with sharp, curved claws furiously attacked clumps of unwanted weeds. There were five individual leggers of this type in varying sizes, working diligently as a team. The largest of the group raised her head toward Vincen before she knew he was there. She was startled at first.

"Why, a good day to you there Vincen," she called. "I trust you have seen that son of mine somewhere along your route this morning? I am sure he is probably running with the Cat today. Quite a pair, those two. Have you seen Mystic? I have a few ideas I need to talk over with him. I think it is about time that he put some work into that dwelling of his. It's beginning to look very worn-down. It was such a beautiful thing once."

The remaining four-leggers slowed their work slightly as they turned to listen in on the one-sided conversation between their mother and the Eagle. They too were wondering as to the whereabouts of their brother. He could perform the same amount of work with one swipe of a single paw as they could all do working feverishly together.

Vincen wasn't sure how he should answer her questions or in what order. Had she already seen Lightning this morning? He decided to answer her first question with a question, "When did you see him last?"

"Let me see...when did he leave his den? He was headed out early toward the fort. He had his sack of food with him. I figured he would be gone for a while. He needs to get back soon. We have a lot of work to do here."

"You have seen him already this morning? Really?" Vincen warily asked in return.

"Actually Vincen...no, I am confused and worried. We have not seen him in a few day-rounds. Normally that would not bother me, but since you are here speaking with me and not out trekking with him, I'm afraid I let the time slip my mind. He left...oh when did he leave?"

Another of the furry creatures ceased his weeding chores to join in on the conversation. "It was five day-rounds ago, Vincen. Like Hazzel mentioned, we were not that concerned until we noticed that you were here and not with our son and Bubba. Is Mystic with them? Why are you asking us where he is when normally we are asking you?"

Vincen felt stalemated. "I am curious. I have been with all three of them today. I left them earlier to fly back, but now it seems they have taken a detour. I thought they would be coming directly back. We had quite an adventure. They should be here soon."

Hazzel and the other four- legger stopped weeding entirely. They scurried closer to Vincen and looked up. Even the low hanging branch was too high for them. "We wish you would come down here to chat with us, Vincen. Our necks begin to ache if we look up in the trees for these extended conversations. It would please us if you would come down here."

Vincen's mind was spinning. How many questions did they have? How many of those questions should he answer? He was hoping the questions would not require detailed answers. He immediately hopped off his perch and lightly set down at their noses. "How can I be of service to my favorite pair of Badgers?" He hoped he could throw them off track.

"Vincen, you are so cunning. That is not what you should be asking. Let us ask the first questions. Where is Lightning?" Then the

18

questions were asked in quick succession by both of Lightning's parents.

"Where is Bubba?"

"Where is Mystic?"

"Were you with them?"

"How come you came back and they did not?"

"Where did they wander off to this time?"

"When will they be returning?"

"We heard Bubba came running through here in a panic, then left just as quickly toting Lightning's ax-pike with him. What was that about?"

"Why did Mystic act so strange that morning?"

"What is going on, Vincen? We need to know!"

Vincen imagined this is where the meaning of badgering came from. These four-leggers wanted answers. Vincen glanced around. He noticed the other Badgers had returned to their chores. He asked, "Can we step into Lightning's quarters to continue this conversation?"

The Badgers looked at each other. "Sure Vincen. Why? Is there something wrong that his siblings should not hear?" Hazzel was now concerned for her youngest son. "Is Lightning alright?"

"Yes. When I left him, he was never better. We had ourselves a nice little adventure."

"Good. Then where is he?" Lightning's father had inherited some of the worrisome nature of his ancestors. He could not help it. In his heart, he knew Lightning could survive anywhere, especially if there were ample food sources to feed his bottomless appetite.

"Just a moment. I'll try to answer all of your questions as soon as we step in here." Vincen knew where he had left them, but had no idea why they were not back already.

***

"I have no idea where we are." Frederick continued to experiment with the rapier while Bubba and Mystic milled around the sleeping Lightning, scanning the landscape, struggling to come to terms with where they were now. "All I can assume is that we are where we are supposed to be. I've been thinking about it all morning and I am in agreement with Bubba. Everything that witnesses the globe's purging or purificating, if you will, is somehow able to take an active part in this journey we have thrust upon us. My bag? I'm sure it has some role to play in a yet unknown way. Lightning's axe or ax-pike or whatever you want to call it opens doors for us, on its own mind you, obviously to places it feels we need to be. I'm sure it has no rational thinking in the matter, but is simply another tool used by whomever or whatever is spinning this yarn. I can't say for certain if that particular entity is a thing at all; maybe it is destiny."

"Yes, destiny. A notion often discussed by my family." Bubba settled down and was lying a short distance in front of Frederick, stretching every tight muscle in his lithe body. "I need to run. Can't we figure out what we need to do and get on with it?"

"Well, am I still the leader of this group or is it the ax-pike of the sleeping mountain over here?" Mystic was standing in front of their snoring friend, glaring into Lightning's closed eyes from no more than an eyelash away. "How can he sleep so soundly at a time like this?"

Frederick smiled as he got to his feet. He walked over to Mystic's side to join the stare-down. "Mystic, of course you are still in charge. You were selected by the Staff. I don't believe the Staff has a mind of its own either, but I can't worry about that right now." He was glaring into the eyelids of Lightning, awaiting their awakening. "What do you want to do now? Myself, I think we need to find out where we are."

Bubba jumped off the floor. "You two wait here with him. I'm going on a run. Maybe I will see something familiar. If I don't? Then, we are really no worse for wear."

Mystic nodded in agreement. "Do as you wish. Please don't run too fast. If something is watching, I would hate to expose one of this group's greatest assets."

"You shouldn't worry about that Mystic. I will be back." Bubba crept over to the edge of the shelter. He scanned the surrounding area for cover. There was none. Wherever he went he would be in broad sight of anything or everything around them. He turned to Mystic. "Leggers, we are right out in the open. Where is the hedge row we came through? I can't see anything but wide open fields. I'll find something."

Bubba quickly took off at only a fraction of his speed. He was out of sight before they realized he was gone.

Frederick raised his eyes from Lightning to watch Bubba fade into the distance. "Mystic, how fast is he?"

Mystic kept his eyes focused on Lightning, "I don't really know. Every time he runs, he gets faster. Vincen can't keep up with him anymore."

"Mystic, now that you mention Vincen, where is he? I have not seen or heard him since we re-emerged. Did he happen to follow us?"

Lightning stirred. His eyes opened to see the Wolf's eyes staring a hole through him.

"Good morning, Lightning."

"Mystic, great Prince, I have felt your eyes on me since I heard you walk over. A stealthy one you are not. What do you mean we are not where we want to be? This place needs to be the Great Forest. I need to get back to my dwelling. My family will not be happy with me, I'm afraid, if I ever do get back." Lightning stretched his thick neck to the light peeking around the leafy roof. "Where is the mountain?"

"Lightning, we don't know where we are." Mystic turned to look beyond the edge of the shelter. "We don't know where we are."

***

Bubba was feeling good. He was created to run. The sun was shining down on the exquisite, shiny coat he inherited from his Mother while the strength from his Father coursed through his sinewy muscles. His speed? It was a gift from something altogether different, but it was his and his alone. No other living creature's speed could compare with his. No sky-traveler, four-legger or two-legger could compete with him over any terrain. His speed was effortless, defining and awe-inspiring at the same time. He was about to need it. Out of the sky dropped a wide shadow. Bubba caught sight of the menacing apparition on both sides of him. He remembered the day long ago when he was scooped off the ground by Vincen. This shadow had appeared in much the same way. Vincen appeared those many years before as a shadow out of nowhere to snatch the small Cheetah cub off the ground and out of harm's way. Bubba shook off the memory. He was much bigger now and so was this shadow. The dark lines on the ground around him thickened as the large creature lowered its approach from behind. This was not Vincen. Bubba could read the slow, graceful motion of the wings, but the size! These wings would have to be two or three times the size of Vincen's. What was this? The Cheetah was not scared; a little wary, but not scared. He knew

21

what he would do. The shadow dwarfed him. He veered off course to allow the sun to do some of his detective work. As he turned, he watched the shadow as it steadily grew. His course had changed enough to where he could easily see a shadow of what was happening beneath the wings. The creature's wings were now settling towards the back of its body. Bubba knew what came next. Two feet with strong, but, straight, blunt talons poised themselves for the attack. It was time to act. If he slowed down, he would be an easy pick for the attacker.

With a burst of speed, the likes of which this sky-traveler had never seen, Bubba shot ahead of his pursuer. He continued accelerating in a wild zigzag course that confused and nauseated the winger. He ran as fast as he thought necessary to put him far ahead of the pursuer. His escape speed allowed him time to turn around and catch a glimpse of the shadow maker. "Oh mercy that thing is big," thought Bubba.

The sky-traveler could not match the speed of the Cheetah. That fact became readily apparent. The Cheetah was toying with the large winger. This was supposed to be an easy catch. The four-legger even had the audacity to turn and espy him. That had never happened before. No matter, he had to get the message to the four-legger. Summoning the remainder of his sapped strength, the giant winger increased his speed and the elevation of his flight. He made a sharp arc at the apex of his rise which, once again, put him on a course to intercept the Cheetah. "Though this may not work, I must give him the message."

Bubba crouched as if he were hunting a prey. He would make a dash for safety if this creature brought on another attack. He had correctly decided that his speed was unmatched by the sky-traveler. He waited, ready to spring. As the winger approached, Bubba was not impressed by the creature's beauty. The body was all black except for white triangular markings under each wing. The head looked to be absent of feathers except for a tuft directly behind the face which was a patchy mixture of yellows, blacks and orange. Its beak appeared strong and menacing enough to rip flesh, but no aggressive action was taken. The creature was not much to look at; still, it was as graceful and powerful as any sky-traveler the Cheetah had ever seen, its size was shocking.

The sky-traveler lined up his sights on the coiled Cheetah. He dove directly for Bubba. He never extended his talons as he had done the previous time. Instead he softened the angle of his dive and slowed as he approached. As he passed over the Cheetah, he calmly stated, "Beware of the intelligents. Godspeed Cheetah." He pointed his beak skyward and was gone with a few powerful flaps of his gigantic wings.

Bubba rose from his crouch. He watched with bewildered admiration as the sky-traveler slowly disappeared into a tiny black dot high in the bright blue sky. "Beware of the intelligents?" He did not know what that meant. He had to get back to the shelter fast. Maybe this was a clue, an omen or just the ranting of a giant sky-traveler. There was no time to waste. Bubba called on his speed again and made a bee-line back to the shelter. This should make for an interesting conversation.

On his return jaunt, Bubba searched the horizon for anything familiar. He found nothing. There was not a familiar mountain, forest, lake, ditch, rise or anything to key on. This area was completely void of landmarks. It reminded him of the plains on which he was raised, everything except for the tall grass. The grass which grew well over his head was abundant. He leaped high above it on occasion, hoping for a glimpse of something only to be disappointed again and again.

*** 

Hazzel, Lemeer and Vincen made their way around the garden watching as the young Badgers made quick work of the weeding. Their large claws and short, strong forearms enabled them to dispatch weeds at a fast clip. Each Badger looked up to give a respectful nod to Vincen as he strode by before returning to their work.

After the three of them entered Lightning's sleeping chamber, Lemeer began the conversation. "Vincen, please answer our questions now. We know Lightning goes off on these adventures all the time, however, it is very odd that he has been gone this long without even a message back to us. It is quickly nearing the time for his long sleep."

"Lemeer, I know you are concerned about your son. When I left him earlier, he was as fit and fed as I have ever seen him. One day, one of us will tell you all about that, but now we have to believe the previous adventure has not ended. Maybe it has only begun."

It was a worried Mother that spoke next. "What do you mean, Vincen? Like Lemeer told you, it is nearing time for Lightning's long sleep. I have never known him not to require it. When will he return?"

"Hazzel, I wish I could give you that information. I cannot. I do not know when he will return. They were to follow the established path back to here once they found it."

"What do you mean once they found it?" Lemeer asked.

"Again, I am sorry Lemeer. I do not have time or the proper authority to speak of what we have been through. Suffice it to say, friend, we have taken quite a wondrous journey. None is the worse for wear and all emerged from the well with a new outlook on our lives here. Maybe in the future, we can take you back with us."

"Emerged from the well? What well?" Hazzel had picked up on the Vincen's slip.

"Oh my, I did say well. I should not have mentioned that yet. Please do not make me speak further of it. Would it be too much to ask that I not have to explain myself?"

Hazzel curtly replied, "Yes."

Lemeer was next, "Vincen, surely you are not speaking of "The Well of the Ground Below? That well cannot exist. I have heard only of it in stories." He fidgeted, "Old tales with no intention of being factual."

"Oh no Lemeer, it is that well indeed. It is real. I have experienced its true brilliance as did your son and our friends. Mystic discovered it in the South Quarter the morning we left or maybe it discovered him. He was the first in. I came for Lightning and Bubba. We gathered our supplies and followed Mystic down the well soon after he disappeared. It was hypnotizing and glorious."

"It does truly exist then? Why did you need to experience it? You mentioned it may have discovered Mystic? Lemeer, I am not enjoying what I am hearing. Remember what your grandfather told us about the well and what followed?" Hazzel remembered. She was not happy.

"No, Vincen, this can't be. They say when the well opens it can only be a portent. Will that be the case?"

Vincen became quiet. He whispered, "With the information we gathered from reliable, yet unique sources, we believe we can rein in the trouble that may be brewing. We have discovered many secrets, as well as strategies that we are now enlightened enough to set in place. Unfortunately, in order to accomplish that, those of us that went need to be together. I apologize for this, but I must get on my way. I must find them. Please do not allow yourselves worry fits. It will do no good to anyone. Go about your normal lives. If you should worry, we will let you know. I'm sorry I must go. Pray all will be well."

Hazzel and Lemeer watched Vincen hurry out. There was a side of Badgers that wasn't to be toyed with. A steely resolve was stirring in each of their eyes. "Hazzel, I don't like what I just heard. The well opened for Mystic."

"Yes, Lemeer, Vincen did say exactly that in a roundabout way. He knows and we know what that means. Please say the "Return" is not happening now. Our family, our lives here, what will happen to us? I never liked what our ancestors said we used to be."

"My dear this charade may be over. It may be time to be what we are. We should humbly begin our preparations just in case. Let the young ones know that it may be coming. They may be disappointed in the beginning, but we are what we are. If needed, we have and always will fight to the end." The steely resolve hardened in the eyes of Lemeer. "We will do what we have to do."

Hazzel looked into the eyes of her beloved mate. She nodded. Her eyes hardened with resolve as she agreed, "Yes Lemeer, we will do what we have to do."

***

Vincen hurriedly made his way out of the den. He hurriedly glanced around, saw nothing of note and took wing. He must find the other members of his group. The fact they had not showed up in the Great Forest was beginning to burden him. Inside his head, questions were banging into each other, knocking reason and logic around like sparks floating above a fire. The lack of answers wafted throughout his thoughts as if each had a mind and agenda of its own. Hazzel and Lemeer had not shown any outward signs of fear when he had told them the condensed version of his story. Did they know more than they were letting on? Were they more prepared that he was? According to Great Forest legend, the Badgers were long a family of seasoned worriers. They certainly showed no signs of that when he left. Oh well, things would either get better or worse. That, he knew, would definitely happen. He flew to his favorite perch. He scoured the land as far as he could see on all sides of the Great Mountain. Where were they?

\*\*\*

Lightning rummaged through his bag looking for a proper morning kake. He found nothing to appease his taste. It was about this time every year when he became excessively hungry. He never understood it. His parents just told him it was the way he was supposed to be. He was sleeping longer and wanting it more. This was not how another adventure should be starting. His companions would be counting on him. He needed to find a way to win the battle over his want of sleep and increasing desire for food. He was not sure how much longer he would be able to keep up the pace.

"Lightning, are you eating again?" Frederick called from the edge of the shelter.

"I'm afraid I am famished Frederick. This time of year, I have to eat more than normal."

"Are you normally prone to a very long nap, once a year after a gluttonous desire for food fattens you up?"

"Yes, you are correct."

"We two-leggers call that hibernation. We don't practice it. It is solely for some of you four-legger species. This is not a good time for you to be thinking about that."

"I'm sorry. I have no control over it. When it hits me, it hits me whether I'm thinking about it or not."

"I think we will have to find a way to delay that habit of yours. The most important role you will ever play in your life may be speeding down a path directly at you and the rest of us as we speak. We will need the best effort we can muster to survive this future of ours if it gets as bad as it may. Lightning, you have to be there for all of us and all of those less fortunate than yourself. There is no other way. You must overcome this. If we are successful, you can take your long nap then. If we are not successful, some creature or happening may make that nap unnecessary for you."

"You mean I may get taken?"

"If that means dispatched or killed then yes. You may get taken. All of us may get taken. There are no guarantees. There are possibly some very bad creatures out there that will not take a liking to what we want to do."

"Agreed. You all must help me. There must be some way to delay this hibernation as you call it."

Mystic was listening to the conversation. He slowly walked over to the pair. "Lightning, I completely forgot about the timing of this. I am so sorry."

"There is nothing you could have done to prevent this Mystic. I will do my best. There must be something we can do." The irregular Badger hung his enormous head in despair. What could he do?

Frederick reached up and swatted Lightning between the ears. "Let us not worry about that now. Time has a way of dealing with things. Let's find that Cat then get on our way. Shall we?"

Mystic nuzzled Lightning's shoulder. "Let's go. Enough of this."

Frederick led them to the shelter's edge. "Now Bubba, where are you?"

Far above Bubba, far above the shelter, far above the clouds, Frederick thought he saw a dark speck circling, watching down on them. "There it is again," he mumbled to himself.

Mystic looked up and saw the speck too. "Well I guess we are not the only ones here are we?"

"No Prince, I guess we are not."

Lightning was not looking up. He was looking at a ripple in the tall grass. The ripple was moving rapidly in their direction. "If that is not Bubba, we may have a problem."

The other two swung their glances in the same direction as Lightning, temporarily distracting them from the flying speck high above. Indeed the ripple was moving fast, heading directly at the shelter.

The Cheetah raced out of the grass never slowing down until he was out of the spying eyes on high. Not even slightly out of breath he exclaimed, "Did all of you see that winger up there?" He sat down and pointed with a front paw. "It came down after me like Vincen did when he saved me from the poachers. It almost had me. I ran a little faster than it flew so I escaped. I got far enough ahead to turn around for a look at it and it came at me again. The second time it did not even try to grab me."

"Whoa Bubba," Mystic was in control now. "What do you mean? It came after you once or twice?"

"It came at me twice. It only tried to grab me once. I saw its shadow. I got a read on what it was trying to do."

Frederick needed more information. "Was it unprovoked? I mean did you make it angry or something? Did you see anything else?"

"No...no...no, I did nothing to it. After I eluded it the first time it came back. The second time, it just flew over me."

Now Lightning was curious. "It just flew over you?"

"Yes, it just flew right over me."

"You mean it knew where you were and didn't attack you again?" Mystic wished Bubba would just get to the point.

"What did it do when it flew over you?" Frederick had retrieved his writing stylus and pad from his bag and was taking notes.

"It spoke to me."

"Did that surprise you?" Frederick was writing down everything now.

"No."

Lightning moved a little closer to the Cheetah. "What did it say to you?"

"That's what I can't figure out. It said "Beware of the intelligents" and "Godspeed Cheetah.""

Mystic stated to them all, "So it was not attacking Bubba, it was warning him, collectively warning all of us. It has been watching since we arrived here, wherever we are."

"Yes," continued Bubba, "It must be a warning of some kind."

Frederick looked up from his notes. "I wonder how that creature spells what it said?"

Mystic replied, "What do you mean?"

Frederick continued, "If he spells the word intelligence; i-n-t-e-l-l-i-g-e-n-c-e it would mean one thing, if he spells it i-n-t-e-l-l-i-g-e-n-t-s; it could mean something all together different."

Lightning laughed a small laugh, "That, two-legger, is a question only you would ask."

"Now wait a minute Lightning," Frederick was on to something he needed to get across to the four-leggers. "All of you listen to me. Our words can have multiple meanings. A lot of the meanings are dictated by the spelling of the individual words. You four-leggers do not get caught up in that necessarily, but whoever gave this message to the winger must have a reason for the wording, thus, a particular spelling. We, I mean two-leggers, don't have a word that is spelled in-t-e-l-l-i-g-e-n-t-s. If that is how this word is to be used then a four-legger or winger would have to interpret its meaning that way. If not, the message would be warning us to beware of intelligence which is something that we will certainly need to get through this. So, I'm asking, which definition do we use?"

"Hmm, you have a valid argument Frederick." Bubba was thinking the way Frederick was leaning. "Can we not call that winger down and ask him ourselves?"

Lightning was looking up and shaking his head. "Nope. It's gone."

\*\*\*

If panic could be seen on an Eagle's face then it was all over Vincen. He had searched every nook and cranny for Mystic's group from one end of the Great Forest to the other. There was not a stone left unturned. They were, simply put, just not there. Vincen raced through every scenario possible in the limited space remaining in his mind. He would have to go back to the beginning. The problem with that line of reasoning was; the beginning was in Nuorg. How could he get back without the Staff? He again flew to the South Quarter of the Great Forest hoping to find some clues to re-open the well.

He flew in a hurry, using pursuit beats only. Any time wasted dilly-dallying could prove disastrous to their mission. How could he have lost a Wolf, a two-legger, a Cheetah and an extremely large irregular Badger? Why had he flown off without them? Had he taken the safety of the Great Forest for granted? That answer was obvious, he had. Again, questions, questions and more questions. He needed answers to all of those questions, but answers were not forthcoming. Who did he know? Who could he trust? Suddenly it came to him. Of course! He remembered a group of sky-travelers who just might be able to help. One, of their bunch, had been exiled from the Great Forest long ago, but the remainder of the group was trustworthy. Vincen hoped they had not fallen under the exile's spell. Now what was the fastest way to their dwelling?

\*\*\*

Frederick wasn't feeling overwhelmed at the moment, he was feeling like an alien. This world of talking animals and talking birds, at the moment, seemed the sort of thing only fireside stories were made of. Not to mention was the very real fact that inanimate objects were now making life-changing decisions for him, pointing his thought processes toward the surreal. He stepped away from the four-leggers physically and mentally. He felt an obligation to the others to determine their location and reason for being but knew the decision was not his to make, it had already been made by a higher power. As he numbly paced the area, he fought urges to abandon the mission and head back to his home, a land only of talking two-leggers. His gift as a Talker was an over-bearing burden at the moment and with no way to avoid or discard it, he felt imprisoned. Should it not be considered a blessing? The very idea that he could so easily converse with animals and birds should be listed as one of the greatest gifts to mankind. Now, it was his lonesome burden. He well knew he was not the only Talker, but he was the only one that existed within the realm of this small group of creatures. Being a Talker was not only a splendid reward, it was a great responsibility. Maybe he was feeling overwhelmed after all. Frederick tensely shook off the feelings of self-doubt to rejoin the others.

"Mystic, Bubba, Lightning...we have to make some decisions and we have to make them now. Which way was the sky-traveler heading? Did any of you see it fly off? We must decide where to go, where to travel from here. The day is burning away from under us. Vincen has obviously been called elsewhere. He was not included when the ax-pike landed us here. Which one of you has a strong thought as to which way we should head?" Frederick was determined to get something started, wrong or right they had to get moving.

Lightning answered, "I saw it as a dark spot heading north. I say we follow it."

Mystic sided with Lightning, "From here, I don't know where heading north will take us, but I agree, we can no longer stay here and ponder our predicament. The Staff is not glowing, so we can assume we are safe for now."

Frederick nodded, "I agree, Mystic. We must pay close attention to the Staff. It knows more than we do of what is happening to and around us."

Bubba spoke next, "I want to know the direction from where the winger came. That might be better to know than where it headed. If it was heading out to warn something else would we not be following it into potential trouble?"

Lightning heard something in Bubba's question. "Bubba, you may be right. What if we do head south? Would we not be running into trouble there as well? Or, would be heading into some creatures in the same situation we are in? Who really knows?"

"I am thinking the same as you Lightning." Mystic's thoughts were becoming more focused. "If that winger is flying the countryside crusading its cause, would we not be more likely to run into others who share our same plight? If there are other groups like ours hunting the unknown, would it not be to our advantage to band with them for a strength in numbers kind of thing?"

"Good point, Mystic." Frederick looked to Bubba. "If that winger was not on our side and he was as big as you say he was, could he not have carried you away with little or no trouble at all?"

"Yes, no doubt. He could have easily carried me off with him."

Lightning perked his ears up and swung his large head back and forth. "So, what will it be? Shall we chase after the winger or chase toward whatever it was chasing before it chased our little Cheetah?"

Frederick stared high and long into the north sky. Seeing nothing, he turned to Lightning, "I am all for strength in numbers. We need a winger. We have no scout with the same eyes or speed as when we have a raptor in our midst."

Bubba reacted a bit miffed, "Excuse me? I am faster than any raptor I know of Frederick."

"Surely you are Bubba, but can you fly? Can you spy happenings from high above the ground as we travel? Can you see far down our path even when we are in low places?" Frederick was not being mean-spirited, he was simply stating facts.

"Well," Bubba stammered, "I uh, I don't…Yes, I see your point. Sorry."

Frederick bent down until his face nearly touched the Cheetah's. "Bubba, I was not doubting your speed by any means. Should we need speed, you will be called first. What I tried to say is that we miss Vincen's ability to espy great distances while he still soars directly over our position. Maybe I should have stated my case in a different way."

"No, Frederick you stated your case well. I'm on edge. Let's get on, shall we?" Bubba headed out of the shelter, looked back at the group then turned south.

"South it is." Mystic followed.

"Wait, Mystic, I have something I would like to try on you." Frederick removed a complicated set of straps from a side pocket on his bag. He fitted it around Mystic's neck and chest. After adjusting a few buckles he looked at Mystic, then the Staff. "May I?" Frederick pointed to the Staff at Mystic's feet.

"Yes, by all means." Mystic was hoping Frederick had just fashioned a holster for the Staff.

Frederick took the Staff and inserted it inside a void between Mystic's strong chest and the bottom strapping. After a few further adjustments, the fit was better than expected. The globe protruded slightly beyond Mystic's shoulders allowing all but the Wolf a direct view in case it began to glow. Other than that, the fit was surprisingly good.

"I will continue to refine this as we travel. I think it is a much more efficient way to carry the Staff than your old way!" Frederick looked on smiling.

"Frederick, my teeth and my jaws wish to thank you. This contraption has already made my future journeys more pleasant." Mystic turned and raced off after Bubba.

Lightning followed the four-leggers with his eyes before turning back to Frederick. "That was brilliant of you. What about this?" He raised his ax-pike to Frederick's eye level. "Can you make me a holster for this as well?"

"I'll tell you what large Badger; I will make you a holster. For now, I will throw it across my back and ride on yours!" He took the ax-pike from Lightning, slung it over his back then jumped onto Lightning's shoulders. Frederick took hold of the coarse long hair at the base of Lightning's neck and shouted, "Make for the south, you great steed!"

The huge irregular Badger did not move. "You great what?"

"You great steed," Frederick reiterated.

"Oh mercy. I don't like how this is beginning." Lightning's face showed traces of a sly smile. "If you think those small four-leggers are the only ones who can run, two-legger, think again!" Lightning nearly threw the rider from his back with an explosion of power which shot them both from beneath the shelter. "Hang on Frederick!"

Frederick was shocked with the Badger's acceleration. He smiled and desperately dug his fingers deeper into the fur on Lightning's strong neck. Ahead of the lumbering duo, Mystic was closing in on Bubba. The Cheetah had slowed to a trot; slow for Bubba, it was almost as fast as his friends could run. Bubba lightly came to a stop. He once again turned back to catch sight of the others. "Mystic, are you three coming or not?"

"Forgive me Bubba. You know we are not as fast as you. It is hard for me to understand, but I believe you are getting even faster with each passing day-round. How can that be?"

"I do think you are correct, Mystic. I can feel it in my bones. There is no doubt. I am faster than I ever was. I'm faster than I was a day-round ago. You too are faster with your new holster I see."

"I think so, yes. I am no longer worried about dropping this Staff or cracking my teeth while trying to hold on to the thing in my jaws. It makes for a more pleasant run at least. We are heading south aren't we?"

"By my measure, we are. Oh, I see Lightning and Frederick are on their way. Let's wait for them. I'm sure Frederick can figure a true southward direction for us."

No sooner than Bubba completed his statement, Lightning came barreling in. The tall grass parted at his feet. "That was fun!" The irregular Badger wasn't even breathing hard. "I think I enjoy running after all."

Frederick jumped off Lightning's back, landing softly on the ground. "What say we?" He asked. "Why have we stopped?"

Mystic answered, "We were waiting on you two. We were not sure if we were indeed heading south. Are we?"

Frederick jerked his chin, up pointing his eyes skyward. Once he located the sun, he took a step back putting both hands on his hips. He exhaled a deep breath. "One would think so. This landscape is so void of anything reliable enough to get a bearing on." He kept staring at the sun occasionally sweeping his eyes about the horizon which stretched in all directions around them. "I don't know. I do know we are not in Nuorg, for the sun in this sky is moving."

Lightning scanned the horizon where it met the blue of the sky. "Do any of you think it will make that much of a difference which way we head?"

"I'll have to agree with Lightning." Mystic could not make any learned decision between the right way to travel and the wrong way. They didn't know where they were, so what difference did it make where they went?

Frederick nodded his head with agreement. "I concur, Mystic. Why bother with our heading? I guess we will know for better or worse when we get to our destination. Bubba?"

"Whatever. I have no idea either. Let's continue. One way or another we are going find out...eventually."

"Very well. If we think south is this way, let us continue south." Frederick pointed the way and jumped up on the Badger's back again. "Southward, shall we?"

Lightning looked amused. "Two-legger, is this a habit in the making?"

"Very well may be, giant Badger. It very well may be."

Mystic and Bubba chuckled. Together they shouted, "Southward it shall be!"

The group traveled with no intended urgency for the remainder of sun time. As the sun began to fade to their right, the horizon began to offer slight hints of contours. Whether mountains or rolling hills, something lay ahead of their approach. The change in the horizon, although still very far off in the distance, brought a welcome chorus of sighs from the travelers.

Frederick had ridden atop Lightning for the entire second half of the day with various maps and notes spread out on the four-legger's table-sized back. "Does anyone think we will feel those hills beneath our feet by sundown?"

Lightning shrugged, "I'm sure some of us will feel them beneath our paws, but if you stay up there I am positive you won't feel them under yours!"

"Now, now Lightning, I have made good use of my time up here. I caught up on lots of note-taking and map reading. I have been researching through my notes concerning the Staff and there are quite a few tidbits of information that are now becoming very clear."

"Like what for instance?" Mystic was very interested in anything regarding the meaning or wielding of the Staff.

Frederick never raised his head from his work. "Later this evening, Prince Mystic, we can discuss a few things I have learned lately along with some revelations regarding the ax-pike and rapier. Well, actually we need to have discussion on how these inanimate objects have been affected by the globe's purification processes."

Bubba continued straight ahead. He added, "I assume there will be some discussion of the ability of my rapier to pass through living tissue without harming it or at least drawing blood."

"I'm not so sure of that, Bubba. I have found nothing that even comes close to explaining that little phenomenon. I have found no mention of that or anything of that nature in any of these notes or map inscriptions." Frederick took his quill and circled a section of his notes that was copied verbatim from the back of the map pages. He continued. "If it were me I would not want to experiment extensively with that trick."

Mystic was not sure of that answer. "Are you saying it was a magician's trick Frederick? Something learned by you two-leggers over in your world perhaps?"

"No, I certainly am not saying that. The rapier definitely performs on its own as it pertains to the piercing action. I don't want any creature outside of our group knowing what it can do. If it is accidently revealed, the secret would be gone and so would our surprise use of it when needed. Be prepared for anything in the upcoming day-rounds. Who knows? Maybe we will need to fake an early demise for one of us in order to save the group later or the real heart of our mission. You just can't know at this juncture."

"I don't know why, but I understand your premise completely." Lightning was learning to deduce certain accumulated facts at an outstanding rate never seen before by his fellow four-leggers. The globe's earlier actions may have something to do with that as well.

Mystic and Bubba looked at each other with a look that could only be described as fascinating. Frederick didn't take notice of Lightning's response. He just kept studying from atop Lightning's massive back. The group kept walking with no further comments or conversation.

Off to the right, the sun was beginning to rest for the day. It lazily slipped past the horizon, offering its opposite partner the opportunity to continue the guide role. The moon was full and bright, ready and able to see the group's entry to the foothills. It gazed down upon the wonderers with a benevolent eye. The moon took note that not another creature of any sort was within seeing distance as the four meandered up the first slight slope of the rolling foot hills.

"Mystic, do you feel a change beneath us. Is it my imagination or are we actually climbing a hill of some kind?" Bubba was thinking they were, but after the long day, he had to ask.

"Yes Bubba, I think the flat land is finally changing shape." Mystic looked behind him and saw that the vast flat land they had covered was now able to be seen in its entirety. There was a clear view back as far as his wolven eyes could see. He voiced silently to himself, "I do wish Vincen was here with us."

**4**

V incen flew with determination. As of late, it seemed to him all of his flying was very deliberate. There was no time allowed anymore for enjoyable floats over the land. Everything now was very driven and purposeful. What once would have been considered exciting was now, more or less, directly linked to life or death. He flew with a panicked intensity now. The mission of the flight added a very handsome quality to the beat of his wings. He flew the entire day without so much as a leisure beat escaping his wings. He knew exactly where he was going. He could only hope the bevy of small but swift sky-travelers would still be where he left them. They were a precocious bunch and more prone to talking down on other creatures than talking with them. In Vincen's mind, it was not necessarily a bad thing, but if one misconstrued the intent of the small creature's lectures, well, that one, if larger, might get mad enough to eat the smaller. The great Eagle scoped the country side with keen eyes, hoping for one small hint of the bevy's location. He located a small forest of trees to his east and took for it. With no further doubt in his mind and running out of options, he dove on the trees. He lit in the mid-branches of a perimeter tree then stared into the thickery.

"I will be confounded," Vincen declared. "There is not a sign of those sky-travelers anywhere within this mild excuse for a forest. Not only is there no sign of them, there is no sign of any sky-traveler or legger of any kind. Why? Why is this happening?"

Vincen was perturbed with his lack of good fortune. Once again, he took wing without a direction. He was understandably frustrated and heading somewhere else. Where? He had no clue. He only reckoned that anywhere else could not possibly be any worse than where he was now. Once again he flew with purpose and speed. This time he made sure to focus on every tiny nook or crevice, be it one tree, bush or patch of weeds. Surely the entire bevy could not have relocated. But, could they have been decimated? With the last thought lingering in his mind, his intention to locate the sky-travelers increased beyond decent measure. He forced a great Eagle distress call from deep inside his inner being. The scream must have been heard by every object with breath or not for hundreds of pursuit beats beyond the measureless confines of what the Eagle could see. Fortunately for all concerned, the Eagle's cry was heard in a crevice of a split boulder at the edge of Vincen's range of sight. A few members of the bevy huddled together, snuggly wedged underneath the large rock. They were terrified not by Vincen's screams, but of those running amok in their short term memories. It had been a horrific past few day-rounds for the sky-travelers. Vincen would soon discover the horrid details that led to the absence of life outside the crevice near the bottom of this boulder.

A young voice whispered, "What was that? Are those things returning for us?"

"I can't be sure, little one. That sounded like an Eagle's cry. I have never known of an Eagle to attempt the barbaric display we have witnessed. Wait here, I must know whether it is an Eagle or another problem."

"You are going out? You are leaving us?"

"I believe the dangerous ones are gone for the time being. I will come back for each of you." He looked at the young Doves huddled with him. "I will not leave without any of you. Do you understand?"

Silently, each of the tweensts solemnly acknowledged the older Dove.

"I have lost as much or more than each of you. I will not lose you too. I must go. I will return. Do not move from here! Have I made myself clear to you?"

The lead Dove carefully made his way out of the crevice. The sunlight shocked his eyes momentarily. As he waited for the adjustment of his beady pupils to the brightness, he clicked his head around listening for the slightest disturbance in the air. His eyes fully acclimated once again to being outside; he quickly spotted a large creature on wing high above. He had no way of knowing the Eagle was circling in desperation, hoping for a glimpse of the living. The Dove took wing and made directly for the much larger sky-traveler. He drew a bead on the shadowy, large mid-section. Racing upward with as much speed as he could muster, the Dove struggled to reach the same altitude where the larger winger seemed to float. The air was thinning; his wings were tiring; he too was desperate. He could fly no higher. He cried out to the Eagle as loudly as he was able. What escaped his beak was barely a peep. This was his lucky day. The Eagle spied him coming his way and immediately adjusted his course downward to intercept the failing Dove. As the small sky-traveler's wings were beating their last beats, Vincen lightly plucked him out of the sky.

"Little Dove, I have been searching for you."

"Vincen, I am ever so glad to see you." The Dove slumped unconscious.

"Why Tine, so nice to see you as well. Have you been betraying any of your friends lately? I'd better get you down to thicker air. Don't leave me Dove!" Vincen dove faster for the ground, his wings beating the denser air senseless. Again he commanded, "Don't leave me Dove! We have much to discuss."

The ground approached Vincen in a hurry. He pulled up quickly, braking with a few altered flaps of his wings. He gently laid the Dove in a soft clump of grass before setting down at its side. Vincen paced around the unconscious winger in a small circle knowing that soon the thicker, oxygenated air would bring him back around. He was correct and his wait was not long.

"Vincen, we have much to discuss. Why are you here? How did you know?" The questions were not asked in a very courteous manner.

"I have come to ask a huge favor of you. How did I know what?"

The Dove's breaths were becoming more powerful with each passing second. "A favor? Hah! First, I will need to ask a huge favor of you since you owe me so much already. How did you know to come here after what happened? Do you see or did you see any signs of life for the last clicks of your travel here?"

"I'm afraid you have lost me. Please explain more of what has occurred."

The Dove hopped to his feet. "Vincen, two moons ago our dwellings, nests, aeries, lairs, dens and everything else was attacked. Deranged wingers, maddened leggers and nasty vile creatures of all sorts descended on us from every direction. My followers...uh, I mean my friends were taken away from me in cages and boxes. Those of us not captured or chased away were killed on the spot. Total carnage. I was able to mercifully lead four tweensts into hiding where we have been ever since. There was no excuse for what happened. None of our dwellers has an interest in anything that happens past my boundaries. We are a completely passive society. We do well by ourselves. As you know, we are not thrilled about incomers or outgoers. Who even knew of us? Did you spout off to some creature about our private community over here?" The Dove's voice inflection was changing. It progressed from a poor, pitiful tone to a why are you here in the first place tone.

Vincen was taken aback by the report of the attacks and initially felt sorry for the Dove. However, the last statement went a little too far in assuming the worst. "You're pushing it Tine. Don't you dare make any insinuations regarding what I might have done. I let you know during my last visit that your tone with me was never justified. If you let your condescending ways continue in this conversation, I will forget I ever came here and leave you to a follow-up visit by your previous marauders. Are we clear about that?"

"Whatever, Vincen. All I know is that my ranks have been decimated. My admirers captured or killed and all of our other inhabitants have been scattered to the numberless corners of the world. Now, out of the sky, you just happen to drop in after the pillage is complete. How did you think I would react?"

"Tine, you are pushing me to where I don't want to be. Your language is very pointy and I will not hear anymore of it. Change your tone immediately or I will for sure leave you as you are. You and your tweensts."

"You would not dare leave me in dire straights!"

"Try me!" Vincen's eyes seared the Dove's grayish feathered body. His stare was unwavering and unnerving for Tine. "For such a small creature you have an inexhaustible supply of arrogance."

"Arrogance has its merits, Vincen. Our society has no room for incomers. We warned ourselves of such a tragedy as this. You were allowed entry and recognition by my peers against my better judgment and look what valuable gain it has brought upon us. Look around you Great Eagle! This is all your fault and your fault alone. Don't you try to back out of your role in this." Tine returned Vincen's stare with earnest.

"I will give you one instant to recant your ridiculous cast of blame on me before I leave here taking you with me. Your tweensts will surely perish without the all knowing Tine here to protect and nurture them, but it's happened before right?" Vincen's stare grew even more intense. "Your time is up!" Vincen lashed out with his beak. He grabbed the Dove's wing crisply and lifted him off the ground. The Eagle took wing with Tine flailing in the wind, struggling to free himself. Vincen dropped the Dove from his beak. Before any attempt was made by Tine to right himself, Vincen wrapped his strong talons tightly around his prey then strongly stated, "You might need to say a prayer for those poor tweensts you are leaving behind. I dare to say, if they don't make it through a long life, it will be completely the fault of your befuddling, unwarranted arrogance."

Far below, the tweensts emerged from the crevice beneath the boulder. They had heard every word of the conversation between the larger wingers. They agreed to follow the Eagle wherever he was heading to personally thank him for saving them from another demeaning word out of Tine's self-serving beak. He had not led them to the crevice, he had followed them. He forced his way into their hiding place, making the small space extremely uncomfortable. He sent some of them out into the open to make sure the attackers were gone. He threatened each individual if they chose to disobey. Each of the young tweensts was certain the Eagle had once again come to their rescue.

Tine was terrified. "You can't do this to me Vincen! You can't take me away. You can't expose me to a world I don't know. You are promising me certain death! They will come for me once I am shown again to outsiders. You horrendous creature! Go ahead and squeeze the life from me. It's better to be killed now than to suffer an agonizing torture at the whim of stupidly spineless creatures other than yourself." The Dove pleaded to uncaring ears.

Vincen was not sure why he thought this paranoid sky-traveler would ever agree to help him. He could not figure why he wouldn't either. The great Eagle only hoped that Tine would live long enough to return to the Great Forest. If he made it that far without suffocating on his own guilt, maybe Vincen could convince him to help out the cause, if Vincen didn't tire of Tine's ludicrous babble and dispatch him first. They flew fast toward the Great Forest. Once there Vincen would intercede in Tine's defense if the arrogant agreed to help. The Dove was not remembered with any particular fondness at home. Vincen fought with himself, he did not want to utter another word during the entire flight. More often than not, he staved off overwhelming desires to crush the breath out of the Dove and suffer

41

any consequences therein. He knew, beyond doubt, that no creature would ever cast blame on him if he did.

A short distance behind, the bevy of tweensts followed the Eagle's every move. Fortunately for the younger sky-travelers, Vincen flew at a lower altitude than normal which allowed them to match his speed. Had he flown higher he would have lost them.

"Vincen, I beg you, please don't take me back. I left on such bad terms. Every living creature in the Great Forest hates me."

Vincen could not stifle his voice any longer, "May I add that it is not without good measure. You were a fool Tine, an arrogantly vile waste of feathers. It sounds to me as if you haven't changed one bit. You will change quickly or suffer the consequences of your actions. Your private society, your elitist pecking order, what a pile of rubbish. They may exile me for returning your conceited blood and feathers. You will face your charges and atone for your wrong doings or I will personally inflict pain upon you that you could never imagine. Now, lest I squeeze your last breath from you at this very moment, I suggest that you not mumble another word until we arrive. I am not taking a liking to what I am hearing. You have not changed at all."

Tine knew better that to press the issue. He had no choice. He would face his past in due time and he also knew that even though Vincen could easily dispatch him with a slight flick of his talon, the Eagle would rather wait and let him suffer through a trial for all to see. The remainder of the trip was flown in complete silence other than the sound of occasional gusts of wind sweeping around them.

***

In the Great Forest, the alarm was sounded. Hazzel related Vincen's story to her closest friends, leggers and sky-travelers alike. There were no tears shed, no hysterical fits thrown, no cowering in the face of the unknown; each inhabitant of the Great Forest knew what would be asked of them and they would answer. Granted none of them had a history of fighting with such intensity as the Badgers, but they knew their place in the order of preserving the lives they had known since the end of the Terrible Years. That lifestyle was worth everything they could throw at it. Lemeer's communications also went well. He spread the word mostly among his male counterparts, again with the same results as Hazzel. All creatures had dreaded the moment when this news would come, but none were innocent enough to think it never would. The joy of the day-round did not totally disappear. What emerged from the spreading news was a togetherness, a resolute confirmation of being a family, extended as it was. No creature was going to come in and take anything from the dwellers of the Great Forest without a fight of the kind they had never wanted to know. Lemeer gave the word to open the hidden dens holding the remnants of the battle gear long since used and never completely forgotten. The systems and methods of old were once again sought from the libraries to study and refine. By the time Vincen returned, the Badgers were determined for a proper yet non-obvious transformation to have taken place. The dwellers had no idea Vincen's return would also mark the return of a very unpopular inhabitant who had been exiled long ago for reasons running a gamut between hideously despicable and cowardly treasonous.

Vincen entered the outer boundary of the Great Forest, aware of, but not acknowledging the lookouts. Immediately as he crossed the invisible border, two smaller coal black sky-travelers took up positions at his side, approximately one-half leisure beat apart. Below and slightly behind him came a trio of swift sky-travelers with wings completely out of proportion with their long tails and brilliantly colored feathers. High above them all loomed a lone spy. Vincen counted his company. With a slight tilt of his wings, he finally acknowledged his escorts and signaled for the middle trailer to move forward to within speaking distance. The trailer approached from below. He was shocked when he witnessed the prey within Vincen's grip.

"Why in the name of all that is right do have you that vermin clutched beneath you while he is still breathing?"

Tine knew the worse was yet to come. Vincen answered the trailer, "I know I am taking a chance, but Tine must perform a task that none of our inhabitants have the luxury to do. Please take word ahead of me. The tribunal must be called to meeting. Mystic will not be attending. Make sure the others are there. I will make my case upon arrival. I will give you three clicks to make arrangements. I know I have some explaining to do and I will argue for you to see my point. Please don't make this worse than it is, Karone."

"As you ask, Vincen. I won't question your judgment, although I think plenty others will make up for my silence." Karone turned from Vincen then headed straight for Lemeer's dwelling. He knew for a fact this could get very interesting. That much was obvious.

Vincen spoke again to Tine, "I pray that you will speak in a fashion appropriate to the facts with which you will be presented."

"Will I have any choice?" Tine was becoming more afraid by the moment. Why did he behave the way he did? The time to discover that was closer at hand than ever before.

"No," Vincen tersely stated, adding a menacing crimp with his talon on Tine's chest.

"Just dispatch me now Vincen. I am not in the mood to face those accusers of mine that struggle to think past the edge of their ears."

Vincen breathed a breath of disgust and squeezed his talons even harder around the arrogant Dove. "You better change your demeanor when we arrive, or you won't enjoy the remainder of your prematurely short life." Vincen remained confounded by Tine's pride. He turned to his left and signaled, the black sky-traveler shadowing from that side nodded then turned away from Vincen with the remaining escorts. They headed back to their assigned lookout posts.

From higher, the spy swooped down from behind the tweensts.

She tried not to spook them and failed. "May I ask where you are going?" The tweensts' grouping immediately fell apart. "Wait! Every one of you come back here. I need to speak with you. Don't make me angry!" The tweensts were scared but logical. There was no way to outmaneuver the entire escort party. They regrouped to answer the spy's questions. "That's better. All of you follow me. We will speak once we are on perch." They followed her without hesitation.

***

Vincen flew on without incident. Word traveled fast. As he flew over his homeland penetrating eyes were raised, struggling to catch sight of the traitor clutched tightly in the revered Eagle's grip. Questions formed in every mind but no creature voiced any opinion. No opinion would be voiced until Vincen had his say, his argument presented. What exactly that argument entailed was any creature's guess. Vincen headed to Mystic's dwelling. The tribunal should be gathered soon.

# 5

The arrow sliced through the air silently as it flew toward its target. Even from 200 yards the archer was deadly accurate. The target perched high in a tree, shielded by a low canopy of thick green leaves. Slightly to the left, his wing stretched across a branch. Between two of the longer feathers was a gap just big enough for the arrow head to pass without harm. The victim closed his eyes partly out of boredom and partly from lack of sleep. The arrow arched a medium height before realigning itself and honed in on the target. With a smooth, barely audible whack, the arrowhead neatly embedded itself between the feather tips just as planned. The unknowing victim suddenly became quite alert and shot out of the tree. His eyes immediately located the archer and as he approached he demanded, "Now what did you do that for? Can I not get a short minute's rest without you trying to impale me with that gadget of yours?"

"Ah don't worry about it. I had no intention of impaling you today! I was just proving to my friend here that you were actually awake in the tree. We had a bet and I think I won, did I not Hemoth?"

"Yes, yes I think you did," replied the friend stifling his laughter.

Far from settled, the handsome Falcon added, "I refuse to be fodder for your jokes or a target for your games! You must respect me, for I am your elder. I told your Father I would always watch out for you. How am I to do that if you kill me? Hmm?"

With a great smile and a little laughter, the archer said, "Sig, you know very well if I wanted to impale you, I would have impaled you. I merely wanted to get your attention. Might I add that I did?"

"I'll say. I promise I will stay more alert for your protection from this day on."

"Oh really, from this day on? Are you joking with me? You are too old to stay that alert!"

"Really, and you talk this way in front of a guest...who I have never met or seen before?" Sig nodded at the friend and offered a wink with his eye the archer did not notice.

The archer could not keep from chuckling at this type of talk. "You always sound so proper when you are mad. I'm so, so very sorry. And may I introduce to you one of my dear old friends. Hemoth, please make your acquaintance with Sig. Sig is my dearest friend in the whole world."

"Why thank you. It is a pleasure to meet you Sig."

"Oh no, the pleasure is mine sir," stated the overly courteous Falcon.

"Well then, so be it. I have traveled a long way to speak with your charge here. Would you mind walking with us? We have lots to discuss and my friend here wants you involved with everything."

"Certainly, I will be honored to share your company."

The small group turned and began walking back to the archer's home. "Hemoth, please tell me why you have made this long journey just to bring me a letter...could it not have been sent by messenger? And, are you sure you and Sig have never met before?"

"I'm afraid not. The messenger was not available and the circumstances are far too sensitive for me not to get directly involved."

The archer's brow tensed, "Well since I have not seen it yet, at least tell me who sends it my way. Sig, please fly a route and let me know of any approachers."

"Yes, Miss." The Falcon was off.

"Very well Madaliene, I will certainly let you see it. Let us stop for a moment and you may open it. Then, you tell me if it is important enough for me to be here or not."

Hemoth gently swatted at a large clasp on his chest. A brown bag dropped to the ground beneath him and he used his snout to nudge it toward the archer. The archer kneeled down next to the bag and pulled an ornately detailed envelope from inside. The hand writing on the face was delicate and proper. The letters were feminine and spaced perfectly. It read:

*For the sole purpose of notifying P.M., your family sends you here the best and most heartfelt wishes on your upcoming engagement. Stay sharp and invite your true friends. The guest list should not be short, as several here wish to make your acquaintance. The new invitees are wanting to combine and bring you a glorious gift. As we were taught, glorious is not always best. Do not write back. You need not make that effort. Love and rainbows. P.E.*

The archer took a deep breath and turned to her friend, "Hemoth, is this a bad message from Evaliene? I can't really tell because it is so cryptic? If it is bad, she must be in a trouble of some kind."

"Very good point, Miss. I honestly can't say. Is it not full of well wishes?" Hemoth paused, "There have been several messages of this same sort being sent everywhere. I think it might be a ruse of some kind."

Sig returned and hopped upon the archers shoulder. "All clear my dear. Madaliene, did I hear you say the letter is truly from Evaliene?"

The archer, struggling to hold back frustration, closed her eyes, faced the sky and shook her head up and down. "Yes Sig. It is from Ev. I think we must go to her. I can't believe she didn't bring this in person. Should we hurry? Do we need to make plans?" Madaliene turned and grabbed Hemoth's shoulder, "Hemoth, did you just say several messages like this are being sent everywhere?"

"Yes, Miss, I did."

"How can that be?" Madaliene asked dumbfounded. "These types of messages were only meant for a select few individuals. Do you think someone may be setting a trap for a bigger catch? Whoever the instigator is will be in for more that they bargained for. I am sure this came from Ev, but she's my sister and I could recognize her style of writing anywhere, regardless of the circumstances."

"You are correct, Madaliene. Several of the messages have been received by two-leggers who are not Talkers. They have no idea what the messages mean. Someone is up to no good here, I assure you. They are wasting a lot of time and effort to communicate with folk who don't have a clue what they are reading."

"Well, Hemoth, don't jump to that conclusion. Do you not think that is part of the larger plan? Maybe besides our code, there is another code between these lines meant for other readers with other meanings. This situation could already be out-of-control. How many of these have you tracked? Where is the origination point?"

"That is exactly why I am here. You are the one with the means to figure that out. We have four-leggers everywhere as you know, but a few key messengers are missing, including Evaliene's. She hasn't been heard from in a very long time."

"You are joking...surely. How did you get this letter if she didn't bring it to you? Who else knows where you are?"

"It was not delivered to me by Ev's messenger. I don't know who told this letter's carrier of my whereabouts and that bothers me. That bothers me a lot."

"We need to let someone else see this, but first I have more questions. Sig, will you please fly again? Keep an eye out for foreign wingers." The archer and the giant Bear continued their conversation, the Falcon rose high into the beautiful blue sky.

***

The messenger returned under duress. Several of her fellow sky-travelers were in captivity. They were held in a decrepit, non-descript barn on the far border of a vast battlefield of the past. It had been used during the recent years as a nurturing area. A plot of land to grow food, raise young leggers, revel in youth or contemplate growing into the late years. Both two and four-leggers enjoyed this bit of land with a reverence for the ghosts of long day-rounds past. There could not be a more unacceptable use of this revered site than its current employment. Inside the failing, long since abandoned structure sat untidy row after row of dangerously tall, wobbly stacks of filthy wooden crates, each of which had seen better and happier days. Crammed inside each crate, various sorts of sky-travelers struggled to move or even breathe. There were countless hordes of Hawks, Pigeons, Crows, Doves—thousands, nearly every type of winger, some which were normally thought to be invincible. Confined for extended periods of time, several were experiencing their last days of existence in this world. Tragically, these were not randomly selected individuals; these were entire families of wingers-from the youngest to the oldest. Stolen away from their homes, they were all captives. The youngest watched as the strongest were sent on messenger treks well beyond normal flight distances. Gone for days on end, they would return within a given time frame or else return to a crate full of unmoving clumps of feathers. The captors showed no mercy on those left behind. Perform the task, return for the next directive or lose your family; that was the painfully simple guideline.

More often than not, messengers came back to lifeless crates...regardless.

She was exhausted. Maybe, if she was lucky, this would be her last mission for these heathens. She stretched open her wings, pulled her head up and slowed down to the speed necessary to enter the void in the barn wall without slamming into it. Famished from a lack of nourishment-there was no time afforded for food, she toiled desperately with her balance. Maybe she should just slam into the barn and ease her suffering. No, she would fight for her family trapped inside. Watching her suffering from very high above, a much larger sky-traveler was also approaching at a rapid pace, much faster than her own. This winger had no intention of slowing to enter the barn. He rotated his body in an instant to intercept her path. In a short blink of an eye he was honed in on his target, strong, blunt talons extended, wings folded tight to his side. He pierced arrow-like through the crisp air. This shouldn't take long and he needed to get back to eat. Just as the rank odor seeping from the barn hit his nostrils, he gently, but swiftly snatched the weary messenger from the opening. With a few wing beats, the immense sky-traveler bore his prey away from the sickening barn and high off into the still crisp air.

She emitted a shriek that sent shivers through the feathers of the wingers still breathing in the crates. "Noooo! My family! They will kill my family..."

A voice completely void of emotion replied, "They already have."

Inside the barn, the caged wingers were terrified but silent. The creatures responsible for the captures and mission assignments were livid. Arguments broke out amongst them all. The leader demanded to know what just happened and who was responsible. Chaos followed. Blame was thrown at every creature not crated. "How could this have happened? What was that thing? Where did it go? How? How? How?" The leader panicked then screamed, "Kill them all! Kill them all!"...and they did. No crated winger escaped. To some, their horrifying end came as a relief. To others, it was dreaded but expected. The scrambling within the barn took a toll on the integrity of the building. Great numbers of falling crates smashed into weakened old poles, chipping away at the barn's fragile structural integrity and crushing the captives within. Without any feeling, good or bad, for the occupants, the entire structure collapsed upon itself. Unfortunately, some of the captors escaped. Even more unfortunately, the leaders were in that group. With an eerie, rabble-spewing, ear-shattering, thunderous crash, it was over. A large stomach-turning cloud of dust and feathers, freedom and hope exploded into the sky where it lingered for a few clicks before silently drifting closer to the ground. That cloud of misery would hover and ferment for days to come. The destruction posed a very unfitting memorial to those brave sky-travelers buried in the rubble.

***

"Ev's winger did not deliver this to you? How else would you get it?" Madaliene asked.

"A Golden delivered it. How she found me still baffles me. I don't think the letter was meant for me. It was addressed to you, but study the impressions above your name. There was another name or location written first then removed. I believe it was to be delivered to someone else first then to you by different means. I think something else was supposed to see this and, by the fact that they did not, we may have avoided a scenario a bit more troubling. The Golden was adamant that I deliver it directly to you. She mumbled some information I could not make out when she left me. I figure she may have stayed long enough to draw three, four breaths? Then she was gone."

"A Golden? A Golden delivered this to you? Are you positive she was a Golden? What did she tell you? You must remember something Hemoth! You must!"

Yelling, "Miss, do you not think I already know that? I have tried Madaliene! I have tried! I am not familiar with the Golden's dialect. It sounded mostly like gibberish to me. I was fortunate to understand what I did. Since she left me, I have been trying to recall exactly what she said. Believe me, I want to know too!" Hemoth was visibly upset with their predicament. He stormed around in a circle, shaking the ground with each fall of his giant paws.

"I'm sorry Hemoth. You know I trust you, but this is so unnerving. Ev has a White not a Golden. If this came from her, where is her winger? Did the Golden do away with her, steal the letter and bring it to you knowing that you would find me? Are we being watched right now? Was she watched?"

"What is it with you two-leggers? Do you think every winger has its own agenda? What is the problem with a Golden? Are they so different from the Whites? No matter. We will certainly take up this conversation later, if we are able. I don't have the stomach for it today. Where is that tiny winger of yours? Did you terrify the life out of him?"

"Hah! That brave little Falcon has seen his fair share of bad times. I certainly did not terrify the life out of him. It would take far more than being shot at with a bow." Madaliene put two fingers in her mouth and blew three strong breaths. The whistle that was emitted from her delicate features was stunning. Hemoth turned his head away to escape the shrill noise.

"My sakes, Madaliene! You want to give me a little warning before you do that again?"

"Oh I'm sorry. I forgot what sensitive ears you four-leggers have. Next time I'll warn you." She quickly, put her fingers to her mouth again and blew a long straight breath. Again the noise was just as shrill and stunning as the one before, maybe a little more so. She coyly smiled, cut her attentive brown eyes to Hemoth and through pouty lips whispered, "Sorry."

"Madaliene!" Hemoth roared.

Within a breath Sig was perched on Madaliene's left shoulder. Three short bursts followed by a long burst called Sig down from whatever route he was flying or roost he was roosting. The bond between the legger and her winger could not be broken by anything less that one's death.

Sig, with a gleam in his keen eyes, asked Madaliene, "Should I dispatch him?"

"Who is he talking about dispatching, Miss?" Hemoth inquired.

"Why you of course my large furry friend!" She answered.

"Me? He wants to dispatch me? You are teasing me. You are...teasing...correct?"

Madaliene and her sister had glorious laughs. Smiles widened, exposing perfect white teeth, their noses twitched and the dimples in their cheeks appeared, brilliant eyes twinkled like bright stars on cloudless nights. Yes she was teasing Hemoth. She and Sig had a good laugh at the big four-legger's expense. Hemoth just looked puzzled and shook his enormous head. "Very well then, I have been spared the might of the little Falcon. How might I show my appreciation, Miss?"

"First, we have to get back to my dwelling. There is a lot to figure here. Night is near and we shall eat, plan and rest. In the morning I hope we can get to the bottom of this, or at least be headed in the right direction. Shall we?"

"Please my lovely two-legged friend, lead the way."

Sig initially planned to ride Madaliene's shoulder back to her dwelling. He wanted to listen in and be a part of the coming conversation. Instead, with one look in conjunction with a tilt of Madaliene's head, he was off to scout the several paths home. Should he discover a problem, only then would he return to her side. If nothing was out of the ordinary he would continue on his own, making his way back to the dwelling as he saw fit. This way, if either of them was seen, no connections would be made tying the two of them together.

The trip back to Madaliene's dwelling was a route taken distant from the paths most generally traveled in the area. There were few inhabitants of this region that even knew she was here, much less any that knew of her dwelling. She always shied away from the normal gathering places since she had nothing but bad memories where large numbers of people were concerned. She had always assumed her parents were still around somewhere. Her family split up voluntarily many years before when word came that the heirlooms were being hunted again. The heirlooms, what would anyone need with an ugly handmade decoration and a bow? The heirloom Evaliene received wasn't satisfying to look at. Madaliene never bothered an interest in it. She had received the bow that was now slung across her back. What value could it have? It was just a bow. She learned to use it early in her childhood. She was a marksman by the time she was four years old. The bow was big for her then and smallish for her now, but it could out-shoot skillfully made longbows, much to the disdain of those expert bow makers. Evaliene was her older sister and only sibling. Evaliene was about 18 years old which made Madaliene closer to 16. She never really kept up with her age much except for an occasional reading of the calendar that sat at her bedside. Madaliene stayed outside more than she stayed inside. The outdoors appealed to her tastes where Evaliene had grown accustomed to either. Both of them could defend themselves whatever the situation, ride Horses or the like as well as any male or better. Madaliene had a strong will and Evaliene possessed a quick temper.

The separation was planned years in advance of either of their births. Plans were made and followed out perfectly in practice runs beginning when the girls could walk. When Madaliene turned 10 years old the practice runs ceased and the actual separation took place. Madaliene ventured to her secluded fort and her grandparents, Evaliene followed her parents where she was met by her guardian who took her to a secret location inhabited by several of her father's trusted and loyal secret-sharers. Each secret-sharer was trained and loyal beyond death. There were no betrayals, no traitors, no non-believers. They shared lives with folk common to the township where the guardian placed Evaliene. This location was left completely up to the guardian. The secret-sharers made their way into the township in small groups, avoiding suspicion, until they blended in perfectly with the naturals. The secret-sharers were a very powerful group of people, linked by blood to the girls' father. No foe could win a battle against them.

After a long walk that saw several clicks pass by, Hemoth began to wonder if they would ever reach Madaliene's dwelling. "Will we see your dwelling today, Miss? Or will we keep walking 'til morn?"

"Oh poor Hemoth, we are almost there. Look up." She pointed directly over her head. High on the cliff to their left was an outcrop of rock. "See the outlook? Just below that is the entrance. You will just squeeze through. The path is narrow, just don't look down. There is a row of fir trees that screen the entrance from approachers and you can use them as a railing."

Hemoth was not feeling at ease. "Do we climb up the cliff to access the entrance?"

"Yes, we have to. There are clefs and steps that you should find very handy. You aren't afraid of the climb are you?"

"Well, I am not keen on climbing cliffs for at least one good reason."

"Oh dear, you will be fine. I will even let you carry me up so you will have a great reason not to fall!"

"I guess that would give me a good reason to make it up," Hemoth added.

"Let us give it a try, shall we? We are here. There is the first clef." She pointed at a rock about two times her height off of the ground.

"Bend down and I'll climb on your back."

"You were serious then?"

"Yes I was. Get over here."

"No promises. If I fall, we both fall, right?"

"Right." Madaliene grabbed fist-fulls of thick fur just behind Hemoth's large ears. "This doesn't hurt does it?"

"No. You would have to pull a lot harder to hurt me. Just hang on. Here we go."

Hemoth climbed the face of the cliff nimbly as a Squirrel. He was extremely proud of himself and knew this was exactly what Madaliene had in mind when she suggested it. Carrying a part of history on his back gave him all of the strength and confidence he needed to conquer his fear of falling.

"Whoa there Hemoth. You are about to pass the entrance. One more clef up to your right, then look down to your left. Swing me onto the ledge, then you can easily climb onto the path. You can grab hold of the trees and step right through, but don't look down!"

"Gotcha."

Without further incident Madaliene and Hemoth both landed solidly on the path in front of the dwelling. After a short stroll past the row of fir trees, Madaliene slid through a round opening in the side of the cliff directly under the rocky outlook. After a little huffing and puffing Hemoth entered the front chamber of the dwelling and was amazed at the amount of room he had to stretch out. He immediately fell to the floor to rest.

"Hey you can't fall sleep right there! We aren't quite inside yet. Come on."

"We're not?"

"No. Just a bit farther in." Madaliene led Hemoth through three larger chambers before turning to the left and traveling down a slight ramp. At the end of the ramp, she turned left again and turned to her guest.

"Welcome to my aerie, Hemoth!"

Hemoth rose up on his back legs and stared in utter amazement at his surroundings. "Who built this for you? This is a palace! I can't believe I have never been here before."

"This is merely one benefit of being royalty my friend. My father, his father, his father's father...their secret-sharers built this for me under extensive direction way before I was born. Evaliene has one just like it, but I don't know where it is. Actually, I don't think she does either. Oh well."

"Madaliene, you are home." A sweet voice echoed from within a side chamber. "I'm glad you sent Sig ahead of you. I had no idea we would have a visitor tonight."

"He is really not a visitor at all Gamma. I believe you know each other."

The large Bear stepped into the smaller chamber. "Hemoth!" Gamma shouted as she hurried over to greet the furry visitor with her toned arms stretched high, reaching nearly to his shoulder. "I can't believe you are here! When was the last time I saw you? You were so much younger and a tad smaller. My, my you are so very big now. I wish I could have known your parents, how big they must have been. How are you? Where is your dwelling?"

A thousand questions could be asked all at once by all parties. Madaliene interrupted the merriment. "Hemoth, show Gamma the letter. She needs to know. You remember she is a pretty smart lady."

The Bear was struggling to understand how this lady could even be standing in front of him, let alone, asking so many questions. "You?" quizzed Hemoth. "You live here with Madaliene? What else do I not know about this mysterious young lady?"

"All in good time my friend. I find it hard to believe she has not told you of me. Where is this letter? Sig told me you brought an important notice to my dear granddaughter. From what I hear, it can't bode well for our future."

"How, how, how are you here? They buried you years ago. I was there. I saw it. You suffered a terrible accident. I saw you after you fell. How did you live? If you are here...it must have been a trick? That was so mean spirited of you. I guess you are going to tell me that..."

Another voice approached from the back, "I am alive as well?"

"Oh my." Hemoth was startled once again. He felt very weak in all four knees. He attempted to steady his enormous bulk. "Gann, you are...you are...I ought to stomp you 'til you can't breathe! I have to lie down. Let me rest. You read the letter and tell me about it when I

55

wake up." With that, Hemoth dropped where he stood and immediately fell fast asleep.

"You might should have warned him about us," Gann grinned.

"Gann, you know I can't speak of either of you outside of this mountain. This letter proves that things are changing again and no one can know of your existence. For all plans and practices, you and Gamma are long since dead and buried."

"But you could have told Hemoth couldn't you?"

"No Gamma. I cannot tell anyone or any creature, period! I am not going to lose you!"

"It's okay Mad, show us the letter."

"Okay, here it is." Madaliene pulled the envelope from a pocket on the inside of her shoulder bag. She removed the exquisitely hand-written letter from the envelope and handed the scented paper to Gamma. She gave the envelope with its broken wax seal to Gann. "What now?" she asked.

"This is absolutely your seal," Gann stated. "The wax is not of the kind your family used in the past... still its quality is sincere. The stamp looks original. It has not been tampered with. Wait..."

"Evaliene writes so beautifully doesn't she?" Gamma had wondered over to a short table near the rear wall, unfolded the paper and laid it close to a large reading candle that illuminated most of the chamber.

"I don't think she has used any words to trigger the code. Let me see..."

"Wait? What do you see Gann? Is there something wrong with the stamping? It all looked normal to me." Madaliene raised her hands to shake her wild hair loose from her silk head scarf. She folded her arms and shrugged.

"No, no dear, most everything is normal here. No sign of panic. It's just that the stamp is not perfectly straight. Evaliene never stamps her work without fretting over every small detail. Hmmm, here is something else. See how the wax is thicker on one side? She did this in a hurry. She would never rush something like this without cause."

"What do you think was her reason for the rush? Why was she in a hurry?" Madaliene asked the same question twice, she was nervous.

"It's okay Mad. We can figure this out. Let's look at the letter before we jump to conclusions." Gann tried to ease Madaliene's thoughts, as he turned to Gamma huddled over the letter. "What have you discovered my lovely?"

"You are so sweet," she answered. "At first read I saw nothing out of the ordinary. I mean there were no trigger words to invoke the code. But, as I read it over and over...something just doesn't seem right. She is trying to tell us something."

"Did you remove the spaces? Did she use a letter count instead of the code trigger words?" Gann loved using his wits to solve puzzles. All three of them knew there was more to this simple letter than one might see at first glance. But what? Evaliene was telling them something important. They had to figure it out. They would figure it out.

Madaliene looked over Gamma's shoulder to read the letter again. This time she noticed something that startled her. "Oh no!" She did not react well this time. "Oh no!"

"What is it dear?" asked Gann.

"It is so obvious. Can neither of you see it? The capital P and M on the first line! Ev always said she would never refer to me as princess unless she were dead! It has been that way as long as I could remember. All of the parties and festivals, we were always two princesses in public or when we were introduced with Mother and Father, but in private? No way. She was oldest, she was the princess. She did not ever let me forget that. Of course she was wrong since we are both real princesses, however in our speak, she was the princess and I was only the little sister. Oh no, she is in danger." Madaliene steadied herself next to the table.

"Now Madaliene, don't jump to a bad conclusion just yet. Let's think about this rationally first, shall we?" Gamma was trying to gather her thoughts as well. The little bit of information Madaliene had just revealed was now troubling her too.

"Now both of you need to collect your thoughts. Gather yourselves. There is more to this. We cannot discover anything if we do not approach this with reason. You must take your emotions out of it." Gann was not going to tolerate this turning into an emotional disaster. "Give me the letter. This is far too important to cry over!" With that he took the letter. He walked to the other side of the chamber, sat in a tall chair and read it again...over and over and over.

"Where did you put the envelope Gann? Let me see it again."

Madaliene walked quickly over to Gann's side as she spoke.

"I have it right here dear. You may inspect it again if you wish, but be sensible! We don't need tears washing away all of the evidence your sister has given us."

"I understand, sir. I will control myself better this time." Madaliene retrieved the envelope from Gann then sat down beside him. She carefully went over every minute fold and crease of the envelope. Where were the other clues?

"Madaliene are you hungry? I can get you something to eat anytime."

"Sure, Gamma, a snack may help me think more clearly. Fruit and tea would be nice." Madaliene continued tracing every delicate detail of the envelope. "There has to be something here," she said quietly. "Gann what are these little marks around the edge?"

"Madaliene have you ever known Ev to write so rudely? The words do not flow as hers normally would. She seems very determined that you not make certain mistakes. Should not, is not, do not and need not. That usage is simply abrupt and rude. What marks are you speaking of dear? Four nots, why four and not five or six? Why any?"

"Here you go loves. Time for a break. I have fruit and tea, Madaliene, just as you asked." Gamma came back in the room and set the table with ornate cups and beautiful green porcelain plates. "Come quickly, the tea is hot. The letter can wait a bit. Oh, the four nots may refer to the four knots that you girls always tied in the cords that secured your diaries. Remember, one knot for Father, one knot for she, one knot for Mother and one knot for me? You still have your diary, don't you Madaliene?"

"Oh spiked tree toads!" Madaliene jumped up and raced to her bed chamber. With one fluid move she lifted her well used diary off her side table, slid the cord from around it and bounded back to the table. She grabbed a large round fruit from the grouping and took a tasty bite out of the fattest, juiciest apple one could imagine. "Thank you so much Gamma for that clue. We may be on to something!" She hurried back to Gann's side.

"Not so fast young lady. Gann you bring her back to this table. Both of you will sit down and you will eat. When your stomachs are full, your heads will work better. Get over here now!" No creature was going to take the call to the table lightly with Gamma. Gann and

Madaliene humbly sat down at the table to begin eating a very decent snack. The possible clues and riddle-like connections zipped through their minds. "That's better."

She couldn't hold it in any longer. "I think the knots on my diary cord are the key to the code, if there is a code in the letter! What do you think about that Gann?

Gann said nothing in reply. He ate his food while nodding to Madaliene. He knew better than to get into an argument with Gamma. The repercussions would be harder to deal with than just waiting until after eating to deal with the letter and the code and whatever else. And she was correct, as usual; a full stomach usually leads to a sharper thought process. He continued to eat in silence. Gamma turned her attention to Madaliene.

"Young lady, if you want to finish your experiment with Ev's letter I suggest that you eat now. If not, I can make that a very difficult process for you."

Madaliene wasn't going to win this fight. She acknowledged Gamma with a nod of her head. Being a smart girl, she kept eating. Not another word was spoken until the last tidbit of food was removed from the platters and eaten.

It seemed to Gann and Madaliene that hours had crept by as they sat at the table trying to enjoy the meal. With each bite, their minds scrambled through the options for decoding the cryptic message that must be hidden within the letter. It must have taken Ev quite some time to assemble the wordage which correctly placed each individual letter. Gann was positive that the true message contained in the letter would eventually show itself. Madaliene was not so sure. Gamma, secretly, wanted to take another look. What could Ev be telling them?

"Should we wake Hemoth? I am sure he could use a bite to eat also." Gamma knew every creature had to eat. Even though Hemoth could easily deplete their immediate stores in one sitting, she was determined to make sure he had the opportunity to fill his stomach.

"No. Let's not wake him yet. He has come a long way on little sleep to find me. We have enough to do on our own. He will awake on his own time. Where is Sig?"

"I assume he is out watching the mountain on your behalf dear."

Gamma began to clear the dishes from the table. "He was a bit perturbed when he could not figure out how Hemoth reached you with him knowing nothing about it. There were, according to him, no signals or mentionings of Hemoth being in this area. It seemed to him like all of the posts were inexplicably abandoned. He hasn't seen or heard from another winger in weeks now. I am sure he will be back soon enough."

"Yes, he was noticeably flustered," Gann added. "But now let us get back to Ev's riddle, shall we?"

All at once Sig came barreling into the den. Flying much too fast within the confines of the dwelling, he crashed into a back wall before tumbling to the floor. Righting himself immediately, he again took wing heading for the table where the letter was spread out in front of the readers. He crashed into the back of Madaliene, flapped his wings and clawed his way up to perch on her shoulders. Frantic, he spoke. "They are all gone! Every post was empty! There is not one watching eye remaining within this whole land. I saw some disturbing sights at some of the posts. Not all. Only some. Those were bad enough. Blood, feathers, signs of struggle. They are gone. They are all gone!"

"Sig, who is gone?" Madaliene was distraught after she saw the look in her Falcon's eyes. Normally a brilliant brown, they were now a dull black. His feathers slightly tousled from the brush with the wall, showed wear from flying at a high speed.

"Madaliene, they are all gone! There is not a sentry left at any post from here to forever. I checked going, I checked coming back. I found blood. I found signs of great struggles. I found lots of feathers. I did not find one sky-traveler! Not one! Where are they? Who could have taken them all? Who?"

"Calm down, Sig. You need to eat and drink. We will take care of you first, then, we will listen again to what you have to say. Not another word until you gain some strength from food." Gamma knew something was amiss. It would be no use to sap Sig's willpower at this instant.

"Madaliene, let Gamma take care of Sig. She will let us know when he is better. Now we must decode this letter from your sister.

"You are right as usual, Gann. What do we have so far?" Madaliene picked up the exhausted Falcon and laid him on a soft chair cushion near the hearth. He didn't need warmth, just rest and food.

Gann cleared off the rest of the big table. He used a flat knife to scrape the crumbs into his hand before tossing them away. He laid the letter and the envelope on the clean table. "Madaliene, we should not expect to leave this table until this riddle is solved. If it takes all night, so be it. Are we in agreement?"

"Yes, Gann, no one here wants to know more than I do. What do you want me to do first?"

"You take this envelope and that string of yours. Use your brain. Think like your sister. What would she naturally do with her string if she were sitting here next to you? How would she bide her time with it? I will go over this note stroke by stroke until some pattern emerges. Your sister is as brilliant as are you. Unfortunately, I can think like neither of you. You two got the smarts from your mother's side of the family."

"Right Gann, I'm sure we did because you and Gamma are as dumb as rocks! Please." She began twirling the string in her hands, wrapping it around her fingers, tying her hair back, just about every use for the string was exhausted sooner that she hoped for. "One knot for Father, one knot for she, one knot for Mother and one knot for me." Madaliene said this short poem repeatedly. "One knot for Father, one knot for she, one knot for Mother and one knot for me. Come on Ev, what did you mean?" She placed the string on the envelope. She went through every geometrical design she could by lining up the knots on her string with specific nodes on the envelope. Suddenly she shouted, "I need another string! Quick Gamma another string! I must tie it exactly like this one. Please hurry!"

Gamma left Sig recovering on the cushion. She rushed to her bed chamber and came trotting back holding a string almost identical to the one Madaliene was using. "Her you go child. You nearly stopped my heart."

"Thank you Gamma. I may be on to something."

Gamma moved behind Gann, wrapped her arms around him and gave him a great hug. "How's it coming, old man?" she asked before returning to Sig.

"I don't know if I'm getting anywhere dear. If I think I am, I will let out a holler just like Madaliene did." He winked at Madaliene. She returned it.

Madaliene successfully tied the knots in the new string in exactly the same spots as the knots in her original string. She had more trouble maneuvering the two strings across the envelope than she bargained for. She laid one string across the top of the envelope and a thought suddenly occurred to her. "How clever is Ev? This is so elementary." She reversed the two strings then laid them side by side. The knots were not equidistant from each other, which left every other knot between the originals. "Gann, please hand me the note. Do you see how she has left her spacing completely random? She never writes like this. Now, I am going to lay these strings over each line of words. I want you to write down each word and letter that falls under each of these knots. I will reverse the strings on every line. When we are at the end of the note, let's read what we have left."

"Madaliene, that sounds a little too easy, don't you think?"

"Well Gann, in order to even try this you would need one of our strings. If this works, like I think it will, you would need the two identical strings to figure it out. Who else would have that?"

"You may be onto something Mad." Gann leaned forward in his chair ready to write down whatever Madaliene told him to.

"Let's try it Gann."

*Solepurposefamilyhere*
*yourandyour*
*listnotwishyour*
*wantingcombinegiftwere*
*notbestneedthat*
*rainbows*

"Those are the words, let's get the letters."

*eye*
*ydr*
*lnwo*
*tefw*
*obnt*
*w*

"I am afraid this says nothing Madaliene. It is nothing but gibberish."

"Gann, there is something there, I know it!"

"Well, let's find it then my girl."

"Gamma, do you have a sharp knife? We need to cut some holes in this envelope." Madaliene's mind was spinning. "Gann, may I borrow your quill?"

Before she realized it, Gamma handed her a thin bladed knife. She placed the knotted string over the envelope in the shape of an "E" and marked the spots where the knots fell. She then did the same in the shape of an "M" and marked those spots. She cut out slots where the marks were. She placed the envelope over the words Gann had written down.

The visible words were:

*Sole purpose combine family gifts*
*need you here*
*were your wish rainbows*
*not the best*

"I don't get it. This should have made sense."

Gamma took a look at it. "Why Madaliene it does make sense. Your sole purpose is to combine your family gifts. She needs you with her to do so. If you thought you could avoid trouble with your bow that would not be the best method of solving the problem. You have to find her. Before anything good can happen, you have to find her. You and Evaliene are the family gifts, not anything you have."

"All of that puzzling for that? It is so cryptic, why did she not just write it plainly so we would not have spent so much time on it!"

"Madaliene, that is not the only riddle there dear. The letters you found beneath the words are the real puzzle."

Madaliene and Gann both looked at Gamma simultaneously, "Huh?"

"Believe it. That is the real puzzle. Let me see what I can do. Gann, you go check on Sig, he needs to eat. Madaliene, you need to wake Hemoth. I'm sure he is very hungry as well. I'll figure this out for you two. You have done the hard part. Let me have some fun with it."

63

Gann stoked the fire with another log. It wasn't cold. They merely enjoyed hearing the crackling and popping. Its randomness eased the deafening silence of the cave. They had lived here for several years, since Madaliene was 10 years old. She was now closer to 17 than 16 which meant this cave had been their dwelling for close to seven years. If it had not been for the safety of their granddaughter, he and Gamma would have taken their chances in the old family manor. The "Terrible Years" had displaced so many people. Factions of instigators continued to roam the world of the two-leggers.

It still wasn't a safe place for the families of the Defenders. His ancestors raised everyone in their family the same way. The difference between right and wrong was never a grey area. It was black or white--right or wrong. Gann knew several acquaintances who could not define the difference between right and wrong and several of those were caught up in the middle ground of the debates that sprung up in the years after the "Terrible Years". Now, he correctly assumed, some of the remnant factions were growing, bent on forcing the issues again. They were easy pickings for any of the polar opposite groups. He hated that aspect of social change. Unfortunately, the world of the two-leggers was changing and would never be simple again. His job was to protect Gamma and Madaliene to the death and he would do that. His son and daughter-in-law had not been heard from since they sent Madaliene with him and Evaliene with her Protectors, who were the surviving families of the Majestic Guard. It was too dangerous to keep the family together in their homeland. It was too easily approached by their enemies. The family was split up so that each daughter could be raised under different circumstances in order, hopefully, to be reunited at some point in their future. This was a dangerous theory, which Gann had argued up until the day they separated. He was of the mind that if the girls were raised in completely different environments, their opinions of what was right for one may not be what is right for the other. That way of thinking was dismissed by the most intelligent person most people had ever met-his wife, Gamma.

\*\*\*

"Sig, are you back with us now?" Gann stroked the feathers on Sig's head. The Falcon looked completely different now than he did before his nap. His feathers had laid down nicely, his breathing, once again, steady and light. "Sig, wake up. You need to eat."

Across the way, in the front chamber, Madaliene was having more trouble awakening the sleeping Hemoth. "Hemoth, get up you huge furry beast! Get up!" Madaliene pushed, prodded, poked, pulled, shoved and pinched the sleeping, snoring mountain of a Bear. "Good knights of yore! Get up you snoring beast!" Madaliene took a few steps back; she readied herself for a running leap onto Hemoth's heaving back. "Here I come; you are going to wish you had awakened sooner!"

She propelled herself a few steps and jumped with all of her athletic grace and strength. She aimed to land atop Hemoth's backbone in the middle of his shoulders, grab his ears on either side of his monstrously large head and shake violently until the Bear came to. Madaliene did jump, very high and gracefully. However, during her flight, Hemoth opened one eye, caught sight of the airborne lass and timed his next move perfectly. While Madaliene was gaining height with her jump, Hemoth rolled towards her while holding up his giant front paw. Madaliene saw the movement too late to correct her direction. "You're gonna pay for this you stubborn oaf! Uumph."

"Am I really?" Hemoth held his paw high, Madaliene wrapped tightly around his trunk of a forearm. "Were you about to pull my ears lassie? You know that is not a wise move."

Madaliene slid off slowly like a slug crawling down a rock to the cavern floor. There she sat. She blew out a long perturbed breath, puffed out her cheeks and rolled her eyes and neck up at Hemoth who was now towering above her. "One day I will best you Hemoth. Dread that day beast. Dread that day."

"Madaliene, although you are an arrogantly diligent lassie with loads of spunky charm, may I politely say you will never best me. Hah! What does Gamma have for me to eat? I hope she has rooms and rooms of food, because I certainly feel like I could eat for days." He extended a paw to Madaliene. "Truce?"

Madaliene took a hold of the Bear's paw with both hands as he easily lifted her off the floor. "We have lots of food, but if you eat it all, I will have to throw you off the mountain. Is that clear?"

"My dear Madaliene, you never quit do you?"

"Never, you overgrown toad, never."

## 6

The spy led the tweensts higher above the forest floor. On the side of the mountain, beneath Vincen's aerie, a natural void in the rock formed a perfect, semi-circular room. The room was well-used with a cozy air to it. She perched at the front edge and watched as each of the younger birds landed before heading inside. She positioned them so each would have an unobstructed view of her and her of them.

"First of all, none of you should fear me. Neither I, nor any other winger here in the Great Forest has any intention of causing you harm. That can't be said for your elder in Vincen's clutch. Had I been sent to retrieve him he would have never made it back breathing on his own. Also, had I known his cowardly existence was within my flying range, I would have sought out his worthless living carcass and transformed it into a lifeless rotting carcass not even good enough for the lowest form of slimy, crawling maggottry to digest." These callous statements were presented in a smooth, calm voice void of any emotion.

The delivery did nothing for the tweensts except cause even more nervous tingling beneath their feathers.

"Now for the quadrant of you," the spy eyed each of them individually as if she was making plans to enjoy them as four separate meals. "I know you are too young to know anything of any importance regarding your leader, however, I want to know what you know of the past few day-rounds. Why is your small group following him? Are there anymore of you out there? Do I need to round them up also?"

"No ma'am." One of the tweensts answered. "There are no more of us that we can tell. The rest were killed or removed during the attack of two moons ago. We had hidden, as we were told, beneath a large boulder. The one the Eagle clutches saw us go into hiding. There were six of us. He bullied his way into our haven, forcing two of us out into the open. We never saw them again. We have assumed they were killed or eaten or taken away by the attackers. We despise the elder we flew with."

A second voice continued. "We were pursuing him to whatever end he might find. Had we been older, maybe we would have done him in ourselves. A pitiful whining creature that one. Pitiful."

The spy listened as each of the young Doves recalled the attack in detail up to the time they went into hiding. The eye-witness descriptions were followed by explicit details surrounding Tine's appearance and occupation of their hiding place. Each tweenst despised him for forcing their friends out. That much was very clear.

"Well young Doves, you each have found approval with me. Tine is despised around here. It is hard to believe Vincen brought him back," she turned her head from side to side, looking around the small room, "...breathing. You will be safe here. Make yourselves at home. I will return for you."

***

Vincen lit on an ornate cupola rising from a steep section of a rear roof of Mystic's dwelling. From here, he viewed the gathering tribunal and curious onlookers. Nearly every Great Forest dweller was in the crowd or accounted for. "Well Tine, it's now or never. I hope the powers that be accept my offer to throw you on the mercy of the court."

"Vincen, what plans do you have for me? What makes you think I will accept any offer you make me? I could very easily flee once you loose your grip on me." Again Vincen grimaced at the words spoken by the arrogant Dove.

"Tine, let me make this obvious for you. Should you try to escape me, you will not make it. You will not make it to the edge of the Great Forest. You will not make it to the edge of the yard. You will not make it away from my shadow. I will personally cleave you in half with one snap of my beak. Should that happen, my co-dwellers here would have a grievance with me for not allowing them the opportunity! You are hated here, Tine. Can that not be made more clear to you?"

"That doesn't scare me Vincen and neither do you. You could loose me this very instant and I would be clear of this assembled rabble before they knew I was gone."

67

"Very well then, as you wish." Suddenly, Vincen raised his claw, loosed his talons setting the Dove free. "Let me see for myself how far you get."

Before Tine left Vincen's shadow, he was once again in the grip of sharp talons. "Going somewhere Tine?" Karone spat the question out like the words were poison.

"Let go of me, Pheasant! Let me go and I'll do away with you!"

"As you say fool," Karone loosed the Dove.

Tine fell from the Pheasant's grip. He was instantly in the clutches of the spy's claws. She was not happy with the tweensts' stories; actually, she was livid. She was here to witness Tine's tribunal appearance. She only hoped she would have the duty of dispatching him after all was said and done.

"Not so fast coward!" The black Crow squeezed the breath from the Dove. "Quite the bragger now aren't we?"

Vincen looked on as Tine quivered in her grasp. "What were you saying again? You would escape me and all the rabble collected here? I think not. Take him to the podium, Arlis."

"Can I not just dispatch him now, Vincen? We are wasting too much time with this worthless molt."

"Please, let me state my case. If he refuses what I ask of him and the tribunal denies my request, then I will turn him over to you. Will that suffice?" Vincen knew the pain Arlis would inflict on Tine. Fortunately, so did Tine.

"Whatever, Vincen." Arlis flapped her wings heading to the southern part of Mystic's back garden. The tribunal awaited the accused and Vincen. She lit on the podium releasing her grip slightly on the still arrogant, but quiet Dove. She stared into his eyes with a kindled, burning gaze.

Vincen composed himself before nodding to Karone, "If Tine escapes us again, do what you must with him. Do not let him escape." He swooped down to join Arlis and Tine. Approaching the podium, he could only imagine the questions he would soon field. The foremost question on his mind? Why, Vincen? Why did you bring that traitor back here? After all he brought down on us, why would you bring him back? The Great Eagle could only hope the rest of the tribunal would see his reasoning.

***

Riding along on the back of Lightning, Frederick lost track of time. He was as confident as he was intense. He had set his mind on unraveling every thread of every riddle imbedded in every word, drawing, scratch or scribble in his notes. Slowly he was making sense of the entire history of the Staff, its past guilders, bearers and owners. Like a slow growing tree, the seed had sprouted in the cavern beneath the "Forever Trees" and it was growing taller with each passing moment. Frederick relented to himself that even at his current pace he would not know all there was to know about the Staff for many years to come...unless it decided to tell him. This seed was meant to grow a very tall tree.

"You still up there, Frederick?" Lightning asked. "You know I almost forgot about you."

"Yes I am, Lightning. I have been studying the whole time. Where are we? What do you make of our position?"

"I have no idea where we are, but the Wolf and the Cheetah are convinced we are heading to higher ground."

"Really?"

"Yes really. I have to believe them for I have seen nothing to the contrary. The land behind us is fading into darkness. So much for figuring how much higher we are than when we started out earlier."

"Well I know I have been of no help at all. The more I find out about that Staff, the more questions I have pushing me farther and farther into these notes and diagrams. It may be the death of me, but I will find out what it is all about."

"I believe we will need you breathing if you are to help us further."

"I was speaking metaphorically dear Badger."

"Oh I understand Frederick. I'm simply making conversation. I think we need to stop and eat, don't you?"

"To be honest, Lightning, that thought has not crossed my mind."

"You little creatures, how can you go without eating?"

"I think the urge to hibernate is beginning to affect your thinking." At that moment or maybe a little earlier, Frederick felt Lightning slowly lower to the ground. He instantly heard great snores coming from his mount. "Lightning! Lightning!" Frederick climbed down the huge front shoulders before plopping onto the ground. He spied Bubba and Mystic some distance ahead as they were disappearing into the grey of middle night. He decided his safest option was to stay put next to his large friend. He stepped back to Lightning's side, yawned and took a long, deep breath. He sat down between Lightning's head and his front shoulder. He never remembered dozing off because he fell asleep instantly.

Mystic and Bubba were traveling in silence. Not a word had been spoken for quite some time. Bubba instinctively turned his head to get a glimpse of their companions. He stopped as soon as he realized they were not their normal distance behind. "Mystic, hold up, we are missing half of our group."

Mystic turned around to see for himself. "You don't think any trouble has found them do you?"

Bubba did not answer immediately, but instead perked his ears up and took several steps back down the path. "I don't think any harm has become them, still we should find them. We can't travel separated. We can't separate at all. Follow me!" The Cheetah did not wait for a response from Mystic. He took off at a fast pace followed closely by Mystic.

If there was panic on the faces of the pair, it was soon displaced with large smiles as they came upon the sleeping leggers. "Well Bubba, I think they had a good idea. I wonder why they didn't let us in on it?"

"I couldn't agree with you more, Mystic. Shall we?" Bubba crawled to Lightning's side while Mystic lay down beside Frederick. Suddenly there were no problems in their world. Sleep came upon them soon; a heavy, restful sleep. At sunrise they could continue their trip to wherever they were going, but now all was well. High above them a large dark sky-traveler circled effortlessly, borne by air currents and a large dose of curiosity.

\*\*\*

The melee of questioning started even before Vincen figured it would. No sooner had he lit near Arlis when he heard the first barrage of questions hurled in his direction. "What were you thinking Vincen? How could you do this? Are you out of your mind? Let the coward go, I dare you." There were all kinds of expected questions and demands directed at him, but he brushed them all aside.

"Hold on!" he exclaimed. "I am in charge here. If you would allow me the time, I will explain the reasoning behind this so-called outrage." Vincen was now eying every creature in the garden. "May I explain?"

With respect to Vincen's plea, the crowd hushed. Though some still grumbled to themselves, the crowd and tribunal gave their full attention to the Eagle. While some hoped Vincen's argument would quell the uprising, others were hoping that the cowardly traitor would succeed at making one final attempt to break free of Arlis' tight grip. If he did, the uproar would soon be over and Vincen would not have any explaining to do, for the Dove would be dead and the Eagle's desire for bringing him back forgotten.

"As if all of you don't know already, we have a problem. Using Tine may be our fastest option for getting the word out. I know that each of us have pre-described duties in and around the Great Forest, but this little slug-eater has no responsibilities here."

Some creature in the throng stated, "You are not telling us anything of importance now Vincen. We know the worthless rubbish you brought back here never took responsibility for anything while he dwelled here among us. Get on with your plan."

"That's enough!" Vincen firmly answered. "Tine here owes us with his life. That is not in question. I am of the opinion that we coerce him into running an errand that will either help us greatly or end his life. Either way is good for us."

Tine twisted his head up at Vincen. He was not sure of where this was going. He tried to speak until Arlis' grip closed even tighter around him. She looked menacingly down at him, growling under her breath, "Give me an excuse to take you Dove, any excuse at all..."

Vincen continued speaking. "There is, outside of our land, those that have been sworn to help under dire situations like those that may befall us very soon. The thing is...no creature knows where those are. I can only imagine they dwell many, many day-rounds from the edge of our forest. I can't go out on any chase with no end for I must stay here, with you. We must study our plans for defense and enact them. As many of you do not know...Mystic, Bubba and Lightning did not return with me from our last adventure. I will explain more on that later when I am able to put more of the details together. Anyway, as of this moment, I am in charge. I will not take that lightly. I suggest to the tribunal that in order to pay in full for his unacceptable behavior in the past, Tine be persuaded to find those who can help us. He must locate them, explain our plight, bring them to us or die trying." Vincen cast a glance at Tine that almost burned the life from him. "What do you have to add? Anyone?"

Lemeer stepped to the foot of the podium. "Vincen, as first juror of the tribunal, I need more information before I trust this useless bag of feathers to do anything. I assume you have more you would like to share with us or is this it?"

Lemeer was soon joined by the remaining jurors, ten of them in all shapes and sizes. Each of them nodded in agreement with Lemeer.

"Very well jurors, I have no more details. I am relying on facts I have heard since birth. As each of you well know, my birth was long before each of you came to be. It was told to me after the 'Terrible Years' ended that we had an opportunity to reach out to others experiencing the same trials we struggled through. We didn't. From sheer ignorance, pride or stupid self-reliance we fought the wars alone. Our families paid dearly for those poor judgments. Do any of you think we can or need to bear a burden like that alone, again? None of your parents and very few of your great-grandparents were around to witness any of the horror brought to our ancestors or the aftermath of losing so many brave loved ones. My question is why chance it again? Face it friends, evil is out there. It is once again spreading. Our idyllic life within the borders of our Great Forest could be now and forever in jeopardy. I propose we send Tine out after answers. If he successfully returns here, it will only be with the help we need. If he doesn't return, he will be out of our lives until time ends."

A juror spoke up, "What makes you think he will perform any duties we assign him, Vincen? What has he to gain?"

"You have asked good questions. I will answer the second question first. What has he to gain? He can gain his self-respect back. Believe me, that is very important to him. Now to answer your first question, Tine is not stupid. He knows he will never see the light of another day-round if he refuses our assignment. Too many of you gathered here want to see him suffer for the irreparable pain he caused us. I must admit I cannot see how he could suffer enough, but plenty of you have ideas of how to make that happen that I won't get into. If he refuses to help us, Arlis will turn him loose. Does that satisfy any of you?"

Arlis was the first to speak. "Oh yes Vincen that satisfies me. You have no idea how much it does."

Vincen looked at her, "Arlis, I think I do have an idea. But I think each creature here has similar ideas. That is why I don't think Tine has any option but to do our bidding."

The Dove tried to say something and Arlis didn't flinch or try to speak, she simply tightened her grip ever so slightly around his chest.

"Anyone have any better ideas? Please speak up now. Time is slipping away from us. We must act soon." Vincen hoped for no further discussion.

Lemeer was fidgeting with a shiny round cylinder in his paw. "Fine with me Vincen, have him do as you say. If he refuses, have Arlis release him. Let me say to you, my fellow jurors and all others gathered here, life can be painful." The Badger looked directly at the terrified Dove. "Very, very painful."

***

She remained high above the sleeping leggers, her flight path growing in ever widening circles. Keen eyesight, at her altitude, was not what she relied on for guidance. She was more in tune with her instinctive feelings. Feelings that never let her down. A certain air of discernment on which she trusted her entire life. It's time they should move. She had watched over them all night. Nothing had interfered with the sleep they desperately needed, but now it was time to go. She lazily made her way to the ground. Scanning the ground for something to toss their way, maybe to startle them awake, she discovered the remnants of a long ago fallen tree. Gliding over, she clasped a solid section of the trunk in her strong claws. Without hesitation, she began ascending to a stealthy altitude. It wasn't long before she was over the group of sleepers. Slightly upwind of her target, she dropped her cargo 10 to 20 two-legger paces away from where the group slept. It landed with a loud, deafening boom, shaking the ground violently. The leggers were, at once, involuntarily awake and alert. With no time to shake off the groggy, after-sleep syndrome, each came to their feet attentively looking past all four corners of the compass. High above, she continued her circling and grinned.

"What on this world was that?" Mystic called out to all.

"It sounded to me like an explosion of some kind." Frederick was well versed in the study of explosions, not so much the four-leggers.

73

"I would have guessed the crashing of a tumbling boulder, but there are no mountain sides from which it would come." Lightning too, was at a loss to explain the interruption.

Bubba eyed the aftermath of the falling tree. He stepped away from the group to get a closer look. "Over here!" Bubba stared at what was left of the tree trunk then he stared into the sky. Up and down, up and down. "Where did this come from?"

Frederick walked to Bubba's side. He kneeled down to inspect the wood shrapnel scattered about and the crater created when the quickly falling trunk hit the ground. "This is not a natural phenomenon where I come from."

"What could have caused this?" Mystic, like Frederick, was inspecting the splintered wood remains as he stepped around the crater. Whether by instinct or wariness, each legger kept one eye on the sky and one on the mess of wooden debris. "Something dropped this with intent. I want to know if its aim was off."

"Or did they miss on purpose?" Lightning wasn't searching the ground anymore, he was searching the only place left; the sky. "There is no reason to think otherwise; this was either dropped for our benefit or theirs."

Frederick scooped up several shards of wood. He rubbed them together in his hands. "This wood is not rotten. Had the aim not been slightly off, these splinters alone would have caused serious damage to all of us, probably killed one or two as well. Yes, this was no accident."

"But who or what could have dropped something this big out of the sky?" Mystic remained puzzled.

Bubba squinted skyward. "I know something large enough to drop this. I told you the winger that chased me was big. It could have easily dropped this from very high above us. High enough that we would have never known it until it hit. That is exactly what happened. Whatever came after me is still up there."

"Too bad Vincen is not here to get up there with it. Maybe he could identify it for us." Frederick still held pieces of the tree in his hand. "This wood is remarkable. I've never seen anything like it. It must have been felled years ago, but it shows no sign of rot."

"Or get taken by it." Lightning kept his gaze high, craning his neck to its stops hoping to see even higher into the bright blue space.

"Okay, was this a warning or a miss?" Mystic needed to know.

Bubba had the only answer, "Does it matter who or what dropped this? For whatever reason, we obviously need to move on. A moving target is much harder to hit than an assembled, stationary group. Shall we?" The Cheetah motioned forward with his head. "I suggest we move now?"

"Sure, sure, I agree Bubba. Let's get going." Mystic stepped to Bubba's side. "Lightning, shall we?"

"What about breakfast? We have to eat breakfast."

"You can eat while we are on the move. I'm serious, let's get going."

Mystic took charge. "Frederick, you coming?"

"Yes Mystic, of course. I'm taking some of these splinters with me. I'll catch up to you." Frederick hurriedly stuffed all sizes of splinters and shards in his bag. "There, that should do it." He slung the bag over his shoulder then rushed to join the others. "Mystic, Bubba, Lightning, I suggest we keep some distance between ourselves. If another something is dropped on us, I would hate for it to take us all out at once. It would be better for our efforts if some of us survive to complete this trek, for whatever reason that may be."

"I agree Frederick. Let's keep at least four or five of your paces between us." Mystic was thinking clearly. "I will lead, Lightning you behind me, then you Frederick. Bubba you trail us. You are quick enough to avoid most falling obstacles and fast enough to escape if that need arises. This is hard to say, but we can't spend a lot of time caring for our wounded. Should something terrible happen, we must continue. Do you agree?"

"Yes, of course we agree Mystic." Bubba was taking his place at the back of the line. "I don't believe single file is the best way to travel either. Let's make the next attack on us more difficult. We will put space between us and fall out of a straight line. To put it another way, let us wander along together. We will all take different paths to the same end. Does that make sense?"

"Sounds good to me, but I have to eat." At the moment Lightning would agree with anything if it meant he could begin stuffing his belly.

"Lightning, think about it. How much food do we have to eat? We brought only enough to get back home, right now we don't know how far we are from there, furthermore we have no idea where there is! We have the sweet mud, a few kakes and the Nuorg water. We aren't going to use the Nuorg water to drink, at least not now. Is that clear?" Mystic was in charge now. There was no doubt.

"Fine, if we do find food fit to eat, I will gorge myself. Take that anyway you like. I will eat my fill."

"Fine with me. Hopefully, we will find something soon. We won't if we don't move ahead though. Are we good?" Mystic was tiring of the talk. He had other things on his mind. "Let's go."

Mystic led the way with Lightning behind to his left. Frederick followed off to Lightning's far right. Bubba trailed slightly. He stayed directly behind no one. His chosen course zigzagged behind the others.

***

She liked what she saw. Finally they were learning and adapting. They might make it after all.

# 7

G amma sat at the table, poring over the jumble of letters left after Gann and Madaliene's attempted deciphering of the puzzle. "Dear, are there any other letters that could have been under those words? Unless Ev was delirious when she wrote this, I cannot imagine what she is trying to say." Gamma wrote the individual letters down on a large sheet of paper to ease the strain on her eyes. "Look at this, it's enormous and I still can't see anything in it or on it. I have been in this cave too long."

Gann brought Sig over to the table. He was alert enough to ride on Gann's arm. Gann sat across from Gamma folding his arms on the table. "I am at a loss too Gamma. I still can't see anything in that mish mash of letters."

Sig looked down at the large sheet of writing paper laid out in front of him. He was stunned. "I did not know either of you knew the language of the Eagle's so well. Who wrote this?"

Gamma alertly raised her head from the table. "What on this earth are you talking about Sig? You can see something here?"

"Of course I can. You cannot? Gamma I am surprised. First, you are reading it upside down. It is as clear to me as you are."

"Well? What does it say?"

"Must...find...Nuorg...Window. What is Nuorg?"

"Nuorg? How are you spelling that?"

"In your lettering, N U O R G."

Gamma wrote it down. "N U O R G? That doesn't spell anything."

"That is what it says. It is very clear to me."

"Is it backwards?" asked Gann.

"No, that would be G R O U N. That doesn't completely spell anything either does it?" Sig was confident that the letters spelled Nuorg.

Hemoth stuck his nose into the discussion. "Groun? Did you mean to write ground? Where is the D?"

Madaliene was next, "Must find ground window? Wouldn't the other words be backwards too?"

"I'm telling you it says "must find Nuorg window" and the N is upper case. You would not spell ground g r o u N, would you?" Sig knew the Eagle's language, these leggers did not.

"You sound sure of yourself, Sig. I have no reason to doubt you." Gann did not know what to make of it.

"What or where is Nuorg?" Madaliene asked.

The others all replied, "I have no idea."

*** 

Just outside the cave, on the low, thick branches that cleverly hid the entrance, a nervous and exhausted winger perched. Alert eyes darted in every direction. She was not absolutely sure if she had been followed. "I hope this is the place." Earlier she had been plucked out of the sky and carried far from her dwelling. Separated from family as they were under attack, she was convinced she would be promptly dispatched and eaten. While she was lifted higher and higher into the dark sky, she listened in horror as the other members of her family were swept away by wingers and caged or beaten senseless by leggers whose origins were unknown to her. A winger had removed her from the attack zone much to the dismay of the attackers. "What was that?" She heard one of the attacking wingers scream. The winger took her high and drifted on the currents higher than she had ever flown before. In silence they soared, the gigantic black winger never bothering to utter a word. All she could make out were large white spaces under its wings. She was held loosely with one claw. She noticed the other claw was not like a normal winger-- the talons were straight and blunt, while hers were razor sharp, though she never tried to inflict any damage on the rescuer. They soared for several clicks and the larger winger never flapped a wing. Higher. They went even higher. The air was getting cold and thin. She wasn't able to breathe at this altitude. They soared in complete silence, the wind moving them along at its pace. She was at peace. Her memory of the attack became foggy, her breathing slowed. Just before passing out, she took in the serene beauty of the land far below, wishing it would look that way if she ever got down to it again.

The wind was buffeting her face. She awoke. The huge winger was descending rapidly, forcing air into her lungs. Her world was coming into view again. What was going on here? Why had this winger spared her? She saw mountains. They did not look familiar. The winger was slowing with deft adjustments of gigantic wings.

After a complete flight in total silence, the rescuer spoke with a deep, nearly unintelligible voice, "You are alone. Stay silently where you fall. They will find you. Beware of the intelligents." The stealthy winger released his grip on his passenger, flapped his wings once or twice and was gone over the mountain.

The terrified captive, released, fell directly into the lower branches of the large trees. There she stayed. "Who will find me?" she whispered.

***

Hemoth's spacious stomach growled. "I'm sorry, Gamma, I need to eat. Do you have enough to spare?"

"What kind of question is that, Hemoth? I have stores enough for a family your size. Have a seat on the floor. I will fill this table for you." She motioned for Gann to clear the table of the papers.

"Sig, let's take a walk. I need to get out of here to clear my jumbled head. I need to find my sister, but first I have to clean the vestiges of that riddle off my mind. How about a moonlit target practice?" Madaliene loved shooting her bow day or night.

"I will gladly accompany you Miss if you promise not to use me as the target this time. That is growing quite redundant." Sig hoped onto her shoulder.

"Gamma, we shouldn't be long."

"Be careful dear." Gamma returned to Hemoth with a platter full of berries and freshly baked doughy rolls. "This should get you started. Gann, here is a pint of mead from your latest vat. It should be well aged by now."

Hemoth politely began gorging himself with the array of ripe berries. Gann retook his seat with the stein of mead, a mustache of foam on his lip. "Cheers there, Hemoth. Let's enjoy a nice break. We will be up to our necks figuring out what a Nuorg is soon enough!"

***

Madaliene stepped outside into the fresh air. She was alive outdoors--she yearned for it. "Well, Sig," she asked as she drew a

79

slender arrow from the quiver that never left her shoulder, "What should I shoot? A cone from a pine? A tusk from a boar? A hair from an ogre's chin? What will it be?"

"I don't have the foggiest idea child. Why not shoot an enchanted arrow high in the air? Let it find its own target. Why should we always make that decision?" Sig was preoccupied, his mind wondered back to the missing sentinels.

"Well that is an easy answer. I have no enchanted arrows. I'm thinking you have been reading too many bedtime stories." Nocking the arrow securely on the string, she gently placed the shaft of the arrow on its rest. Her bow hand, which was her right, held the bow loosely at her side, two fingers of her left hand cradling the nock. She studied the sky for a moment then closed her eyes to read the wind. "Sig, if I did shoot this enchanted arrow at a star, do you think I would hit it?"

"Knowing how well you shoot, I would never doubt it could be done."

"You are so kind, Sir Falcon. I think I shall aim for the brightest star I can see." Madaliene raised the bow. She scanned the sky for a suitable target. With her bow arm pointed in the general direction of her chosen star, she drew the string to the anchor point on her cheek being careful not to overdraw. Holding steady, she finely tuned her aim. As she released the nock, the arrow glided smoothly off the rest, the fletching gently grazing her hand as it began to stabilize the flight. It elegantly pierced the night, sailing toward the brightest star with a flowing arc before settling into a downward decline.

"Far be it from me to challenge your aiming, Miss, but it appears to me that your aim for that bright star may be slightly off." Sig was nervously tracking the arrow's flight with eyes much more capable than Madaliene's. The Falcon's eyes were adept at following small, ground-bound objects from high aloft. In this instance, he was using them in reverse by standing on the ground following a flying object.

"I'm not sure, Sig, I think I aimed correctly. Why?"

"Because your arrow is now heading directly back to us. Is it a boomerang arrow?"

"Sig, I don't have enchanted arrows and I certainly don't have a boomerang arrow!"

"Well then, fair enough. That being said, I suggest you duck immediately."

"Really?"

"Really!"

Madaliene managed to duck in time to avoid the returning arrow as it made its own course unswervingly over her head. "Good night! That was close!"

Sig zeroed in on the arrow as it whizzed over Madaliene. "Indeed it was." A sharp flick sounded behind them. "I believe your arrow has struck and held in that large spruce tree yonder."

Madaliene was still crouching on the ground. "I believe it has as well, Sir Falcon. Shall we retrieve it?" She was laughing at the predicament and Sig's choice of words. "A tad proper are we?"

"Be my guest."

"No, my liege, after you. Age before beauty." Madaliene enjoyed it when she and Sig laughed together.

"Yes my dear, as you wish." Sig flew straight to the arrow, "Here it is archer. Here rests your enchanted boomerang arrow."

Madaliene trotted up the slight incline in the trail to where it stopped dead in front of the trees. She reached the arrow and wiggled it free. She held it up for Sig's benefit. "Well the flight of this arrow will make quite a story, will it not, Sir Falcon?"

"Indeed it will, Miss." Sig sensed another winger in the tree. He spotted a shivering mass of feathers approximately eight branches higher. He whispered to Madaliene, "There is another winger higher up in this tree."

She whispered back, "Well ask him, or her, what business it has in our tree."

"What do you want me to say?"

"I don't care. Say be you friend or be you foe. I don't know. You have to say something."

"Are you going to shoot it?" Sig replied.

"Do I need to? We don't know why it is here yet. Go ahead, ask it."

"You there, in the tree, be you a friend or be you foe?"

Madaliene squeezed her eyes shut, clenched her lips together and crossed both of her arms over her chest in an effort to contain her laughter. She managed to get out one more furtive whisper. "I can't believe you said that." She returned to containing her laughter, her body heaving.

"It was your idea!"

81

"Shhh! How is it reacting?" She was still struggling to contain the laughter.

"It is now looking at me as if I were a newt."

"A newt? Did you actually say a newt?" She was crying now.

"Well, it hasn't flown away yet. Shall I ask again?"

Madaliene was fanning her face with one hand and wiping away tears with the other. "Newt? You said he was looking at you like you were a newt." She resumed her laughter.

"I know what I said, Madaliene!"

"A newt." She was tearing up again.

"What do you want me to do?"

"Go up and get him or her. Please, I can't help you now."

"If it attacks me, you will shoot it won't you?"

"Yes, yes I will shoot it. Go make a new friend or something. If I have to shoot, make sure you are clear. I promise I won't use my newt arrow." She was still giggling uncontrollably.

"Yes, quite hilarious you are, Miss, quite hilarious." He hopped further up the tree. "Hello there winger, what are you doing here? Come on, answer me straight away."

A scared voice replied, "Does she really want to shoot me?"

"Not if you identify yourself to us properly instead of stalking us from up in this tree."

"I need help. I was told you would help me. My family is gone, carried off by attackers earlier. They were wiped out. We were the sentinels south of Glacier's Crest. Please don't let her shoot me. I am so scared."

"There, there, you say Glacier Crest? That is a very long flight from here. How did you get here?" Sig felt awful for the winger.

"May we please find cover? I am very scared."

"Madaliene, have you recovered? Are you presentable now? We have a young visitor who needs help. Do you mind? And, don't shoot him!" He looked again to the visiting winger, "Oh yes, I almost forgot, she is a Talker."

She had regained her composure. She needed that laugh. Everyone needs one now and again. "Yes Sig, I am quite composed now. Bring him down and I won't shoot him."

"Does she mean that, sir?"

"Yes, she means it. Let us get you inside. There are others that need to hear your story. Hop down and perch on my two-legger's shoulder. Madaliene, will you give him a ride inside? The poor lad is tuckered out."

"I absolutely will. Send him down."

"Well, go on lad."

"Yes sir. Thank you."

"Never you mind. We will talk more inside." Sig lit on Madaliene's arm.

The frightened winger lit on Madaliene's shoulder, and looked up to her with sad eyes. The preceding events were coming back to him now.

"Winger," said Madaliene, "We will do the best we can to help you. We will need to hear your entire story. Are you okay with that?"

"Yes ma'am."

\*\*\*

The crowd slowly dispersed leaving only the jurors, Vincen, Arlis and Tine in the garden. There was too much preparation to undertake for the Great Forest dwellers to hang around waiting on Tine's decision. He was on their minds, but the least of their worries. Vincen glared at the Dove still imprisoned by Arlis' clutch. "Well, Tine, what will it be? Will you do what I ask, or are you going to try an ill-fated escape...which is exactly what the majority of the dwellers here hope you try. It's up to you. I need an answer now. Arlis is growing bored with you."

"What makes you think I won't escape this miserable place again? None of you had any right to hold me captive after the accidents. What I lost was more than any of you could imagine."

"That does it!" Arlis squeezed Tine within a few breaths of lifelessness. "You! You worthless piece of rotten molt! How dare you address us with those remarks?"

Tine could barely breathe. "How do you think I dare? You are nothing but a scavenger, preying on the deaths of other creatures for your sustenance. Of course I'll address you anyway I see fit!"

Vincen was stupefied, "Tine, you remain an arrogant, condescending, self-righteous boor. A slow miserable death would be too good for you. Part of me hopes you take this assignment and succeed just so you can live the remainder of your life in that morbid, lonely existence you call a life. The rest of your years spent growing more hateful and resentful until the final breath oozes from your pitiful, decrepit body. I am growing tired of you. What will it be? Yes or no?"

"If doing your bidding will gain the un-needed forgiveness of this wretched place and all of you ridiculous creatures, then yes I will do as you wish. Yes. Yes. Yes! I don't need your blessing to live out my life as I see fit. I never did anything wrong to any of you! None of you ever had any business accusing me of any wrongdoing. I was taking care of myself. I was looking out for me!"

Arlis lost her restraint. She released Tine only after giving him a death-beckoning squeeze. "Tine, you allowed your hatchlings to starve to death. Your mate, rest her soul, gave her life laying her eggs and then you sat by and watched as your hatchlings slowly gasped their last breaths because you said you never wanted them in the first place. You had the audacity to tell us that the hatchlings were her idea! You killed them! You let all of them die and you watched! You never, ever offered to feed them while you left the nest to eat as you pleased! You don't deserve to live! Ogres and monsters would not find favor with you!"

Arlis paced maddeningly around the still motionless clump of feathers, staring holes through him. "Then after we dealt with you on that matter, you convince hordes of our numbers to venture out past the limits of our lands knowing full well the dangers they would face! You knew then the price two-leggers would put on our heads out there. Most of them never came back and not because they didn't want too! You used your slick talking to lure them to their deaths at the hands of those meat-eating two-leggers who live far beyond the Black pond. The offspring of the worst of the two-leggers that decimated the Wolves! What did you have to gain by that? How did their sacrifices manifest a reward in your pathetic life?"

"It was done to prove to all of you once and for all that I am the smartest creature within these scraggly tree lines. If I can talk you idiot creatures to your deaths, then there is no limit to what I am able to acquire for myself. I am the only thing that matters to me. I have the nerve to watch my birdlets die in front of me and feel no remorse. I have the intelligence to talk others to their deaths, what can you possibly do here to stop me? There is no satisfying my desire to ruin you all."

Vincen, if he fails or changes his decision, please let me know. I can't bring myself to look at him anymore. My stomach is churning. I must go." Vincen nodded as the Crow took wing.

"Tine, you are the lowest form of life I have ever known. There is no way to atone for your past. No way to beg our forgiveness. Your only saving grace will be to help us as we requested. You will never be welcome here again, but our dwellers will forget about you. We will not pursue you again, ever. Is being left alone worth anything to you?"

Tine managed to flip over and get to his feet. He was barely able to speak. "Vincen, as much as I loathe you dwellers of the Great Forest, I will do as you ask, but you will never convict me of wrongdoing. What do you want me to do in order to rid myself of you forever? Remember, there is no guarantee from me that I won't betray this miserable place to anyone and everyone I meet, if they only promise me to wipe the Great Forest from existence."

Vincen was keenly aware of the many pairs of eyes watching for the outcome of this discussion. Tine, if he was aware of them, did not acknowledge any threat. Secretly, Vincen wished Tine would attempt an escape. This sky-traveler had no reason to live in his mind. Should he try to escape, well... he certainly wouldn't live for very long. "Tine, fly east over the mountains, the plains and the large waters. Ask around for the Falcon Master. He will have the knowledge to take over where you leave off. Once you make contact with him, tell him of us. After he accepts your offer to help, you will be released from your duties. You will be free to live out your pathetic life as you see fit. No creature from here will follow you or threaten you for the remainder of your life. If the Falcon Master does not agree to help us, you must return here and I will grant you your freedom. Now be off at once before one of the dwellers changes their mind."

"I just fly east until I find the Falcon Master? That's it? That is all you are going to tell me? You are an ignorant oaf, Vincen, whose time has passed. Very well. I will fly east. I am sure your highness that I will find everything just as you say. And I'll be back. You better believe I'll be back. I'll come back just to hear you acknowledge my freedom in front of the insignificant and stupid masses that inhabit this regretful place." Tine slowly regained his composure to take wing. He was off. "Ha-ha! Goodbye Great Forest. Goodbye for now!"

Vincen watched the grey Dove disappear into the bright sunlight. He turned to the trees where so many eyes were watching. He nodded solemnly then paced around the podium. He was not sure if he had done the right thing. The pairs of eyes scurried off to continue their business leaving Vincen to his own thoughts.

***

Throughout the lands of the many worlds they surveyed, attitudes were changing. The fresh air breathed in was not the same as the tainted air breathed out. There were creatures searching for power, searching for wealth, creatures who had never known either were now intent on having great masses of both and having it all now. Not every world included these creatures, but many worlds did. Those creatures had a unique way of communicating among themselves. It had to be more than happenstance. These problematic hundreds schemed more wisely than the bad doers of the past. Some wise folk said the evolution of bad was more intent on succeeding than was the evolution of good.

This was what they needed to stop. They had to stop or, at least, reverse the evolution of bad. They were a powerful group themselves, led by a creature few had ever believed in and fewer had ever seen. As a matter of fact, most of them had never seen it either. Still it was good. There was no doubt about that.

She was sent from it. As she hovered far above her clutch, her thoughts wandered...why her? Why this group? Other members of her clan were thinking the same thoughts, she was sure of that. How many others were there? Her mission, "Do whatever is needed to guard your clutch. Direct their paths as you see fit. You are the good here." That was it. That was all of the mission's directive. Was it really that simple? So far she didn't think so. What was so special about these characters anyway? No questions were allowed and no further answers given. There was one secondary and ominous warning given to each of them as they left, "Beware of the intelligents." What did that mean? She decided not to try to understand it, she would find out soon enough. Then, she would retreat back to the mountains, reunite with her clan and live peacefully as they had for so long before.

# 8

His land was bleak, hot and dry. Where there was enough water in the ground to sustain them, trees grew scattered about in clumps separated by far-reaching fields of sand. Other than the trees and sand, only dry river beds and lots of hard, dusty ground that sometimes stretched for days of walking helped to break up the landscape. Jahnise enjoyed this land. The only surviving child from the last ruling tribal clan, he was very tall with a slight, slender build, aged somewhere within his middle years. His exact age was of no importance to him or any of his folk. His cheerful, deep-set eyes were dark brown. A woven-wide brimmed hat atop a hairless head and wraps made of fine thread and his friend shielded dark cocoa-colored skin from the glaring sun. He loved his land. He enjoyed his people. He enjoyed being royalty. His folk found ways to cope with nearly every obstacle the land put in their way. Jahnise was a wise man. He settled disputes among his folk with honesty and common sense. He never let arguments get out of hand and found favor with rival tribes as a result of his unselfish leadership. If called, he would journey for days in order to settle even the slightest of bickerings. The food of the area was not tasteless. But on occasion, Jahnise wandered the fringes of the land searching for something different to eat. This day happened to be a very lucky day for his folk. On this day, a new food source would be added to the menu. The travels Jahnise would carry out in order for that to happen would change his land in a good way.

Jahnise had been travelling for a good three-quarters of the day. The sun had not started to set and his insides were telling him it was time for a short break from the heat. He had grown to trust his insides and took heed. As beads of sweat formed tiny rivers that ran down his rounded cheeks and over his strong square jaw, Jahnise came to a stop on a small rise that was barely noticeable if one were not directly on top of it. Oddly enough, it was not even off the beaten path. Jahnise stuck his walking stick in the sand, sat down, retrieved his water sac and took a few needed sips of water. Once his ration of water for this stop had passed his pronounced lips, he replaced the seal with his long muscular fingers and with a twitch of his wrist swung it around to his left. He glanced around to reset his bearings and noticed to his surprise that a wet spot was developing near his right foot. A bit startled, he double checked the seal on his water sac to make sure it was not leaking. A leak would be disastrous in this land. Jahnise pulled his legs beneath him in an attempt to stand but the right foot disappeared into the ground. He quickly grabbed his walking stick hoping to regain his balance. He couldn't. The wet spot was now a very real water hole and his leg was immersed up to the knee. The hole was tugging at him. He could do nothing to counteract the suction as the water started to spin and change colors. Almost as quickly as it began, the water claimed Jahnise. He was rushed down through the vortex. He gave up fighting to stay afloat. He smiled. "It must be my destiny," he quietly noted as his head passed out of sight. Once the hole swallowed Jahnise, it simply closed leaving only a few wet drops as evidence that it had ever existed.

There was no creature around when Jahnise was consumed by the mysterious hole. No creature was there to give assistance or call for help. Sadly, that seemed to be the one drawback to being alone.

Jahnise was not the kind of man to struggle with the unknown. Living alone for most of his life he had become accustomed to adapting with whatever was thrown his way. He approached this odd turn of events with the same perseverance anyone who knew him would expect. He calmly accepted the circumstance and vowed to make the most of the situation as it revealed itself. In his mind, destiny was much more powerful than any man could defeat. He chose to use his strengths to acclimate with that particular destiny rather than fight a futile attempt to overcome it. Jahnise relaxed as the liquid enveloped him and sped him away from his homeland. He took a deep breath, closed his wondering eyes and a wide grin lit up every facet of his face.

***

"Do you feel that? Something is coming through!"

"Yes, I do feel a small, irregular vibration. I think you are right. Shall we wait for the arrival over behind that outcropping of rock in case we don't like what we see?"

"I agree. Let's expect our guest from over there."

From behind the medium sized boulders, two pairs of watchful eyes awaited the visitor. These eyes were relatively young and never before bore witness to a window opening. They were very excited. Soon, just as it had been explained to them, the ground began to shake and little rocks began to quiver. Suddenly an opening appeared in the designated spot, as predicted, just under the trees. A fountain of purple and green water burst forth shooting high into the trees. In an instant the fountain dissipated and the window was closed once again.

"Did you see anything come through?"

"No, I can't say that I did."

About half way up the tree was sprawled something that did indeed come through. The two-legger was soaked to the skin with the colored liquid. His hat sat lazily a few branches above him. His water sac, still hanging around his neck, was draining dry through a large rip in its side. A walking stick tumbled to the ground landing with a soft thud in the grass beneath the tree.

"I think we have a visitor," one of the small four-leggers stated to the second. "Should we inquire as to his state right now or just see what happens?"

"Let's wait and see if he makes any move on his own to get out of there. We really must work on that entry if we are to expect more visitors. That could be quite an uncomfortable arrival."

"Yes, I suppose you are correct."

"I hope he is still able to make quick travel."

"Of course he is. You know what that water is capable of."

"Yes, yes of course I do."

Jahnise opened his eyes. He was not familiar with this type of tree with the thick leathery leaves and huge branches. The last stage of the ride was a blank. He remembered sitting on the small rise and stowing his water sac, the warm cocoon of liquid that surrounded him...then this. He would have to figure a way down to get a clear grasp on his location. He noticed his hat was slightly out-of-reach and above him. He stretched his long sinewy arm towards it and just had it in his grasp when he lost his balance and fell down through the branches. He landed hard in the grass at the foot of the tree.

"Do you still think he is healthy?" asked the second four-legger.

"I hope so. The water is still all over him. See the sheen? He should still be okay."

"Yes, I should think he is."

Jahnise felt fine. He hopped to his feet before glancing high in the tree above to locate where he thought he had fallen from. "Great wishes," he said aloud. "Great wishes."

"Looks like the two-legger survived. What do we do next?"

The first four-legger answered, "Well, we need to find out who he is."

"What if he is not a Talker? What then?"

"I thought he had to be a Talker to gain entrance here?"

"Well, usually I guess they are."

"Usually? Does this happen enough for you to say usually? Has it ever happened with you before?"

"No, I guess not."

"Well then?"

The second four-legger knew the conversation was going nowhere. "Stop. I'll just go over there and ask him who he is and what he knows."

"Be careful, if he is not a Talker, it could be dangerous. Look what he has over his shoulder. It could do you serious harm."

"I will be careful. You watch for any more. There could be another one in that tree."

With that, the second four-legger nervously walked from behind the boulders to approach the visitor. "Ahem, ahem," the four-legger cleared his throat. "Ahem, excuse me!" he shouted.

Jahnise heard the shouting and looked around nervously trying to locate the origin of the chatter.

"Hey two-legger, down here!"

The tall two-legger lowered his curious eyes down, way down until he was looking at one of the most unique little creatures he had ever seen. With a low baritone he addressed the four-legger, "Aha, say little one, what may you be?"

"I may be a bit of trouble for you unless you explain to me who you are and why you are here."

"Excuse me little one, I can't make out what you say. Can you speak louder?"

"I said I may be a bit of trouble for you unless you explain to me who you are and why you are here! My sakes legger, can you not hear me at all?" The small creature shouted.

"Oh no, no, no little one. You are no trouble for me. You must be a runt of a Rat. Does your mother know you are out causing trouble for giants?"

"You don't understand...what? A Rat? I am no Rat. And I am no runt either thank-you! You just wait until I get..."

"There you go again little one. You must talk louder. I am way up here and you are way down there," Jahnise laughed. "What kind of land have I entered where upon my arrival I am greeted and threatened by the tiniest of creatures with the biggest of attitude?"

"You are in the land of Nuorg sir," came a reply from beside his ear.

Jahnise turned his face to the voice. Sticking precariously on the side of the tree, a second tiny creature attempted to carry on the conversation. "Good day to you too little Rat," he chuckled. "The land of Nuorg? I have heard of this place many times."

"Please, dark two-legger, what is your name and what business do you have in Nuorg?" the balancing four-legger asked.

In his thick accent Jahnise answered, "Why little one I have no idea why I am here. I never knew I would truly wind up here. I must be summoned here by a force bigger than I, bigger than you. I was sitting near a path I travel very often, taking a sip of water when all at once I was sucked into this place through a swirling passage of a strange liquid," he explained with violent hand motions which frightened the precariously placed four-legger. "I can tell you this. I am Jahnise Equakembo from the Great Plains. May I be at your service?"

The second four-legger scurried up the tree to get in on the conversation. "You certainly cannot be of service to us until we check you out and that may take a while! You will have to follow us back to our Burg and meet with our Keeper. She will then decide if you are worthy of living, much less!"

The first four-legger shook her small head, "Please pay no attention to him, sir. He suffers from what we call here, small creature with a large ego syndrome." She threw a stern look at her companion. "He is quite harmless. All squeak and no bite. Oh, also we are not Rats. We are lowly, mild and meek. We are simple field

Mice. Rats are unfit to follow our paths...a disgusting lot, all of them."
She spat her last words onto the ground.

"I understand clearly now. So little brave one, when can I meet
your Keeper? Is she nearby or do we travel to her? If we travel, I
suggest you ride along with me. You will tire quickly. I take long
strides and may even break into a run if I so desire." As he spoke, he
adjusted the brim of his hat back into shape. "Now, if you will do me
the honor, please scamper onto my hat and you can direct the path
we shall take."

"Scamper, I'll show you how I scamper," replied the second
Mouse. He leaped for the hat at the very instant Jahnise offered it to
the first Mouse. In his haste, the second Mouse missed the hat
entirely and slammed into an adjacent tree knocking him out cold.
Just before he fell to the ground, a large dark hand caught him and
carefully placed him on the hat.

Jahnise laughed hard and directed his question at the first
Mouse, small creature with a large ego syndrome is it? Ha-ha...hah.
This trip may be a lot of fun little one."

The first Mouse stared off into the distance and shook her head.
"Quite possibly," she said. "Quite possibly."

***

"Bongi, has anyone seen Grendl or Kohlyn?" the Keeper asked.

"I believe they had watch this day-round Keeper," came the
answer. "Who is it they were to expect?"

"A royal from the Great Plains is what I heard. Mystic flew by here
and told me to expect the fourth key very soon. I can only suspect
that he or she would come from that area. We have contact with the
first key and we have messages out for the other two. There is a lot
going on above but we have to focus on getting the key holders here
at the same time for the plan to work."

"But won't having the four here at one time leave a huge void in
the protection of the lands up there?"

"Yes it will, but only the Wolf is aware of the power the staffs can
wield. I would be surprised if the others knew anything at all other
than the fact that those things are so clumsy."

***

While one Mouse slept, Jahnise began to question the other one. He had lots of questions. "So, do you have a name little one?"

"Yes, I am called Grendl and my sleeping mate over there is Kohlyn. He is very protective. He means well, but, well you saw what happened."

"Ah yes I see your point. Very mouthy that one. Are you two a pair?"

"Yes we are and we have many offspring to show for it."

"Hah, I shall look forward to meeting them. You say we are in the land of Nuorg? Where exactly is this and have you any idea why I am here?"

"Yes, you are in Nuorg. I can't tell you anymore than that. When we get to our Burg you can ask the Keeper and she will answer any further questions you may have."

"Fair enough, Grendl. I trust you can lead me there?"

"Yes I can. Once you clear these trees, take a left onto the Beaten Path. It will be easy to spot. We will follow the Beaten Path all the way to the Burg. It isn't that far traveling with your legs, but with our legs, it takes much, much longer."

"Ha-ha, I would think so, Grendl. To the Beaten Path we go."

\*\*\*

"Where exactly are we going?" Jahnise asked to either of his passengers.

It was Grendl that answered. "Our Burg is a meeting place of sorts for two-leggers such as yourself and four-leggers as well."

"Does your Burg have a name, tiny one? Or is it simply called 'The Burg'?"

"Good legger, we cannot give you that kind of information yet. We don't know if you are the one we were expecting or maybe, like the others we have expelled, an accidental comer. You will find out most of your answers once we arrive and you have your meeting with the Keeper."

"Very well. Please don't get bothered with my endless questions then. I don't normally get to speak with four-leggers. My land is vast and my friends are few and far between--very far between. I will watch the sun set many times on my journeys to see them."

"Oh are you lonely where you come from?"

"No, no, not at all. I do not need to speak to leggers as you say to be happy. I have my land and my beliefs. I am alone most of the time, but I am not lonely as you put it."

"You're speaking truthfully, aren't you?" Grendl had never been without constant company, so this tidbit sounded very odd to her.

"Yes, I always tell the truth, Grendl. It is how I do things. It doesn't always make everyone happy at first, but eventually they come around. At least, they will more often than not. I have upset the melon basket a time or two." He grinned a wide toothy grin that exposed his flawless teeth. He laughed. His big eyes did twinkle although they seemed to be masking something way down inside the tall, dark man.

Grendl began to fell sorry for the two-legger. It was a mothering instinct that she could not push away. Once a mother, always a mother. She turned to Kohlyn still asleep on the brim of Jahnise's hat. She smiled at her brave little mate and got comfortable at his side. "If you need directions, just ask," she mentioned.

"Rest yourself, Grendl. I will alert you should I find myself wandering off the pathway."

\*\*\*

Bongi was an odd looking but handsome animal. He looked to be a cross between a Giraffe and a Zebra with a touch of Antelope thrown in for confusion. He blended in well with his surroundings. Much similar to a tall Horse in size, he was quite a looker but drew no additional attention to himself, if he could help it. Most of the time, he couldn't help it. He was very striking to see. Curiosity overwhelmed most creatures that came in contact with him. "Just what is he?" they would ask both to him and those in his company.

The Keeper was ordinary to look at. No special markings or oddities to make her more noticeable, she was just what she was. Tan in color from her head to the tip of her long tail, she was a Lioness. She was not abnormally big or beautiful. She was a Lion from a land near the Great Plains who left long before she became attached to mothering. She would have made a wonderful mother but felt a call of a different kind. She had not decided to seek this land on her own accord although pressure to lead was exerted on her at times from those wizened by the passing of time who could see deep into her reasons for being. She had quickly tired of the mundane existence on the plains. No family trouble, no dire circumstances caused her to leave her homeland, she wanted to do more with her life. Like most of the creatures in Nuorg, she was magnificently wise. "Brilliant mind. Too stubborn. Adoring. Loyal. Much more than intelligent," they said. Eekay left her pride on the plains with no promise of ever returning. Loved by her family, they told her when she broke the news to the council that she would always be welcomed back. The pride was strong. Made up of several generations of Lions, they would miss Eekay, but they would survive. Her mother, father, sisters, brothers--each of her relatives would survive and wanted the best for her. She decided the best for her was leaving. She came to Nuorg with curious mind and clear conscious. Bongi had welcomed her in on her first day. The two quickly became inseparable.

"Eekay, what do you make of our little welcome party? Where are they? Should they not have returned already?" Bongi asked this question knowing what the Keeper's answer would be.

"In their own time my friend. That pair can take care of themselves. Anyway what harm could come to them here?"

"I cannot help but worry for the little creatures. I know they are seemingly hard to spot, but Kohlyn can be heard far and wide."

"Yes, you are right. What do you want me to do? Shall I send another pair of creatures out to spy on our first set of creatures who we sent to spy on whoever may or may not come through the window?" Eekay sounded perturbed. She wasn't. It was just her way.

"Again, I will agree with your reasoning. There is no sense throwing something else into the mix."

Eekay was pleased with the response. "Bongi, do you not realize that I am just as concerned for those two as I am every other creature here? We are to expect another guest here today also. The Eagle from Burg one will be paying us a visit soon. As we know there was an incident with that a short time ago." She pointed toward the glowing yellow orb in the sky.

"Ah, I remember it well. Arms of light shooting out of it trying to grab something. I will feel better, I hope, once I get an explanation of that activity."

"Me too. I suspect one of our visitors will explain it in detail." Eekay ended the conversation by abruptly turning and walking away. She was not much for small talk or good-byes.

Bongi watched her for a moment, still not sure of why she acted as she did, then turned back to walk the bridge. Maybe he would see or hear the spies returning.

***

"My good friends, do I see your Burg in the distance there?" Jahnise asked while he walked the crest of the large round hill. He had walked without stopping for quite some time now. He always traveled without a lot of stopping, figuring that when it was time to rest, he would have a good, long rest. He paused at the hill's peak to take in the rolling stretch of land that lay in front of him. "My little friends, you have a beautiful land here. Look at the dark greens of the hills and grasses. My land is not so green as yours. Look at the mountains too, magnificent they are. I am curious. There is no snow at their peaks. This is odd to me. Oh too, the yellow light, that is not unlike the sun where I come from, yet it does not move. Yes, I have many questions when I meet your Keeper. Many questions little friends."

Kohlyn was awake now. He and Grendl were spending their time waiting for conversation from the two-legger which never came. This legger was not very interested in conversing while he traveled. "At last he speaks," he whispered to Grendl.

"Good awakening Kohlyn. I hope you rested well. Am I taking us in the correct direction?" Jahnise pointed his long, slender finger toward the walls of the Burg ahead of him. "The walls, are they to keep creatures in or to keep creatures out? Oh I am sorry. I know you can't answer that. On we go. Let me know if that is not where we are going."

Kohlyn peered down the brim of Jahnise's large hat, "Yes just keep walking. They should see us soon enough. They will send a welcome from the Keeper out to us. Only then will we be allowed to enter."

"Very well Kohlyn, I will do as you say."

Grendl twitched her head rapidly then whispered, "They will send a welcome from our Keeper out to us? What was that all about? Eekay won't send anyone out to welcome us! When we get to the bridge she will either let us in or she won't!"

"Shhh!" Kohlyn whispered back, "I want him to think that we are being watched and that he had better beware!"

96

"Oh my little friend, you whisper very loudly. Beware? Beware of what? Now you have opened a honey jar to the bees. I was looking so forward to a welcome." With that Jahnise grinned his wide grin before continuing to the bridge.

"One day Kohlyn, I hope you will learn to keep your whisper to a whisper!" Grendl slowly shook her head.

## 9

M ystic led Frederick and Lightning for most of the uneventful journey. Meadows and occasional clusters of trees made up the landscape for the day. No small mountains or even higher hills were to be seen. Ahead Lightning noticed a grayish mist floating above the ground at about tree top height. He paid no attention to it until the four-leggers began to notice a ghastly smell wafting towards them borne on the slightest breeze of the day. Lightning stopped the parade and stood on his back legs to get a clear view of the phenomenon. Once he was standing upright he took special notice of it. "Do any of you smell what I am smelling? It is dreadfully awful."

The other two four-leggers had noticed the odor, but it had not distracted them. Mystic poked his snout around in the air, "Yes, Lightning, I caught wind of it earlier, but I can't say I know what is causing it. It's not terrible smelling."

"What? You are not smelling high enough." He bent over, "Hop on my back, Prince. I think you can smell it from there."

Mystic took a few quick steps and launched himself up on Lightning's platform like back. He raised his nose as high as possible and took a long breath in through his nose. He could not have imagined the potency of the stench had be been properly warned of it. Before he could react, he became uncontrollably dizzy and tumbled off Lightning's back and fell hard to the soft ground. He struggled to his feet, trying to shake and cough the nauseous rot from his lungs. "Good mercy, what is that? I can't get it out of my body. Bubba, jump up there. See if you are able to smell it."

Without questioning Mystic, Bubba leapt onto Lightning. He jumped much higher than Mystic. So overwhelmed with the stench, he cleared Lightning and he too tumbled to the ground fighting the stench as if it was some kind of enemy. "For the sake of my life! That is horrible. It smells worse than a hundred deaths. What is it?" He rolled over in the grass, huffing the blades of grass into his snout hoping to either brush the smell from his nostrils or clog them from further exposure to the merciless stink. "Frederick? Can you not smell that?"

"No Bubba, I can't." In this moment, in this place, Frederick was never happier to have a sense of smell several times weaker than the tortured four-leggers. "Is it that bad?"

"Oh my lord," shouted Mystic. "It is the worst thing I have ever witnessed with sight, sound or smell. It won't go away. It is getting worse as we live and breathe."

Frederick opened his bag and pulled out an old rag he had stuffed deep inside. He hurriedly ripped it into pieces. He then rolled the remnants into tight rolls. Once he had six pieces, he doused them by dripping a precious few drops of Nuorg water over them. Quickly, Frederick stuffed one into each opening of each four-legger's snout.

"There, those nose plugs should tide you over for at least a little while."

Mystic noticed the difference immediately. "Nice work Frederick. All I can smell now is 'Sweet Gulley'. That was close. What can be causing that stench?"

Bubba and Lightning were taking deep, comforting breaths through their noses. Lightning was now getting hungry, even though the smell had initially made them all nauseous. "Frederick, do you happen to have any of that 'Sweet Gulley' goo in your bag. These plugs are bringing back some pretty flavorful memories."

"No, I'm sorry about that. No goo, nothing but the water."

"You know, that is really too bad. What I would give for a nice long dip in that gulley about now."

"I can taste it too, Lightning, tastes pretty good." Bubba wiped at the tears coming from his eyes. "Are we heading into that rank? I mean are we going to make a conscientious effort to get closer to it? If we are, we...I think we need to...uh, rethink that plan."

Mystic agreed, "We need to rethink it a lot!"

Frederick shook his head, "Sorry Bubba, we can't do that. Remember, the ax-pike took us where we need to be, not where we want to be. It is obvious to me that we are where we are because of that smell. I am getting little whiffs of it now. I don't like it either but we have to do what we have to do. If we have to go into that stink, then we will. We can re-wet the plugs as long as we need. I want to experience what you three have experienced before I plug my nose. I'm assuming that is part of the experience we are here for. Come on all of you, there is no need to discuss where we should travel now. We know. Let's get on with it. Follow me."

"Follow you? Hah you can't even smell the stench yet. You follow us." Lightning was adamant about that.

The four of them spread out in formation just as they had earlier, although the formation was not quite as wide. None of the four-leggers had any intention of moving too far from Frederick and the Nuorg water. To an individual, they concluded correctly, the smell could only get worse.

The gray mist was darkening before them as it descended closer to the ground. As it darkened, it thickened like a storm cloud. Actual droplets of the stench floated about within, bumping into each other, creating an appalling atmosphere. The group inched closer together with each unsettling step. Before entering the thickening gloom, Frederick got a strong whiff that knocked him to the ground like a hammer. His eyes crossed, his breath was thrown clear of him. He became nauseous and threw up his lunch.

Bubba was at his side instantly. "So it seems the two-legger's nose finally caught up to the four-leggers'. What do you make of it Frederick?"

Frederick could not think of more than one thing at this moment. Gasping, he grabbed the remaining rag from his bag, hastily sprinkled a few drops of Nuorg water on it then clenched it tightly to his face. He motioned for each of the others to get a wetting too. As they came near him, he shook a few drops onto each plug without removing them from their placements. He figured removing the plugs might do irreparable damage to the four-legger's sensitive snouts.

Now the gray mist was transforming into a living grossness. It not only stunk, it settled onto the fur and skin of the leggers as if it were there to consume them. As they made their way deeper into the muck, they had to physically move it out of the way. There was no sense in turning back now, they were in too far. Lightning was carving the widest path, with the others instinctively forming a line behind him. The stench was beginning to permeate through the plugs again. Suddenly Lightning stopped. He was not sure of what he saw before him; still he tried valiantly to swipe it away with a powerful sweep of his paw. He was not successful. Whatever lay in his path was heavier than the surrounding cloud. Mystic, Bubba and Frederick lined up at his side, each trying to distinguish what lay in front of them. Not only was the obstacle heavy it was also big. Frederick reached down to get a feel of it. His hand grazed what he thought was a piece of wood, a plank maybe? He lifted it with one hand still holding the rag firmly to his face.

"This was a large dwelling of some kind. This piece of wood, I think, came from a small door, or a crate of some kind. The hinges are still on it. Lightning, can you pull out a few more pieces? We need to get as many pieces as we can to carry back with us."

"Carry back with us? Where are we going now?"

Mystic understood where Frederick was going. "We are getting out of here, Lightning. We can take pieces of this place outside of this stinking cloud to get a good look at them. Maybe we can determine what it was. Please, let's get some pieces and go. This is overwhelming!"

Bubba nibbled at a few of the wooden pieces until he found one he felt was the right one, although he had no idea what the right one could possibly be. In reality he wanted to locate something of significance quick and get out as fast as possible. The sooner he could breathe without the nose plugs, the better he, and everyone else, would like it. Not soon enough, he lifted a smooth metallic strap out of the pile. It came complete with several other complimenting pieces, he gripped it tightly. Frederick picked up several different pieces of both wood and metal. Mystic decided to drag a heavier metallic piece with him. He tapped Bubba on the shoulder then signaled his willingness to leave. Frederick followed with Lightning carrying a huge chunk of debris with him. Hoping to make a little sense out of anything, the group hurried, as they could, back the way they came. None bothered to communicate until the haze was far behind them.

Mystic dropped what he was carrying, "Is this far enough?"

Frederick answered, "No," and kept walking. With numbing mouths, hands and noses beginning to force a will of their own, Frederick called a halt to the retreat. "You each know that we are going back in, don't you? Once we decide what this is or was, we are going back to discover why we were brought here in the first place."

Bubba was astonished, "Frederick, you have to be out of your mind. We can't go back in there!"

"Yes we can and we will. There is something back there we need to find. We are not leaving without it!"

"Mystic, do we have to?" The hair on the back of the Cheetah still stood on end.

"I think we do, Bubba," Lightning was of the same mind as Frederick.

"There is something bad back there. We only tasted it."

"That is not a good way of saying whatever you are trying to say. I tasted it through my mouth, I tasted it through my fur, and I tasted it through my eyes. We may never rid ourselves of whatever is back there!" Bubba was not happy.

"I'm sorry, Bubba. I still agree with Frederick."

"Then it is settled. Bubba, please calm down. We will figure this out." Mystic stood over the pieces he brought out with an inquisitive eye. "Frederick, what is this?"

Frederick squatted down beside Mystic. "I can only guess here Prince, but I think that is one of several sections that at one time formed a holding cage of some kind."

"But the color? What do you make of the color?"

Frederick picked the piece up. He held it close to his face studying the color intensely. "At first I thought the color may be a certain color of ugly paint." He removed his nose plugs and inhaled a long breath through his nose. "It is not paint Mystic, there is paint under this coloration, but this, I'm afraid, is blood and lots of it. As a matter of fact, this piece was soaked with blood at one point."

Mystic recoiled from the thought of the cause. "Where would that much blood come from?"

"Don't get too excited yet, you two, look at the piece I dragged back." Lightning dropped his load near Mystic's find. "Look at this. These pieces were also soaked in blood. That has to be half the cause of the stench. The other half; must be other carnage."

Frederick stepped between the pieces dropped by Lightning. "My, all of these parts comprise a much bigger whole than I thought." In front of him laid a tangled mess of wood, metal and worse. "These were once gates used to fence in livestock for farming, but they have been modified. Something changed them to hold smaller creatures. This was a crude modification, hastily done. Look at the unnatural bends in this metal. This piece must have been very high before it crashed to the floor taking bits and pieces of creatures with it as it fell. See the residue here?" He pointed to several stained spots all over the materials. "These stained areas are made up of more blood and other things."

Bubba quickly grasped what Frederick was saying, "What you are trying to say in a genteel way is that these clots are flesh and bone from the victims here, correct?"

"Yes, that is exactly what I am saying Bubba. What did you salvage?"

"I am not sure. See for yourself." Bubba dragged his clangy find over and laid it by the growing collection. "What is it?"

Frederick stared at the latest part. "This is a device used to trap creatures by maiming them. It is a spring loaded and very dangerous. What were these used for? Who put all of this together? I don't know. We have to go back for more clues. We have to go back before sunset. The sooner we can figure this out the safer we will be. Whoever or whatever left this doesn't have a conscious that cares too much for the welfare of others. Mystic, are you going to lead us back or am I?"

The Wolf was struggling. He tried to comprehend what Frederick was implying to them all, but could not. "If it is okay with you Frederick, you lead us back. It really makes no difference to me. You must first plug our noses back up."

"I will do that Mystic. I tell you what, let me try something first. He plugged the snouts of the four-leggers and tied his rag tight around his face. "Lightning, in order to validate my thinking, please raise your ax-pike. I want you to ask it where we should go. Don't be shy, raise it, point it and ask it."

Lightning grumbled a bit then did as he was told. He held the ax-pike in the opposite direction of the stench hoping he could influence where they would end up in some small way. "Ax-pike, take us where we should be."

Before the last word escaped Lightning, the group was immediately plunged into the center of the reeking mist. Not only into it, but deep into it. If the smell sickened them, what they saw now would leave indelible, ghastly images in their memories. Memories clogged with sights impossible to unsee. They were standing among several piles of sickening rubble and hundreds, if not thousands of rotting winger carcasses. The thick mist welcomed them by raising above them the height of a short tree. Along with the mist, the stench rose as well allowing for slightly better breathing conditions. The stink was not gone, but it was considerably weakened.

Bubba stared directly at Frederick, "I guess you were correct. What do we look for now?"

After a quick glance around, Frederick made some decisions. "Lightning, take your ax-pike and dig the biggest hole you can manage. Mystic, I want you and Bubba to help me. Please locate the remains of as many wingers as you can. I want to give them a burial. Find some long sticks that can serve as lifting devices. Use your mouths and the sticks to collect as many carcasses as you can. Identify as many as possible and keep up with the numbers. Stack them by species. I will place them in the hole."

Bubba was sickened at the thought. "As you say, Frederick. I may need several breaks. I don't think I can stomach this."

Mystic agreed, "Frederick, I have never been this close to so much death."

"Fine, we can take as long as we need. We are here for now. We will stay until the job is complete. We can't leave these creatures like this. After the slaughter of the Wolves all of those years ago, I could not live with myself knowing I could have shown these dead respect but chose to abandon them instead. The sooner we get started the better. Lightning, from the looks of this...you need to start digging now."

Lightning lifted up his ax-pike, "Now exactly how am I supposed to use this?"

"I'll show you." He walked with his burly friend just beyond the devastation's edge. "Here, hand it to me." Frederick took the ax-pike firmly in his hands. He eyed it. The big wide end was pointing up so he spun it in his hands so as the narrow side pointed up instead. "You use it like this." The two-legger lifted the tool high over his head and pulled it forcefully down, embedding the wide end deeply into the ground. He jerked upwards on the handle and removed a clean chunk of sod and dirt. "That's about it big fella, just start digging. I don't think you will get too deep, too fast."

Lightning dug for all he was worth. He soon found out he enjoyed the digging. He used it as a release from the destruction around him. He became very adept at swinging the ax-pike in exactly the spot he needed to deepen or enlarge. "Hey, Frederick, I think I might like this whole digging thing. My family tills a lot of ground back in the Great Forest. I need to show them how this is done!"

"Wonderful Lightning!" Frederick turned to Mystic and Bubba who were less than enthusiastic about their task. "Hey you two, I know this is difficult. Somewhere under this carnage lie reasons for what happened here. It is up to us to discover them."

"Whatever, Frederick. I am at a loss to explain how or why this could happen. There are untold numbers of dead sky-travelers mixed in with the wood and metal and who knows what else." Mystic was not sharing Lightning's enthusiasm.

Bubba lightly stepped around piles of feathers, gently lifting each lifeless carcass with the end of his stick. His jaws quickly became numb from the repetition. "Frederick, I have a question. Why us? Is this all a part of the Nuorg thing or is it part of the here and now thing?"

"Bubba, I think it is equal parts of both. Who knows for sure? I certainly don't. I have already counted three piles of over a hundred wingers each. There were over twenty different types of wingers in here and we are not nearing the halfway point yet. Once we get all of these poor things buried, only then can we search for clues to their demise."

Mystic was busy searching under larger pieces of wreckage. He discovered a knack for sniffing out the unfortunate wingers who lay buried deep under the rubble. Oddly, he was rooting beneath a large shingled section of the roof when he noticed the area become unexpectedly illuminated. "Hmm, where is this light coming from?" He mused to himself. He pulled himself from under the large piece and was met immediately by Bubba.

"Oh Prince, its glowing again."

"What? What is glowing?"

"The globe on the Staff, it's glowing again."

Mystic glanced down to his chest where the Staff was secured and temporarily forgotten in its handy holster. Sure enough the globe was glowing, not radiantly, but just enough to initiate a small amount of panic inside the smaller four-leggers.

Mystic hollered out for the others, "Frederick! Lightning! We may have a problem." Mystic gingerly removed himself from the ruins, hurriedly making his way over to Lightning with Bubba closing in.

Bubba easily passed the slower Wolf by leaping completely over him. He landed in front then turned swiftly around to face Mystic and the globe. "Should you roll it?"

Mystic stopped but not before he bumped into the Cheetah and sent him to the ground. He fought to release the Staff from the holster. He could not get a grip on it at all. "Frederick, you made this holster, get the Staff out!"

Frederick released the locking strap. Pulling the Staff free, he held it in front of Mystic. "It is not glowing that brightly."

Lightning noticed the faint light, "But it is glowing!"

Bubba urged Mystic to roll it. "Roll the globe Mystic. If it is glowing, it needs to be rolled!"

"Now let's all calm down." Frederick seemed to be the least bothered by the warning sign. "I have studied the globe, remember? This is not a blatant sign to stop our lives and roll it. This just means that evil is present. This may actually be a clue to what we are looking for. Mystic take us back to where you first noticed this. We have to search thoroughly under every splinter in that spot. Lightning, bring your ax-pike, the digging can cease for the time being."

"Now I just have to remember where I was." Mystic looked to Bubba, "I think you probably know where I was more than I do."

"You're right. Follow me. You were over there under that section of roof."

Frederick smiled, "You four-leggers sure impress me with your broad knowledge of the world of two-leggers. You call a roof a roof too? Hmmph."

"Well what else would you call it?" Lightning was smiling too. A little humor was not a bad thing right now. If it could be found among the devastating circumstances, they would take full advantage of it.

They moved over to the spot without the normal, enthusiastic aplomb. Dire consequences darted through the mind of each individual creature. The globe had dimmed some since Mystic removed himself from under the fallen roof.

"Here is the very place Frederick, see the paw prints in the dust? Those are mine."

"Ah, there is no doubting that Bubba. Where were you Prince?"

"I was jammed under this as far as I could squeeze. Why? I have no idea."

Frederick called on Lightning, "You are the strongest Lightning. See how much of this you can move for us. It should all be attached, at least from what I can tell."

"Alright you little cubs back out of the way and give me some room to work." The irregular Badger grabbed two large support beams with his massive paws then lifted them up to shake off the smaller, residual scrap laying atop the roof material. He bent his back slightly and backed up with no luck. Lightning dropped the piece to the ground to think about another plan of attack. Instead of using his paws, he bit down on one of the timbers and used all four legs to tug at the mass. Slowly but surely it began to budge, one step then two, then three turned into four. The large section was moving and drawing several smaller pieces along with it.

"You can stop there," Frederick shouted. He scrutinized the uncovered area with probing eyes. "Do any of you see anything out of the ordinary? It looks pretty much like everything else around here."

Bubba stepped into the center of the space and began pacing. "I think there is something else here. Call it curiosity or whatever killed the Cat, but I think this," Bubba clawed at a bare spot near the edge, "might be something of note." His claws struck something metallic, when he did the screeching sound made the hair rise on the back of Frederick's neck.

"You have definitely found something Bubba, but please stop raking your claws over it!"

"Oh, sorry...you mean this?" Bubba pulled his claws over the object one last time just because.

"Yes that!" Frederick tried to get angry with the Cheetah, but could not find it in himself to do it. "Please Cheetah, back away from your find, back far away!"

While the four-leggers chuckled, Frederick found a heavy stick and began to scrape around the edges of the metal, the shape became very apparent.

Mystic saw the outline and shook his head. "Are you serious? This is like a crazy bedtime story. Every time we get close to solving a problem, another mystery beckons. Could that be...oh, I don't know...a trap door?"

Frederick got tickled and so did Bubba and Lightning. "I don't know, Prince, it could be an entrance to your secret lair. Would you like to open it and see?"

"Not on your life, Sir Frederick. Not on my life or your life or the lives of the Cheetah or the Badger. I shall order Lightning of the Great Meadow to do the honors."

"Wonderful choice, Prince Mystic," added Bubba.

"Huh? Why me?" Lightning was none too happy with the declaration.

"Because Lightning my great friend, we smaller creatures need to be far away at a safe location, as you fight the evil doers that will surely come attacking from the depths hidden beneath that lid." Bubba loved to put Lightning on the spot.

"Safe place you say?" Lightning lunged at whatever it was, reached under the edge with one huge paw and before the others knew it, wrenched the metal thing from the ground. He flung it over the heads of the dazed others. "Come and see what evil we've unleashed my brothers!" The brave Badger moved backwards giving ample room to whatever was coming out of whatever the metal thing once closed.

"Ahhh!" Bubba raced to Lightning's side. "I can't believe you just did that! Are you out of your mind? With the experiences we have had of late, you do that? Do not ever turn your back on me Badger, I will have my day. I promise you I will!"

Mystic wasn't afraid of the hidden void in the ground. He looked down for the globe, he only saw the faint glow the same as it was before they uncovered whatever it was. "I think we will be okay, don't you, Frederick?" The Wolf and the two-legger inched closer to the uncovered whatever it was. They peered over the edge and discovered a thin, rickety wooden ladder leading them to a shallow cellar. "After you two-legger, I believe you are the only one of our group who can use one of these things."

"Oh yes, I'm afraid you are correct. I mean, I am not afraid anyway...simply a figure of speech." He glanced at the others hoping one of them would try talking him out of his next move. As he slowly and carefully climbed down the ladder, his eyes were nearly bulging from his head, silently pleading with the others to watch his every move. "If I don't come back out of here soon, pull up every board in this floor and find me! Do you understand?"

"Don't worry two-legger. We won't leave without you." Lightning meant every word.

"Mystic, while I am down here will you and Lightning begin burying the wingers? Leave Bubba here with me."

"Certainly, it is the least we can do."

"Thank you. Please bury the neat stacks first. I have them documented."

## 10

B ongi casually made his way to the bridge located between two tall trees on either side of the Burg's large entry gate. Main entrances to every Burg in Nuorg were designed in this manner. He greeted each Burg creature he passed by name, wishing them well. Unlike other Burgs in Nuorg, this bridge spanned no river. It steeply sloped to a lower level making the walk down much more enjoyable than the walk back up. At the end of the bridge was another steep ramp made from the ground which allowed for a nice view around the surrounding landscape, though the best lookout location was high in the gate trees. For obvious reasons Bongi left those particular perches to creatures much, much smaller than he. He glanced down the Beaten Path. "Hmm, I believe Grendl and Kohlyn might have welcomed a creature through the window after all. I must alert Eekay of their return."

"And why must you do that?" Eekay asked. She had quietly stalked him down the bridge. "That is a tall dark legger. I have seen plenty of his kind where I am from. I hope he is for us rather than against us. If not, we will defend ourselves and he will disappear." She turned away and headed back up the bridge without another word to Bongi. Unlike her second in command, she said nothing to those she passed heading back in.

Bongi was past being startled by Eekay's methods. He paid her no attention as he continued watching the legger approach. "I only assume that Grendl and Kohlyn are close at his feet," he said to himself before he peered around to see if Eekay had indeed returned within the gate. "This could get interesting," he thought. "Why is she so, so without emotion?"

It had become a common truth among the inhabitants of this Burg--Eekay was not a warm, loving creature. Eekay did not care who knew it. She had her way and she had no intention of changing. She never showed a side of her that would lead others to believe she ever had a softer side. Like it or not Eekay was not a creature to engage in small talk of any kind. She was not one to be amused with frivolous or funny stories. She was all business. In the days that followed, that trait would become even more obvious and, possibly, save a lot of beating hearts.

***

Jahnise continued his long, fluid stride. He headed directly for the entry ramp to the Burg. He amazed his two tiny passengers with his tireless gait. "Ah yes my new little friends this is your home. Very interesting. I see creatures much, much larger than you on the wooden hill. What number of creatures do you have in there? Do you all get along? Oh. I am sorry. Too many questions. All of my questions will be answered soon I hope. I must say, that is one very strange looking creature at the top of the dirt hill. I must ask him of his origins."

"You must be speaking of Bongi. He is our Keeper's first helper. A very pleasant creature. Odd, but pleasant," Grendl informed him.

"Is he odd? I'm sorry, if you think he is odd...wait until you meet the Keeper." Kohlyn had a way with words that Grendl never fully appreciated. "She is not odd to look at, but oh my, if you seek a conversation, I would look elsewhere."

"Oh my, that was not a very complimentary thing to say about our Keeper in front of our guest! Do you think you could be a tiny bit more flattering when you mention her?" Grendl shook her head and gazed straight ahead.

"What?" Kohlyn asked to his dismay. "She is odd. No creature has ever held a conversation with her that lasted long enough to bother with. At the very least, most have quit trying. A very different thought process that one. A very different mind indeed." Kohlyn normally said exactly what was on his mind. Unknown to many, Eekay preferred that. She respected the tiny little creature for that very quirk in his personality.

"Let us move on, shall we? I look forward to meeting your Keeper and her first helper. I hope you both will be so kind as to introduce us very soon." A smile grew on the face of the two-legger.

The ramp was no longer off in the distance. They had reached the first ramp and Jahnise marveled at the size of it. The Burg sat near the top of a very large small mountain He stopped at the foot of the first ramp and placed the long walking stick in the ground at his side. Removing his hat, he placed it and the two passengers on his other side. He then kneeled on the ground and bowed his head.

"What are you doing sir?" Kohlyn was curious why Jahnise had not continued up the ramp.

Jahnise raised his head to answer, "If you permit me, I am asking for a blessing on your Burg before requesting permission to enter. Where I am from this is our proper way of paying respect to the dwellers here. If I am not permitted to enter I will be on my way with no bad feelings."

"Please Jahnise, go right ahead with your custom. I hope my nosey mate did not disturb you." Sometimes Grendl wished to muzzle her vocal mate.

Again Jahnise smiled. "As you say little one."

With eyes closed, the tall dark two-legger once again lowered his head to his chest. He raised both hands high above his head. "My Provider, I ask that you bless all inhabitants of this dwelling with wisdom, strength and health. May my visit here be fruitful and hospitable. Let us seek the truth and the good in all creatures. If I can be of service or help to these creatures let it be done. I do not understand why I am here or why I was summoned to this new land. I trust you know and will let it be known to me in the near future. Let it be done."

Jahnise opened his eyes, raised his head and nimbly got on his feet. He carefully raised his hat to his head and set it in place. He pulled his walking stick out of the soft ground. With both hands around it, he placed it in front of him and brought the ornately carved handle tightly to his chest. With reverence in his movements, he again bowed his head. Using both hands, Jahnise lightly lifted the stick and tapped the ground four times. He used the stick symbolically to steady himself as he positioned his body on his left knee. Releasing his grip with his right hand, he reached to his side and retrieved a well hidden knife. The long blade shimmered brightly in the light before turning dull. The two little passengers looked on with apprehension of what was coming next. Jahnise studied the reaction of the blade with curiosity.

"That reaction does not bode well," he said softly. "However, I will do what is asked of me." He took the knife to his left arm. He slid his left armlet down and made a slight cut just below his shoulder where the armlet had been, drawing a steady rivulet of blood. As the blood ran down his arm he replaced the knife in his wrap and dabbed three long fingers in the stream of blood. With two fingers he placed a drop of his blood on the ground on each side of him. The third drop of blood he placed above his nose between his eyes. Lastly, he slid the armlet back over the cut and tightened it to slow the blood flow. He raised himself to his feet, bowed his head again and waited.

"Hmmph," said Kohlyn staring over the brim of the hat. "That was strange."

Grendl was more inquisitive. "Jahnise, why the ceremony?"

Jahnise's demeanor changed. His smile faded, "I have just seen the approach of evil, Grendl. I am doing what I can to limit its power within my presence. The light of this land is not natural. It is strong but not of good. I feel my visit here may have been a trick."

"What? A trick by whom?" asked Grendl.

"Maybe a trick by the dwellers of your Burg."

"I do not think so!" exclaimed a dismayed Kohlyn. "How dare you make that statement!"

"How else to you explain it little one?" asked Jahnise with a new serious tone to his voice. "Are you in trouble? Is your Burg in trouble? I am a great man where I come from. I can help if you or any of the others here need me. Just say so and it will be done."

"We must speak to the Keeper now Jahnise. Let us enter the Burg." Grendl was nervous.

"He must invite me in." Jahnise pointed to Bongi. "I cannot enter unless I am invited. It is not my home. It is yours."

"Bongi! Bongi! Invite us in...quickly!" Grendl squeaked as loudly as she could.

Bongi had been watching the actions of the two-legger in awe. He was stunned by the reverence of the legger and a little frightened by the sudden change in his disposition. He heard Grendl's plea. He hurried down to greet the party at the ramp's edge. He sized up the legger with a few glances. "Please dark two-legger, at the request of my tiny friends, I graciously invite you into our Burg. Please come with me."

Jahnise simply replied, "As you ask." He silently followed the clomping of Bongi's cloven hooves up the long ramp, then finally through the large opening between the two giant trees. "Bongi, I need to speak with your Keeper immediately. The peace I once had on entering this land has grown weak. I want answers to my questions now. Do you understand what I am asking?"

The answer came from behind him just as Bongi began forming the words in his mouth. "Yes, he understands what you are saying. I am Eekay. I am the Keeper of this Burg."

Bongi turned his head towards Eekay and snorted. "I guess I won't have to locate her for you. Here she is. Keeper, you can make the introductions on your own and someday will you please let me in on your stalking secrets?"

Grendl and Kohlyn looked at each other. Their beady little eyes grew wide. What would come next?

"I'll answer the last question first Bongi. I am a Lioness. If I can't stalk, I can't survive. It's that easy." Bongi took a few steps back out of respect. Eekay looked the very tall and dark skinned two-legger up and down. "So, who are you and why are you here?"

"Very well Keeper. I am Chief Jahnise Kotumanrunda Equakembo from the Great Plains. I am here because someone or something summoned me. It was not of my own doing."

She appeared startled for a moment, "Why the ceremony at the foot of our door step?" She monotoned.

"Dear Lioness, I was saying a prayer for our protection. I never assume that I have taken a journey that was not led by a power much bigger and much wiser than myself."

"And the drawing of your own blood? Was that part of the prayer too?"

"Not exactly. That was a sign of my trust in you. I will wear a drop of my blood on my forehead as a reminder to those I come in contact with that I will shed it for you too if the need arises."

"Well, I guess I should be thanking you for that. Maybe groveling at your feet or something?" Eekay was a hard-willed creature.

"Do as you wish. That is not for me to concern myself with. I am only here to serve."

"Really? Well that skin you wear around your shoulders might tell another tale to creatures like me."

"Oh this? Jahnise stroked the adornment around his shoulders. There is a story about that I will share if you are interested."

"Yes I am interested. I am very interested and so is every other four-legger in this land. I'd say we all will want to hear the story together. Bongi, call to raise the bridge. I do not want this two-legger out of our sight. We will have a gathering when the shutters close in the middle court. Alert all of the Burgs to send four-legged representatives, especially the big Cats!"

The field Mice were anxious and a little scared. "If you could please let us down now Jahnise, we will scurry back to our dwelling for a short rest."

"Absolutely little friends." Jahnise lifted his hat off of his head. He tilted it down so the Mice could run off right on the ground.

"Grendl, Kohlyn, before you two go too far, remember, I want you both there at the meeting." Eekay was very demanding.

"Yes Eekay, we will be there. Middle court. Right." Kohlyn looked at Grendl and nodded.

***

Bongi hurried to the base of the gate trees. He craned his neck back to get a glimpse into the trees. "Hello up there. I need a sky-traveler now!"

A voice answered back, "Do you need a fast one or a slow one?"

"Answer me this, how many Burgs are there in Nuorg?"

"Do we have to fly to all six other Burgs in one day?"

"Actually, I need a messenger to fly to every one of them by the second half of this day-round...and bring representatives back."

"Are you serious?" One of several non-committed replies fell on deaf ears.

Bongi nodded his head up and down, "Yes, I am very serious. A matter just came up with our latest visitor."

"Latest visitor, do you not mean our only visitor?"

"Yes, yes our only visitor. Can you do it or not?"

The leaves of the immense tree shook as several wingers swooped out of all areas of the trees. They lit on Bongi's head, neck and back. A few landed near his front hooves. "Here we are Bongi. Should we pair up?"

"Wait, did I call you all down from the birdlet tree? Do any of you even know where the other Burgs are? I'm not sure some of you can even fly that well yet, can you?"

The several balls of tufted feathers that landed on his back let out a disappointed chorus of no's. The one perched between his ears also said no. That only left about four wingers that could even start the trek.

115

"Okay, I'm sorry but you birdlets have to stay here. You there, the grey one on the ground, don't you have some other wingers in your family?"

"Yes I do."

"Do you know where they are?"

"Yes I do."

"Can you go get them?"

"Yes I do, I mean yes I can."

"How many?"

"Six wingers total."

"Good, how about the Golden there?"

"Yes, I can get two more to join with us."

"With you three Seagulls that makes 12. One of you will have to pair up with a Golden. That won't be a problem will it?"

"Nah, shouldn't be a problem. I mean it won't be a problem for me, if they can keep up," replied the Golden.

"I'm sure they can. I want to assemble right here in one click. I want to see 12 of the best flyers we have in this Burg. Is that clear enough?"

"Yes Bongi. Right here. One click." They were off.

***

Jahnise had taken on the face of a troubled man. Eekay had not left his side since officially barging in on his introduction to the Burg. His eyes still twinkled. His smile remained radiant. However, his demeanor, since seeing the reflection in his blade, had changed. He tried to retain his upbeat personality, but it was difficult. What kind of land was this? Where was the evil that he saw so clearly in his blade? The characters he had met did not seem even the slightest bit evil. Not even the Lioness. She was very cold, not evil. How did all of the animals stay so friendly? Did they not sense the threat of evil as he did? Was he the only one right or the only one wrong?

"So, what do you think? Do you think I'm cold-hearted too?" The question rolled off Eekay's tongue with absolutely no emotion. "I have seen your kind before in my homeland. I have to say I never thought I'd ever be this close to one of you without a bloody spear sticking out of my side. I guess you wore that Cat skin here just to show us who was in charge? Your kind baffles me. I was told I would be dealing with your kind when I became the Keeper here. I intend to keep my word whether I want to or not."

"Ah the brave Lioness, speaking emotionless phrases full of emotional words. My kind is an assorted lot. There are the good and the bad in every type of creature. Why do you think I am the bad kind? I have gone to great measures to make all of the creatures I have met comfortable with my visit. I did not awake in my village with the intention of venturing into a land I know nothing about. The Cat skin is a long story. I ca..."

"No. You won't tell just me the history behind it. You will tell the assembly of representatives from every Burg in Nuorg the full story of how you came to wear one of their kind on your shoulders. There will be all types of creatures there. There will certainly be plenty of Cats, so I can't wait to hear your story, I really can't. What they decide to do with you will be a collective decision. If it were up to me...well I can't get into that now."

"So Lioness Keeper, are you holding me prisoner? Am I free to roam within your walls?"

"No, you are not my prisoner and no, you are not free to roam within these walls. When Bongi returns you will be his charge until the assembly. Your amount of freedom will be up to him."

"Very well. I will wait with you, here."

Jahnise could not read this Lioness at all. Somewhere during her lifetime she had been hurt. She had never reconciled that pain. At this rate, it might never happen. They continued the wait in silence. Eekay's eyes never left the two-legger. Occasionally she would shake her head in a confounded way, but she never looked away. What is it she was looking for? Jahnise hoped he could figure it out for her. He closed his eyes, bowed his head to his chest and prayed.

\*\*\*

"Eekay, you have been summoned by the pride council. There has been great interest shown in you by advisors to the council. Can I tell them that you will welcome the opportunity to speak with them?"

"Mother, why must I speak with them? Do you believe they always have our best in mind? What do they want with me? I am nearing the age to have cubs of my own. Do they want to take that away from me? Do they want to take that away from you? What has Father said to them? Is it his idea? Why did you not have any sons?

117

Aren't the sons supposed to be summoned by the council to go start a new pride somewhere? Why me?"

"Eekay why do you want to argue every time we speak? You should consider it an honor to be summoned. They must see something special in you. You are so young Eekay. Why make yourself miserable second guessing every decision you make? I wanted sons. I wanted lots of them. That did not happen. It was not the way things were to be. Is that worth you punishing me every day?"

"No Mother. I did not mean it like that. I want to be upbeat. It is just not my way. Why am I like this? Why am I not happy with my life?"

"Eekay, maybe the council elders can help you discover that. I have not been able to since you were born to me. I want you to be happy. Maybe you just can't be happy here, with us. Maybe you need to go out in this world and find what makes you happy."

"Mother, I...I...sure, tell the council I will meet with them. I hope it is the right thing to do."

"Eekay, I will let your Father know. He is so proud of you."

"Mother, if he is--why doesn't he tell me?"

# 11

"**G**amma, this platter is almost empty. Hemoth looks to be enjoying it. Would you mind bringing him another? I don't want to confront an angry Bear of his size." Gann took another swig of his mead. "Hemoth have you ever heard of a Nuorg before?"

"No Gann, I have not. I don't know whether it is a thing or a place. I do know it must have windows or else Evaliene would not have mentioned it. Gamma, this food you are offering is hitting the spot. I hope you have enough."

"Hemoth, you never mind that. We have plenty. Over the years we have dried, preserved, bagged about everything edible we have found. We have accumulated enough food stuffs for a small village of leggers. This cave is deep and wherever we have wandered within it, there is now food. Eat as much as you like."

"She is telling you the truth Hemoth. The deeper you go into this cave, the more food you will find. What else are you going to do for all of these years, for lack of a better term, in hiding?"

"Yes," Hemoth was saying through a mouthful of green leafy vegetables, "I see your point. Thank you, Gamma, this latest platter is full of completely different tastes than the first."

"Just keep eating, Hemoth. Let me know when you need more." Gamma was searching every crevice of her brain trying to scrounge up a memory or mention of a Nuorg. Absolutely nothing came to mind.

Madaliene and the wingers she carried quietly entered the cave. "There are three other leggers in our dwelling young winger. Do not be surprised. None of them will harm you in any way. There are two like me, only older and an extremely large four-legger. Are you okay with that?"

"I realize that I may not know you, but I believe you. I have no other choice. I trust you as much as I can. If you say they will not harm me, that is good enough."

"Fair enough, let's introduce you." Madaliene lightly stepped to the den's threshold, "Gamma, Gann, Hemoth, we have a visitor and a terribly frightened one at that. Shall I bring him in?"

All eyes turned to Madaliene as she entered. They spotted the frightened winger on her shoulder. "Bring that birdlet in here, Mad." Gamma walked over to Madaliene. "Here you go little fellow, hop on my arm, I'll carry you to the table."

"Thank you ma'am and I am not mad."

"Well, I don't think you are mad little one." Gamma looked at Madaliene with surprise. "Why would you be mad?"

"I'm sorry, you told her to bring the birdlet in here mad, but I am not mad. I promise."

"Oh, no, no, no. We call our grand daughter Madaliene. Sometimes we just shorten it to Mad during our conversations. I'm sorry."

"Madaliene is such a pretty name and Mad seems so angry. I have not been in the company of many Talkers before. Your speak is the same, but much different than mine. I understand. Please forgive me I am still very scared. Who is that?"

Gamma answered, "Which one? The two-legger or the four? The two-legger is my husband and Madaliene's grandfather, you can call him Gann. The large fellow there with his paws into the food is Hemoth. He is a giant Grizzly Bear from the north and a long, dear friend of Madaliene's."

"I appreciate making your acquaintances, each of you." The birdlet politely nodded to each legger individually. "I hope my being here doesn't inconvenience any of you. If you can't help me, I can be on my way."

"Hang on a bit there little one," Hemoth's eating had slowed down a bit, at least long enough for him to have a say. "This is not my dwelling, but I can assure you that you are not an inconvenience to these two-leggers. What is your story?"

"Thank you, Hemoth. My story, I fear, is a sad one. I don't want to burden you with bad news."

"Oh, go on now young winger, we are sifting through some bad news of our own right now. Knowing yours may help us deal with ours more easily. Let us hear it if you will." Gann cleared a spot on the table for Gamma to set the winger down.

"Here you go," Gamma rushed off to get another smaller plate full of nuts and berries for the young winger.

"This may sound unbelievable to you all, but here goes." The birdlet relaxed.

Gamma was scrambling to get back before the story began. "Just a minute. Don't start without me." She sat the plate of morsels in front of her newest guest.

"I am from a family of Peregrine Falcons. We made up the sentinel colony south of Glacier's Crest. My family was large, several generations strong. I am called Perrie for short. Obviously, that is not my given name. I can't even pronounce my given family name yet. I may never know it since I doubt I will ever see my family again. You referred to me earlier as a little fellow. Actually I am a daughter. The coloring of feathers for my kind is very similar with both sons and daughters. We daughters grow much bigger than the sons. I am not yet a full year old. I don't know if you speak of years or day-rounds or many other synonymous variables of years. My kind are very intelligent creatures, we are taught by several different teachers on several different levels. I am the brightest of my class and I am also the fastest flyer in our sentry group. I think I am all alone now. Before I was snatched in mid-flight, I witnessed a near slaughter of many of my kind, including family members. If they were not killed, they were captured by two-legged barbarians or snatched by dreadful wingers I had never seen before. It was appalling." Perrie shuddered at the memory. "The group, to my knowledge, included no Talkers. You three are the only Talkers I have ever had contact with. During my studies, there was talk of you, but only in legends. Under different circumstances, I may have been more excited to meet you. My feelings are numb now. I'm sorry."

Hemoth had a question, "Perrie, you came from Glacier's Crest? That is forever from here. How did you find us?"

"Hemoth, you are correct. Glacier's Crest is in the northern quadrant of the upper half of the world as we have learned. Where are we?"

Gann answered, "Worded like that, we would be in the lower middle quadrant of the upper half and to the east."

"Very well. I was brought here by a silent soaring winger whose wings were like 10 of my own. Without a doubt, he was the largest flyer I have ever known, seen or heard about. Even the largest

Eagles are only three times larger than the largest of us. His talons were not even sharp. I have no idea what he was. I say he even though I am not convinced that he might have been a she. As I said earlier, he grabbed me in mid-flight with one claw. He wrapped it around me loosely so I could continue to breathe. He was intent on rescuing me. I never felt threatened. He flew higher than I knew could be flown by a winger. He flapped his wings only to gain altitude, once we were at the height he wished, we just soared. I was having trouble staying awake in the thin air. Eventually, I went to sleep. I have no idea how long I was out. The last I remember, he was diving in the direction of your mountain. Just before he let me go, a low utterance came from him. He had not spoken the entire trip. He said, 'You are alone. Stay silently where you fall. They will find you. Beware of the intelligents.' I did as I was told. I perched in the tree directly under where he dropped me until I was spotted by Sig. I was too afraid to call out, but then they found me. I apologize if I was too general with my descriptions. I should be able to go into more detail as my memories return."

"My dear, you did very well. Now eat and rest. It is time for sleep. In the morning we will get after these mysteries once again." Gamma was as adamant about sleep as she was about eating. No one argued with her. "Madaliene, give Perrie space in your chamber. Sig, you are out here with Hemoth."

Madaliene took Perrie into her sleeping chamber. Before she doused the lit candle she asked, "Perrie, have you ever heard of a Nuorg?"

"I'm sorry, a what?"

"A Nuorg." Madaliene repeated.

"No ma'am I have never heard of that."

"Alright, maybe we will find out tomorrow. Sleep well Perrie."

Sleep came quickly to all of the creatures. The morning would arrive soon enough.

\*\*\*

The new day broke. Gamma, as always, was the first to greet the day with a short time of solitude outside the cave entrance. She began each morning in this manner. There was only so much time one could spend in a cave before taking on lethargic qualities. Gann would join her for their daily morning routine which consisted of watching the sun rise, scanning the horizon for any sort of visitors, long talks and short walks over the top of their mountain. It had been so long since they had two guests at once, they hardly knew how to be hospitable anymore. As a matter of fact they had not had any guests since they resigned themselves to dwell in the cave nearly 10 years ago. They once worried how Madaliene would cope with the loneliness, but had given up on that many years ago. Their granddaughter had never given any hint of being lonely. Now they seemed to worry more about how she would fit in if they were ever to move back to a populated land.

Gann exited the cave with two steaming mugs of sassafras tea sweetened with a thick syrup made from thumb sized black berries that grew in abundance on the mountainside. "Good morning, Gamma, thought you might like a hot mug of tea to help you ward off the chill in the air this mornin'." He gave her a sweet peck on the cheek.

Gamma smiled back, "Thank you kind sir. I'm afraid the chill in the air this morning is not because of the air temperature. I have spent my entire night trying to determine what a Nuorg is, either in thought or dreaming about it. Do you realize how difficult it is to dream of something when you don't know what that something looks like or feels like? All night--nothing but big empty dreams of big blobs of something. Do you think it is a thing or a place?"

"You got me there. I experienced the same kind of night. Racking my brain over and over, I got nothing. Woke up this morning still nothing. I'm more tempted to think of it as a place rather than a thing, or maybe a thing in a certain place."

"It sounds like you accurately interpreted my thoughts." She took another sip of tea. "My, the tea is good today. One lingering question, how does Evaliene think we are going to locate this place or thing? We sapped every bit of information from that poor letter. I'm of a mind it might just jump back in the envelope and seal itself up if we try to wring it out again." Another long sip of tea. "My goodness Gann, how much syrup did you pour in here?"

"Ah, not that much. Mine's not that sweet. I guess you must have stuck your finger into yours."

"Oh well, aren't you the slick talking one this morning. Gann, what are we going to do? Where do we go from here?" She moved closer to him and put her arm around his waist.

Gann put his arm around her shoulder, pulling her closer to him as they stared wistfully through the trees. He took an extra large gulp of tea. "We are going to figure out where Nuorg is. We will all draw on our experiences to get Evaliene out of trouble."

"So, you think she's in trouble?"

He took another gulp of tea, "Yes I do. I think she is in trouble, but this time not of her own causing. Her temper may get her out of this trouble, but I don't think it got her in it."

"Let's go back in and eat some breakfast. Mad and her guests should be awake by now." They walked back into the cave in search of their oldest granddaughter.

Hemoth was stirring. He lumbered around the spacious living area like a caged animal. He was not particularly distressed physically, but emotionally, that was another story. He pounced on the elder couple as they entered. "Did either of you discover anything about Nuorg? Whatever it is has stymied my mind. I have never heard of one, talked of one or ate one, though now I could eat about anything. All night long...tossing, turning, flipping, growling...for naught! For nothing! I hope I didn't keep you up."

"Goodness no, Hemoth, Gann and I were the same. We mentally pursued every lead we could imagine. Same as you--for naught."

"Oh this is not good. I have a bad feeling."

Madaliene pirouetted into the chamber in her long, purple, flowing sleeping gown. "Good morning all. Unlike the others, she had slept soundly with nary a dream to disturb her rest. "What can we do today?"

Shortly behind Madaliene, Sig and Perrie followed with a less enthusiastic display of morning behavior. Sig was dragging. Perrie showed signs of being physically beaten. Her body ached from the stressful happenings before she was rescued by the giant winger. Her delicate crown feathers crinkled and her cere was dull, not shiny like it would normally be on a Falcon of her age.

Sig was the first winger to speak, "Morning. I would like to know which one of you guilty parties snored last night. Any volunteers? Come on, speak up now. I won't hurt you." He wearily flew up to perch on a small dried tree Gann set up for him several years before. "Do I need some tea?"

Perrie was next. "I do hope that I am not intruding on any of you this morning. If it is better for you, I can wait outside until you are ready to deal with me." She looked toward the exit.

"Absolutely not, Perrie. You should be the first to the table. Hop here Falcon." Gamma patted a spot on the table. "You have the host's ear. What would you like to eat first? Anything you like is yours. What will it be?"

"Well again I don't want to make a nuisance of myself. Normally I would have a few mice for breakfast if I could find them or maybe a mole or a small rabbit."

Hemoth raised his eyes, "We may have a problem here."

Sig was all ears, teetering on the very edge of his perch awaiting the next response from any of the Talkers. "This should be interesting."

Gamma clasped her hands together, "Hmm, that is a very delicate menu option you just requested Perrie. I don't quite know how to tell you this..."

Gann nervously crossed his arms over his chest. "But..."

Madaliene put her hands on her head, pulling her wild hair into a mess on the top of her head, "We don't..."

Sig was next to chime in, "Eat..."

"...each other, Perrie. We are Talkers. We don't eat each other. Where exactly are you from?" Hemoth was stunned. He vaguely knew of this activity, even he devoured those slippery, slimy creatures that lived under the water by the cart loads but never another living, breathing animal.

"Oh my, I'm regretfully sorry about that. I sincerely hope I have not hardened your feelings toward me. Where I am from, there is a complicated, though necessary structure which, over the years, has been refined. There are clear distinctions drawn by class, size, natural ability; a ranking of creatures so to speak. Even among wingers, we can and do have the option of eating lesser creatures such as a quail or a dove for instance. They are smaller, less intelligent...food. From the time we are branchers, we are taught to distinguish the lower classes of creatures which sets them up for later consumption. I thought that practice was carried on here since I have not seen a raptor or standard winger since I was dropped here. I had every assumption that the winger that rescued me was, in actuality, merely collecting his next meal."

"You present a very unsettling case, Perrie." Although Hemoth heard of these practices, he never studied these types of societies during his many travels, nor had he ever encountered a participant until now. "So, Perrie, I am one of the largest Bears in the entire world as we know it. There is nothing higher up on the food chain than me. Even the big Cats of the far off lands would not have a go at one of my kind. Given that, do I have the ability to pick and choose any creature I cross as my next meal?"

"The answer, where I come from, is yes."

"So if I get hungry, I just take a bite out of any of these two-leggers here or eat the whole thing. If I am still hungry, I can eat you as well?"

"Again...yes."

"Hmm," Hemoth turned away.

"Well, this is a splendid morning isn't it?" Gamma asked. "Perrie, I'm afraid you will be restricted to non-breathing meals here. Once you return to your lands, feel free to eat as you choose. Our stores may bore you, however it will nourish you."

"Thank you for your understanding, Gamma. I will do only as you say. I'm sure my appetite will be quenched adequately."

With that said, the others nervously studied Perrie. She didn't look all that imposing, but they were not completely sure.

"Gann, Madaliene, help me serve our guests." Gamma was off to the pantry.

Madaliene had never heard such talk. She was excusably pale. She shuffled quickly after Gamma and Gann. "Is she telling a story, Gann? I can't believe she was expecting to eat four-leggers for breakfast. What would be her big meal for the day? Us?"

"No child, in her world she would fear us."

"So in her world, if I got very hungry, I'd just take hold of Sig and start munching?"

"No sweet thing," replied Gamma, "You would pluck his feathers and cook him first."

"No way! You are joking. Does that really happen?" Madaliene didn't know what to believe.

"Mad, we have a bigger problem now. We must feed our guests with our selection of food. Then, after we eat, we must make plans to find your sister. Got it? That is all you need to concern yourself with now."

"Yes ma'am."

As Gann carried a bushel basket of fruit back to the table, he tried to understand why a winger from a completely different world would be dropped on their doorstep. "Dear, why is Perrie here?"

"I don't know, Gann, what is a Nuorg?"

"More than ever I'm beginning to think of it as a place rather than a thing. Evaliene must have known where it is or what it is. We certainly never told her of it. Do you think she just heard of it or experienced it?"

"Well dear, I haven't a clue as to what she was thinking. She has always been more like your side of the family. Maybe it is something she grew up hearing about from some of them. You know how strange they could sometimes be, wandering about, raving about all kinds of silly superstitions and the like. I am so glad you became one of the normal ones."

"Why, that is so sweet of you to say. You worded it so carefully to avoid hurting my feelings or stirring my temper."

"You know full well what I mean! Some of your people are oddities and those nuts didn't fall far from the tree. Thankfully, when you hit the ground something came along and kicked you completely out of that forest."

Gann had to laugh. "Even under the cloud of this mystery, I can find that humorous and I'm sure when I'm gone you will tell wonderful stories of that day, how you were my saving grace, how you were the one that pulled me from the grip of the insane. Did I ever thank you for that?"

"There was never a need for that Gann. I knew it from the moment I looked into your eyes. You were smitten with me. From that day on you have lived every day thanking me."

"Really? Smitten? Every day?"

"Yes, every minute of every day since you first laid eyes on me, you have been thinking of me. There is no need to voice it, I just know."

"Oh my, you are so humble, is that why I love you so?"

"Obviously!" Gamma laughed out loud.

Gann, with love and respect for her beaming from his eyes agreed. "Obviously."

Madaliene walked over to them, "Gamma, are you two recalling the days when Gann rescued you from your crazy side of the family?"

"Madaliene! You know better than to say that out loud! That is our secret!" Gann exclaimed beneath a howl of laughter.

Not only was Evaliene like her grandfather's side of the family, but Madaliene grew with the same temperament and love of life and adventure as her sister. Gamma's family was a stoic, intelligent and quiet group of ruling monarchs. Gann's family was nearly the complete opposite. How they ended up together was another story entirely of its own.

"What are we going do to research this Nuorg thing? Should we send Sig and Perrie out to scout information? Should Hemoth and I go on a mission of our own to find out about Nuorg and then actually go there? What about Ev? Someone has to go after her, don't they?" Madaliene was tossing out question after question. The answers to those questions were not as easily forthcoming.

Hemoth lumbered into the conversation. "Madaliene, I can't see the benefit of sending out the wingers. According to Perrie's accounts, there are none left out there for them to communicate with. Did she not say she had seen none during her trip in? You and I will have to go with or without them. I think they should accompany us, with Gann and Gamma's blessing of course."

"I agree completely, Hemoth." Gamma nervously looked at Gann. "Don't you dear?"

"I'm afraid so, Gamma. We will be safe here from whatever is after Evaliene. Nuorg must be found. If the secret to Ev's rescue is there, it must be located quickly."

"But, Gann," Madaliene searched the chamber with her eyes for reasoning, "How can a place or thing we know nothing of be found or discovered quickly? How can it be found at all?"

Gann's strong fingers rubbed his chin and he shook his head, his lips pursed tightly together. He stammered for a moment then answered very unsurely, "Maybe Nuorg can't be found. Maybe you can't discover it. Maybe we are pondering a lost cause. But, maybe we aren't. Listen, all of you, does it really matter if we can't find Nuorg? Does it matter if we can't figure the mystery out? My answer to that would be no. The only thing that does matter is rescuing Evaliene. However mystifying it may be, Evaliene is more connected than any of us gave her credit for." He turned and stared at Hemoth, "Big fellow, I am putting my complete trust into your capable paws. I am giving you an order to return to me both of my granddaughters.

There will be no other option. You will discover Nuorg, you will rescue Evaliene and you will return here with both girls in a safe condition. Is that clear?"

"Yes sir, it will be my honor to take on that task for you."

Gamma silently agreed with Gann. After forcefully nodding her head, she added, "Hemoth, you know the consequences of failure as well as you know the consequences of any action taken on behalf of our family. To say that our girls are important to the future of us all is tantamount to any point drawn on this matter. They are the future of everything. When the time comes they must be prepared. Should either of them not return, the consequences will be grim. You should leave soon. Take what you can. While Madaliene and I prepare for your departure, you, Gann, Sig and Perrie work out some kind of plan for discovery and communication." Gamma turned to the long hall leading down to the store rooms. She motioned for Madaliene to join her. "Come with me."

"Sig, you and Perrie need to hear this. Follow us. We have some planning to do." Gann led Hemoth up a second hall from the large living chamber. This hallway led high up into the mountain while the others snaked down into the mountain's depths. The wingers perched on Hemoth's back. They traveled in thoughtful silence.

## 12

"**K**eeper, I am back. The messengers have been sent. Twelve in total, six pairs to six Burgs. I am afraid our dwindling population of wingers is most distressing. I am ready for my next task if you wish one for me." Sometimes Bongi was more courteous than Eekay wanted to deal with.

Eekay stayed in her trancelike state even after Bongi's entrance.

"Excuse me, Eekay, I am back. Excuse me?" Bongi stepped a little closer to the Keeper. "Eekay! What do you want me to do now?"

Eekay jumped. She shivered when she became aware of Bongi's presence. "Bongi, you handle this. Whatever happens, you handle it. Our visitor must be here for a reason. If the representatives do not expel him tonight, put him in the middle of it all. Let him carry out my duties. I can no longer do it. I don't belong here. If they do expel him, I will go with him back to my home land. I have unfinished business there. I should have never taken this position. If they do not expel him, I name him as my successor."

"But Eekay, you have no authority to do that. You have a duty here. You cannot abandon this appointment." The moment Bongi had feared for some time now was imminent.

"I can and I will abandon this appointment as I see fit. I have decisions in my head to make that have nothing to do with this place. Reality needs me. This Burg, for me, is not reality. Like I said, if they will have him with that Cheetah skin and all, good riddance. I must go."

With that Eekay lunged out of the doorway into the Burg. Shortly after, she came running at full speed for the gate. She took one leap onto the gate, striking it about one-third of the way up. Her extended claws raked the wooden planks until they found solid grip. She yanked her body up another third of the gate then leaped over the top. Once on the other side, she flipped her body around reversing her grip to lower herself to the bottom ramp. She threw her head from side to side searching for the ground. She quickly found it just outside the reach of a long jump. She dropped the remaining distance, landing on all four paws. She turned to look back up the gate marveling at the height she had just scaled with nothing but sheer determination. She had to be free of the responsibility of this place. She roared a menacing roar heard through the Burg, turned and never looked back.

Bongi shuddered at the veracity of the Lioness' roar or scream. He shuffled his body to face Jahnise, "I am sorry you had to witness that. I knew it was coming, I just had no idea it would be today. Something about your arrival triggered a side of her that she normally kept so well hidden."

"Bongi," Jahnise stood very saddened, "Our leaders are creatures that live their lives just as we do, breathe the same air we do, they have trials and tribulations just as we do. If she was selected for duty here, somewhere inside her is a strength she has yet to find. I know what she is going through. The pressure to lead is overwhelming at times. It is not how you face it immediately that sets your legacy, but how you deal with the ramifications of not leading when you should that makes you strong. A leader is a leader whether they lead or not. Now or later is not the issue. When you find that gift inside you, only then can you become what you are."

Bongi was fascinated by Jahnise's response. "You came here to be our Keeper?" he asked. "Did you know any of this before you entered through the window?"

"No I did not Bongi," Jahnise replied solemnly. "And no, I knew nothing. It is not complicated my Okapi friend. Most of the time spiritually I find myself blowing with the wind. Wherever I am supposed to be, I will be. Whoever I need to be I will try to be. I am now here in your Burg. I will trust my life to who made me, the one who knows what is best for me and knows me best. I will not let you down my friend. Let us make preparations for the gathering this evening or shutter-closing time as you say."

"Very well spoken, Jahnise. I hope you can speak as eloquently later to the representatives. The matter of the Cat skin should be very interesting."

"Bongi, I will speak as I do at the gathering to all those who wish to hear. The matter of the Cat skin is a very interesting matter indeed. You may be surprised. I will stay here until you call me. I have much to prepare." Jahnise smiled a soft smile at Bongi before sitting down cross-legged near the outside wall of the tree. He laid his walking stick across his lap, bowed his head and began humming a song from his past.

Bongi respectfully left Jahnise alone to prepare. He stepped out of the tree then closed the door behind him. He had much to do. He spread the word about the gathering and tried to calm the storm of talk surrounding Eekay's sudden bolt over the gate. Yes, there was a lot of work to do. His next job was to get the gate opened. He did.

\*\*\*

Eekay ran for the window back to her home. She retraced the route taken earlier by Jahnise and his hosts. She hoped the window would still open to take her home. She left much more of herself at home than she had left at the Burg. She wanted to tell her mother how much she missed her, how the time away had made her promise herself to quit arguing for no other reason than arguing. She wanted to make her father admit that he was her father and not only the pride leader, that she meant something to him, how he wished she had been born as a son if that is what he was wanting and holding against her. After all it was not her fault she was a daughter. She had no choice in the matter. She had questions for the elders who deemed her fit for the appointment in the Nuorg Burg. She just wanted to go home.

\*\*\*

The couriers were arriving on a regular basis about two or three clicks apart. Bongi sent the pairs out according to the speed at which each pair was able to fly. The first pair of Seagulls got the closest Burg. One of the Doves swapped with the Golden to pair with the third Seagull. The pair of Goldens got the Burg farthest away, the Golden and fastest Dove got the next farthest. The remaining two pairs of Doves were assigned the average distanced Burgs which were left. As they returned, Bongi was waiting for each of them with a scribbler close at foot. There was not an over-abundance of two-leggers in this Burg since Eekay had made it known to all that she would rather not deal with any of them. That being the case, Grendl volunteered for the job. Her exceedingly neat scribbling was on a scale proportionate to her size. The larger creatures could read it with

132

the aid of a magnifier. It was easier for her to read it aloud once she scribbled it down. She kept her logbooks in a room beneath the Gate welcoming room. Kohlyn's job was to keep the logbooks tidy and in order. As a team, they worked together very well, with only an occasional disagreement.

As the messengers returned, Bongi asked each pair the same questions:

1. Did you speak with the Keeper?
2. Is he or she sending representatives, if so how many?
3. What are the names of those he should expect?

Every pair stated for the record that they were well-received. Each and every Burg was sending at least three representatives to the gathering.

"So Grendl, how many total visitors should we be expecting?"

"Let me see Bongi, hmm...Burg One is sending five, Burg Two is sending three, Burg Three is sending three, Burg Four is us, Burg Five, coincidentally, is sending five, Burg Six--three, Burg Seven--four. That makes 23 total. They should be arriving shortly."

"Very well done Grendl. Thank you very much. Let's prepare for the arrivals shall we? Kohlyn, please spread the word that we have 23 representatives that should start arriving shortly." Bongi was good at his job. He enjoyed it thoroughly.

"I certainly will, Bongi. Do we have a beginning time?" asked Kohlyn.

"We will start three clicks after the last representative arrives. That should provide all the visitors ample time to rest and ready themselves. Are we all set? Shall we proceed?"

"By all means we shall." Kohlyn was off.

Grendl tidied up her scribbling. She carried it down to the library and filed it away. She got a new roll of writing material and marked it:

*"Nuorg Gathering for the authentication and validation of Jahnise Equakembo. To welcome or expel."*

Bongi quietly pushed the door to the Gate welcoming room open far enough to stick his head in to check on Jahnise. He had not moved. His stick was still in his lap and his head bowed. He was breathing deep regular breaths which told Bongi he was sleeping

133

soundly. Having no immediate need to bother him, Bongi let Jahnise sleep and made off to continue the preparations for the evening.

Over the course of numerous clicks, the representatives arrived. Each group arrived together whether they were leggers or wingers. Bongi and his party welcomed each group personally. Nuorg was nothing if not graciously accommodating to all fellow Nuorgians. Most of the guests knew each other from similar gatherings, so there were no new faces in the crowd except for one old Eagle from Burg One. He arrived with Hugoth, Donkhorse, Rakki and Karri.

"Hugoth! So good to see you up and walking. We heard about your run-in with Charlie, that conniving fiend."

Hugoth gave Bongi a smart slap on the shoulder, "Yes Bongi, it is also good to see you! I am afraid his attempt to dispatch me would have been much worse had it not been for the Wolf and his Staff. I feel wonderful now. Why were we summoned on such short notice? Where is Eekay?"

"I will have to address those questions later Hugoth. This must be Mystic. Sir, it is an honor to make your acquaintance."

"I have heard much about you Bongi. Such clever markings you possess." Mystic had never seen such a four-legger in all of his travels.

"Thank you, sir. Donkhorse, you look...rather normal."

"As do you, Bongi. Normal is not that bad, is it?"

"Rakki, handsome as ever and Karri! You are still the most beautiful Hawk in Nuorg! What is your secret? If you ever go up, I'm afraid the male Hawks may not let you return to us." Bongi was good at his job and, unlike in the lands surrounding the Great Forest and other places above Nuorg, he actually meant every word he said.

Rakki acknowledged Bongi's compliment with a nod. He was just about to address his host when Karri fell all over herself, blushing through her facial feathers. Her eyes lit up, sparkling. "Bongi, you are so handsome yourself. You don't know how good you make me feel. It is so wonderful to be thought of as a lovely creature. Do you really think the other Hawks would like me up there? I would never hear words that sweet from this pack of creatures!" She hopped up between his ears then gave him a flirty peck on his brow. Rakki grimaced and shook his head.

Bongi saw another group headed up the lower ramp. "Kohlyn, please show this group to middle court it you don't mind."

"Certainly Bongi. My pleasure." Kohlyn scurried up to Hugoth's massive shoulders to lead the way.

"So teeny, tiny little friend, what do you know about Eekay's absence?" Hugoth was surprised when the moody Lioness did not greet them at the gate in her less than jovial manner.

"I can tell you that I do not know the entire story, Hugoth. I can tell you it happened very quickly. You know how impulsive that one is."

"Yes she is impulsive and moody, but there is a unique quality to her honesty that was needed around here. After all, our tasks are not all fun and games. She can see right through creatures. It almost seems to me that she sees right into their souls. She is an excellent judge of character. I miss her." He laughed at how odd that sounded. "I do miss her. Do we know where she is?"

"Hugoth, you may be the only creature in Nuorg who sees her that way. We all know she has our best interest in mind, but still...her moods are hard to take. You see her early in the day, she wants to ignore you, you see her later that same day, she wants to eat you! Or, at least, I thought so anyway. But who am I to say? Right?" Kohlyn's gaze turned back towards and past the gate. "I do so hope she is alright, Hugoth. I do."

"We should find out more at the gathering, should we now? Bongi knows what is going on with her. What about this new two-legger? What is he all about?"

"You are talking about Jahnise? Grendl and I welcomed him through the window before the shutters were opened this day, a very tall, dark man. His color is deep. The same as one sees with his eyes and shutters closed. He is very tall for a two-legger. Very tall, but not thin like a young tree, his shoulders are wide, his arms strong. Jahnise has much energy. He is very steadfast in his ways. He met with Eekay earlier before she...well earlier today. Bongi knows more. We will wait for him to tell more. My talking is just talk."

"Very well, Kohlyn, I will ask no more about her. Is that good?" Hugoth had gathered enough information to start putting a theory together.

\*\*\*

Eekay neared the grounds where the window resided. Ahead of her were the same boulders Grendl and Kohlyn had hidden behind when Jahnise came through earlier. The tree where Jahnise landed appeared on her left. A fuzzy haze covered an opening between two Nuorg junipers. "Good, the window is still here. I have to get in it. I have to get home." She continued running full speed. Just as she approached the junipers she leaped into the haze above them. Eekay was on her way home. She was immediately encased in the watery liquid. She had been here before so she was not afraid. She breathed the liquid as air. This part of her journey over, she relaxed her entire body.

***

Every Burg was represented. The pomp shown to the visiting Nuorgians was not overly dramatic. There were no banners, no festival type atmosphere. The gathering had not attracted a horde of un-passionate, disgruntled or sad creatures. It had, however, attracted a very determined and diverse crowd of wingers, two-leggers and four-leggers. The majority of Nuorg two-leggers were not Talkers. Most of the two-leggers remained in their respective Burgs. The two-leggers that were present were from Burg Five. All five representatives from Burg Five were two-legged Talkers. These two-leggers did not feel the least bit awkward within the grouping of wingers and four-leggers. The hearts of these five were genuinely devoted to the protection and future of the Nuorgian credo. Burg Five was the only Burg with a two-legged Keeper since the entrapment of Burg One's liar. Hugoth had performed his tasks flawlessly regarding the removal of that problem, especially given the fact that the Wolf and his cohorts had arrived complicating the dilemma. Burgs Two, Three, Four, Six and Seven sent randomly selected representatives from their populous.

Per Eekay's instructions, the verbal invitations, although not terribly detailed, were worded to draw several big Cats. She had not been thrilled to see the two-legger striding over the hill in the first place, much less wearing the skin of a Cat draped over his shoulder. If Jahnise was allowed to stay in Nuorg, which she doubted, he would have his work cut out for him. Wearing a four-legger hide in Nuorg was rare, so rare that it had never happened before and should not ever happen again. The list of forbidden acts was long, and within that list were several grey areas, but as a rule, four-leggers did not wear or eat two-leggers and vice-versa. Jahnise would have to tell a fantastic tale to the gathering in hopes of explaining his choice of

136

coverings. And although it was to be a varied group of Nuorgians, there would still be several Cats.

***

After checking on Jahnise, Bongi asked a few of his fellow Burg dwellers to assist with and oversee the needs of the representatives. He found more volunteers than he needed. Every creature responded positively before Bongi could finish asking. It seems that Eekay's vault over the gate was big news around the Burg. Not every creature had seen it, but the remaining wingers in the trees certainly had. They wasted no time spreading the news of the biggest event to happen there in...well, since she arrived to become the Keeper. The Burg was abuzz with chatter of Eekay's departure. Bongi tried to quell it. It was no use. The dwellers were going to talk and they had that right. There were a lot of creatures that never fully warmed up to Eekay. She was hard to like. There was no debating that.

A sturdy four-legger walked up to Bongi, "So do you want the two-leggers in front or in back? Do we seat according to size or age? What do we do with the Cats? I'm thinking they should not be on the front row if our Visitor is wearing one of them on his shoulders!"

"All good questions Stewig. Do as you wish. I must fetch our speaker. If you doubt your decisions, run them by Hugoth. I know he is not our Keeper, but at the present, we do not have one. Either Hugoth or Ian, one of them will have a say one way or the other. Thank you for your help."

"Alrighty, I'll take care of it. Where is Ian? Have you seen him?"

"I only saw him long enough to welcome him in. He was with his family. Look through the crowd, they are probably following him." Bongi made his exit and headed for Jahnise. He hoped what was to follow would be civil.

Stewig swung his unwieldy head from side to side many times before he spotted Burg Five's family of two-leggers in the growing crowd. Ambling over he found both Hugoth and Ian in the center of a smaller crowd, undoubtedly entertaining the onlookers with their stories. These two long standing Keepers were loved and protected by all. Many wondered if these two set the standards for Keepers. How was Eekay ever considered for such a prominent position? Hugoth's mass combined with Ian's large boned two-legged frame made for an imposing pair. Stewig nudged his way through the horde, being careful not to step on any stray foot, paw or claw. "Excuse me. Coming through. Mind your paw there."

"...next thing I remember was a brilliant flash of light. Everything the sages have written about the Staff number One is true. Contained within the handle is a trove of information, maps, notations... everything as written. The Wolf? Oh yes, a marvelous legger, the Cheetah too. Wonderfully fast." Hugoth was telling of his latest adventure. "My friend here, this old Eagle, is one to whom we owe much gratitude as well." Hugoth pointed to the ancient Eagle perched on his massive shoulder.

"So, Hugoth, you say that this Wolf is actually the particular one for whom we have been waiting?" The two-legger was not doubting Hugoth's revelation, just verifying it.

"Yes, Ian, without a doubt."

"A Wolf? I heard he came with a party of four and left with a party of five? How is that? Did one of yours return with them?"

"No, Ian, the two-legger, Frederick Mounte, was here unbeknownst to us all. He lived beneath the mountain for some time. He went through the same globing process as the rest of us and came out no worse for the wear when the blast cleared."

"Interesting. So there was a Wolf, a Cheetah, an Eagle and a Badger?"

"Oh yes, and what a Badger Lightning is!"

Stewig had bulled his way to Hugoth. "Hugoth may I have your ear just a moment? Ian, if you would as well, this way?"

"Certainly, Stewig. How are you?"

"I'm rather okay."

"How can we help you?" Hugoth stepped out of the crowd, pulling Ian with him.

"I'm not sure if you know all about the visitor and the reason for this gathering. There is a very fragile matter at hand that you two should be informed of. Once you give it some thought, I need to ask your advice on the placement of the audience."

"Why would you ask that, Stewig? Let everyone take any place they want." Hugoth did not see the importance of this questioning yet.

"Hugoth, Ian, there is a potential problem with our two-legged visitor. He um, he is, he ah..."

Ian wanted to pull the question out of Stewig. "What is it boy? Does the man have two-heads?"

Hugoth didn't know where that came from. "Ian...two heads, really."

"No, I don't mean literally Hugoth." Ian turned to Stewig, "I mean really, Stewig, what is so terrible about this man?"

"He is wearing a Cat on his shoulders."

"What did you say?" Hugoth was paying attention now.

Stewig repeated himself. "Jahnise is wearing a Cheetah on his shoulders. A dead Cheetah!"

"Oh my!" Ian was stunned.

"Exactly, so I was more than a bit concerned with allowing the big Cats to get too close to him."

Hugoth agreed. "I can see your point. I hope he has a legitimate story to tell us about that. Some of the big Cats do not take well to that kind of display."

"That doesn't matter if they take well to it or not Hugoth. Ciruss, Duister, Luiperd and the rest of them better watch their step. I know they are worthy of being in Nuorg, but if they step out of line they know what will happen and do you know what I mean by step out of line?" Ian was not in the mood for this.

"Ian, yes I know. We must speak to Ciruss now. Stewig can you bring her to us? We may settle this before it starts."

Stewig looked around. "Hugoth ask your Eagle friend over there if he could fly up and spot her for us. I can't see over this crowd."

"Mystic." Hugoth's loud voice carried well.

The old Eagle heard Hugoth's summons. He made his way to Hugoth's shoulder with one flap of his wings. "Yes, Hugoth?" He nodded to Ian, "Your wife and children are charming sir. What can I do for you?"

"We may have a problem developing here and we want to squash it before it begins. We don't have a lot of time for explanations so will you pop up over the crowd and locate the largest striped Tiger here? She has a tear in the top of her left ear. She is gruff, but harmless...we hope. Tell her we need to speak now."

"You hope she is harmless? Me too! Of course. I will do it right now. Do I lead her back here?" Mystic was eager to hear the rest of this.

"Yes," said Ian. "Bring her back quickly."

"I'll do my best."

"Stewig, are you sure Jahnise is wearing a Cheetah?" Hugoth asked.

It was Ian's turn. "Are you absolutely positive he is wearing a dead Cheetah on his shoulders?"

Hugoth, "Beyond any shadow of a doubt?"

"Actually, I haven't seen it myself, but Bongi relayed the information to me."

A squeaky voice sounded from Hugoth's shoulders. "It is true. I have seen it with my own eyes. It is a Cheetah and it is lifeless. Grendl and I noticed it when Jahnise first arrived."

Hugoth had forgotten Kohlyn was still on his shoulder. "Hah Kohlyn, did you need a nap?"

"I guess I did Hugoth. What is happening?"

"Much more that I bargained for. So you did see the Cheetah?"

"Yes I did. As I live and breathe. Grendl and I were shocked."

Ian's hands fiddled with his coat while he shook his head, "Hugoth, we must defuse this before it grows with the wind. Let us find a dwelling or some place with a little privacy. I don't want Ciruss making a scene. Especially not now with what you know is coming. Oh why can't we just deal with one thing at a time? Stewig, the gate room in the tree, can we meet there?"

"I think that would be as good as any place. I'll take you there."

Hugoth, with Kohlyn still on his shoulder, and Ian followed close behind Stewing as he pushed his way through the growing crowd. When the crowd thinned, Stewig whispered to a four-legger standing at the edge of the middle court, "Can you take over here? I need to take care of a little problem."

A deep voice rose from deep inside the creature, "I can do that. Please hurry. The shutters are soon to close. Excitement is brewing."

"Thank you Faun." Stewig led the way back down the path to the gate.

They passed a myriad of potential spectators as they traveled. Ian was confused. "How many Nuorgians were invited to this? As I understood there were only to be 20 or so. I was counting those in the crowd earlier, now I have lost count at over 100."

"I can only offer you one word to answer that: wingers." Stewig enjoyed his life in Nuorg. The wingers never ceased to amaze him. They were a very social breed.

"Stewig, can we hurry? There are too many here to let this get out of control." Hugoth was concerned with the growing crowd and the large number of Cats coming by. "Do any of you suppose Eekay stirred this pot on her way out?"

"Out of where? Where is she? She should be here. She did call this gathering, did she not? Hugoth, what do you know?" Ian saw the gate trees ahead. He also spied Bongi's head coming out of the door. "Uh oh." He broke into a trot.

His pace was soon equaled by Hugoth and Stewig. Ian shouted at Bongi, "No, no get back inside. We need to have a chat."

Bongi raised his head then ducked back in the room right before Ian crashed through the door followed closely by the others. "Where is your visitor, Bongi? Where is he?" Ian begged.

"I am here." Jahnise emerged from the dark side of the room, almost as if he simply materialized right in front of the group. "What can I do for you?"

Bongi put himself between Jahnise and Hugoth. "Hold on a click here. What is going on with you? Stewig, who is placing the audience? Never mind that. What are you three doing here?"

Kohlyn popped up out of Hugoth's thick fur, "That would be four of us, Bongi."

"Oh terribly sorry, yes now I see you, Kohlyn. Again, what are you four doing here? I was about to escort Jahnise to the court."

"About that," Hugoth interrupted, "I think maybe we should have a little meeting ourselves with him first. Eekay is not here to fill us in on the details causing her to call this gathering and we have received some troubling information regarding Jahnise. We are concerned for his safety."

"You must be joking, Hugoth! Here in Nuorg? Why would you be concerned for anyone's safety?" Bongi was angry at the accusation.

"Bongi, the scars on my shoulder are fresh reminders of just how unsafe we can be in Nuorg. I want to hear the legger out, but several others may not be that interested in his story."

There was a sharp peck at the door. "May I enter?" The old Eagle stepped into the room. He held the door open as a large Tiger followed him in. "Hugoth, I brought Ciruss to you as you requested."

"Good to see you again, Hugoth, Ian, Bongi." Ciruss was very polite addressing the group while she stared directly at Jahnise. "Oh. I'm sorry, good to see you also, Kohlyn. I knew I smelled a Rat."

141

"Field Mouse, Ciruss, I am a field Mouse."

"Whatever. Bongi, I guess this dark two-legger is the reason for the gathering?"

"Yes, Ciruss, he is. Eekay thought it wise that we introduce him at a special gathering."

"Why, is he visiting or does he intend to stay here?"

"I cannot answer that, Ciruss. Eekay is no longer here." Bongi was now nervous. Hugoth and Stewig could subdue Ciruss since they were both larger and stronger than her or any of the big Cats, but the claws and the fangs were menacing.

"What do you mean she is no longer here? Did she call this gathering or not? Who has she appointed to replace her?" Ciruss' way of speaking was soothing. She never spoke too loud or too soft. She never lost her temper...yet, and was the undisputed leader of the big Cats.

"Actually, Ciruss, she appointed Jahnise here to be her successor." Bongi now wished Eekay had written down that proclamation.

"What?" asked a surprised Ian. "Is Eekay not coming back? Why would she leave without warning?"

"My dear Ian," Ciruss explained, "Eekay never intended to be here. She certainly didn't intend to stay. She was too young to take the reins here. The elders of her pride saw something wonderful undeveloped in her, as did I and Hugoth. Am I correct, Hugoth?"

"Yes, Ciruss, I had no idea she could not handle the pressure."

"Yet, Hugoth, she could not handle the pressure yet. Where was I, yes, anyway if Eekay appointed this two-legger as the new Keeper of this Burg then it is fine with me. She has, unknown to her, a powerful gift of discernment that she has never come to terms with, She hated it because she does not understand it. I don't have it, but you do as does Ian and his daughters."

"I am not sure that explains everything to my satisfaction, but if you say so, I will side with you, Ciruss." Hugoth could not understand why Eekay would just quit.

Ian was listening carefully to Ciruss. "Ciruss, the reason we wanted to meet with you before the gathering has nothing to do with matters relating to Eekay. Our concerns are with Jahnise and what he is wearing. You are a Cat, how does it strike you? Will it cause any trouble at the gathering? Jahnise, please step out of the shadows there. Please everyone, let us step outside. Hugoth, if you will, could you, Stewig and Bongi block the view from the path to here? I want Ciruss to see this clearly."

Hugoth, Bongi and Stewig did as Ian wished. They stood side-by-side facing the door, forming a solid wall between the path and the tree. Ciruss was the next one out. She took her place in front of Hugoth. Ian stepped out next.

Jahnise stood in the open doorway facing his small audience. He ducked his head low, leaned down on his stick and stepped through the opening. Once outside, he again stretched his tall body to his full height. After his rest, Jahnise had cleaned himself of the dust and grime he had collected during his journey. He had wiped down his walking stick, washed himself with the miraculous water from Nuorg and beat any remaining dust from his clothes. He did not look like the same two-legger who had climbed up the ramps earlier. His skin glowed luxuriously, his smile radiated warmth. Dark eyes exposed onlookers to the depth of his soul. The radiant colorings of purple and gold woven into his clothing alluded to royalty not known throughout Nuorg. Only two pieces of apparel seemed out of place. His hat was beaten and dull. The second piece was the Cheetah skin. It was a magnificent hide, albeit very controversial.

"Good evening glorious creatures of Nuorg. I am First King Jahnise Kotumanrunda Equakembo, King of the Great Plains and Chief of all tribes therein."

The small crowd was stunned. Jahnise was far more than a casual visitor to Nuorg. All of the four-leggers from the lands that bordered the Great Plains had heard of him and the great deeds he had done for all living creatures within his kingdom. Where they came from, Jahnise was a common name given to males of any family. In most, not all translations, it meant man-child. His name never caused a stir before because he had not given it, in its entirety, to any creature but Eekay. Even then he did not mention First King.

Eekay was correct when she told Bongi that Jahnise could be her successor. She was honored to give him her position. Why, she had wondered had he wanted it? It was at that point when she decided to go home. This Burg would be in better hands than it had ever been and she wanted her young life back. If it meant starting over, she would.

Jahnise kneeled in front of Ciruss. She was mesmerized by his manner. "Ciruss, I see you have become a great Tigress just as I expected. I have heard much of your exploits in your homeland. Do you remember the day we first met? I had visited your country after the death of your grandfather. He was a dear friend to me. You were no more than this big." Jahnise held his hands a short distance apart. "It is a great pleasure to meet you again, Queen."

Ciruss blushed as tears filled her eyes. "I do remember you. You picked me up, very high off of the ground. It scared me."

"Yes I did. Do you remember what happened next?" Jahnise was smiling.

"I do, I tried to free myself. I swatted the back of your head when you rested me on your shoulders. I remember trying to grab your neck to brace myself. You were bleeding."

"Oh yes, Ciruss, I bled." Jahnise removed his hat. He bent way over exposing the back of his neck for all to see. "See these four scars?" He pointed to four visible lines of scarring that ran from the middle of his neck to his shoulder before fading away. "Those were made by your baby claws. Should that happen now, I doubt I would survive it."

"My mother felt so bad about that."

"I know, she told me over and over again. But no worries, Ciruss. When I pick up cubs now, I hold them differently. How is your family? I haven't been that way in a long time."

"They are aging, but healthy." Ciruss was visibly crying tears of happiness. The more she remembered of Jahnise, the more she cried.

Ian looked on in wonder. "Oh my, I never saw that coming. Jahnise, who else do you know here?"

"Oh, could be more than I can count sir. More than I can count."

Ian stuck out his hand. "Ian, Ian Patrick Mecanelly. Glad to meet you, ah, should I call you King?"

"No, no, Mister Ian. Call me Jahnise."

Bongi and Stewig were captivated by Jahnise. The person Bongi saw now was not the meek, humble visitor he welcomed on the ramp, but a strong, confident leader who had seen his share of the world above with great success. "Bongi, the Okapis are a magnificent breed of creature, quite shy but magnificent. Stewig, yes you are a sturdy creature. Your parents named you well and are very proud of you I hear. Your kind is becoming rare. I am not happy with that. Hugoth, I have even heard of you. I never traveled to your country, still you must know, your past brings a great joy to many people far and wide. Shall we proceed to the gathering? Do not be concerned for my safety. I can handle myself. Once they hear my story, the big Cats will not have a problem with me. When can I see Duister and Luiperd? Will they be here?"

Stewig led the way to middle court followed by Bongi. Jahnise walked with Ciruss on his right. Hugoth, Kohlyn, the Eagle and Ian brought up the rear.

Hugoth looked to his shoulder at the Eagle, "Mystic, you were shockingly quiet."

"Hugoth, I was and still am amazed. I have nothing to say. I'm utterly speechless."

Hugoth then smiled at Ian, "Doesn't that beat all? Here we are all worried sick that the big Cats will want to eat Jahnise and he might have raised them. Oh the mysteries of Nuorg continue."

"Yes, Hugoth, baffling isn't it? Absolutely baffling."

# 13

Frederick reached the bottom of the ladder. He reached into his bag, found and lit his handy candle. Cautiously, he held it out in front of him. The candle cast an eerie glow on objects foreign to his eyes. He slowly moved down a tight main corridor cluttered with old cages and containers of every shape and size. To his side, a journal very similar in design to his own rested on a makeshift table. A sudden breeze snuffed the candle. It was quickly relit. As Frederick raised the candle back to eye-level, his gaze fell on an indistinguishable pile of parts. "This couldn't be what I think it is?" he whispered. On a shelf behind him, an object teetered before it crashed to the damp floor. More objects fell from the shelving and before long the entire unit collapsed at his heels. Frederick whirled around, his candle once again snuffed out. He tripped over the collection of fallen objects at his feet, plunging headfirst into heaps of something which originally lay hidden behind the stack of shelves. He fumbled to get his candle lit again. It took longer than his previous efforts. He rolled onto his back, frantically striking a flint on his belt, breathing rapidly. Finally, a spark emerged from the darkness followed by the warm flame of the candle's wick. He sat up, took a deep breath and again looked around. Frederick was sickened at the sight he beheld. He was laying in a row of long dead, slightly mummified bodies...of two-leggers. Who or whatever placed them here did so in no particular order. To his horror, all of their identifying features had been removed. He had seen enough. He scrambled to his feet, trying to regain his composure. His hands clawed for something solid to grasp, and his voice was silenced. No sound escaped from his lips. He looked around again and gasped for breath. Respectfully, as he sat his candle on a nearby shelf, he reached over to the nearest bodies he saw and searched the clothing for some piece of identification, some trinket or bracelet, something that would give a clue to who these people were. His hands, as if they were guided by fate, found several items. Grabbing as many things as possible, he stuffed them into his deep pockets, picked up his candle and snatched the well-worn ledger book. Pausing for a moment, he uttered to the dead, "I hope one day I can give you all the respect you deserve." His stomach now spinning, Frederick raced back up the ladder, extinguishing his candle as he exited the top. "Bubba," Frederick was shaking. "Bubba, it is not good down there. It is not good at all. Please cover the opening with something and do it fast. We have to get out of here. Cover that up, please! Find something, anything!"

Bubba had no time to think. "Anything?"

"Yes anything and the more the better." Frederick, visibly shaking, teetered around searching for answers to a new nightmare and a place to sit down. With nothing but destruction surrounding him, Frederick continued stumbling away from the debris soon finding himself on the opposite end of the collapsed structure from Lightning and Mystic who were performing their gruesome task as well as could be expected. He was almost clear of the wreckage when he collapsed to the ground, heaving and vomiting uncontrollably. As he fought to control his involuntary reflexes, sobs began to wash over his dust caked face, taking streams of pale mud down his neck. As his physical being was plummeted with body blows, his mental state began to deteriorate in tandem.

Bubba dragged anything he could find to the opening, before he knew it; he could no longer reach any higher to stack even the smallest scrap of wood on the pile. He scanned the immediate area for Frederick. Bubba spotted Frederick's dark jacket and sprinted to it. He found the two-legger on his hands and knees, shaking uncontrollably.

"Frederick? Frederick, are you alright?" No response. "Frederick! Frederick!" Bubba nudged him with his front paw. "Hey! Hey!" Still no response. "Frederick!" Bubba pressed his head into Frederick's chest forcing the two-legger to fall over on his back. Only then did the Cheetah see the result of the cellar experience mirrored in horror on Frederick's face. Bubba was unnerved. He sat down beside his mortified friend in silence, resting a paw on his heaving chest.

Mystic and Lightning were busy moving the organized stacks of remains into the burial pit. Lightning excavated a large hole that would adequately accommodate every lifeless carcass. They used a large wooden panel as a sled to move the dead wingers to their final

147

resting place. The mist rose higher as they worked allowing fresh air to sweep the rotting smell downwind of their toil.

"I wonder how many of these sky-travelers died in this collapse." Mystic was perplexed by the high number of casualties.

"Mystic, I am more concerned with why the collapse happened. If it was accidental that would be one thing, but why were these poor creatures in there to begin with?" Lightning pulled the sled to the edge of the pit, tilted the panel and carefully slid another large group into the hole.

"Did Frederick say he counted all of these?"

"He said he documented them. I don't know why. Maybe it's a practice in the two-legger's world. I really don't see the need at this point. There couldn't be that many survivors or extended family members. We have placed entire family flocks in the hole so far, everything from tweensts to elders. This is the saddest thing I have ever seen."

"Well, it probably happened so fast, don't you think?"

"I think the end may have been fast, but I don't think the deaths were. These creatures suffered. I hope the instigators suffered the same fate as their captives. If not, I rue the day we meet."

"Rue the day, hah, where did you hear that?" Lightning answered an unheard voice. "What did you ask? Oh Mystic? Oh yes, he rues the day for those evil doers. Rues the day!" He smiled at Mystic, "Rues the day?"

"Yes, I rue the day. That means..."

"I know what it means, I just think it sounds funny coming from a Wolf."

"You would. Where is Bubba? Is he still with Frederick? We are about done here."

"Let me get the last of these in their grave and we can go check on them. Frederick needs to get the rest documented." Lightning slid the remaining wingers in the hole before dragging the sled close to another, undocumented pile of feathers. "That's it for now. Let's see what they are doing. Frederick should be above ground by now."

The pair gingerly stepped back through the disaster. They became concerned when they saw the pile of junk stacked high over where there had, a little while ago, been an opening. Lightning stretched a paw out to knock away some of the upper stack...

"No! Don't touch that! Frederick is not down there anymore. He's over there and not doing well. He must have seen something that really got to him. He is resting well away from here." Bubba nodded toward the two-legger's location. "Come quickly. He is not good, not good at all."

They hurried to where Frederick lay prone on the grass in a near paralyzed state, his eyes unfocused, mouth agape, hands trembling, breathing regular but very labored. Lightning bent down to speak with him. "What happened down there?"

"He's not talking, Lightning." Bubba assumed the position of mediator.

"He is pale as a...as a...I don't know what he is as pale as. I've never seen a breathing two-legger this pale. I've never seen a breathing one either except for him and Charlie, but I don't think Charlie was a real two-legger. What do you think is wrong with him?"

"I can't say."

Mystic got a closer look. "He looks terrified. Something in that hole traumatized him."

"Traumatized him? First it was rue the day, now it's traumatized? Who are you, Mystic?"

Bubba looked at Lightning oddly, "Rue the day? Who said rue the day?"

"Prince Mystic here. Plain as it could have been said, rue the day."

"Really?"

"Yes he did." All of this chatter took place as Frederick remained their only focus. "Rue the day."

"Whatever! We have to get Frederick back to our world. Any ideas?" Mystic soon regretted his previous choice of words.

"I have tried everything I know to do. I suggest we wait it out. He has to come around eventually, doesn't he?" Bubba wasn't positive.

"Should we go back over there? See if we can find out what did this to him?" Lightning was all but headed back when Frederick suddenly lunged for his front leg.

The two-legger shouted, "No!" and fell backward.

"Whoa! That was strange." Lightning stopped in his tracks. "I guess we won't be checking it out after all."

"I am not sure about you two, but you couldn't make me go back in there." Bubba was sure of that.

Mystic sat next to Frederick with several ideas whirring about. "Should we use the water? Is this considered life or death? Or should we wait it out?"

"Let's use it. We have to get going. It will be dark soon and I don't want to be near here when it arrives." Bubba begin to scratch at Frederick's bag. "How do we open this thing of his?"

"That is a problem I didn't think of. I guess we will wait." Mystic rose to his feet, sniffing the air for a scent of anything. "Do either of you smell water?"

"I think you are the only here that has a nose for that Prince Mystic." Lightning rolled his eyes.

"Fine, I will go hunt for some water. There has to be some near here. Everything looks too green."

"If you want to go looking for water, I'll go with you. We can leave Lightning here with Frederick." Bubba took a step nearer to Mystic. "Where do we start?"

Mystic wasn't at all sure, "Let's wander over to that line of trees. There may be a stream nearby. Bring that rag hanging out of his pocket."

Bubba pulled the rag out with his teeth. "Leth's gah."

"Lightning, hold the fort. We'll hurry." The Wolf and the Cheetah headed off to find the water side-by-side.

Lightning watched. As they faded from view, he turned his full attention to the matter at hand or, better put, the two-legger at paw. "Frederick, do you hear me?"

The two-legger, entrusted to the Badger, did not respond. Instead his gaze remained vacant and drops of drool slowly followed the curves of his bottom lip before dropping down on his jacket. Nothing seemed to be reaching Frederick as his glazed eyes studied and hands toyed with several different types of two-legger ornaments he pulled from his pockets, dangled and placed back. Lightning stood at Frederick's side, wishing for even the slightest sign of coherence from the two-legger since none of the happening's pieces were fitting together as of yet. Occasionally Frederick would sit-up, shudder for a moment then relax into a fixated stoop. Lightning nosed around at the bag slung over Frederick's shoulder, but that was it, he couldn't even begin to get it open with his huge paws. If it came to it, he would rip the bag open with a tiny flick of one claw, but he knew now was not the time for that. A couple of times, Lightning prodded Frederick with his snout to no avail, knocking him over then picking him back up.

"What have you done or seen," he wondered aloud. "I have a mind to go inspect that hole for myself."

"No! You can't. You are not prepared for what you will see!"

"Was that you?" Lightning asked the comatose legger. "Hmm, when I mentioned the hole..."

Again Frederick shot up and remained alert long enough to plead again, "No! Please leave the hole as it is!"

Lightning wasn't surprised with the outburst this time. Any mention of the "hole" shocked Frederick or some reflex within him to respond immediately. "The hole. The cellar. You walked down the ladder. What did you see Frederick? What did you see? You don't want us to go back down the hole? Do you want us to let you go back down the ladder?"

"No, no, no, no, no! Don't uncover the hole. Don't go down the..!"

Frederick suddenly slumped completely over as if he were stone-dead. No movement of any kind. Lightning became frantic. He swatted the legger to and fro with tiny flicks of his paws.

"I have to get in that bag!" He slipped one claw under the front flap and curled it down in a sawing motion. The flap loosened. One more time and the inside of the bag became accessible. Only the closing buckle was damaged. As lightly as he could, Lightning rummaged through the bag. There it was. The container of Nuorg water slid effortlessly into a big paw. Lightning cupped it and held it over Frederick's face. He gently squeezed the sack until a few drops made their way down the side of the bag. He squeezed a little harder and a steady flow of droplets began dropping onto the pale, dry skin above the two-legger's nose. The water began to splatter into the glazed eyes, crusty nose and dry mouth. First, the lips begin to quiver, then, the eyes fluttered. Gradually, Frederick came around. Lightning released the pressure on the bag just enough to allow the droplets to continue their chosen paths.

The water was remarkable. Since they first tasted the liquid in Nuorg, each member of the group yearned for more, racking their minds for the best excuse to drink more of it. Frederick involuntarily won the contest. His eyes popped open with all of the sparkle they had on the day Mystic first brought him into the confidence of the

Staff. The color came back to his face as if it had never left. He was fine... again.

"Lightning, how much water did you use on me?"

The proud Badger smiled, "No more than amounted from a few trickles of drops." He held the bag up for proof. "See, it is almost like I used none at all. Here, put this back in for safe keeping. I'm afraid you may need to repair the flappy thing there on your bag."

"Oh never mind, if that is the only problem, it will be quite fine really. Where are the others?"

"They went hunting water to revive you before I messed up your bag. I couldn't wait. I thought we had lost you there for an instant."

"Lightning, we will never go near that hole again, at least not without the threat of death hanging over our heads. Awful. I will never speak of what is in there so don't bother asking. If the others bring it up, you tell them. I am done with that atrocious cellar."

"What could it...?"

"I said no! Absolutely not! Fetch the others. We need to get as far away from here as we can. I am not thrilled about even being here now."

"But the sky-travelers we were burying? Should we not lay them all to rest?"

Frederick sighed, "Yes, we must complete that task. Let's get on it while the others are out. I am not documenting any further, I have all of the information I need. Suffice it to say, there are no more sky-travelers, wingers, birds or what have you around these parts anymore. They and those from many lands here abouts are in those piles of feathers we are burying. Come on, let's get a move on. It's a grim task. I want to be rid of it."

"I'm right here with you on that. What did you say about no wingers?"

"You heard me correctly. There are no more around here. That's all I want to say about it now. Please respect that wish. I will tell you more in time. I have a journal from the cellar. I hope it will shed some light on what led up to the end." Frederick led Lightning around the perimeter of the debris. He did not intend on going back through it, ever.

Lightning filled the wooden sled up with pile after pile of the winger's remains. Some carcasses barely resembled a sky-traveler and some resembled a type neither he nor Frederick had ever seen.

The colors ranged from brilliant to gray, shiny to dull. Some were nearly the size of a two-legger and some smaller than a sparrow. Whatever the case, there were far too many dead ones. They worked on in silence. When the last winger slid into the pit, Frederick said a few words then asked for some time alone while Lightning covered the remains with dirt.

Lightning watched Frederick as he slowly walked away. He was allowing him alone time, but he was not allowing him out of his sight.

As he walked, Frederick slipped the worn, dusty journal from his side pocket. He scanned the first few pages for a glimpse into the life of the author. He found a few round boulders protruding through the green grass and used one for a seat and one for a table. He laid the journal down then reached into this bag to retrieve his own. The similarity was uncanny. Both had a large gilded "H" in the center of the cover with script below. They were the same width and height but his contained at least triple the amount of pages. He opened them both. Having nothing in his stomach, he took a fruit out of his bag and ate as he began to read. Page after page of normal life in the Hewitt clan was told in everyday terms. He was not familiar with this particular branch of his family. There were no mentions of any of his close relatives, which caused him to believe, on more than one occasion, that the initial similarities may just be that; very strange similarities.

With only a few more pages left, the tone of writing changed. Where once Frederick was reading of the normal trials of life, he was now reading of capture, imprisonment, torture and weird screeching voices; he had to take a break. He opened his journal, raised his pen and wrote.

*For those of you who decide to read my journal through mere curiosity or necessity I must warn you, these next few pages can only begin to tell you of the horror I have witnessed just today. Fortunately for the others in my company, they were spared the agonizing realization of what went on within the remnants of the once fine barn that rests behind me to the north. Oh, the torture that must have taken place within those innocent walls, the wailing that must have been heard by the magnificent trees that surround us to the west. What could have brought the savagery down on these poor, poor creatures? Was it us? Was it the two-leggers as we are called? Or, was it some rogue sect of four-leggers or did the wingers, the birds take out their own. I have never seen evidence of such brutality so widely available to my eyes. Sure, I have heard of it, but...we found a cellar, I can't even describe it. Awful, I have no words for what I saw with my two unbelieving eyes. I escaped with a journal, a "Hewitt" journal. For a split second, I thought it was my own. It was a very strange experience. The poor animals with me were so upset for me. The biggest one of the bunch, Lightning, the irregular Badger, Duke of the Great Meadow stayed with me as the others went in search of water. It is getting late and they still are yet to return. The cellar...*

"Frederick!" The voice was clearly the deep resonant bass voice belonging to Lightning. "Our two weary travelers have returned. Let's get out of this place."

Frederick was never happier to close his journal. "I'll be right there." He rushed to join the others. He could not wait to thank them for taking care of him. "So, did you two find any water?"

"Yes we did, I am happy to report!" Mystic came running for Frederick, his tail wagging, ears up and alert. Bubba was slightly behind and closing fast.

They hit Frederick mid-stride, knocking him to the ground. "What happened to you?" "What did you see?" "Did you hear anything we said?" "Are you okay?" What did you see?" "You already asked him that!" "So?" "We found water." "Get up, we need to go. Lightning is in a mood."

Rapid fire questions asked faster than anyone could hope to answer. The four-leggers were overjoyed with Frederick's new-found health. They helped him up as best they could and walked at his side back to Lightning.

"I am fine...now. Regarding the cellar and what it contained, well you will never know. As I told Lightning, I am not nor will I ever be willing to talk about it. Drop it shall we?"

"Drop it? What you saw down there nearly destroyed you." Bubba did not like this answer.

"Bubba, you will never hear it from me, so please, never ask me again."

Mystic read Frederick well, "Bubba, we don't need to know. Let's get these two to the water."

"But, bu, bu..."

"No. The matter is not to be discussed, unless...?" Mystic raised his head to Frederick.

"Absolutely not. If you ask regarding the cellar again I have instructed Lightning to sway your opinion in an opposite and all together much more pleasant direction. Is that clear?"

"Yes. If it has to be, it is."

"And you, Bubba?"

"Yes, yes for me too. I'm very hungry. Can we eat at the water's edge?"

Frederick had no problem with eating, all he had since the unfortunate stomach emptying incident was that one fruit. "I sure hope we can."

Unknown to Frederick and Lightning, Bubba and Mystic were pretty close to exploding from their feast earlier at the lake. Yes, it was a lake, not a pond but an extremely large lake, a lake that would make the Black Pond pale in comparison. It was hidden beyond an unnoticed rise at the tree line. Bubba and Mystic gorged themselves on a feast of reddish fruits that fell from the trees and big juicy fruits bigger that their heads. They ate water-livvers, tasty water-livvers that nearly jumped right out of the water and into their wide-open mouths. They hurried back to the imploded barn where they were overjoyed by the news of Frederick's improved condition. Until now, they kept their secret to themselves.

Bubba urged the group on. "Let's hurry here. We need to put distance between there and wherever we may be going before sundown."

Frederick checked his time piece, "I'm afraid that won't be long now Bubba. How much further?"

"Just past those trees. About three leisure beats from here. If we pick up the pace, we will be there before we know it."

Lightning wasn't falling for the "oh boy" act. "If I were a smarter Badger than I am, I think that you two have already been where we are going, you already ate a great feast and, only then, did you decide to return and tell us of your magnificent find. Could I be correct?"

Bubba couldn't resist, "You could be correct, if you were a smarter creature! Hurry up! I need a second helping!"

Mystic broke into trot. "You stragglers follow us. It's a straight shot from here. We'll set the table for you." And, off they went.

Frederick beamed. "Lightning, maybe our extraneous work paid off in a big way. Maybe we earned our dinner."

"And, from the sound of it, all of tomorrow's meals and the next and the next..."

"Hold on, we still have to pack our meals. There is no need to take more than we need. Someone or something is looking out for us, but I agree with those two, let's speed it up. Let me jump on your back. You can run faster than you have let on."

"Is it that noticeable?"

"Yes. From what I hear you climbed that cliff under my cave entrance as nimbly as Hugoth. That's very admirable...for a Badger!" Frederick climbed up on Lightning's back and held on for all he was worth.

Lightning chuckled, "Yep, for a Badger, I climb a pretty serious cliff." The huge four-legger took off, setting a pace to nearly take over the two smaller friends. "I am so hungry."

Bubba and Mystic arrived back at the lake shortly before the bigger pair of leggers. Immediately, they began eating more of the delectable offerings. "We need to eat our fill before Lightning gets here. He may not leave much for us to pack up. He seems very hungry." Mystic was scooping water-livvers from the shallows with his front paws, eating them whole.

Bubba was devouring any Mystic missed. "These are so tasty. More please."

Lightning slowed to a trot as he neared the tree line. His nose was picking up a heavenly aroma. "Food!" He exploded through the trees, nearly landing in the lake and pulling Mystic and Bubba in with him,

Frederick hanging on with every ounce of energy he could muster. "Where is it? Where is it?"

"Patience, Badger! Look, it's all around you. Melons and smaller fruits, vegetables, and these delicious water-livvers that swim right up to the edge for you." Bubba did not like being in water, instead he scooted a few Mystic had thrown him over for Lightning to taste. "Try some."

Frederick slid off the famished Badger's back just as Lightning's snout dove for the squiggly, wet treats. "My, you two have sure found us an ample spot." Frederick walked the area, tasting melons and vegetables as he inspected the many different plants.

"Why do you suppose all of these plants are in the same place, Frederick?" Mystic was lying down, his over-stuffed belly heaving with each fulfilled breath.

"I am not sure, Prince. It may have something to do with the way the lands around here drain to this lake. It is quite possible that over the years plants and seeds have made their way here totally by accident and taken root. I wish to thank whatever made this happen though. This is a fabulous occurrence. There are far too many different foods here to sample at one time."

"I beg to disagree." Lightning was foraging through the plants eating an assortment of everything he was offered.

"Okay, I want to amend that statement. There are too many foods for a creature of normal size to sample during one sitting."

"That sounds more plausible, Frederick. Thank you for that clarification." Lightning continued to eat.

"My biggest concern right now is trying to decide what we can easily take with us. There is so much to choose from and some things here we can't possibly pack out of here."

Night was falling. Mystic was beginning to snore a satisfied stomach snore while Bubba's actions were getting slower as he too fell under the sated hunger sleep phenomenon. Lightning even quenched his voracious appetite. Frederick sat alone, contemplating what had happened that day. Since it was too dark to make entries in his journal, he sat under the starry, night sky listening, toying with his bag and thinking alone. Soon, he was asleep with the others.

# 14

The tunnel wound high up inside the mountain; so high, in fact, every ear popped on more than two occasions. Hemoth was amazed at the craftsmanship exhibited by the tunnels. "When were these built, Gann?" Hemoth was growing more curious by the step.

"Hemoth, these are old tunnels. They were started when my great-grandfather's father was a young boy. They were built in many sections to avoid discovery. The only period when these tunnels were not maintained and extended was that time of the Terrible Years. There is only one map of the top corridors and it is in the lowest part of the caverns. The map of the lower caverns is hidden away up here somewhere. I never needed it, so I never looked or asked to see it. If anything happens to me...well, I guess that would be bad. You need to memorize everything you see up here. Sig has flown a few of these routes, haven't you Falcon?"

"I'll say I have and that I had no choice. You tied me to your gauntlet so I wouldn't fly away and find myself lost in here. Yes I know most of this mazern, but not nearly all of it."

"Mazern? I've never heard of a mazern. Is it a real word Gann?" Hemoth didn't need to question the Falcon, but it was a unique word.

"As far as Sig is concerned it is. I imagine he got it into his mind years ago, you know the caverns below and maze of tunnels up here. Yes, I think it does fit all of the qualifications of a word; you can say it, you can spell it, it means something. A word it is, indeed."

Perrie was not convinced, "A what? A mazern? Maybe so."

"Don't let it bother you young one. There are a lot of words used around here that may or may not be real words in some other places." Gann continued leading Hemoth higher and higher in the mountain. "We are almost there. We have a station coming up soon."

The leggers and wingers continued spiraling up high inside the mountain. Hemoth began to breathe more heavily than normal. "How high are we, Gann? I don't remember working this hard to breathe ever before."

"We are almost at the top. As a matter of fact, here is our stopping point now." Gann ambled to the side of the tunnel where a wooden door awaited him. "I know it doesn't look like much, but believe you me, it is a wonderful spot to watch the world go by or come at you." He stepped to the side of a gangly contraption and threw off the dark cloth cover. It consisted of three skinny legs ending in a pivot point, from there a long round cylinder rested on top. The tube was larger on one end than the other with clear lenses at each. Gann spun the tube around easily, inspecting it for damage. "Nope, good as new."

"Perrie cautiously eyed the device. "What is that? There is nothing like that where I come from."

"Perrie, this is a telescope. It is used by two-leggers to study the sky. Since we can't fly, we have to use one of these to get closer to it. It brings the moon and all of those other specks up there in the night skies into focus--really a very ingenious instrument. It can also be used to scan our borders for signs of visitors, both good and bad. Let me open the window and see if we have any out there."

Hemoth was interested to hear more. "Can you see all the way around the mountain Gann?"

"Oh no, we have three of these set up." He pulled a rope tied to a wooden shutter that opened easily on greased rails. With the window open a creature could see far off into the distance. "Sometimes I find myself up here scanning the horizons for days on end. I even think one day I might get fortunate enough to catch a glimpse of the future. Do any of you think I could really see that far?"

Sig needed to nip this conversation in the bud. "Gann, you know you can't see the future until you are there and since the future is always the future we are never essentially there. Now, do you see anything?"

"Well said, Sig. And no, this side of our world looks normal. Let me shut the window and cover this up, we will proceed to station number two." Gann hurriedly went about his business then led the group around the circular corridor to station two.

"I could learn to like this. Are there accommodations for Grizzlies up here?"

"You are always welcome to stay up here Hemoth. Mind you though, it can get extremely monotonous, but to each his own. Here is station two." He went through the same procedure as before. The stations were identical except for the direction they faced. Gann spun the second telescope around with a very skilled motion. He stopped, pulled his eye from the viewing lens, blinked his eyes and looked again. "Well that is odd. We seem to have visitors far off near the lake. This time of year those trees are so full of leaves I can't see the old barn anymore. Of course, it is hundreds of pursuit beats away. Sig, do you think you and Perrie might go check it out for us? Be careful, the sky is oddly void of wingers. That is strange, but it is consistent with Perrie's recollections. What do you say, Sig? Have a go, will you?"

"Do you think Madaliene will be angry with me?"

"I gave you to her, so I can override her decisions if I feel so inclined."

Sig cut his eyes to Hemoth then laughed, "Sure, of course you can as long as she never finds out!"

Gann agreed, "I suppose you have a point there."

"It should be okay, Gann. It is a straight shot as the Crow flies, right?"

"Yes. Fly over there, find out who they are, what they want, why they are here. Tell them to leave if they start talking crazy. If they do seem legitimate, I mean...uh, I don't know what I am saying. Use your judgment. If they know what a Nuorg is, bring them all back!"

"Oh, okay, just how should I bring that up?"

"That, my winged friend, is totally up to you."

"Very well then, Perrie, are you up for a stretch of the wings?"

Perrie was visibly distraught and trembling. "I uh, I, I am not sure I want to fly out there in the open right now. It should be dark soon, can we wait until then? I do not want to be ambushed from on high again if I can help it."

"Absolutely you can wait. Let's get a bite to eat. When the moon rises you shall go."

Hemoth was not going to argue that. "Gann, do we have to go all the way back down to eat?"

"Oh no, we have stores up here as well. We stock them with the riser. This way." Gann led the way to a spacious but not overwhelmingly large room towards the center of the mountain. After he opened the normal looking door, the guests were greeted by the sight of a large banquet table. The room was set up to entertain many guests, as many as 40 or more two-leggers at a time. "Please, make yourselves comfortable. I will get some snacks." He entered a nice sized pantry returning with a basket of hard breads and non-perishable foods like dried fruits and vegetables and a basket of clay jars holding sweet water. "Here you go. Eat as you wish."

Hemoth was stuffing his mouth full of everything he could grab. Gann just snacked on a loaf of hard bread. The wingers devoured sacks of small nuts and seeds. Once the stomachs were substantially filled, Hemoth asked, "What do you make of the visitors you saw? You think they are here for a purpose? Do they know anything?"

Gann quickly finished chewing his mouthful of food, and as he swallowed the last crumb he answered Hemoth, "I can't say that I know any answer to your questions. They looked nice enough."

Sig added, "Yes, and this little Falcon perched next to me doesn't look like she would want to eat you either, but given the chance? Well...I just don't know."

Perrie nearly spit seeds out of her mouth, "Excuse me! We have already discussed that and the matter is closed!" She continued snacking. "Wonderful sense of humor you have Sig, awfully wonderful...oxymoron by the way."

The time flew by, edibles eaten; the group cleaned the table then headed back to station two. Gann again led the way. "Perrie, it is dark outside now, are you ready to give it a go? I will watch you with my scope from the time you leave. Fly low to the ground. Stay lower than the trees, try right above the grass, I know you won't see as well, but try it. If anything tries to attack you again, when you are flying low they will never get a good bead on you. Sig has flown that way lots of times and he always comes back."

Sig did his best to lessen the younger Falcon's fears. "He is right you know. There is no way anything can catch us flying fast and low."

"You both may be correct, but I remain nervous as a butterfly in a spider's web. I can't keep my feathers from quivering. Let's get on with it then."

Gann nodded his head in agreement. He stepped to the window and opened it wide. The brilliant twinkling stars were lighting the way for the wingers. "Remember; stay low...whatever you do, stay low. Sig, take care of her and you come back as well. I don't wish to break bad news to my granddaughter after breaking the rules of conduct with you about you. Understand?"

"Gann, I want to return safely also. Your worries don't need to be for me, but for you just in case I do not."

"Well thank you, Sig, I'm glad to know you are always thinking of me first. Go now. Again, fly low."

The Falcons rose to the open window, lit for an instant then took off quietly. The wind rushing around their sleek profiles made no noise. They flew incredibly fast. Gann had not known the exact distance, but it was easily several hundred full pursuit beats. The wingers flew it with ease. The strong flaps of their aerodynamic wings spurred them on as fast as they desired to go. Sig had speed remaining, but it was not so with the young one. Perrie was flying as fast as she could. Unlike Sig, she did not have the years behind her to build strength and endurance. She may have still been a fast winger, but she could not match the older Falcon's endurance. If flying close to the ground had any advantages other than stealth, Perrie would have loved to know what they were. Several times during the flight Sig would suddenly change directions or altitude to avoid obstacles normally reserved for land-walkers or leggers as they called them here. Many close calls with rocks, downed trees and errant clumps of brush, made for a traumatic experience. They flew on, Perrie within a beak's width behind Sig's last tail feather. Every 50 or so beats Sig would rocket skyward; catch a glimpse of direction then fall back to the ground. Each time this maneuver was completed, Perrie sent her food back to her stomach. If it wasn't for unknown peril, she would have thoroughly enjoyed this race under the star-filled night sky.

\*\*\*

On and on the Falcons sped over the ground. At full pursuit beat, these wingers were mere blurs in the sky; close to the ground it was even more difficult for any eye to get a clear focus on them. They passed stationary objects so quickly; no judgment could be made for an interception point ahead of them. She just watched them from far above as a constant moving line drawn by a very fast hand. She earlier wondered if this chance meeting might take place, hoping it would.

***

Perrie was tiring, but Sig was not in the least winded. Gann had long lost sight of them without the ability to catch the bright sun reflecting off of their shiny feathers. Even the long eye of the telescope was of no use to him now. "Hemoth, there is no more we can do here until morning. Let's go back down to our quarters and find out what the females are planning." Gann reluctantly shut the window and covered the telescope. He again led Hemoth into the mazern.

The journey down was much easier. It did not take nearly as long as the trip up, at least Hemoth didn't think it did. In fact it did take as long. Hemoth found himself just as hungry at the bottom of the trip as he did at the top. "I apologize, Gann. I am very hungry yet again. May I have another basket of snacks?"

"Of course you may." Gann stepped into the living chamber then headed directly for the pantry. He returned with another fully loaded basket of goodies, this time solely for Hemoth. "There, that should do you for a while. I'm off to find the girls." He left Hemoth to his eating and headed down the lower tunnels. "Follow me when you're finished."

***

"Gamma, all of this, I don't know...stuff, why have you kept it locked down here for all of these years?" Madaliene was standing with Gamma in a cavernous lower chamber stocked floor to a high natural ceiling with armaments. Everything from arrows and fine bows, to large experimental metal tubes of every shape and size sat patiently waiting to heed their call. Handmade crates with strange symbols on their sides lined one entire side of the room. Down the center was painted a series of lines with several sacks filled with heavy cloth at the far end. A circular target sat halfway up the pile.

Madaliene stared at the pile of sacks, they had to be at least four or five short runs away. They looked so small from where she stood. "Remember when you first brought me down here? I was thrilled to be here. It was such a mystery then and is still somewhat of a mystery to me now."

Gamma was opening an ornate wooden box. She lifted a fine, well built piece of equipment from inside. Quicker than a flash of lightning in a low sky, she snatched an arrow from a quiver, nocked it in her bow, pulled the string taught then let the arrow fly with a slight upward bend. The arrow sailed smooth and straight. It ended its flight with a slight thunk sound. "Well Madaliene, let's take a walk. I want to see if I have still got it!"

Madaliene smiled wide, showing a mouth full of teeth. "Let's."

They walked to the target passing by several years' worth of food stuffs, clothing, and other necessities stacked high with occasional ladders or stair cases leading to the upper levels. This room has always been an interesting place for Madaliene. She never questioned its need while growing up, only now was she beginning to figure out exactly what it was for. Grandmother and granddaughter walked side-by-side for the entire length of the gigantic room chatting occasionally. Finally they stepped up to the target. Imbedded to the fletching rested Gamma's arrow, not in the center of the fist sized spot on the target, but not at the outer edge either.

"Well child? Do I still have it?"

Madaliene shook her head in amazement. "Even after all of these years you still have great skill Gamma. Was there ever any question?"

"Madaliene, there are always questions. You just never know until you try it again. It's a gift my dear, it's a unique gift. You have it as well as Evaliene. I hope she had her chances to practice since she left."

"Can Gann shoot the arrows like we can?"

Gamma laughed, "No, Madaliene, he can't. Poor man can't figure out which end of the arrow to aim unless he hurts himself with it. No, Gann's skills lie elsewhere."

"So, why are we down here? There are plenty of provisions up there." Madaliene pointed to the ceiling.

The pleasantness of Gamma's face changed to a stern, concerned look. "Practice Madaliene. I want to see you shoot. Your life, ours and those of your friends may depend on it very soon. I want to see for myself, with my own aging eyes that you can still shoot. I don't want any creature lurking around outside to see your skill level. I want you to be at your best when you leave here. No one needs to know how good we actually are. Leave them guessing. Trust me when I say there is no one anywhere that can best us with the bow. There may be those who think so, but they are wrong. You may even see some trick or shooting exhibition that leaves you doubting yourself, but believe me, even the best the outside world has to offer will fall far below your skill level. Now load up your quiver."

Madaliene did as she was told. When Gamma got that look on her face, doing anything other than what she said was met with great disdain. She was in full protection or maternal mode right now and everyone around her knew better than to challenge her. "Shall I fill it full?"

"Yes. You will fill it and refill it if need be."

Madaliene opened a large tall box behind the target area. Inside she pulled handfuls of unused arrows from individual slots. She filled her quiver and both hands. "Is this enough to begin?"

Gamma's expression relaxed somewhat, "Yes that should get you started. As we move back to the zero marker I will give you calls. When I finish the call, I expect an arrow to have hit its mark. Is that understood?"

"Yes ma'am." Madaliene tried to nock an arrow. She struggled with both hands already full of arrows. "Well I can see this won't work. Do we have a larger quiver?"

"Yes, but it will slow you down. I will show you how to carry more arrows when you are done shooting. Section eight, row three, right side corner, first box."

Madaliene whirled to her left, drew and nocked her arrow. She released it. It flew perfectly, hitting the exact spot Gamma had called out.

"Section eight, row three, left corner, second box."

Again Madaliene let her arrow go. It hit as it should.

"Section 56, row 11, middle middle."

As did the others, the arrow hit perfectly. This exercise invigorated Madaliene. Up and down the aisles they walked as Gamma made the calls and Madaliene made the shots. "How am I doing?"

"Very good so far. Continue walking to the zero mark. Listen for my calls. They may be loud, they may be quiet. You have to hear them."

Madaliene did as she was told, no questions asked. Gamma stepped over near a stack of brightly painted crates. "Section 14, row one, left box, right side corner."

Madaliene spun halfway around and let the arrow fly with total concentration. Only after it left her bow did she realize where it was headed. The arrow's flight path was taking it swiftly to Gamma. The older archer did not twitch as the arrow silently tracked her. She had her hand placed on her hip with elbow bent. The triangular opening made visible the left box, right side corner of row one, section 14. The arrow stuck in the center of the triangle with a thud.

"Nice shot Madi, I'm so glad I taught you to count!"

"Gamma!" Madaliene exhaled the breath she had been holding for what seemed to her like an eternity. "Why? Wh…What were you thinking?"

Gamma only responded with two words, "Keep walking."

Madaliene, again, did as instructed.

"Section 23, row two, middle box, middle, top rail."

The arrow again was loosed. It headed directly at Gamma again. It hit its mark with another thud. Madaliene again realized where she had targeted only after the arrow hit. Gamma was standing in the middle of section 23, row two with a beautiful, finely made arrow placed less than a finger's width above the center of her head. "Again Madi, nice shot."

"Gamma! I've got to stop this. What if I hit you?"

"Well then I guess I'll know you are not prepared to leave this room yet."

"Really? Could you maybe not use yourself as a target anymore?"

"I'm afraid it's the only way for me to judge your skill level. So far, I see no reason to complain."

"Uh, you think so? If I kill you, I'll never know will I?"

"Yes you will dear, if you kill me then you aren't ready now are you?"

Madaliene said nothing out loud in reply. She closed her eyes tightly, let her chin fall to her chest then bobbed it up and down. She let out exasperated breaths while slapping the bow on her leg. "Gamma, Gamma, Gamma," she whispered softly.

"Section 36, row nine, right corner, left box."

Again an arrow flew penetrating another poor box in the exact location called out. This practice went on for hours. A call, a shot, sometimes Gamma was standing in front of the arrow, sometimes she was moving in front of it. No matter what the situation, Madaliene's prowess with the bow was unquestioned. After numerous quivers of arrows pierced numerous targets in numerous locations, the stacks of crates and boxes looked like a large Porcupine had blown up in the chamber. Arrows stuck out of every conceivable spot.

Gamma smiled as she glanced around admiring her granddaughter's competency. "I think you are ready Madaliene for whatever you may face out there. You will certainly be able to protect that Grizzly friend of yours."

"Isn't he supposed to protect me?"

"Ha-ha! If you only knew Madi, if you only really knew. Let's go find the others. I'm sure its getting late. You need a full rest in order to leave." Gamma helped Madaliene load up with arrows, strings, a spare bow and other items. She gave the young archer a warm hug which was returned whole heartedly and began the climb back to the living quarters.

"What did you mean back there Gamma? If I only really knew?"

"In time child, in time."

# 15

The crowd was assembled. The area which comprised middle court was full of creatures. Over 100 Nuorgians had ventured to this Burg to witness for themselves what the ado was about. The invited representatives took their places at the front of the lawn. Ian's family sat in chairs borrowed from a nearby dwelling. The remainder of the four-leggers and wingers gathered around sitting or lying next to each other while a few perched on chair backs or shoulders of the leggers. Mystic, the Eagle, flew from Hugoth to perch on the arm of the chair designated for Ian. Hugoth stayed back to protect Jahnise just in case things got out of hand or crowd control became an issue. Behind a tall hedge which designated the front of middle court, Jahnise stood proudly between Bongi and Stewig. His head towered over them both.

The two four-leggers could not help beaming with pride. This could be a historical event in the documented history of Nuorg. Never had royalty volunteered to stay in Nuorg. In fact, no true royalty had ever been to Nuorg, at least not royalty recognized in the land above. There were a few princesses and princes, a queen or two, such as the Wolf-- Mystic, Prince of the Great Forest and Ciruss, Queen in waiting of the Indojaneer Jungle, but no real sitting royalty.

Jahnise was true royalty. He had been in power, ruling his country and the lands abutting it for more that 30 years as the two-leggers wrote it. He was hailed as king when his father fell ill. Jahnise was only 14 years old. When his father succumbed to the ravages of the consuming disease, Jahnise was sworn in as king at the age of 17. He was one of the most revered leaders in the two-legger's world by the age of 24. Under his leadership, his country had resolved itself of all conflicts whether internal or external. Other countries used Jahnise's methods to resolve their own conflicts or invited Jahnise to take care of it himself. From the age of 24 to 44, Jahnise forged a legacy which was unequaled in any land. He was now 47. For the last three years, he had lived as a nomad. He dressed like the normal people of his land and traveled as the normal people of his land. Everywhere he traveled he heard of or witnessed firsthand the fruits of his diligence and leadership. What troubled him most was that no one recognized him as he was. His people were looking for a king who lived like a king, who dressed like a king, not a man who was humble in personality and appearance. Although disheartened, he stayed his course. He heard of Nuorg during several journeys, but not from two-leggers. Two-leggers scoffed at the thought of such a place, but four-leggers knew it existed and told him tales of the many experiences from Nuorg. He wanted to see it for himself. Now with trouble of some sort brewing at every stop he made combined with word of more troubles abroad, he decided it was time for his visit. It was then he told his family of his wishes. He left no indication of not returning to them, but made no promises either way. He felt led to do what he felt in his heart was the right thing. His children were grown with families of their own and his wife trusted his decisions without question. One day he told them farewell and followed the legendary paths relayed to him in the many stories he'd heard. There was no map to Nuorg or absolute method to get there. He followed a pure heart yearning for the good of all creatures.

"Excuse me Hugoth, Bongi, Stewig, please excuse me a moment. I need to have some time alone to pray." He politely bowed to them individually. "Just call for me when you are ready." He proudly walked further down the thick, green barrier.

Hugoth walked up to Bongi, "The crowd has gathered. Go before them and get this gathering started. You know the process, thank them for coming, give them a brief reason for being here then introduce Jahnise. I think he can handle it from there."

"Very good idea, Hugoth. I have just one little problem."

"And that is?" asked Hugoth.

"I can't speak in front of large crowds. You know, I get kind of nervous. A little flighty one might say."

"Bongi, Stewig and I are right here. Don't worry."

"Why of course I will worry, Hugoth, I was just saying I also get a little nervous."

Stewig was tickled. "Of all the creatures in Nuorg to be bashful, it has to be him."

169

"Bongi, I am counting to six, if you are not out there speaking by the time I get to five, you will never hear six. Are we clear?" Hugoth was trying to keep a calm face.

"Yes, Hugoth, here I go," He turned back, "See, I'm walking out."

Hugoth turned to Stewig, "Did you know that about him?"

"Yes I did."

"And yet you said nothing?"

"Wasn't my place to say."

Hugoth reached over and slapped the tall horn at the end of Stewig's leathery face. "You and your manners, get out there."

After being politely coaxed to the front of the crowd, Bongi got on nicely. It turns out he was quite the speaker after all. He spoke for a few minutes and then got to the point. "Without anything further to add, may I present to you all Jahnise Equakembo."

Behind the hedge, Hugoth summoned Jahnise. He made his entry without much excitement. The crowd fell silent at the sight of his chosen wrap. He could not help but notice the icy stares and hear the heated whispers as they began making their way through the crowd from the front rows to the back. He respectfully stood still and tall. As he waited for the clamor to die down, he lifted his hands with their long fingers high on raised lanky arms. Turning his palms up, he waited and bowed his head. No one kept a record of the length of time Jahnise stood before them in complete silence. Eventually the clamoring died away and the icy stares thawed. Only then did Jahnise attempt any movement. Still as a statue, he soaked in every good or bad feeling from each and every creature in attendance and he heard every unfriendly whisper. When he finally raised his head those in the front could see the tears streaming down his dark cheeks. In a quiet voice, he addressed the gathering.

"I am Jahnise Equakembo. I have nothing to prove to any of you. No winger, no four-legger, no two-legger here has the right to do anything but listen to me. You cannot talk about me because you don't know me. You cannot stare at me with hatred because you have not seen through my eyes. I do know each of you. From the least of you to the most powerful of you, I know you. I know you because I am you. I have seen what you have seen. I have heard what you have heard. I have cried the tears you have cried and I have laughed the laughs you laugh in humor or at the expense of other creatures. Most of you are staring at my friend lying around my shoulders. He is not dead. He is with me as is each of you. If I had the mind, I would toss him to the ground. I would say to him as he lay at my feet, get up and run. If I said that--he would get up and run. He would get up and enjoy my life with me as he did for so many years. He did not die for me, he lived for me. He saved the lives of many of my family on occasions too numerous to name. He has killed creatures for me, not to feed me but to protect me. He dragged two of my children to safety when a brush fire ravaged our country."

Jahnise held the pelt for all to see. He pointed at a burn mark at the end of an unnaturally shortened tail. He then pointed to a scar visible on the neck. "The point of this spear was meant for me. He threw himself between me and my attacker. That is not what killed him. He died of a broken heart. His family was decimated by two-legged poachers. When we returned from our duties, we found what was left of them. My Cheetah asked me for permission to kill the poachers. I did not give it. He died years later after his heart ran out of love. He said to me, Jahnise I have nothing left for you. The love I knew before is extinguished. There is not a drop left. Why did you not allow me to take my revenge on the poachers? They robbed me of what I had left of my life. I answered like this, had you killed out of revenge, you could not have lived as long as you did on the love you had for them. The revenge would have killed you and the poachers. Acting out your revenge would have ripped the love from your heart too early. You had too much of your life to finish. It was not your time. As his days walked away, he told me to take him with me wherever I go, to remember him as I traveled. He said he would always protect me even when he ran out of love. He is here with me now. Believe me, there is a hurt within my heart too big to tell you. I left his body out on the savannah for years as I carried on my life. The day I decided to pursue Nuorg I went to the savannah to reclaim my friend for the journey. He decided to come with me. If any of you should try to separate me from my old friend, you will not succeed. What I have discovered in my travels is diversity among the vast and different regions of the world. No creatures think the same, no creatures react the same. There are, after all, only two basic differences in all of us. Those differences are easily defined as good and evil, there is no in-between. I am good, what are you? Where do you stand? Is it possible to do evil for the sake of good? Yes it is. Is it possible to do good for the sake of evil? Again the answer is yes. The difference, my friends, is the ability to make that distinction."

Jahnise took a break from speaking. He lifted his friend from his shoulders and laid him down in front of him. He then raised his hands high above the crowd. He spoke with more passion than before. "Hear me Creator. Among those that you have entrusted to me, you have placed those who are wary of me in this crowd, do as you wish. Those that will believe in me believe in you, you have already prepared them, those that do not, they are yours to do as you wish."

Jahnise lowered one arm. He picked up his walking stick and aimed it at the audience. With a powerful stroke he slammed one end into the ground. A flood of light pooled around the impact area. It spread from within like it was being forced out by a strong gust of wind. The light became so bright that it obscured the light from the glowing ball in the sky above them. The cloud of light began seeking through the crowd.

A warm familiar feeling took over Hugoth. He mentioned to his fellow four-leggers, "This looks very familiar. You might want to pay close attention for the next few moments."

They listened but could not completely comprehend what he was saying, remaining mesmerized as he had been with Mystic's globe. Unlike the explosion of light from the globe, the light from Jahnise's stick hovered around them. It was thinking before reacting. The Cat skin on the ground was not disturbed; instead, it glowed brilliantly. The light was making decisions now. Several creatures gathered in the audience were selected. They were brought to the front involuntarily, all of them struggling against the pull. But no matter how vicious their struggle, they could not escape the light's hold on them. Two-leggers, four-leggers and a few wingers were selected. The cloud of light became more and more intense as more were chosen. As the light reached full intensity, eyes were shut out of fear. Hugoth watched in awe, his eyes completely open. Jahnise did nothing nor did he speak. The cloud crawled through the entire crowd before it began to tighten itself around the creatures gathered in front of Jahnise. Soon the cloud was only big enough to surround the selected.

Jahnise looked down on the besieged mass. "Inhabitants of Nuorg, before you stand the traitors to your land. These creatures do not belong here. They have come to learn your secrets and carry them back to plot against you. They have no right to be free in Nuorg or the lands and worlds above." He looked sternly at the selected, "You have made the wrong choice."

Jahnise placed his other hand on the stick. It began to tremble. He suddenly flicked it upward, and with his full strength swung it at the yellow ball above. "Rid this land of these wrong doers!" A stream of pure light shot from the stick. The thin, bright beam headed for the ball carrying the chosen with it. When contact was made with the yellow ball, Jahnise collapsed to his knees. He held the stick firmly as the beam fought him wildly, begging for forgiveness and release. Jahnise held on, unwavering. In a moment, the spectacle was over. He bowed his head and prayed again, silently.

Hugoth smiled at Bongi and Stewig, who he was happy to see still at his side. "I told you so."

"That was amazing, Hugoth. How did you know?"

"Let me just say I had a hunch."

Stewig only stood there staring at the yellow ball, speechless.

Jahnise used the stick to pull himself up. Once again, he was standing and facing the crowd. He closed his eyes, clutching his walking stick to his chest. "My heart is breaking for any of you who have just lost someone close to you. Righteousness has no conscious. Those of you remaining, should you want an explanation, let me say this: I cannot offer you any explanation right now. I am only a messenger."

Strangely, no tears for the selected were shed. The light had given those that remained the answers each needed. No further explanation was necessary.

Jahnise lifted his wrap from the ground and slung it over his shoulder. He walked to Bongi. "Friend, pick those with the most authority and bring them to me. This includes the three of you," he motioned with his stick to Hugoth and Stewig. "I am tired. Give me seven clicks to compose myself, then, we will meet. Send the Mice for me or a winger. I will be resting on the hill outside the Burg, near the river. We don't need to involve the entire audience. There will be more time for that. Just those now who can handle some bad news." Jahnise left alone with no further words for either of them. He walked down the path tall and proud, occasionally conversing with his wrap.

"What just happened here, Hugoth?" Stewig was coming out of his stupor.

"You have just witnessed a purification process. It seems to be the thing around Nuorg lately. The light emitted from Jahnise's stick is similar to the light emitted from the globe atop the Staff of Hewitt."

"What staff?" asked Bongi.

"Oh yes, I haven't told you about that experience yet. Bongi, dismiss the gathering. Tell them we will be in touch. Ask them all to stay in this Burg if they will. I am sure they will want to hear explanations. Catch up to us when you are finished. Stewig, come with me."

Bongi did as he was told. He was relieved to find no creature lingering about afterward to question him on the happening. He bid good day to the crowd and galloped down the main path to catch Hugoth and Stewig who were deeply immersed in a conversation.

"How did it go?" Hugoth hoped there had been no question and answer period. "Any questions?"

Bongi shook his head, "No, thank goodness. I don't know what I would have said. I'm clueless as to all of that."

"Me too." Stewig rolled his eyes. "It seems that our friend here just experienced a similar event in his Burg not too long ago. Seems to follow him around, I'd say."

"Come now, Hugoth, what is going on? All of this seems very mysterious to me. Is there something we need to know? Your Burg seems to be the only one with answers. Why is that?"

"Bongi, please... you know why. I am the leader of this entire land of ours. There is a reason I am the keeper of Burg number one."

"I suppose so," Bongi answered.

"Hugoth, do you have any theories about Eekay's sudden exit?"

"I'm not sure, Stewig. She wasn't happy here. She felt this was not her place. She may find herself one day and return. There are certainly no guarantees."

"I'd be remiss to say I badly miss her. She can be a real pain in the rear end. I never witnessed such mood swings with any other creature here or above. Really irked me at times."

"There now, Bongi, don't say something you might regret." Stewig warned.

Hugoth added, "It's alright, Stewig. Sometimes you have to speak your mind."

"I'll say." Bongi continued and questioned Hugoth. "What was that back there...the purification? How did Jahnise know what to do? How many people did he zap out of here?"

"Hah, nice way of putting it, old friend. Jahnise did not zap anyone anywhere. His stick did it."

"His stick?" Stewig tossed his head back.

"Yes the stick did the choosing. There is a shift in the balance of good and evil taking place above. Evil is pushing very hard to win the day."

"A little dramatic maybe...I hope?" Stewig spoke softly.

Hugoth smiled back, "No Stewig. I am afraid not."

"I want to know what happened here." Bongi was irritated.

"Here it is. That little light show just let everyone in attendance know who was and who was not welcome. The ones who got zapped were sent to the yellow ball for safe keeping. The rest of us passed the test. That means we have only good intentions. We can help balance or sway the shift above because we do not have ulterior motives opposed to the restoration of good in the world above, which means our lives have meaning. If the evil wins out over good, Nuorg will be no more. We will be forced to return above and live out our days knowing we let our mission slip out of our control. Does that make any sense?"

"No." Stewig could be contrary at times.

"Sure it does you armor plated dunce! What do you mean no?" Bongi could be contrary too.

"Yeah, yeah, yeah."

"That will do." Hugoth cut the bickering off. "Where can I meet up with my contingent? I need updates."

"Use Eekay's dwelling. It's not as spacious as yours, but it will do. I'll send a winger for them." Bongi trotted off to find the Goldens.

"Stewig, if it becomes necessary will you go back up?"

"Of course I will Hugoth. I will do whatever is needed. You know there is no need to ask."

"Thank you."

"Don't mention it." The two continued walking to Eekay's dwelling.

# 16

One more quick jump from ground level would be the last one Sig needed to hone in on the tree line. They would land below a tree and hop up however many branches required to scan the lake bank. "Perrie, can you see them?"

"No I can't. I can't hear them either. What kind of creatures are we looking for?"

"Some type of leggers I guess. Gann didn't elaborate on it. Probably should have asked him I'm thinking, but I desperately needed to get out of that mountain. We've been cooped up in there too long. You know a winger's got to fly."

Perrie simply nodded her head and with one exceedingly long, drawn out, condescending word acknowledged him, "Right..."

"We need to stay together if you see fit to live through the night, understand?"

"Yes I do."

"Very well then, we are going to perch high in those branches. Take a look, and then fly short bursts. We won't fly as low to the ground as we did coming in, just below the lowest branches. You still with me?"

"Yes sir, I am."

"Here we go."

Once they landed beneath their first tree, Perrie followed Sig. They jumped from branch to branch, staying out of sight until they were almost at the top of the tree. Sig scanned below their immediate tree and saw nothing. He signaled to Perrie. With her right on his tail they flew parallel with the tree line for approximately five leisure beats. Not seeing anything, they promptly lit in the next tree. The pair performed this maneuver over and over again.

Sig was showing frustration, "We may have made the wrong decision to head this way."

"Excuse me sir, I did not make any decision. You may have made the wrong decision."

"Fine, I made the wrong decision. We need to head the other way now. Would you like to lead the way?"

"Yes I would, this is so exciting. I had no idea old birds could fly as well as you do."

"Please!"

"Shhh, follow me." Perrie led this time. They made it back to their starting point and regrouped. "Maybe they have gone from here."

"No, I don't believe Gann would have sent us out this far if he didn't think they were staying the night. Lead on."

With Perrie flying ahead, Sig trailed a little farther behind. He took double takes at every object of interest. After a few more flights they stopped again. "Sir, do you still think they are here? We've flown almost this entire line of trees."

"They are here. Let's try a few more times. We will locate them."

Sig was correct. On the second jaunt under the trees, Perrie nearly crashed into one of the visitors immense bodies covered in a blanket of thick fur. "Oops," she exclaimed as she at once cut for the nearest tree. Fortunately the legger took no notice of the near miss. Once in the tree she was trembling again. Sig was at her side instantly. "Sir, I uh, we uh, we found them or at least one of them."

"Yes we did, Perrie. Calm down. There are four of them the best I can tell. We have a Cat, a Wolf, a two-legger and that huge dark creature you almost smacked into. The moon isn't reflecting off of him. We need to get closer to see if they are dangerous."

"Okay, you do that and if they kill you I will fly back with haste to report your death to everyone."

"Now why did you put it like that?"

"Because that could very well happen! Are you serious?"

"Unfortunately, I am serious. Stay here. I'll be careful. Watch the other three while I check on the two-legger. Stay alert!"

"Don't do this sir. I don't think it is wise."

"I have done deeds in my life much more perilous than this. I can assure you of that. I will be careful. Watch my back."

"Yes sir."

Sig softly took wing. The two-legger was lying on his side, prompting Sig to land at his back. He carefully stepped around the length of the two-legger, his eyes darting up and down, searching for any clue to this group's intent. He noticed the shiny rapier, the bag and a hat all lying to his side. A worn but well made jacket lay over the legger's chest. After studying his find, Sig flew back to Perrie.

"He looks innocent enough. I read no malice on his face or his body positioning. He wasn't lying there as if he had anything to hide. I will go check out the Cat next. Again, watch my back."

"Yes sir."

Sig landed near the Cat and with the same caution studied every nuance of the Cat's being with trained steady eyes. Seeing nothing unusual, he flew again to Perrie's side.

"Two down, two to go. Wish me luck."

"Please be careful, sir."

Sig landed at the Wolf's head. Just as soon as he landed, the Wolf half opened one eye, "Do you know how much noise you are making?"

Sig answered before he realized he was being questioned. "Was I that obvious?"

"Yes. The others snore, but I sleep with both ears open. Who are you and where are you from?"

"I think I should be asking the questions, Sir Wolf."

"It's Prince Wolf to you, winger."

"Prince Wolf? Royalty then? Well isn't that quaint. Prince Wolf who?"

From behind Sig came the whispered answer. "Prince Mystic of the Great Forest. Last of the Great Gray Wolves. Do you request more?"

Frederick had crawled up behind Sig during the earlier questioning. Sig was startled. He shot a glance into the tree where he saw his lookout trembling and pointing a wing in his direction. "Well so much for my lookout. Please do unfreeze yourself, Perrie, and come on down here. These leggers pose us no harm. If so, they would have killed me already. That was the truth? Please correct me if I am wrong."

"You speak the truth. I am Frederick Mounte of the Hewitt family, although I dare not claim them all, nor do I stake any claim or fondness to their past deeds."

"And who might they be?" Sig motioned to the Cat and the sleeping hulk.

"The smaller one is Bubanche of the Great Plains--we call him Bubba. The larger one is Lightning, the Irregular Badger, Duke of the Great Meadow."

"Thank you." Sig spoke directly to Frederick, occasionally making glances at Wolf and the Cat. "I am Sigourne. My terrified watch dog in the tree is Perrie. We were sent by my family to ask your business here." Sig took another glance at the larger, still snoring legger. "Excuse me, Frederick; did you say that legger over there was a Badger? Looks like a really big Badger."

"Yes I did. He is our good friend Lightning, the Irregular Badger."

Sig looked at Frederick. He then walked over to the nose of Lightning. He studied the Badger judiciously. "A Badger? Really? He sure looks like something else." He stepped back and called to Perrie. "Young Falcon, would you do us the favor of joining us?" Perrie reluctantly shook of her tremors. She lightly flew to Sig's side then nearly crawled under his wing.

The Wolf noticed her uncontrollable shaking. "Perrie is it?" He looked at Sig. Sig nodded. "Perrie we mean you no ill will. We have no intention of harming any living creature that brings no harm to us. You are safe in our circle. Do you believe me?"

"Yes sir, I do. I mean...yes, Prince Mystic, I believe you."

"Then it is settled. For goodness sake, please relax."

"I'll try."

Sig asked Mystic the next question. "How are you so sure we mean you no harm? We could have legions of attackers just beyond the ridge ready to rip you apart at our command."

Mystic shook his head. "You could have, but you don't. It is only the two of you. I heard you fly in earlier. I have also heard your many short flights up and down this tree line."

"In addition to that Sig, since you have been chatting, I have run this entire area and I have seen nothing." The Cheetah was talking now. "There is nothing over that rise except a stretch of mountains in the distance. I noticed them shining in the moonlight. A handsome grouping I might add."

Mystic and Frederick were as surprised as the wingers. In unison, they replied, "You really did?"

"Yes, and as I said there is nothing between us and those mountains."

Sig was curious, "How fast are you, Bubanche?"

"Call me Bubba, it's a long story. I would guess that I am about, I don't know, eight times faster than you."

Frederick's eyes popped wide open. "Eight?"

"About that, yes. Eight sounds good."

Perrie was impressed, "That seems very fast for a legger."

Bubba answered her, "Yes young Falcon, it is very fast. But I am blessed with tremendous speed. The more I use it, the faster I get."

Sig brought the conversation back on point. "We must get back before the sun rises. I don't want to scare you all, but Perrie told us some very unsettling news. She was mysteriously dropped on our doorstep a few nights ago. We are leery of the day sky. Either we stay here the remainder of tonight and tomorrow or we head back to our mountain immediately. The choice is up to you."

"But the food," Bubba commented first. "We have to leave all of this food."

"There is plenty of food where we are going. This is one of several gardens we have throughout the area. This one was an accident, but a very plentiful accident." He motioned to Perrie, "The water-livvers here almost jump into your mouth. If you are interested in a real treat, try them out."

"I can eat water-livvers? Are those the same things as swimmers?"

Sig felt a need to apologize for Perrie. "She is not from around here. Yes, Perrie, I assume they are. You know the creatures that spend their entire life under water?"

Frederick took up for Perrie, "Yes little Falcon, in some places they are called water-livvers or swimmers or fish. They have several names. I do agree with Sig, they are very tasty."

Mystic and Bubba both turned to each other with shocked expressions on their faces. "Two-leggers eat water-livvers too?"

Frederick stretched his arm out to Perrie. "Hop on, let's go try a few."

Sig smiled, as best he could and said, "Please hurry. I'm serious, we need to get back."

Mystic walked a short way with Frederick and Perrie. "What do you think Frederick? Should we make haste to the mountain?"

"Let's leave at first light. The globe is completely dark. I would worry if it were anything else."

Mystic rejoined Bubba and Sig. "The decision is made. We will leave at sun-up."

"But we could all be in danger in the light." Sig was not happy. "Are you completely, absolutely sure we will be safe?"

"Yes, Sig, I am. Let's spend the remaining part of tonight resting. This is just one more stop on our journey. No more talk tonight. There will be plenty of time to talk tomorrow."

The answer satisfied Bubba. Sig relented. Lightning never moved.

Frederick stepped to the edge of the water. Several of the tasty water-livvers swam to the surface, frantically begging to be eaten. "See for yourself Perrie." He sat down. Perrie hopped off his sleeve and began readily picking snacks from just beneath the water's surface. "Perrie, where are you from? The north, the south?"

"Why do you ask? I have to tell you, you are only the third Talker I have ever seen! I heard the stories growing up, but I've never seen one before this particular trip. How many of you are still out there?"

"How many? I'm not sure. You know two more? What a coincidence. What we saw earlier today begs me to ask the question."

"It is not a pleasant story sir. The short of it is I was nabbed mid-flight by the largest winged creature I have ever seen from a horrifying display of destruction carried out by horrid wingers and leggers. I am lucky to be speaking with you."

"Tell me as many details as you can remember…if it doesn't upset you too much."

"I can't remember that much. I had been thinking the creature stole me away, but now I am changing my mind. I think he or she saved my life. Why? I certainly don't know, not now anyway. Every winger in my part of the world was killed or captured, Frederick. There were hundreds of us. They were all wiped out. Every one from the smallest to the largest…except for me. I guess it was my lucky day." Perrie hung her head in shame. "Yes, my lucky day. I shouldn't be here. There were so many better than I who could have done so much more."

"So your family is gone?"

"My family? Yes, I'd say they are. I saw most of them die right before I was taken. I am still reliving it. I haven't had the time to cry yet. My entire life is gone. All I have left is my breath. What do you know?"

"We do know of a massacre similar to what you describe. There is what's left of a barn a ways back that was destroyed. We were led there by a foul stench. It drew us in, wouldn't let us escape it. We found the barn collapsed, inside were hundreds and hundreds of dead wingers. We buried all of them we could find."

Perrie began to tremble. "Can we talk about this more when we get safely to Sig's mountain? I really can't hear this right now. Please, let's get back with the others."

"Very well. We will rest here tonight and head out at sunrise."

He held his sleeve for her. She hopped on and they headed back. Frederick noticed the group had settled closer together directly beneath the trees in a defensive arrangement. He situated himself between Mystic and Bubba. Lightning held one entire side at bay. Sig woke on their arrival and Perrie huddled next to him. They stayed that way throughout the remainder of the night.

Morning broke uneventfully. Frederick stood, stretching his arms and legs, working out the stiffness brought about by his sleeping arrangements. Out of the corner of his eye he caught a quick glimpse of a large dark shadow that rose from the trees before it disappeared. He felt uneasy but sounded no alarms. "Everybody up! Come on. You got plenty of sleep. It's a new day. Let us make the most of it!"

Slowly the creatures came around. Lightning was the first to climb to his feet. "I feel great and hungry. If you don't mind, Frederick, I'll start eating my breakfast now."

"Be my guest."

Sig and Perrie were up next, then Mystic and Bubba.

Frederick was very upbeat. He was anxiously awaiting the introduction with the Talkers Perrie spoke of. He waved his arms at the four-leggers, "Come on you two, if you're going to eat this morning, get on with it. Find you some food for the trip. We are leaving here shortly."

Each one sought their favorite food to start the day. They had plenty. Frederick finished swallowing his last bite and gave the order. "That's it. Time to move on. Sig, exactly where are we going? Lead the way if you please."

"I will ride with you if you please. It's a straight path. Head to that middle mountain there."

"I'm sorry, Sig. I can't see the middle mountain or any mountain out there yet. My eyes are not quite yours. You may ride with me, but keep us on course. When the mountains come into view for the rest of us, I will feel a little more at ease."

"You two-leggers can't see far enough ahead of you to run fast. I don't know how you do it." He hopped to Frederick's shoulder. He pointed with his wing. "That way."

Perrie hopped a ride with Mystic. Lightning was the last to join the group. He came rushing in with the rind of a large melon falling out of his mouth. He hurriedly gulped it down.

"Were you leaving without me?"

Sig was amused with the four-legger. He and Perrie exchanged looks of surprise. They had never seen him on all fours. Sig whispered something to Frederick. "You are positively sure that he is a Badger?"

"That's what he says."

"Very well then. Shall we?"

***

They began the trek to the mountain with replenished stomachs and good chatter. Hopefully the trip to the mountain would be uneventful. And from high above it all, a mysterious shadow watched and circled. She was elated with the turn of events.

***

"Gann, have you any plan yet? Come morning, Madi and Hemoth should be leaving. Gann? Gann, where are you?" With Madaliene following closely, Gamma searched room by room. "Where did he lead them off to? Gann, Hemoth? Sig? Anybody?"

There was no answer. "Gamma, they could not have gone far. How much could they have done up there?"

"Oh child, there is plenty they could have gotten into. I was hoping they would not get sidetracked. You know how your grandfather is. Never mind, they will be back before morning. We need to get some rest ourselves."

Gamma went to the kitchen. Madaliene found Evaliene's note lying on the table. She picked it up, turning it over and over in her hands. "Dear sister, what have you stirred up this time?" She walked back to the den and made herself comfortable in Gann's big stuffed chair. "Gamma, are we reading too much into this letter?"

Gamma came in carrying a tray of goodies, including a large pitcher full of water mixed with fruit juices. She sat the tray on a short table, poured Madaliene a cup and handed it to her as she sat down. "Mmm, no, I don't think we are. Do you mean are we making it too complicated? We won't really know that until we ask your sister. Oh dear, you must find her. There is so much at stake."

"You and Gann keep saying that type of thing. Why? What is really at stake? What part do we play in a world we are not even part of?"

Gamma ate little bites as she talked. "What is really at stake? Gann should really be here to fill in the blanks. Let me say this--you and your sister are more important than either of you could ever imagine. Why do you think such great pains were taken to build this fortress of yours inside this mountain?"

"Fortress? This is a fortress? I imagine that adds more to this evolving mystery."

"Dear, there are places and things in here I don't even know about. The lower tunnels for instance, did you ever wonder where all of those doors lead?"

Madaliene blushed, "Uh...yes...I wonder where some of those go."

"Madaliene, how many of those doors have you opened?" Gamma's face became stern again.

"A few...maybe less?"

"Uh huh, like maybe you should clue me in on which ones?"

"There were not that many really. I was much younger then. You know...just curious..."

"Madaliene, you are only 16 years old, maybe a year more, when could you have been much younger?"

"Um...I can't say for sure, maybe last summer?"

"You said you were sick! You stayed in your bed, you had us worried."

"Well, I may not have been in my bed the entire time."

"How did you get past us?"

"We are in a cave Gamma. It gets dark in here. I just snuck out in my stockings and padded my way down. I hid some candles in a few corners. Long story short...I got bored. There was nothing I saw to make me curious, so I got well."

"Why did you not ask us to take you down there?"

"Where is the adventure in that?"

"Oh, I guess you are right." Gamma leaned back in her chair, sipping her drink.

"But this letter," Madaliene held it up, "This letter intrigues me."

Gamma sat her cup on the tray, "Let me see it again, will you child?"

"Sure."

"It intrigues me too, Madi." Gamma held it to the light of the nearest torch. "What strikes me as odd is that she made it so cryptic. That is not like her. If something is black, she calls it black, if it is white, she calls it white. There is no gray with her. I am beginning to think maybe she was forced to write the words while someone else spoke them."

"But what about the Eagle language in the code? What is the significance of that?"

"To be honest with you Madi, I think we made that up or it was a coincidence."

"Huh? I mean ma'am?"

"The olde Eagle language was translated too many times. What Sid picked up in the leftover letters could have been anything. I don't know. I just don't trust it. Something inside me is telling me this is not exactly what it seems to be. Here, read it again as you would read anything else Ev writes you."

"Sure, I'll give it another try. But, what about the Nuorg?"

"Just read it." Gamma handed the letter back to Madaliene who relaxed deeper into Gann's chair.

Madaliene scrunched her forehead then looked past her eyebrows at Gamma, "Just like I always read her letters?"

"Yes."

Madaliene read and reread the letter, over and over and over. About the tenth time she came to a stark realization. Madaliene dropped her hands to her lap then turned, staring at Gamma, "How did you know?"

"That's what grandmothers do."

Madaliene raised the letter back up to her face and looked at Gamma yet again. "But, how did you know?"

Gamma raised her cup again and saluted her granddaughter, "That's just what we do."
"Glorious."
"Exactly!"

## 17

Hemoth emptied the basket of snacks and hurried to catch Gann. They walked down through the mountain's many levels, carrying on conversations of subjects that had not been broached in years. Each had many, many questions for the other. What had happened after Hemoth saw the end of them? How long had it been planned? Who knew? How did they stay holed up in the mountain for this long? When had Madaliene arrived at their door step? Gann asked questions about the outside world. How had it changed, how many leggers were out there, what was the consensus on government? The questions were all answered to the best of the answerer's knowledge and ability, of course neither of them told the other everything. It was better if they remained ignorant of some details for their own safety.

They came into the den laughing too loudly. Gamma and Madaliene were startled. They immediately sat up yawning, stretching their hands high over their heads.

"What have you two been up to? Where are the Falcons?" Gamma stood up to get them drinks.

"We had to let them go. They couldn't bear this Bear anymore." Gann waved his hand at Hemoth.

"I beg your pardon. It was not all my fault."

"On a serious note, Gamma, we have visitors at the lake. I sent Sig to check them out. Perrie flew with him."

Madaliene's mouth fell open.

Gamma sat their drinks on the big table, a filled cup for Gann and a filled basin for Hemoth. "You think they will be safe?"

"Yes I do. They flew very low. The moon was dim. I lost them shortly after they leveled out. I couldn't even spot them with the telescope."

This news surprised Madaliene. "You sent Sig out without consulting me? You have a telescope?"

Hemoth jumped in after lapping his basin dry, "He has three telescopes up there. At least I know of three."

"Three? Gann, how come I never got to use them?"

"We were afraid of what you might see with them. You are more than welcome to use them now." Gann did not tell the whole truth.

"I guess there are doors yet unopened for you, Madaliene." Gamma walked over to Gann and put her arm in his. "So, when do you expect Sig to return?"

"They should be back soon. I'd think shortly after sunrise if all went well."

"And if it didn't?"

"Then I think you and I will go after them."

These last words prompted looks of mild astonishment on the faces of Madaliene and Hemoth; well the best a Grizzly Bear can look astonished. "What?"

"If they are not back, we will go find them. It's nothing really Mad, it will be just like our younger days." Gamma gripped Gann's arm tighter. It was difficult not to notice the twinkle in their eyes.

Gann brought the conversation full circle. "Hemoth, get a little rest. When Sig returns, you and Madaliene will be leaving. Madi, the same goes for you, rest up. Gamma and I will return to the lookout station. If we see anything, we will let you know immediately. Be alert, some things around here might surprise you."

Madaliene tried to disguise an incredulous look, "No doubt."

Hemoth was tired. He thought he comprehended the conversation, but he was not sure. He nodded to Gann, "I'll get some rest. You three carry on." With that said, the Grizzly wandered off to a cozy corner and fell fast asleep.

Madaliene watched as Gann and Gamma began the trek up the mountain. She spun around, smiling from ear to ear. "Oh my." She sat in Gann's chair again, and fell fast asleep.

***

For Frederick, the mountains were finally coming into view. Still a long distance away, he was at least recognizing the faint outline where they melded with the bright blue sky. "Sig, we are still a long day's journey from your home. Do you need to fly ahead and let those concerned for you know that you and Perrie are safe?"

Sig though about his answer for a moment. "Just between you and me Frederick, that flight last night nearly wore the feathers off my wings. I was trying a little too hard to impress the youngster back there. She's fast. It took all I had to best her. I think I'll stay right where I am if you don't mind."

Frederick laughed quietly so as not to embarrass Sig. "Okay, you stay just where you are. I believe we will get you back soon enough."

"Thank you." Sig read Frederick as one who could be trusted. He hadn't the pleasure of conversing with a Talker other than Gann and Gamma for several years, he couldn't even pinpoint the exact date that had occurred. "So, what is it like out there now? Out there... outside of this land?"

"Well we have it from several sources that bad times are looming. Seems something is up with a certain group who have motives not in line with our own. We had a scare a few days ago when the Cheetah was almost nabbed from our group. From what he explained, an extremely large winger nearly snatched him off the ground. If he hadn't outrun it, well...who knows? I certainly don't. The Cat was very upset."

"I'd say he was. That seems eerily similar to what happened with Perrie back there. She claims to have been dropped on our door step by a huge winger. She says she was snatched in mid-flight as her own were being slaughtered. Mid-flight mind you. That young Falcon can fly very fast. Do you have any idea what kind of skill it would take to snatch her like that?"

"Sig, I can only imagine, not being a winger myself. The story holds true for Bubba also. He told us he outran the winger and I assume he did. That one must be a formidable foe."

"See that is what intrigues me. If it is a foe, why did it rescue her and bring her to us? No creature was supposed to even know of our existence in the mountain, yet a stranger to us drops another stranger nearly at our feet. Something is amiss or has been planned without our knowledge."

"We have stories of our own that may sound strange to you as well. From the evil to the surreal, I do hope your friends offer us some hospitality. We could sure use it about now."

"Oh don't fret. They will be excited to hear your stories. They are wonderful people."

"So they are two-leggers as well? That will be different, pleasant but different."

***

Gamma and Gann walked quietly up to the observatory level, as they had done for so many years prior. Hand in hand, each one silently remembered the early days when they were invincible. The days when their family ruled with a heavy hand, the days when a promise was a promise, the days when they could be seen mingling with the public. Those days were long past. What happened to their family? Where did it go wrong? Will the girls ever remember what happened to their parents? Why they were left with their grandparents? Gamma and Gann never got over what had to happen. Was it for the best? They thought so then and they thought so now. Will the sisters ever know or want to know what really happened? Gamma and Gann hoped and prayed they would never ask. An accident? No, not really...

Gann broke the silence, "Shall we take a look towards the lake? They should be coming in range about now."

"I think so. If they are in trouble of any kind, I'm not sure I could bear it right now."

They stepped through the door. He uncovered the telescope. She swung it around, sweeping the landscape. "This is a charming piece of equipment you have here. You say you built it?"

"Thank you and yes I did."

"I always knew there was something more to you than good looks."

"You don't say?"

Gamma surveyed the fields stretching to the lake. "Ah, I see them. Nothing seems out of place there. They are still a day's walk out. Can't really make out the group very well. How did you ever see them at the lake?"

"I didn't really, more of a hunch. The telescope can't see that far. Sig was getting restless. I gave him an errand to run. The fact that he found visitors is happenstance. Are you going to tell him that?"

"No."

"Wise choice."

"How soon will they be in range?" Gamma was full of anxious questions.

"Range of what?"

"Range to make out what they are with the telescope of course!"

"Oh, four or five clicks I think." Gann was a little annoyed with her, but let her talk.

"Then we will wait. I'm going to the library. That Nuorg thing is bothering me."

"Oh, by the way, Ev did not write that letter."

"I know."

"Really? And you didn't let me in on your little secret?" Gann looked hurt.

"Didn't think I had too. Thought you knew."

"Glorious?"

"Yep?"

"Madi finally got it. For such a smart girl, sometimes she overlooks the obvious."

"I know. What do we do about that?"

"We can't do anything other than what we have already done. She must learn the rest on her own. She's getting there. It just sometimes takes longer than it should."

"She's like her Father. Ev is like her Mother and that is what bothers me." Gamma kept sweeping the horizon with the telescope. It never failed to mesmerize her.

Gann stood leaning against the door frame with his hands in his pockets. "Can she still shoot?"

"You wouldn't believe what she can do with that bow of hers. She scares the wits out of me."

"I hope we don't have to find out. I cannot loose anymore members of my family to needless wars and violence. The Terrible Years? I can't do it again. Ridding this world of that took too much out of me."

"Me too." Gamma gently lowered the viewing end of the telescope to its stop. She walked over to the door and reached for Gann. She put her arms around him tightly. He hugged her back with strong arms. They closed the door behind them and headed down the tunnel to the library.

\*\*\*

Lightning was tiring of the boring, uneventful journey. Suddenly, he had an idea. "Stop! Everyone, I have a brilliant idea. Can I try something?"

Bubba was fine with it. "I can't see you as having a brilliant idea, but sure give it a shot."

Mystic acted interested. "What have you in that massive head of yours?"

Lightning rushed to Frederick's side. "Look all of you, if we are supposed to be in that mountain, we can be in that mountain. Can we not?"

Sig shook his head and whispered to Frederick, "Are you absolutely, without a doubt, completely sure he is a Badger?"

Frederick whispered back, "Shhh."

Lightning swung his ax-pike around in a circle, twirling it around his neck.

"Look, he can do tricks!" Bubba stated with a teeny bit of sarcasm.

Lightning was unfazed, "If we use this, we can be in the mountain instantly... can't we?"

"I'm game. Give it a try." Mystic wasn't sure if it would work as they wanted, but he was tired of the uneventful hike as well.

"Frederick, what do you say? You have a logical way of thinking." The Badger eagerly waited the answer.

"I reckon now is as good a time as any to see if we are heading in the right direction. Go ahead."

"What is he doing?" Sig was not keen on the idea, of course he had no idea what any of them were talking about anyway. "What does he plan to do with that thing?"

"Don't worry there Sig, just hold on tight. Perrie, you might want to tighten your grip there on the Prince's neck. Get on with it Lightning."

Perrie clasped her sharp talons mightily into the fur on Mystic's neck.

"Owww! A little tight there girl!"

Perrie breathed a slight chuckle, "Oops."

Lightning swung the ax-pike at the mountain. He became all proper with his speech for the sake of the new additions to the group. "Oh hallowed ax-pike," he held it high for all to see, "Take us to the mountain, if indeed that be our proper destination!"

Without pomp or circumstance, the ax-pike blacked out the morning light. No fancy swirls or mystical clouds enveloped the group. Without the slightest hesitation, all six creatures were instantly transported to the exact mountain Sig described to them earlier.

"Wow! Badger or not, that creature wields a powerful weapon." Sig took in the surroundings. He made sure this was the correct mountain and not some other place that may not be as welcoming. He flew from Frederick's shoulder straight up the mountainside. He was shortly lost from view. He sped past the well-hidden main entrance to the cave in order to keep its location secret. He hoped he remembered where Gann's station two opened to the outside, if not he could be flying around all day long. Nothing looked familiar to him. To save time, he looped over to head back to the group. He lit on Frederick's shoulder again. "Perrie, do you remember anything about the window we left from? I cannot find it, nor can I remember anything of it except that it was dark and maybe I should have paid more attention to it."

Perrie shook her head, "I can't recall a thing about it."

"Wonderful! Well then, everyone look back the way we came..."

"No wait, we are making this too difficult." Lightning once again held out the ax-pike. "Where in this mountain are we to be?"

Without hesitation or incident, the group disappeared, reappearing in the ante chamber outside of Gann and Gamma's living chamber.

"Whoa, that thing is good." Sig motioned for Frederick to move closer to the wide opening ahead of them. "Over there, let Perrie and I go in first. We will call for you."

Frederick, Mystic, Bubba and Lightning all had the same appearance on their faces, wide-eyed, dropped jaw expressions of overwhelming proportions.

"Okay, no problem, we can wait here." Bubba eyed the spectacle of the cavern. "This is nicer than..."

"That's enough. Don't mention where we were." Frederick clenched the Cheetah's jaws shut with one hand.

Bubba nodded his head.

Lightning whispered, "I could grow to love a dwelling like this."

"Who lives here? Good gracious, this is more than I expected."

***

Sig, followed by Perrie, flew into the den. They landed on the short table in front of a sleeping Madaliene. "Wake up Madi, wake up. Where is Gann or Gamma? We are back."

Madaliene rebelled against awakening. "What? Let me sleep. Go away."

Sig moved closer, "Wake up Princess!"

"Uh...no...I'm having a wonderful dream...please let me sleep a little longer."

"Wake up!" Sig was not having any success. "Madaliene, we have guests."

"Go away Falcon!" She turned her face to the comfortable chair going back to sleep with no trouble.

"Well I never..." Sig became irritated.

"You never what?" Hemoth lumbered in from his corner. "My, you have an irritating voice this morning. What news do you have for the sleeping beauty there Falcon?"

"At least someone will wake-up when called." Sig jumped to Hemoth's shoulder. "Where are Gann and Gamma? We have visitors!"

"Visitors? How could we possibly have visitors?"

"It's a long story. Where are they?"

"Up in the mountain I'd think. They headed up to scout for you and your little one there. Is the sun up yet?"

"Where in the mountain? The rooms? The observatory? Where?"

"The observatory, I think." Hemoth was sluggish from a deep, peaceful sleep.

"Can you go get them?"

"Now? How do you expect me to answer that? It's a long way up there." Hemoth stared skeptically at Sig through still sleepy eyes.

"Fine, everything is just fine. Perrie, please tell our guests to wait where they are. They are not allowed in here unless invited by Gann or Gamma. They cannot come in here, do you understand?"

"Yes sir. I will let them know."

"Thank you. Bring them close to the entrance but not all the way. Leave them in the middle somewhere. Then, come back here and try to wake this lovely lass up. She needs to be coherent when we all get together."

Sig flew to the pantry, lit on the bottom shelf and loosed a lever. A smallish door swung open. He squeezed by the contraption inside and flew straight up the carved shaft to the top level of the fortress. He scratched open the highest door, bounding through it out of breath. "Where to now?"

He flew the mazern like a crazed Bat. He checked all three stations on the observatory, the meeting rooms, the sleeping quarters, the dining halls and finally the libraries. Fortunately, Gann and Gamma were seated in the first library surrounded by stacks of antique books, most of them opened to "N" related subject matter. "Thank God I found you two."

Surprise would be an understatement. Gann was way beyond surprise, astonishment or any other emotion when he laid eyes on the panting Falcon. "Wha..? Ho...? Whe...?"

"I know, I know. I will explain it all later, maybe...if I can. We have guests down in the entryway. You two should get there as soon as possible. You may be surprised more than you think."

Gamma tried to speak, "But...I just saw you a day's walk away no more than a click ago...through the telescope and I just barely saw you then! Ho...how did you get here so fast? You are all here?"

"Yes, enough of that. Let's get you down to our guests. Must you walk? Can you not use the other method?"

"We haven't used that in years. It's liable to kill us all!" Gann was not going that way.

"Come now Gann, maybe we could. It might be fun."

"Oh no. You too?"

Gamma gathered some of the chair cushions. "Grab a few Gann. We may need them for the landing!" She flitted around like a child, excitement beaming from her eyes.

"Gamma, are you sure about this?" Gann hesitantly chose some of the plushest cushions for his use. "Absolutely sure?"

"Absolutely. We need to hurry. Sig, we will see you there."

Sig rushed back to the shaft, hopped in and flew back down or rather dropped back down. He landed none too gracefully at the bottom and stumbled out into the pantry. He wobbled through the kitchen then into the den.

"That was fast. What happened to you?" Perrie felt sorry for the old Falcon.

Sig staggered to the foot of Gann's chair before settling in a heap of wings and feathers. "Gann and Gamma will be here shortly." He closed his eyes, imagining the pain he would feel for the next several days.

Gamma hurried out of the library. She waited for Gann to come through the door and closed it behind him. He was holding a small mountain of cushions in front of him, barely able to see over them at all. "So dear, what should I do? You have quite a collection of priceless antiquities in your grasp. Shall I just pull you?"

"Your humor astounds me. And the antiquities? The softest cushions I could find."

She led him around to a large closet behind a normal door. Inside they dropped the cushions and slid a wooden panel to the side. Gamma peered far into the dark void. "I can't believe we are doing this!"

"If we are going, let's go!"

Gamma crawled inside. She positioned herself on a short ledge. She tossed a few cushions ahead of her, held one cushion between her feet, the last one held firmly behind her head. "Wish me luck!" She pushed herself off the ledge and began a quick plunge to the lower living levels.

Gann prepared accordingly and shoved himself off the ledge after allowing Gamma adequate room to get clear ahead of him. He plunged down the slick rock slide with abbreviated gusto and plenty of second guessing. Around and around they went. Cork screwing to the lower levels blazingly fast, screaming like children, they rode the cushions like big chunks of ice sliding down the side of a glacier. This was definitely the fastest way down the mountain and much safer than jumping off the side. Gamma saw the lead cushions pass through the trap door ahead of her. She relaxed her body in preparation for the exit. She shot out of the sprung opening landing against the opposite side of a small chamber on top of her cushions and lots and lots of clothes. Gann popped through seconds later.

"Let's do that again! What do you say? Please!" Gamma meant over half of that.

Gann smiled at her, "Always the adventurer. I guess that's one of the reasons I love you so much! Maybe we'll ride it again later, after we take all of these cushions back up. I forgot we landed in a wardrobe closet! We didn't need the cushions anyway." He grabbed her hand, pulling her to her feet. "Let's go meet our visitors."

It was not far from the wardrobe closet, down two corridors and through a set of twin gathering rooms to the den. The couple made the distance in record time fueled by the electrifying rush of adrenaline injected into their aging bodies by the slide. They entered the den from the back.

"Here we are, Sig!"

The weary Falcon looked at them in amazement, "You didn't?"

Gamma bounced up to him. She looked down as he lie crumpled on the floor. "We did!" She exclaimed with glee.

"Oh my, what have I done?" Sig shook his head in disbelief.

Gann strode in behind Gamma, "Where are they Sig? Call them in, if you can get off the floor."

"I will do my best sir."

Gamma prodded Madaliene, "Come on you, get up. We have guests. You must look presentable. Quick, to your room, at least put on a fresh set of clothes will you?"

"Yes ma'am." Madaliene shuffled off to her closet.

"You too Gann, make yourself pretty. I need to spiff up myself. Sig call them in and have them make themselves comfortable. We will return shortly."

The two-leggers each went in different directions to get ready.

Sig did his best to recover from the shock his body was experiencing. He slowly made his way to the den's entry door. "Hemoth, I know you are rather new here. Still, do you think you could help me here?"

"Sure, what can I do for you?"

"Open this door and call in our guests. I can't fly up to the portal in my current state."

"What if I just hold you up there? Then you can call them in properly."

"Very well."

Hemoth lifted Sig to the opening near the top of the door. Normally it was how he entered or exited the rooms throughout the mountain, but now? Flight was beyond him at the moment.

"Excuse me, Frederick, Mystic, all of you." Sig loudly called to them. "Perrie, bring them on in. Gamma and Gann have given them permission to enter. Please step this way."

Mystic heard Sig's voice. "What's wrong with him?"

"What?" Perrie asked.

"I believe Sig is calling us in. He sounds weak."

"I understand," Frederick added, "He may be weak. He has been through a lot recently."

"Yes, I hear him now." Perrie nodded to them all, "We have been called. You are welcome here. Walk toward Sig's voice. It's not that much further."

Perrie led them as she rode on Mystic's back. Bubba, Frederick and Lightning followed closely. After the last turn, a huge wooden door beckoned them to enter. It swung wide as they stepped up to it. Sig hopped down to the floor.

"Welcome to each of you. Make yourselves comfortable, eat if you like. Your hosts will be out soon."

Hemoth remained behind the door. He would close it once the last visitor entered. Each guest was in awe. The caverns under Nuorg were bigger than the den, but the ornate craftsmanship within these hand-hewn walls went far beyond the utilitarian workmanship there. Each guest walked around the den gawking at the detail and furnishings of the place.

"This is fantastic." Frederick was reminded of royal palaces he had only heard about in stories.

Mystic imagined that, in the glory days of his dwelling, it might have come close to the elegance of this dwelling, but he was not willing to stake much on that thought. Bubba had never seen anything like it. That went equally for Lightning. Their wait was not long.

Gann was the first host to stride into the room, Gamma glided in from another entrance. They met in the middle of one side of the room to address the guests. They only saw three at first. Gann bowed his head slightly to Gamma before welcoming them.

"We welcome you each to our mountain castle. Consider this your home during your stay with us. As long as you have nothing to hide from us, you are welcome. Should we detect the need to protect ourselves, you will never see the outside of this mountain again. That is not a warning, it is a dire fact. Once we have all gathered, we will make all necessary introductions. I see three of you, where is the fourth?" Lightning stepped into view behind Bubba. Gann smiled. "Well there he is."

Gamma raised her arms from her side, clasping her hands above her waist. She became very prim and proper. "Hemoth, please step from behind the door and bolt it." She noticed as the guests tensed slightly.

"There now, no worries. That door is always bolted while we are inside. Let me introduce an old friend of ours. This is Hemoth, a dear friend of my granddaughter whom you will meet later."

Hemoth stepped out of the shadows. As each of the guests turned to recognize him, they went silent, their gazes turned to uncomprehending stares, jaws dropped and words failed each one of them. "Good morning to you all. I am Hemoth from the far north. I am from the clan of the great Grizzly Bears."

# 18

High north, nearly at the top of the world, on the cold tundra and snow covered mountains, a clan of Bears lived a normal existence. Their country was natural and free of the dreaded twos that had brazenly invaded so many of the lands farther south. Word was spreading within this four-legger community that the twos would eventually arrive to claim the wilderness, although not a single elder Bear dared to believe one word of the rumors. The twos would never survive in this country with their frail little bodies and lack of thick warm fur. Preposterous was the favorite word bandied about when those conversations arose.

The midling Bears eventually stopped involving the elders in these conversations concerning twos altogether. They would have to shape their own decisions and deal with the infiltration of the twos as they saw fit. As time ticked away, the elders passed down sage advice loaded with knowledge and experiences only years of living could provide, except for their determination to discount or even recognize the possible invasion of the twos. As life would have it, the non-believing elders eventually died off from natural causes, leaving the upcoming generations to carry on the blood lines and decision making. A new, smarter and more wary generation followed. The future of the Grizzly was in good standing. Several generations of Grizzlies came and passed without incident. Maybe the elders had been correct all along.

***

She was not a large Grizzly, but she was a large Bear. Those two words, Grizzly and Bear, used in conjunction spoke volumes for this sow's size, demeanor and motherly instincts. Although her size for a Grizzly was normal, the same could not be said for her cubs. The pair that was off frolicking in the distance was often mistaken for two year old cubs. They were in fact a mere six months old. She had weaned them only a few weeks before, although her instincts told her it was far too early. She could not help it. They were just too big. Fortunately, everything about the cubs turned out fine. The cubs took instantly to hunting the many ice cold streams for swimmers. Obviously, the more of those slippery, scaled creatures they caught, the more they ate and the bigger they grew. The twins became more proficient at catching swimmers than any one Bear could do on his or her own. These two were identical mirror twins. They were constantly confounding creatures with their ability to think alike, finish each other's sentences without hesitation and carry on conversations with others as if they were one creature instead of two. The brothers developed their own language and were never out of one another's eyesight. That all changed on a very mild, overcast day.

The twins and their mother were traveling back to their den for an afternoon nap after a fun-filled morning of rough-housing, tree climbing, survival lessons and eating. Walking a trail used every day by several types of four legged creatures the cubs would lag behind for a while then scamper up and pass the sow before dropping back into formation at her side. The trail was wide where it passed through the open country, then, narrowed as it wound very tightly around the mountain. On the right side was a steep drop-off to the valley far below, a river that ran through the valley and jagged overlooks which offered magnificent views. On the trail's left side, underbrush, rocks, cliffs and an occasional cave offered endless possibilities for young ones to frolic. As the mother led her cubs along the trail, an occasional breeze blew by, bringing, with its cooling sensation an awful odor. The heavy stench found its way to the Bears' sensitive snouts, growing more intense with each step they took toward the river's overlook. Soon, the trail reeked of the dreadful smell. It was so rancid; the cubs began to feel sick as their tongues soaked up the taste of the smell through their snouts. "Mother what is that--it keeps getting worse--the closer we get--to home--it's awful--awful smelly?" The twins asked together in parts as they normally did.

The mother Bear knew very well what was causing the stench and avoided answering the question by directing the cubs to the outside of the trail near the edge. She could not give them a truthful answer yet, so she tried to stall, hoping eventually it would all go away. "I am not sure," she eventually replied.

"It smells--awful mother. Like--swimmers that have--been left out in the sun--too long," the cubs continued.

"Yes, it smells a lot like that. It surely does." She nervously kept up a steady pace hoping her worst fears would not materialize, swinging her massive head around searching for the instigator or instigators of this savagery. There was one thing she was sure of; twos had a way of making their presence known. This could be nothing other than the work of twos. Soon, after rounding the next corner, she was thankful she had re-positioned the cubs, effectively blocking their view of the oncoming, sickening sight. She broke into an anxious trot followed by the cubs. "Don't ask questions now, either of you. When I say run, you run. Okay?"

"Yes--Mother."

The carcasses of several dead four-leggers piled in a heap just to the side of the trail, all in various stages of decomposition came into view after a few more steps. As she kept the cubs moving, several individual carcasses appeared, littering the side of the path blocked from the cubs' view. A few of the deceased four-leggers had not been there long at all. The mother picked up her pace to draw the cubs' attention to her. She did not want to chance them seeing the carnage, especially since one of their relatives was near the middle of the scattered bodies. She gasped at the familiar face staring at her with blank eyes before accidentally letting out an audible moan which signaled their presence. Terrified for her cubs, she again picked up the pace.

The enemy was waiting for that mistake. A small group of twos staged for their bit of fun hid cowardly behind a thicket and a few large boulders. As soon as the sow came in range, they became giddy with excitement. Behind the first large boulder next to the thicket came a loud command, "Now! Take all of them!"

Arrows hissed out of the thicket directly at the mother Bear. Two sunk deep in her front shoulder, three in her back and they kept coming. The hunters reloaded with a vengeance. "Don't let any of them get away."

She had no time to warn her sons. She forced herself on. She turned to spot her two terrified cubs at her side. She was being forced to the outside edge of the trail by the relentless sting of the arrows. She knew it was the time to make the decision she had no option to live to regret. As the arrows kept hitting their marks, she shielded her cubs and forced them closer and closer to the edge of the overlook. Her only thought was for the cubs, not of her own safety. "This may be completely unjustified," she thought out loud, "But it is all I can do to spare them of my horrible end." With her last words, she intentionally forced both cubs over the edge. She roared angrily and slammed her full weight into the cub nearest her who, in turn, rammed the second cub even harder, sending him sprawling helplessly through the air. Still defiant, she roared again, veered directly for the edge of the path then slammed a second time into the remaining cub. He stumbled for a split click, too startled to glance back at his mother. His outside paw landed on a loose rock which gave way, sending him tumbling through empty space on an unyielding path to meet his brother. Still furiously clinging to hope for a miraculous escape, she ran as far as she could. She succumbed after only a few more steps, crumpling to the ground in a heap, she was almost over the edge herself.

"The other two escaped," one of the hunters exclaimed.

Another two grinned as he rushed over to the edge where the two cubs disappeared, "Yeah, tha' might 'av escaped us, but I'm sure tha' didn't live to tell bout it. An such a pity tha' were so big. Tha' meat would feed our crawls eh and them hides, yeah them hides would keep lots of us warm during 'ese bone chillin' nights! Ah, too bad." He turned back to the others. He changed his grin to pursed lips as he tried to get some small piece of food out of the gap in his front teeth and shrugged.

All of the twos laughed before hustling over to examine their latest trophy. "Pretty good size Grizzly here. I'd say it's been quite a good day so far."

\*\*\*

The cubs were shoved off the trail where a rocky crag extends well beyond the face of the jagged cliffs below. Their mother knew what she was doing. The river here runs deep between a set of breaks that slow the current before it enters the next set of rapids. The cubs spent their entire life in and around the water, so if they survived the fall they would survive the water. After falling fast and far, they crashed into the river plunging through the surface of the cold, deep blue water simultaneously sending white, angry plumes of water skyward. The water did not slow their downward progress much as they descended almost to the river bottom. The frigid temperature of the deeper water shocked the cubs back to reality after the crash with the surface knocked them out. They easily swam up to the surface, located each other, drifted with the current and waited for their mother to arrive.

"Where's Mother?" one of them asked. "I don't see her."

"I can't see her either." The second cub began to swim for the shoreline. Maybe their mother was already there.

The current was steadily gaining speed although the cubs were too busy searching for their mother to notice. "Mother, Mother-- Where are you?"

During his swim to shore, the second cub reached a point where he did notice the current's increase in speed. From that point there was no turning back. Drawn by an inherent magnetism, he turned back for his brother. Each of them frantically made their way back to the deepest part of the current to be there for each other. "Its okay-- We'll be alright--She will find us." These were a few of the pledges made from one cub to the other.

The current was picking up speed quickly. "We are heading for rough water--Let's hang on to each other!" Each cub grabbed a layer of fat and fur on the other's neck and clamped down. This was a tough area of hide which had been playfully bitten on several occasions, but this time they bit hard enough to draw each other's blood. Eye contact was the only means of communication and there was only one thing their eyes were saying; "Hold on to me!"

The water turned unkind quickly but they held on. It battered and tossed them around helplessly but they held on. The river pulled the pair along at break-neck speed as it raced from rapid to rapid. Finally, with desperate grips slipping and jaws tiring, the current politely abated. The cubs released their teeth from each other's necks. They released their grip too soon. The first cub attempted to ask the other a question as the false sense of calm lulled them into state of comfort. In an instant, the river became violent again. Had they been able to float up-right and head-first, they would have seen the trouble before it caught them. Instead, they were bobbing with the current on their backs looking rearward, hoping for a glimpse of their mother as she pursued them. The water was whipped into a frenzy downstream as they accelerated uncontrollably toward an unexpected and fast-approaching split in the river. White water pounded between a combination of enormous water-worn boulders and poor, drowned parts of assorted trees. Traveling in opposite directions, the dividing river immediately fought for control of the cubs. A thrashing, wet tug-of-war ensued between the bigger, stronger south fork and the much narrower, but faster west fork. The terrified young Grizzlies were caught in the middle. They tried valiantly with no reward. Big and powerful as they were, the cubs were no match for the determined rivers. They missed the opportunity to ride the same flume by the length of their snouts. Jaws lunging and open, neither brother made contact with the other as they again and again reached out for each other in vain. The menacing water would not be kind this time. It ripped the young cubs from each other without conscience. Both river forks had somewhere else to go, some other date with destiny. The two young cubs were, for the first time ever, unwillingly separated. The cub going down the right fork in the river cried out to his brother going down the left fork, "Hugoth! When the river parted-"

Hugoth answered, "- so did we!"

It was a very sad day indeed for these young Grizzlies. No chance for traditional goodbyes, hugs or words of love. From that moment on, these large, charming cubs were completely on their own to fend for themselves, to educate themselves and make their own decisions--right or wrong. Their mother, if she were there or ever able, would be proud of the decisions these two would independently make. She most definitely would.

***

Hugoth's branch of the river headed westward, Hemoth's headed eastward. The cubs were too busy staying on top of the water to worry about the separation. Those feelings would be dealt with later. Survival was the only thought in their heads at this point.

Fate has a mind of its own. When the cubs awoke earlier in the cozy den they called home, their mother was so close to them they could feel each and every breath she took. The playful fun climbing all over her, using her for tug-o-war practice, begging her to take them out to play, were all distant memories now. Fortunately for them, they were old enough to remember her as a nurturing mother the rest of their days, whether those particular days were now or later. Why had fate called for them to separate in this menacing way? Will that question ever be answered? Not necessarily. Fate answers to no creature, two or four legged. Destiny is different. A creature can have a share of their own destiny. Decisions made, actions taken, the direction one decides for themselves steers their destiny. But fate trumps destiny in the end. A creature's destiny may allow an alternate path to the ultimate fate, but fate will always win.

Hugoth was the thicker of the two. Hemoth was a bit taller. Hugoth was wiser, a long thinker. Hemoth was smarter, a short thinker. The same personality filled both cubs. Hugoth's demeanor was the exact same as Hemoth's under any condition. Hemoth's mannerisms were mirrored in Hugoth. Hugoth favored his left side for strength, Hemoth favored his right side. Twins in every way.

Hugoth rolled over on his back as the current subsided and glanced at the landscape passing him on the south bank of the river. Hemoth rolled onto his back and glanced to the right toward the south bank of his river. Maybe they were not separated that far apart after all.

Hemoth closed his eyes. As big tears were rolling down his heavy jowls the gentle waves were washing them away just as quickly. He, on more than one occasion, fought the urge to swim to the river bank, crawl out and head back home. He had already been carried far past the edge of where their mother let then roam. He had passed that boundary long ago. From here, every patch of ground or clump of trees was a new frontier. He was taught well. He would make it. There were other clans of Bears throughout the lands. He didn't think it would be too hard to find one. Maybe the first clan he came upon would accept him as their own. He hoped so. He decided to ride with the river until it felt the urge to send him aground. One day he would see his brother again. He knew it.

Hugoth watched with interest as his world passed by him. He was distraught and excited at the new path given him. He would play this game as he played all others, fair and to win. The separation would not defeat him and neither would it defeat his brother. The tears welling in his eyes ceased for lack of replenishment. He was cried out. He noticed a tight bend in the river just ahead. There he would start his new life. As the water current slowed, the river widened. Hugoth rolled off of his back to begin his swim to shore. His powerful legs and thick fur allowed him to swim in any direction he chose. The water became as smooth as a well worn path, as wide as any lake he had ever seen back home. He headed to the south bank. Although he couldn't immediately see it, he knew it was there.

Hemoth's river twisted and turned for the longest time. "I have to get out of here soon. I believe it's time to eat." He too rolled over, putting his strong legs beneath him. As he rode the current to river's edge, it wasn't very long before he felt a soft, spongy layer of sand beneath him. He clawed at the unstable river bed until he began to feel the sand stiffen beneath him. He was soon walking to shore under his own power. No more a captive to the river's meandering ways, he plodded out to a dry shoreline. He curiously took in the scenery around him. It was not as barren as much of the land up river. It seemed warmer than he thought. The trees were different too. Different shapes, different colors. How much was going to change from this point forward was obvious; everything.

Hemoth studied his predicament. "Need to eat, head for the trees, should be able to find something in there." He stretched his snout high in the air, sniffing for the faintest aroma of anything edible. Satisfied what he was searching for was not on the riverbank, he cautiously headed through a scraggly grouping of trees beyond the sandy, sloped shore. What he hoped to find remained a mystery to the young Bear. He was determined to succeed. His mother would want it no other way. The young have built-in defenses against extended times of sorrow and despair. Defenses that enable them to move quickly on with their lives, either triggering a survival mode to live or relying on a smaller storage shed of memories, which doesn't weigh them down with grieving over time gone by. Sometimes the young don't fully understand at early ages that tragedy is not the way things normally happen. All creatures are young only once. As far as the cubs knew maybe all mothers are taken from their cubs early. What teachings have they encountered prior to this event could lead them to think another way? They never lost a mother before. They were never separated before. As creatures age and see tragedies take dire tolls on different beings, minds condition themselves on the seemingly proper reactions. Where a mother or father may have a mind conditioned over their life span to fairness, togetherness, sadness, happiness, tragedy, love or loss of love; a young cub cannot feel the same amount of loss or despair since they have no previous experience dealing with it in whatever form. The cubs were sad. However, the time for sadness or the time to celebrate sadness was drawing short. It was time to live. This experience, like many others to come would be filed away by an intelligent mind. The reaction to the individual circumstance would be catalogued and called upon at later times if necessity dictated it so.

Hemoth sensed the newness of this strange wilderness. He raised his snout again, sniffing continuously for the smell of edibles. He perked up slightly when he caught the fragrance of over-ripe berries drifting across his wet nose. Carefully, he followed his nose, hoping it was not misleading him. He came to an area covered by thick, thorny vines intermingled with stoutly grown bushes complete with sturdy trunks. Each vine was heavily laden with hundreds of dark purple berries roughly the size of his smallest claw. He sat down a safe distance away to study the berry patch. Remembering a rule his mother never let him forget, he patiently waited for some other creature to eat a berry first. If the berries did not make that creature sick then he could eat his fill. He waited. The wait wasn't long. Soon after he found a suitable place to sit and watch, a small, lithe creature approached the berries from the other side. Hemoth watched silently as the four-legger carefully avoided the sharp thorns in order to nibble the berries. The creature was tall and looked sort of familiar, but was very thin and gangly compared to the type he was accustomed to seeing. Growing curiosity got the best of him, "Excuse me. Legger, are you a small, sickly Moose?"

The creature's eyes widened to their stops, eye lids bounced up and down erratically. The neck and tail straightened. The creature twitched its neck ever so slightly to track the sound of Hemoth's voice. Hemoth could not help but notice two fan shaped antlers on the legger's slender head. "Uh no."

"Hmmph, but you sure look like a small, sickly Moose. You have Moose antlers, at least a small, sickly pair of Moose antlers." Hemoth did not understand, surely this creature was a small...sickly...Moose. Hemoth's voice was a typical cub's voice, strong and relatively high pitched.

"Well I'm not!"

"If not a small, sickly Moose, what are you?"

"I am a Fallow. What are you a giant Grizzly Bear cub?"

"A Fallow? Yes, I see. I am a giant Grizzly Bear cub or at least that is what I was told."

"Preposterous!"

"No, I am not a preposterous. I am a giant Grizzly Bear cub!" To prove his point Hemoth bellowed a grand roar for the benefit of his new friend. "Rooooaaaaarrr!"

The Fallow stood his ground, continuing to eat his fill of berries. "No, I did not call you a preposterous. I meant you can't be seriously considering me to believe you are a cub. You are a full grown Grizzly as I stand here."

"No, I'm not."

"Yes, you are."

"No, I'm not."

"For the sake of my mother! You are a Grizzly cub. Why are you here?"

"To eat some of those berries."

"No, why are you in this land? You are too far south and east for a Grizzly."

"I don't know why I am here. I was thrown in the river. My twin went one way and I went the other where the river first forked. I have drifted with the current for...uh...uh...I don't know how long."

"Oh, you poor little creature." Another smaller Fallow appeared next to the first with its head lowered, taking advantage of the thick abundance of middle-growing berries followed by more rustling below the lower half of the bushes. "You be nice to this young cub. I trust I won't hear another harsh word said to him?" The smaller Fallow never raised its head as it spoke and picked berries.

The large Fallow did not flinch. He continued eyeing Hemoth, took a few bites of berries and replied, "Perhaps, my fine doe, you should have a look at this poor little creature before you become further enamored with his cute cub voice." Unfazed, he kept eating.

Below the second Fallow came a soft voice, "Mother, there is a tree on the other side of these bushes...and it's moving."

Another soft voice, "Mother, why is the big tree moving?"

The doe answered the two soft voices, "Why you two know trees don't move." She smiled and continued eating.

"Oh," came the reply. "But that one is moving, Mother."

Hunger was drawing Hemoth closer to the berries. Almost involuntarily, he neared the clump of vegetation with hardly noticeable tiny steps. He nibbled a few of the large berries, checking their taste. They tasted delicious! Sweet, tart, juicy. Hemoth discovered an immediate affinity for these particular berries. "These are the best berries I have ever tasted," he said to himself. He began eating the berries in earnest. He was too busy eating to look up. "What kind of berries are these? Are there more nearby?" More messy eating. Unlike the Fallow who judiciously selected each berry eaten, Hemoth was devouring every clump his snout came in contact with.

"Pace yourself cub. You eat too many of these and your gut may explode."

Hemoth stopped eating instantly. "My gut might explode?" A sad look came over his face, "Really?"

Suddenly the second Fallow raised her head. She fired a quick comment to her stag, "I told you not to be harsh with this little cub." At last she took a look at Hemoth. "Oh dear."

# 19

Mystic stood stone still as if he had seen a ghost, as did Bubba, Lightning and Frederick.

Gamma was quick to notice the ear-shattering silence. "What is wrong? Have you seen a specter?"

Frederick was the only guest able to speak and he spoke directly to Hemoth though he looked at Gann and Gamma, "Who are you?"

"I am Hemoth. Why do you ask in such a tone as that?'

"Uh, er...please forgive me Hemoth, rather forgive all of us. We are shocked. We just left you, did we not?"

"What do you mean, you just left me? Is that a joke of some kind?"

"No, we just left you. On our last journey, you were there. You led us around. You were the Keeper where we were."

"I have never laid eyes on any of you. Keeper? What is this Keeper?"

"You were there. It had to be you."

Lightning found his tongue. "Frederick, you are mistaken. Hemoth was not there. This Grizzly is not as thick as the Keeper. He is also taller." The Badger stepped toward Hemoth, "If I may?"

"Sure, if you may what?" Hemoth pulled back slightly. This line of questioning was eerie.

"Let me step to your side for comparison." He did. "See Frederick? Hemoth here is taller and thinner."

Frederick stepped up to the two of them. "The resemblance is profound. How could this be?"

Gann stepped in, "Now I have to know what is going on here. What are you two talking about?"

Frederick moved backward as Gann entered the fray. "If I may explain sir, this creature, this Grizzly Bear bears a stunning resemblance to a dear friend of ours. From the shape of his paws to the tip of his ears, he is our friend, only Hemoth is taller and thinner."

"Thinner? How wide is your friend?" Gann did not understand.

Lightning spoke to Gann, "Sir let me introduce myself first. I am Lightning, the Irregular Badger, Duke of the Great Meadow. Hemoth he..."

Gann cut him off, "Did you say Badger?"

"Yes I did. I said I am Lightning, the Irregular Badger. My friends are Bubanche, Cheetah of the Great Plains, Mystic, Prince of the Great Forest and Frederick Mounte, two-legger extraordinaire. Why do you question me?"

"Because dear creature, you are a..."

Hemoth now cut Gann off, "Grizzly Bear! You are just like me. You are not a Badger."

"Really? That explains a lot." Lightning took two steps back and fainted to the floor.

Hemoth laughed a big belly laugh. "All this time he thought he was a Badger? Oh me! Now while he rests, let us get back to me. Who is this friend of yours?"

Bubba was now ready to speak. "Our friends name is Hugoth. He is also a great Grizzly Bear. Do you know him?"

Hemoth's eyes became spinning saucers. "Hugoth?" Hemoth tried to steady himself but it was too late. He also fainted dead away, landing soundly on the floor.

Gamma was watching the big creatures falling like flies. "Excuse me Bubanche, where did you meet him?"

Bubba faced Gamma, "Yes my lady, we met him in Nuorg."

Gamma's face blanched white as snow, "Did you say Nuorg?"

"Yes my lady."

It's a good thing Gamma had moved closer to the sitting area. Upon hearing Bubba's utterance of Nuorg, she too fainted. She fell to the middle of the couch then, in a very un-lady like fashion, rolled off onto the floor.

Gann rushed to her side, "Oh my, this is great news."

Mystic and Frederick looked at each other, "Great news?"

As Gamma made her way to the floor and Gann made his way to her, unannounced on the other side of the room, a transformed Madaliene made her entrance. She elegantly walked across the room in a sparkling blue gown fit for royalty complete with hundreds of sparkling jewels and matching tiara. Holding her head high, in royal fashion, she had not noticed the collapsing creatures around her. She entered the circle of guests and promptly stubbed her toe on a leg of the short table that had been pushed aside as Gann rushed to Gamma's side. She grabbed at thin air as she tried to catch her balance. The thin air did nothing to stop her fall. She tumbled into Frederick's open arms, knocking him down in the process.

As Madaliene fell to the ground on top of Frederick she couldn't help herself, "What the...?"

Mystic and Bubba looked up for Sig and Perrie who were laughing so hard they could not stay on perch anymore. They fell to the floor, rolling with laughter. The Wolf and the Cheetah carefully stepped over or to the side of the floored others. Bubba was beside a chuckling Mystic, "Now that was funny."

Mystic sat down, "Yes it was Cheetah. Yes it was."

"What do we do now?"

"I guess we could eat something?"

"Good idea, I could use a bite now that you mention it."

"Shall we?"

# 20

Hugoth did not fare much better, for as far as Hemoth traveled in one direction, Hugoth had traveled at least that far in the other. The scenery Hugoth noticed was not drastically different from that of his homeland. He climbed out of the rocky riverbed only to find larger round rocks covering the shoreline. The trees here were the same as home, only smaller. The mountains too were the same, only smaller. Hugoth immediately came across a hollow, fallen log. He was tired. The sun was high in the sky. He laid down somewhat shaded by the log to rest. He quickly fell into a deep, deep sleep. Fantastic dreams peppered his sleep, but did not wake him. He slept peacefully the remainder of the sun-time and all through the night.

Hugoth awoke to the lively sound of wingers speaking in an odd, sharp, curt quacking speak. From the sound of it, Hugoth recognized most of the clamoring was directed at him. He slept on his side with his back snuggly against the log. It certainly wasn't the same as sleeping in a cozy lair next to his mother and brother, but he accepted it. All the action was taking place on his side of the log. From the looks of it, quite a crowd had gathered.

Most of the talk was unrelated to Hugoth actually being there. It was not where he was that disturbed the crowd; it was what he was! Feathers were rattled, beaks were squawking. Hugoth stretched his neck forward and peered past the end of the log. His gaze was met and returned by a floating armada of stern-faced wingers. When they noticed him noticing them, they glared back. The entire group menacingly began paddling straight at him. Hugoth was amused. What did these swimming wingers intend to do with him? Should he be afraid of them? Nah, he threw that possibility away. He quickly discovered that they might possibly "quack" him to death. So far not a single winger made any attempt to directly talk with Hugoth. They were going to win this battle by sheer numbers and determination.

That was until Hugoth spoke to them. "What kind of wingers are you?"

A thunderous cacophony of beating wings and quacking commenced instantly. A dark cloud of wingers took to the sky as one. They quickly climbed high in the sky to begin circling the area. It looked to Hugoth to be an uncountable number or wingers in the air. A line of tiny swimming wingers couldn't take off with the large group. They began a frantic struggle to reach the shore as far away from Hugoth as possible. In single file, the tiny wingers courageously fought against the mild backwash of waves lapping the shore. Hugoth was amused at the sight and troubled with the defenseless posture the little ones exhibited.

"Where is their mother?" he thought. Without warning, an enormous swimmer lunged from beneath the surface of the water. Completely airborne, menacing jaws lined with rows of needle-sharp teeth open, aimed at a confused straggler at the end of the line. With one gulp, the swimmer swallowed the last winger then vanished, slicing into the water without a splash. Hugoth watched in horror as another swimmer broke the surface. There may be a reason for these actions and he might get around to that later, but this was not an act he condoned. He didn't care much for swimmers anyway, a stuck-up creature to say the best. With speed unseen by the panicked wingers remaining on shore, the giant Bear cub leaped to his feet and into the water. He without hesitation positioned himself between the airborne menace and the row of little quackers, (that is what he would call them now). On instinctive reflexes alone, he swatted his front paw at the leaping attacker. The swimmer smacked into Hugoth's thick paw with a thud. He sent the swimmer soaring through the air. It slammed into the hollow log before falling to the rocky beach. Hugoth had no time to savor the moment. Another one, followed by many others also broke the surface. One by one, sometimes two by two, Hugoth whacked each of them into submission. A pile of the swimming attackers was growing near the log. Hugoth kicked his back legs at the little quackers sending wave after saving wave in their direction, forcing them closer to the river's edge. He caught a glimpse of the lead quacker leading the parade gingerly up the bank. He caught his breath and exhaled. He turned to the little quackers who were forming a side-by-side row safely away from the water. "Where are your protectors?" he demanded.

The quacking speak on the shore elevated to a nauseating volume as Hugoth exited the water. He never experienced anything like this before. They were cheering for him. He proudly continued his way to the pile of swimmers. He eyed the pile a little embarrassed by the commotion around him, then turned to the row of little quackers, "What am I to do with these little monsters?"

They answered Hugoth in unison, "Breakfast!"

## 21

Eventually, as creatures regained consciousness, order was restored. Little by little, the magnitude of the previous revelations came into focus. Gamma sat on the couch as Gann held a wet compress to her head. Madaliene was propped in Gann's chair with a wet compress on her foot. Frederick sat in Gamma's chair holding his face in his hands while Madaliene held a compress on the large knot forming on the back of his head. Lightning lay dazed on the floor next to Bubba as the Cheetah shook his head wondering how he would ever make anyone believe the story if he ever got the chance to tell it. Sig and Perrie huddled close together in a nook overlooking the entire room. Mystic sat near Hemoth, trying to convince him that Lightning was a Badger.

"I'm telling you that he is a Badger."

"No, he is not."

"What makes you say that?"

"Do I look like a Badger?"

"No."

"Do you notice any similarity in the way I look as compared to the way Lightning looks?"

"Yes, you look very similar."

"You are correct, because we are both Grizzly Bears!"

"Well...he thinks he is a Badger."

"But he is not!"

"He was raised by Badgers."

"So what? I was raised by a herd of Fallow Deer! Does that make me a Deer?"

"No. You are a Bear."

"Then he is a Bear too, only he was raised by Badgers like I was raised by Deer!"

"Can we call it a draw?"

"No we can't call it a draw. He is a Grizzly Bear!"

"Whatever."

Frederick rubbed the sides of his head. "What did I hit when I fell?"

Bubba, never one to miss the opportunity to rub salt into a wound, answered, "The floor. You hit it square and hard. I haven't heard a more solid thunk in my life."

"Great. Thanks so much Bubba, for clarifying that for me."

"No problem at all."

Madaliene reached down to rub her sore foot. "Gamma, I am never wearing these shoes again. If I had my real shoes on I would have never fallen to begin with."

"Oh now be quiet Madaliene, you look like a real princess in those shoes."

"I am a real princess, how could I not look like one?"

"Well, I had to wear shoes like that for special occasions and so do you. I'm afraid you will simply have to get used to it. Okay...now... who wants to tell us where Nuorg is?"

Frederick sat up. "How did you even find out about it? We just left there."

Gann motioned to the letter. "Madaliene's sister wrote us a letter. When we figured out the hidden message within it, it spelled out Nuorg."

"It was written in the letter?"

Sig flew down to the back of the couch. "Actually, it was hidden inside individual symbols that I remembered from the olde Eagle language. It was only then that the word Nuorg was recognizable."

Gann acknowledged as much. "Sig here is the only one I know who can read that old mess anyway. Eagle language...I'm not sure I believe there ever was an Eagle language."

Frederick reached for his bag. He retrieved his note pad and began shuffling through the pages. "The olde Eagle language is real, but there are many versions of it. These notes found in the Nuorg library confirm as much."

"Please tell me more about Hugoth, will you?" Hemoth could not stop thinking about him.

Mystic stood up. He moved within an ear's width of Hemoth's face. "If it weren't for the differences in width and height, I'd say you two are the spitting image of each other."

"We are the spitting image of each other. We are identical twins."

The room fell silent. "We were separated when we were not even yearlings. We fell into a river in the north; he went one way, while I went the other. I can't believe you know where he is. You must take me to see him. I have many questions for him."

"Well isn't this like opening up a big barrel of coincidences." Gann was realizing there was more to this meeting than first imagined. "Tell me Wolf, what is hiding in your holster there? That implement Lightning brought with him and the rapier worn by Frederick over there suggest your group is on more than a little adventure."

Lightning got to his feet. He carried the ax-pike to Gann's side. "Sir, I don't know what this is. I've been dragging it around since I was young. I got it near the same time Mystic found his Staff. This is what brought us here."

"What do you mean it brought you here?"

Frederick explained, "Gann, Lightning's ax-pike there transported us to this mountain, to you. When we stepped onto the ground near the Great Forest, Lightning held it up and more or less asked it which way to go. We never entered the Great Forest. He asked it a few more times and we wound up in your ante chamber. Who knows?"

Lightning continued, "Our first stop was a barn west of the lake. We didn't like what we found there."

"I'll agree with that." Bubba had hoped that subject would not be discussed.

"What barn?" asked Gamma.

Frederick described it for them. "From what I could tell, it was a large barn once used for normal farming. We found leftovers of typical what have you. We also uncovered a horror. We discovered literally hundreds and hundreds of dead wingers within the debris."

"What do you mean when you say debris?" Gamma leaned in closer to Frederick.

"I mean the barn had been reduced to rubble. There was not a stall left standing, no door swinging. The roof lay on the ground, hiding the carnage beneath it."

Mystic swung around to join the conversation. "What attracted us to it was the smell. It drew us in like a burnt meal. We couldn't turn away. The stink was enough to kill on its own. We would not have survived without the snout plugs. Dreadful."

Gann glanced at Perrie. "Our young Falcon told us a story that ties in perfectly with what you are telling us about the barn."

"Perrie, did you get any glimpse at all of whom the attackers were?" Frederick sat his Nuorg notes to the side. He was now jotting notes from memory regarding the barn.

"I'm sorry, I don't. I was rescued early and remember nothing."

"See, that's what is so disturbing to me. We have been shadowed by an enormous winger since the ax-pike brought us here. It rescued Perrie and nearly scared Bubba to death. What does it want? Why would it scare him and rescue her?" Mystic could make no sense of it. "As for my Staff, I'm not sure we have time for that story."

Gann stretched his legs. "We need you all to help Hemoth and Madaliene find her sister." He said this as if none in the group had a choice in the matter. "Nuorg seems to be the key here for numerous reasons."

Bubba asked the obvious, "Who is the sister and what do we know about her?"

Gamma fiddled with Madaliene's tiara, which was worth more that several towns all added together. She elaborated for Bubba, "We have two granddaughters, Evaliene, the oldest, and Madaliene. Their parents are gone. It happened years ago. We try to forget it. We have raised Madaliene here with us. Evaliene was raised by another family. She, for reasons unknown to us, left that family several years ago. We lost contact with them. It's like they fell in a hole or something."

Mystic suddenly looked at the members of his group with an "it could happen" look on his face.

"We thought everything to be fine. Then...Hemoth brings us this note that is written to make us believe it is from Evaliene. In our haste to read it, we completely missed the clue telling us either she did not write it or she was forced to write it. It never made sense to any of us until we each read it without paying attention to the circumstances."

"How do you know that?" Frederick stopped taking notes to ask the question.

"One word...glorious. That is the key word."

"So the use of the word glorious is not permitted in your writing etiquette?" Frederick scribbled.

Gann continued, "By no means is it not permitted. We just don't use it twice in one paragraph. If an event or a thing, if you will, gains enough status to be considered glorious, then any following thing can't be considered the same or it would render the first glorious thing to be a little less than glorious. That is the key, the way we see it, simple and efficient. Evaliene is in trouble. Somehow the letter was intercepted and given to a Golden Eagle who gave it to Hemoth. Is that correct as you remember it?" He looked directly at the Grizzly Bear.

"Yes Gann. It wasn't that long ago. I remember it perfectly now."

Perrie was not ready to skip over the barn and the dead wingers topic yet. "What else do you know about the wingers? Were there literally hundreds as you say?"

"Hundreds and more," Bubba told her. "I'll never get that sight or that stink out of my mind. We buried stacks and stacks of carcasses. It was horrible."

"You need to be more sensitive, Bubba, when you talk about it like that. All of those we buried were some creature's family, although I'd venture to guess they were included in the whole lot." Mystic was trying to forget it all.

"What plan can be so complex that it would compel its initiators to wipe out or attempt to wipe out an entire level of creatures? I mean what would be the next level to eradicate?" Gamma was trying hard to fit the pieces together.

Hemoth had thought about this. "It makes perfect sense if you allow yourself to put some distance between yourself and the turmoil. Think about it, have any of us gotten any messages from the other lands? I hardly think so. What they have done is..."

Gann stood up and paced. "Isolate us. They have successfully isolated every land by taking away the lines of communication, at least, rapid communication. Hemoth, how long did it take you to get here with Ev's message?"

"I'd say at least eight or nine full days, easy."

"There you go! We have to open these lines back up. The quandary we find ourselves with is how do we do that? Do we split this group up or anybody...?"

"I'm not in favor of that, Gann. Once we split up we become vulnerable. We don't need that." Frederick continued to notate the conversation and prepare his documents for the Nuorg presentation.

Frederick watched closely as Gamma gently sat Madaliene's tiara on the table. He noticed her wrists most importantly.

Gamma sighed, "Madaliene I must say you looked more lovely than you normally do while wearing this. We need to prioritize our topics. I realize the importance of each of them, but we need to see the whole puzzle here, not just bits and pieces. Frederick, you are taking notes right?"

"That's all he does!" Bubba wished he could scribble better.

"Yes, Gamma, I have too many I think."

"No, you don't. Okay, what is our first priority?"

"My granddaughter!" Gann answered loudly.

"What else?"

Perrie obviously answered, "The disappearance of wingers!"

"And don't forget Nuorg is pretty high on the list." Mystic knew Nuorg would tie a lot of this together, or he hoped it would.

Gann was holding up three fingers. "So far, there are three. Are there more? Come on now. Let's get them all out on the table now."

Gamma mentioned the letter. Hemoth mentioned Hugoth. Sig sided with Perrie wanting to know more about the barn.

Gann held up fingers four, five and six. "Anymore? I know I want to know about the ax-pike and your other fine implements. So, that will be number seven."

Gamma stepped to Gann's side. She raised her hand and clasped it around Gann's. "That is enough to start with dear. My vote is to put Nuorg at the top of the list. Any arguments against?"

The room was silent.

"That does it. Who wants to tell us about Nuorg? Frederick?"

"No, Mystic is more familiar than I am with Nuorg. He wasn't there as long as I, but he saw much more. Too bad Vincen is not with us. He could tell you even more than the four of us combined."

"That may be true, Frederick. Let's hear it, Mystic." Gann positioned himself comfortably in a chair, "Start from the top."

Madaliene, Hemoth, Gamma, Sig, Perrie and Gann focused all of their attention on the Wolf. They settled in for what would be a long story.

Mystic began, "I had no reason to be where I was that day. It had been technically off limits since we were much younger. That day found me doing more odd things than I have ever done before..."

Outside the sun was passing the middle of the sky. Mystic held the rapt attention of all listeners, including those who had been to Nuorg with him. The sun kept moving across the sky and began to settle in the west. From time to time Lightning, Bubba or Frederick would add to the story where Mystic wasn't involved. Around sunset the story was coming to an end.

"So then there we were, right back where we started. We planned to go directly to the Great Forest until Lightning's ax-pike led us to the beginning of this part of the story." Mystic laid down on the floor, drained from story-telling.

"That is one nearly unbelievable story you have experienced. So the ax-pike, the rapier, the Staff and possibly the bag were purified by the light emitted from the globe?" Gann, being very pragmatic, wanted more verification.

Frederick answered, "As we see it, yes they did. There are some peculiar goings on with those things now. For example, the ax-pike leads us to where we need to be, not where we want to be, or else we would be in the Great Forest now. The rapier performs its own unique deeds and my bag can now hold anything. I am telling you all now. I hadn't thought it a big deal, but it just kept holding whatever I put in it. Kind of hit me out of the blue. Here, let me show you." Frederick sat the bag on the table. He reached deep inside it. When he pulled his hand out, it was clutching a small melon.

Bubba nosed closer, "I am not impressed."

"How about this?" Frederick reached in the bag again with both hands and pulled out a large, heavy green melon. Do I impress you yet?"

"Not yet, no."

"Maybe this will convince you, if I can find it." Again Frederick reached into the bag. He began pulling out fruits and vegetables out as fast as he could toss them around to the others. Soon, there was a small stack of edibles in front on each creature in the room. "There is more in here if you wish to see."

Bubba was almost impressed. "You got any water-livers in there?"

"As a matter of fact, I do." Frederick pulled out several large damp leaves, each wrapped securely around a pair of nice sized water-livvers. "Here Bubba, just for you."

"Now I am impressed." The Cheetah took his snack back to his spot and quickly devoured them.

Madaliene titled her head and winked at Gamma. "How many arrows could that bag hold?"

"As many as you would like me to carry." Frederick offered the bag to her for inspection.

"It doesn't look heavy either, does it Gamma?"

Frederick held it out for Madaliene to inspect. "Be careful, a lot of stuff may fall out of here."

Madaliene stood up to take the bag. Immediately after Frederick released his grip, the bag fell to the ground. It landed with a pronounced whump.

Bubba looked up from snacking, "That was pretty odd. Is it that heavy?"

"I don't know what is wrong Frederick, I'm so sorry I dropped it. Is everything in it alright? It got so heavy when you let go of it!"

"Really?" Frederick bent over and picked it up with one hand.

Hemoth raised his paw, "May I try?"

"Sure."

Frederick hung the bag's strap over Hemoth's outstretched paw. Hemoth immediately placed his other paw under the first to keep the bag from dropping to the ground again. "Grab it quick, Frederick."

As the group watched, Hemoth fought the weight of the bag with both of his massive front paws. It nearly fell again until Frederick easily lifted it from Hemoth.

"Now I must say, that is odd." Fredrick held the bag high, spinning it to get a good look. "I don't guess I knew that would happen. At this point, Princess, I'd say I could maybe carry a Horse for you in here if the need should arise. Hmmph!"

Gamma spoke, "Gann, what do you make of it"

"I'm not at all sure of what I think. This is just one more mystery to me. It should be very useful though. I'd certainly love to have it. Albeit, Frederick seems to be the only one here who can tame it. Mystic, may I examine the Staff?"

"Be my guest." Mystic walked closer to Gann. "Just pull it from the holster."

Gann slipped his hands around the globe. The Staff slid out effortlessly into his grip. "Magnificent work here. Do you have any idea where it came from or how old it may be?"

"So far," Frederick commented as he spread more notes on the table, "We have not been able to date it or determine where it was made."

"That's the wrong word, Frederick. This Staff was crafted, it was not made. The tables in this room were made, the chairs were made...this was crafted by a craftsman more skilled than any I have ever come across. It is flawless, absolutely flawless. You say it comes apart, but there is no visible line indicating a joining seam of any kind. Please, take it apart for us." Gann handed it back to Mystic.

Mystic was taken aback by the frankness of Gann's request. He looked to Frederick, Lightning and then Bubba in case anyone thought it a bad idea. He got no looks or words to deter the action.

"Gann, this is how it works." Mystic practiced flipping it a few times as he had become so adept at doing in Nuorg. He was a little rusty. Soon enough he got the hang of it again. Without warning, he flipped it, caught it then banged it against the floor. He did this as necessary to separate the compartments. As each one separated, he had Frederick pick them up and spread them out on the table. "There they are, all present and accounted for."

"What about the globe?" asked Gamma.

"Unless it is glowing, there is no need to go through that. It can be quite painful." Mystic was not going to roll the globe just to satisfy curiosity; not now, not ever.

Gann moved very close to the parts of the Staff, hovering just above each one as he carefully studied them. He reached to touch the parchments rolled tightly inside the largest section. "Whoa there sir, I wouldn't do that!" Frederick put his arm out to block Gann's attempt.

"Why on earth not? What harm can come of it?"

"That is exactly what I thought the first time too." Frederick shook his head and threw his arm back to emphasize his stance on the matter.

"Oh now, Frederick, the globe isn't glowing, so we are not evil people here." Gamma took up for her husband.

"Alright. Mystic, is it okay with you if this crazy old man touches these rolled up old parchments and shoots himself clear across this expansive room?"

"Fine with me. I hope he is in good shape and lands on something soft. Have him go right ahead."

"Very well, sir. Go ahead, try and pull them out." Frederick stepped well behind Gann to catch him in case he was blown too far from the Staff parts. "Lightning, please step behind me. He may need a bigger cushion than just me."

Gann stared at the commotion behind him with disdain. "I assure you, I am quite capable of handling any situation that might take place here."

"As you wish. Lightning, return to your place, I will do the same." Frederick walked back to his seat, sat down and watched patiently.

Gann straightened up, brushed himself off and bent over the Staff. "That's more like it." He lightly brushed the edge of the parchment. That was all he remembered for the next few clicks. No sooner had his finger touched the parchment before his eyes bulged from his head. His face contorted as if he was being yanked very hard from behind, his body forming a letter "C". He was blasted over Madaliene and Gamma, who had no time to try and catch him. He sailed through mid-air, nearly to the far side of the chamber, which was an enormous room. His body slammed into a stack of blankets and rugs. Fortunately for him, Gamma had placed them there earlier in the week, maybe for this very occasion. He landed with a crunching sound, unpleasant to those listening. Gamma cried out to him. She and Madaliene raced over to his side. The others arrived by him a bit later.

"Gann, Gann are you alive?" Madaliene pleaded.

Gamma pursed her lips when she saw him breathing, Bubba and Lightning both would say for days to come that she was trying not to laugh. Instead, she sat down by him and put her hand on his forehead. "Gann, when you awake, please thank these creatures for trying to stop you, you stubborn old man."

Madaliene appeared a bit cross with Gamma. She stood up, calmed the wrinkles from her gown and excused herself from the den. "I must get out of this." As she walked to her room, Hemoth could not help but notice her attempts to stifle the laughs coming from her gut.

Gamma turned to her, "Are you alright, Madi? He will be fine. Don't cry." Gamma and Madaliene were a lot alike.

Frederick asked, "Ma'am, would you like to try and touch the parchments also?"

"I think not, Frederick, but thank you for asking." She was overly polite. She sat beside her stricken husband for a quiet moment. She could hold it no more. A little laugh started building deep inside her.

Before she knew it she was heaving like her granddaughter. She politely stood. "I, I, I must change into something more comfortable. Please excuse me. If he wakes before I return, please slap him silly for me." She hurried off to her room holding her laughter under wraps until the door to her room shut behind her.

Bubba chuckled, "She won't need to worry about him waking up too soon."

The leggers moved back to the seating area. Sig and Perrie were asked to stay back with Gann. "If he awakes, should we call for you?"

Frederick smiled back, "Yes, please call for us. He will need something to help him feel better and I have just the thing."

Once they were all seated again, Hemoth asked the group a question. "What kind of brother do I have?"

# 22

Hemoth continued gulping down berries at an astonishing rate. Having a new fully loaded mouthful of sweet happiness in his mouth, on his snout and dripping down his jaws, once again he raised his head when the talk turned his way. He could not help but notice the new kinder pair of eyes staring at him. "Hello," he loudly whispered.

Once again, the soft voices near the bottom of the berry vines were chatting. "Who is that, Mother?" "Is the tree talking?" "She said trees can't move. Mother, can they talk?"

The Fallow doe stood absolutely amazed at the gentle voice emanating from the huge creature. "Hello to you," she replied trancelike, her eyes not fully comprehending what they were seeing.

"My, you are a big cub."

"Yes I am. I am a giant Grizzly Bear cub. My name is Hemoth and I don't know where I am from." He stated most of this with a proud look on his messy face. The last line was delivered with a little less zeal.

"It is nice to meet you, Hemoth. I agree you are a giant!"

"Mother, you told us there were no such things as giants." "She also said trees don't move. Now she is talking to a giant Grizzly Bear tree." The soft little voices had no clue what they were talking about, since they were so short they couldn't see Hemoth but they watched attentively as the giant's tree-trunk sized legs swayed back and forth before them.

The stag looked on, still nimbly picking out the ripest berries on his side of the bush. "He does eat like a cub. Hemoth, do you have any idea how old you are?"

He looked around, contemplating the question. "No Deer, I do not. I think...my mother birthed us...hmm...about eight or nine bushels of days ago? It was not hot when we first came out of our den. It was kind of...cool, I think."

228

"You are only eight or nine months old?" The doe responded. She certainly appeared flabbergasted, only Hemoth had not yet learned that look.

The stag looked at her, "He's big."

"Is he a real giant tree mother?" "We want to see it." "We have never seen a giant talking Grizzly Bear tree."

The doe continued, "You said your mother birthed us, is there another cub with you?"

"No. We got pulled in different directions way up-river. I wish he was with me. I hope he wishes I was with him." Hemoth allowed himself a short sad repose.

"You are alone then?" She refused to believe this. He was too young to be on his own anywhere. "Why, you are younger than our fawns. They are almost a year old and together they can't weigh as much as your head. You have a big head cub."

"I have a giant head because I am a giant Grizzly. Roooaaarrrrr!" Hemoth ducked his head back into the berries. Stretching and munching berries as far as he could reach, he noticed eight thin, spindly legs beside the larger stag's small, sickly Moose legs and the doe's small slender legs. "I was wondering where those other voices were coming from. Hello spindly little Fallows." He contorted his head around where he could see them and they could see him.

"Look, the giant Grizzly Bear tree that talks but can't move is talking to us." "Shhh, it might see us." "It already sees us." "Oh...Mother!"

"Now you two calm down. This is Hemoth. He is going home with us."

The stag was surprised. "He's going where with us?"

"I said he is going home with us. I'm not leaving a baby out here in these woods alone."

"A baby? He is a Grizzly Bear. A giant Grizzly Bear." The stag knew it was better not to argue.

The fawns laughed out loud. "A baby? Mother, he is bigger than all of us put together." "Yes, Mother, he is a giant Grizzly Bear tree cub baby."

"You want me to come back to your den with you?" Hemoth felt good, but he also felt sad. "I guess I can. I can't ask my mother." He pulled his massive head out of the bush. Through a forced smile, "I'm sure she would say I can."

229

The stag nodded his head in agreement. Hemoth might be huge, but he was only a baby. "If we are finished here," he nodded to his doe, "Then home we go." He led the way with the two fawns at his heels, the doe next and Hemoth bringing up the rear.

The fawns kept sneaking peeks at Hemoth. "I think he is bigger than a tree." "And he can walk. Mother said trees can't walk." "But he is walking." "I know."

\*\*\*

Hugoth smiled at the line of little quackers. As life on the river bank slowly tilted back to normal, the hordes of adult quackers began to land once again on the river. Hugoth was not often privy to older creatures flying or running off at the first sign of trouble, especially if it meant leaving their young ones behind, but that is exactly what happened here. He was happy to have been the rescuer of the little ones, still he felt the river bank was not a place for him to stay put very long. He looked down at the lead little quacker, "So, breakfast you say?" He eyed the pile of newly caught swimmers with a glean in his eye,

"If I was your size, I'd eat the whole lot of them! They certainly wanted to eat all of us." He fanned his developing wing down the row at the others lined up to his side. The whole row nodded in agreement.

"Well, if you say so." Hugoth ravenously pursued the large pile of breakfast. The older quackers nervously gathered around Hugoth as he ate.

A colorful quacker approached him, "I see you can talk. We wish to thank you for saving our downies. We were wary of you when we saw you sleeping in our nesting area. We thought you might be after more than a sleep."

Hugoth eyed him. This type of winger was new to him. "No, I just needed to sleep. I have been riding the river for a long time. I don't know how long. I need to find a new den, but I was too tired. What is your kind called?"

"I'm not happy to hear that, Bear. We are Ducks. A mismatched lot of Ducks, but Ducks just the same."

"Ducks. Hmm, never seen your kind before."

"We have never seen a Bear as big as you before."

Hugoth did not mind the small talk. He enjoyed the conversation, but now it was time to go. "Well Duck, I have eaten my fill of these mean swimmers, now I'll be on my way. I must find myself a den and a place to call my home."

"Good enough, Bear. We hope to see you again someday. What is your name?"

"My mother called me Hugoth. I am a giant Grizzly Bear cub." Hugoth made his way through the raft of Ducks gathered around him. "Good-bye all of you big Ducks and little quackers. We may see each other again someday. Be careful of the swimmers." Hugoth was off on another adventure.

The Duck watched Hugoth disappear down the river bank. "A giant Grizzly Bear cub? That is worth thinking about."

Hugoth wandered off in an excellent mood. He enjoyed a pleasant feeling deep in his bones after helping those little quackers. Lots of ideas entered his thoughts as he made his way down the river. Maybe, he should devote the rest of his life to helping less-fortunate creatures. His mother would be pleased. He traveled on. Far past the rescue on the river, he turned to his left. A wide open glen lay before him, bordered by a medium forest on one side and mountain foothills on the other. At his back, a deep, crystal blue lake formed where the river widened and slowed, its serene beauty beckoning to all creatures that passed by. Though this country wasn't the land of his birth, he was not finding much wrong with it. Hugoth stood at the glen's entrance taking in relaxing breaths of the clean, fresh air. The early sun radiated a warm glow from the glen's distant end highlighting the wild flowers and plush green floor of tall grass spread wide from side to side. The young cub yearned to share this find with his mother and Hemoth. Sorrowfully, he knew, right now, that was not going to happen.

Nonetheless, he asked their opinion, "Well, Mother and Hemoth, should I stay here and see what this land holds for me, or should I keep searching?"

Hugoth imagined he heard his mother answer, "Rest now Hugoth. We'll see. We'll see."

"Of course," Hemoth answered, "I'll race you to the other end!"

Hugoth reared up on his back legs, smiled a big Bear cub smile and roared an answer to Hemoth. "First one to the other end is a swimmer!" He took off at full speed, all four legs clawing for traction in the luxurious, happy grass.

***

Hemoth tagged along behind the Fallow family observing every new thing in sight. "This is a very different place than where I am from. Your trees have big limbs at the top. All of the trees I know had big limbs at the bottom and smaller limbs at the top. You have more grass here too. We had spots of grass with lots of rocks. We also had lots of water everywhere. Where is your water? Was the river I came out of your only water?" Hemoth had more questions to ask than he could voice.

"Yes, we have more water than the river, Hemoth. We will come to it in a bit. What do you normally eat where you come from?" The motherly instinct was taking over the doe's conversation with Hemoth. "You don't eat creatures like us where you come from do you?"

"No, no, no. We eat red berries, blue berries, plain berries, grass and swimmers! I love to eat swimmers!"

"Mother, are we swimmers?" asked one of the Fawns.

"Of course, we are not swimmers." The doe laughed.

"Are we berries, Mother?" asked the second fawn chuckling.

"No, we are not berries. You two are being silly."

The stag suddenly stopped walking. He perked his ears and tail up. His eyes darted from side to side. "Hush," he whispered. "They are out there."

"Who are they?" asked Hemoth.

"They are very unscrupulous creatures that don't mind eating creatures like us. Actually, they enjoy it." The doe immediately dropped to the ground. Instinctively, her fawns did likewise, curling themselves up tightly beside her.

The stag stood still as a stone, unmoving. Hemoth was afraid. Of what--he didn't know. "Can I see who they are?" He crept up beside the stag.

"You can see them through this opening in the bushes, Hemoth."

"All I can see are those Cats. Are you afraid of those Cats?" Hemoth couldn't understand what was going on.

"I am not afraid of them for me, I am afraid for my little ones. Those Cats would love to make a meal out of my fawns. I can't let that happen. That is why we must stay completely still until they move out of the area."

"Huh? What if I move them out first? Will that work?"

"Hmm, I suppose that could work. Are you not afraid of that kind of Cat, Hemoth?"

"Um, no. I'm not afraid of any Cat!"

"Very well Hemoth. See if those Cats are afraid of you."

"This could be fun." Hemoth slowly crawled through the opening in front of he stag. The Cats were unaware of his presence. Before any notice was given, Hemoth rose up on his hind legs and roared a loud vicious roar. The startled Cats shrieked. They jumped off the ground, landing in a twisted heap. Hemoth bent down, he put all four paws on the ground and bounded menacingly toward the terrified Cats. "Leave my family alone, Cats or I will beat you badly!" He roared once more, sending the nervous Cats running for their lives. Hemoth turned to the stag, standing motionless and wide-eyed. At his side was his doe, beneath them, staring out from between their parents' legs, the two fawns grinned at their new big brother.

"Wow, Hemoth, you showed those Cats who was in charge!" piped the one under the stag.

"We're going to like having you around Hemoth!" The other fawn chimed in.

"Well, Hemoth, that was quite an impressive show. Now, don't ever do it again! You can't always use your size to intimidate creatures. At some point you need to learn to use your intellect. I will teach you how to do that. At some point in the future, you may encounter something bigger than you. It may not be a living creature, but it still may be bigger that you. Some things you will not be able to scare away with your size and ferocious growl." Though the stag was impressed, he remained very composed.

The fawns locked eyes on each other. At the very same time they growled, "Ferocious..."

"That will be enough of that, little ones. What if Hemoth is not always around to protect you? You need to follow our example, most of the time being smart enough will protect you. You two will never be as imposing as Hemoth." The doe tried hard to suppress a smile, but it escaped.

"Enough of this, we need to get back to our herd. There is a lot to do if I remember correctly. Hemoth, fall in line." That was it. A lesson learned, two terrified Cats, two satisfied parents, two giddy fawns and Hemoth, the makings of a functional family group. Now, how would the stag explain Hemoth to his elders?

***

Hugoth ran as hard as he could to the other end of the glen, he was as happy as he could be given the previous events. True, he had been separated from his family, but he was strong enough to live on. At the end of the glen, he found a good size tree to stretch out under. He found the bark too smooth to scratch his back. In fact, all of the trees had smooth bark. He did the best he could. Finally, he ripped off a few low branches, threw them on the ground and rolled around on top of them, sending innocent blades of grass for cover, puffy dust clouds high into the crisp air.

Deeper into the trees, a creature larger than Hugoth watched the cub's antics suspiciously, not knowing whether to be amused or frightened. The creature stood silently. "What is that?" He whispered to himself. "Kinda looks like a big, furry Gopher." The creature inched closer to Hugoth sniffing the air for fright as he moved forward. His father told him he could always smell fear. All he smelled now was damp, musty fur. "That thing doesn't smell like a Gopher, of course it doesn't smell like fear either." He was now close enough to Hugoth to reach out and pat him down.

Hugoth never noticed the large creature moving in on him; that was a sense he had yet to develop. Before he realized what was happening, something reached over his shoulder from behind him. It slapped him hard on the back, again and again and again. All over his back and sides, he was being swatted by some kind of thick fleshy branch. Every time he turned to see what it was, he would be swatted on the opposite side. This went on for an eternity in the cub's mind. The thing spoke to him, "What are you? Are you a giant Gopher?" Swat, slap, swat, it continued.

"Stop! What are you doing?" Hugoth spun around. He came face to face with his tormentor. The creature in front of him was bigger than he was! "What are you? You are huge!"

The larger creature continued to swat Hugoth. "I asked you first. What are you?" Swat, swat.

"I am a great Grizzly Bear cub! My name is Hugoth. What are you?"

In his deepest, scariest, voice the creature answered, "I am Bastony of the Dark Forest. I am called an Ellyphant. I must take you to my leader. Do not try to run away."

"Why would I try to run away? I have been looking for another creature to talk to. Where am I? What if I just walk away?"

Again the deep voice rumbled out of a relatively small mouth for such a large creature. "Do not try to walk away either...I will chase you down. I will trample you."

"Really? Are you trying to scare me?"

"Yes, I am. I am scaring you."

"No, you are not."

"Yes, I am. You are very scared. I can smell fear on you."

"No, you can't. I am not scared!"

"What is that I smell then Gopher?"

"I am not a Gopher. I am a Grizzly Bear, a great Grizzly Bear!"

"Okay great Grizzly Bear, follow me."

"Why!"

"Because, you are my captive. I must take you to my leader who is my father."

"I am not your captive!"

"Yes, you are..."

"No, I'm not..."

The low ominous voice ceased. A normally pitched voice continued,

"Fine, you are no fun. What are you doing here? You want to go exploring with me?"

Hugoth liked this new creature although he didn't know why. He pointed to the long leathery branch sticking out of the fellow's head, "Is that your nose?"

"Yes, it is. Have you never seen an Ellyphant before? Is that your ear?" He swatted at the top of Hugoth's head.

"No. Yes, it is my ear. Have you never seen a Grizzly Bear before?"

"No. Your kind don't run around these parts."

"You are a strange creature."

"You are too. Come on. I'll show you where I live. You hungry?"

"I am so hungry. I ate breakfast, but that was a long time ago. Were you born around here?"

"Yes I was, but I'm not from here. We were brought here."

"Why? From where?"

"Why? Who knows? From where? Far, far from here. All the way across the big, big, big water. Well actually, I was born here, but my parents, well they weren't born here."

"I guess we have a lot on common. I am not from here either. I don't know where I'm from. I suppose I am from somewhere way up river, way, way up river. Me and my twin were tossed over a cliff into the river while we were running away from some twos. I don't like twos. I don't know what happened to my mother. I hope she comes looking for us some day."

"Oh. Well, we don't look like each other at all, but do you want to be my brother? I don't think my parents will mind. There aren't a whole lot of us anyway. You are kinda small, but it may not matter that much."

"Kinda small? I've never been told that before!"

"Oh yes, you are definitely kinda small! How old are you?"

"I don't know...eight or nine bushels of days. Not a full year yet."

"Well that's younger than me. What is a bushel of days? I am two years old. You might be big enough if you keep growing."

"Well, I hope I do."

"Hope you do what?"

"I hope I keep growing."

"Me too, because you are kinda small."

"Stop saying that."

"Stop saying what?"

"That I am kinda small."

"Well, you are kinda small."

"Stop saying that."

"Okay, but you are."

"Well you have a big, long nose."

"Duh! I'm an Ellyphant and it is called a trunk!"

This banter would go on well into the late day. Bastony enjoyed the company of the Grizzly cub. He had never had anyone to share his explorations with. Hugoth was happy again, not as happy as before, but happy. That was a good thing.

\*\*\*

"Hemoth, wait here. I will send for you shortly. I have some explaining to do with the herd elders. It might take some time to explain to them why you are here. I don't want them to be unprepared for your arrival." The stag was not sure if Hemoth would be allowed to stay with the herd. If he could convince the elders that Hemoth could protect them from predators then maybe, however it would be a sensitive subject, especially with one of the elders.

"What about us? Should we stay with Hemoth or follow you in as we normally would?" The doe was determined to get Hemoth accepted into the herd. She figured her best move was to wait with the fawns. When called for she, the fawns and Hemoth would enter together for a show of support.

"I'm sure it would be better if you wait here with the young ones. You don't mind do you?"

"Certainly, we will wait together until you come back for us." The doe smiled.

"Oh great, now we have to wait? We want to introduce the giant Grizzly Bear tree cub to our friends. Hurry father, please?" The fawns knew they would be the center of attention and have full bragging rights for the rest of their days.

"Be patient, little ones. I will call for you soon." The stag left them. He headed straight to the after-lunch gathering of the elders. He hoped this would go well. He wasted no time once he offered the formal greetings.

"Good day to you, young sir." The stag was greeted warmly by each of the elders. "Where are my daughter and her young ones on this fine late day?"

"Good day to you too, Elder. She is just beyond the circle with the young ones. A few more tastes of berries to quiet them down."

"I could not agree more. Feed them often. They will grow to be fine yearlings."

"Yes sir, we agree. Uh, may I have all of your attention, Elders?"

"Of course you can. What is on your mind today? Have you been reconsidering our offer? You know we won't ask just any young stag to join the elders?" The questions were coming from everyone in the elder group, rapidly.

"I wish I could answer each of your questions and I will, just not today if you will allow me? My doe did something today that didn't completely surprise me. I do think it may come as a shock to each of you. We stumbled upon a juvenile orphaned creature today near the berry field. The poor creature just lost his mother and twin. He was very kind but distraught. Of course, my doe, being the nurturer that she is immediately took him in. Well…well…"

The elder in charge was not very patient. "Get on with it young one. What is it?"

Another elder, the oldest, added, "Now, nothing my daughter does surprises me anymore. Please, make your case."

"Very well, my doe," he turned to his Fawns' grandfather, "Your daughter adopted this young creature and brought him back with her, eh…with us. They are, like I said, just beyond the circle."

"Good heavens, what is that commotion to the south?" asked one of the elders. "Sounds like one of the herd has been attacked."

"Oh great." The stag shook his head. He knew exactly what was happening. Hemoth had been spotted by one of the more theatrical old does. This doe just happened to be the oldest daughter of the oldest elder. Never mated and not very nice, she had her own way of getting attention. This was going to be an absolute fiasco.

"Run, my friends, run! Scatter, protect yourselves! We have an intruder to the south." Here she came in all of her glory. Every eye in the herd glued to her antics. She played her audience perfectly. Running about, bucking, winking at the single stags, this was a captive audience and she knew it. Never mind the fact that the fawns and doe were standing unharmed at Hemoth's side; that did not matter right now. It did not matter one tiny little bit. "Run to save yourself. Run from this intruder!"

The fawns and Hemoth scanned the thick bush behind them frantically searching for the intruder. "Where is it, Mother? Where?"

"Don't fret young ones. She saw Hemoth. She is screaming her lungs out about Hemoth, not that she thinks he is attacking us, just because she can. That old doe, she has no idea how to attract a stag. This certainly won't do it. All of you come with me. Enough of this, I can't take her hysterics."

"Her what?" asked Hemoth.

The first fawn attempted to answer, "It's okay, Hemoth, sometimes mothers use big words."

"I think it should be called hersterics!" added the second fawn.

"Oh, I understand now. That was funny." Hemoth chuckled at the witty remark.

The doe turned to them. "That was very funny. Okay heads up, tails down, eyes bright and shiny. If you want to keep Hemoth as a brother we have to sell this alright?"

The fawns answered in unison, "Yes, Mother."

"Hemoth, walk right beside us, not faster, not slower, I mean right beside us. Keep your head down. If you look up you are likely to scare the whole herd. Try to make yourself smaller, if possible."

"Yes Ma'am."

The doe strutted into the clearing like she was leading a parade. At her side the fawns, beside them Hemoth. There was panic among the gathered members of the herd.

"Uh...that is the orphan I was telling you about, sir."

"Oh my!" The oldest elder could not hide the astonishment in his eyes or his entire body for that matter. "What kind of Bear is that? It is the biggest one I have ever seen!"

"Cub, did you say cub? How big does he plan to get? How old is he?" The elder stag was not upset in the least, he was however amazed. "I have no problem with the cub..." He paused speaking for effect and made eye contact with each younger elder. "As long as he doesn't eat one of us!" He laughed.

"He told us that he eats nothing but berries, fruits and swimmers."

"Swimmers? What is a swimmer? Oh, don't mind my ignorance. Bring him over here. I want to meet this great Grizzly Bear cub."

"Really, sir? You think it will be safe?"

"Absolutely, do you think any creature smaller than he will want to do us any harm with him patrolling our spaces? I think not. They won't know what he will or won't eat!" He nodded approvingly at the lead elder.

The remaining herd elders lined up to the right of Vladen, their newly selected leader. At the far end of the elders stood the doe's father, the oldest elder, grinning broader than any other Fallow Deer could. He was proud of his daughter and her stag. He raised her to accept those in need. He never qualified the specifics. She had felt comfortable with this cub so he was not one to argue the point. He trusted her explicitly. This trust paid off over and over with her.

The stag called his doe over. She in turn led the fawns and Hemoth. The closer he got, the more he towered over all of the Fallows. "Good mid-evening, Uncle Vladen. I would like you to meet

Hemoth. By his own description he is a great Grizzly Bear cub of eight or nine months old...we think."

"My good wishes to you as well Anessa." He looked up at Hemoth, "My gracious you are a big creature. You say you are called Hemoth? Is that correct?"

Hemoth bowed as low as he could. His mother raised him to be very respectful of his elders. "Yes sir. I am Hemoth. I am from a very long way up the river. I never knew where it was, because I never expected to leave it and my family behind."

"That is quite alright, Hemoth. It sounds to me like you have had quite a trying experience. Consider this your home now; we Fallows are your family."

"But sir, the hersterical Deer that we saw throwing a fit through the clearing, will she be okay with me?"

Vladen looked at Anessa with a puzzled look. She took the hint, "Hemoth, that was my sister. I told you she was dramatic."

"Your sister, oh my, I am sorry." Hemoth lowered his head.

"Oh, don't bother with her." Vladen giggled a little himself. At the other end of the line, Anessa's father just shook his head. "She is prone to that kind of behavior. You will get used to it. Just tell her how lovely she is. She will be fine...hersterical? I need to remember that. Enough of this pageantry, Hemoth. Anessa, introduce Hemoth to the rest of the elders then show him around."

For the next short click or so, Anessa worked the crowd to Hemoth's favor. She knew it would take time for him to remember all of the names and assured him that sir or ma'am would serve quite nicely. Lastly, she introduced him to her Father Adamir. He graciously welcomed Hemoth into the herd. He then gave Anessa a heart-warming nuzzle on her shoulder and clicked antlers with his daughter's stag. "I am very proud of you Bellon. I am very proud of both of you! I will take the fawns while you two show Hemoth around. Come little ones. Let's go get into some trouble!" The fawns turned to each other, bucked a couple of times and fell in line behind Adamir. They adored him as much as he adored them back.

The first fawn quickly looked up and asked. "Are you going to tell us more stories Adamir?"

"Adamir? Since when do either of you call me Adamir?"

The second fawn covered for the first, "Okay, I'm sorry, will you tell us more stories Grandfather, Adamir?"

"Yes, that is better. Why of course I am! What kind of grandfather would I be if I didn't tell my favorite fawns stories?"

"I told you so, Deakin!"

"So, Darley, what makes you so smart?"

Adamir slowly walked off smiling with the quibbling fawns at his heels.

\*\*\*

"So Ellyphant, what kind of exploring are we going to do?" Hugoth knew Bastony could never replace Hemoth, but at least he now had someone to talk and walk with. "You are a big and friendly creature, Ellyphant. How big are your parents? My Mother was really big too, once. We caught up to her fast though. I don't know if I will ever catch up with you."

"Shhh, Hugoth, we can't explore with all that talking."

"Why not? Are we trying to sneak up on something to explore?"

"No. Hmm, maybe we can talk and explore. I usually talk to myself in my head so I don't normally hear it with my ears. Instead, I listen for secret noises then I go explore them. I guess now that I have someone to explore with we can talk. Okay, it is okay to talk...but talk quietly, you know, whisper."

"You sure have big ears for an Ellyphant."

"Have you ever seen an Ellyphant?"

"Umm, no."

"Then how do you know my ears are bigger than other Ellyphant's ears?"

"Huh?"

"You said I have big ears. All Ellyphants have big ears...I think."

"What is that?" Hugoth stood on his back legs and pointed through the trees.

"Hey, I can do that too!" Bastony stood up on his back legs, again taller than Hugoth. "What is what?"

"Not what is what, what is that?" Hugoth pointed again.

"I can't see anything."

"Over there." Hugoth pointed again.

"Oh that? Hmm, I don't know. Let's go explore it. Be very quiet."

"Okay." Hugoth led the way.

\*\*\*

Soon it was time to head back to Bastony's dwelling. "My Poppa's going to be so mad at me if we don't make it back before the moon comes out, Hugoth, we better hurry. Bet you can't beat me back."

"I could beat you back if I knew where we were going!"

The sight of these two new friends blazing a path was a humorous sight. There was no sneaking up on anything. There were no quiet footsteps. Wherever they traveled an immediate path was laid behind them. They never found many obstacles they couldn't move, trample or plod through. The innocence projected with their intuitive young actions was endearing to all who witnessed the playful interminglings they shared daily. That day and years following passed too quickly for Hugoth.

Bastony's father was a medium sized Ellyphant with long graceful tusks emerging beneath a solemn, but otherwise, intelligent and weary face. His mother was strangely absent. His father spent his days alone, walking back and forth on a trail that now lay bare of anything but solid stone; the soil and vegetation worn away by heavy footfalls of thick, muscular feet over the past two Ellyphant years. Bastone was a sad creature. He was a single father to Bastony. No other Ellyphants to keep him company, he walked the path over and over again, hoping that one day his lovely matriarch would once again take her place beside him for their daily walks. His family group was once he and Bastony's mother, now it was he and Bastony. His head hung low, his trunk worn raw by a constant dragging across the hard path. The only hint shown at happiness was the sight of their lone son bumbling his way to his side every evening before the last meal of the day. It was hard on Bastony to carry the burden of providing his father's only rays of hope; still he did the best he could. Bastony was young, very young. He had his life to attend to. Bastone knew that and accepted it the best a lonely father could. Where the matriarch went when she left was not known. What was known was that she never returned either by her own will, a sudden illness or, as Bastone always reasoned, great harm brought to her by a hardened creature like the ones who brought them to this place from their home only to abandon them during a wet season several years earlier. Back then the two would have done anything to escape the mundane life they were assigned, but now? Now Bastone would prefer that life to his life now. At least back then there were others to socialize with.

He loved Bastony, but he needed his matriarch. He needed her desperately.

"Poppa, I brought us a new friend!" Bastony came trotting up the path with Hugoth in tow. "I know he is small, but he is a Grizzly Bear cub! Can he stay with us Poppa, please, please...?"

Bastone raised his head, eyes twinkling at the sight of his son. He shifted his spirits into caring parent mode and out of despondent lonely mode. "What have we here, young Ellyphant? Have you found yourself a play partner?"

"Yes Poppa, he is called Hugoth. It kind of sounds like huge, even though he is little, but he is friendly and we went exploring way into the jungle today."

"Hugoth, it is my pleasure to meet you." Bastone extended his trunk towards Hugoth, lightly patting him on the head.

"Thank you, Sir Poppa." Hugoth was staring at Bastone's long tusks in awe. "Are those your teeth?"

Bastony looked at Hugoth with shock. "Teeth? No they are tusks! I have some, but you can't see them yet. They are still inside my head. But, one day they will be like Poppa's and I can shake trees with them!"

"You have teeth too?" Hugoth had never encountered a full grown Ellyphant before. He had lots of questions.

"Of course I do, Hugoth. You have lots of questions little Grizzly Bear. Walk with us. We will talk more while we eat." Bastone's eyes twinkled a little bit brighter. He was happy his son now had someone almost his size to take on his daily safaris. "I can assume you eat, correct?"

"Oh yes sir, I eat. I love to eat."

"Well that is wonderful Hugoth. I have lots of questions for you." Bastone led the two youngsters down the path. As is customary with Ellyphants, Bastony grabbed Bastone's tail with his trunk. Hugoth chose to forego that Ellyphant custom. He decided to simply follow at a close distance.

"Is there anything we should be afraid of around here?" Hugoth asked. "Are there creatures here bigger than us?"

"No there is not. We are the biggest creatures anywhere near here," answered Bastony. "Poppa says there are bigger creatures where he is from."

"Is that right, sir? There are creatures bigger than you where you come from?" Hugoth was not sure if he could believe that.

"Yes Hugoth, there is one creature in particular that is much, much taller than I. They eat from the tops of tall trees. I can only reach near the middle of the same trees."

"Wow, they must be very tall."

"They certainly are Hugoth, indeed."

"I think my mother went back to where she came from. I haven't seen her since I was born." Bastony had no reason to think otherwise, Poppa did.

The trio traveled down the path with the young creatures peppering Bastone with question after question. This turn of events, for the time being, was helping him forget the sadness of the past. The loss of his mate, the uncertainty of raising a young son to adulthood alone, so many times he desperately wanted her to return. The bull of his kind normally left the raising of the young to the mothers. This was not an option for Bastone. Whatever he was doing, he was doing it right. Bastony was a lot like his mother. He had her smaller ears along with her keen common sense. She never worried. She always looked forward to life in general. She never had a bad day. Bastone on the other hand did worry; he over-thought every turn in the road and he had lots of bad days. She said one day she would return, so far; she had not.

"Poppa, Poppa. We are here." Bastony was already eating. His trunk was stuck as high into a tree as he could reach. He was using his trunk to pull off small branches heavily laden with a fruit Hugoth had never seen before.

Bastone shook the bad ideas from his head. "I'm sorry. My thoughts escaped me for a time. We are here indeed. Eat up Hugoth. You do eat fruits, don't you?"

"Uh, yes...I think I do. What are these things?"

"Good." Bastony said while chewing a mouthful of the soft fruits.

"Good what?" Hugoth wasn't sure if Bastony was answering his question or mumbling to himself.

"You, you asked what, (more chewing) what (more chewing) these were. I said (more chewing) good. Ahem, these fruits...are... good. Try one!"

Hugoth picked up one of the yellow fruits with his paw to study it. "Hmm, I guess it looks good enough to eat. What are they called?"

Bastony was trying to eat his fill. "Does it matter? We call them food. Just eat it!"

"Okay! My, you're a little testy when you are eating." Hugoth chuckled to himself and did as he was told. He threw the whole fruit into his mouth, bit clean through it then spit it all out on the ground. "That tastes terrible!" Hugoth was spitting every small piece of his mistake onto the ground as quickly as possible. He failed to rid the taste from his mouth.

Bastone trotted to Hugoth's side. "Bastony, did you tell Hugoth to only eat the soft ones?"

"Uh...(chewing) maybe not Poppa. But you didn't tell me not to eat the crunchy ones either...(more chewing) remember?"

"Yes I remember, but Hugoth is our guest."

"Oh yes and I was just your son. Very well, my fault it is. Hugoth, don't eat the crunchy ones, they taste really bad!" Bastony grabbed a few loaded branches and tossed them in front of Hugoth. "These are ripe, Hugoth. Try them again." Bastony hurriedly resumed eating.

"I don't know if I want to eat another one of those!" Hugoth was not convinced.

Bastone lifted one of the loaded branches up with his trunk. He swished it in his mouth to take a couple from the cluster. He began chewing them in his mouth and held the branch closer to Hugoth. "Try one of these, Hugoth. I assure you, you will like the taste. If not, we will find you something else to try."

"Okay, I'm going to try it." Hugoth picked another one up. While holding it in one paw he gently poked it with the other. He noticed how much softer this one was than the one he tried earlier. It was almost squishy, it was so soft. He carefully placed the entire fruit in his mouth. He very slowly bit it. He was astonished and pleased with the taste difference. "My, these are good. These are very, very good." With that he began eating as many of the softest ones he could find. They ate for at least a good, long, satisfying click.

*** 

Hemoth trailed along with Bellon and Anessa for the better part of the late midday. He was warmly accepted by the entire herd, even Anessa's hersterical sister calmed down once she met him.

Bellon walked gracefully around the perimeter of the Fallow's clearing. Anessa left them to go make a bed for Hemoth. "Well great

Grizzly Bear cub, now you are an honored member of our herd of Fallow Deer. Our ways will be strange to you. Don't lose your natural Grizzly ways. If we don't see eye to eye, have a talk with us. Don't let us confuse who you are to yourself. It will be easy for you to take to our ways even though you are completely different in every way from our type. From time to time the elders or I will send you out to reconnect with yourself. These will be trying times for you if you lose too much of the Bear in you. We will discuss this later, but remember every one of us have your best in mind. We are Deer. We are not Bear. Listen to us. Pay attention to what we say. We will teach you as best we can."

Hemoth gazed down at the wise stag. Suddenly, the Grizzly cub began heaving uncontrollably. Gigantic tears rolled down his furry cheeks like small rivers. The sobs were loud and passionate. He fell backward on his hind legs as they crumbled beneath him. His forelegs lost all strength and they too crumpled. The great Grizzly Bear cub lay flat to the ground, crying tears long overdue. Bellon watched in agony as the cub's huge sides bellowed with sorrow heaped upon his shoulders. The time had come when all of the past days worth of loneliness suffocated the young Grizzly's world. He was alone now. No mother to nurture him, no brother to play with him; a large Bear in a small Deer's domain. Now the finality of the moment set in on him. More than likely, his mother would never find him and more than likely he would never see his twin Hugoth again. If not for the motherly instincts of Anessa, he would be roaming the wilderness upset with no one to comfort him. He was, after all, not even a complete year old. The other Deer heard the painful moan. Anessa rushed to his side. She silently slid by Bellon, kneeled on her front elbows and nuzzled into Hemoth's thick neck blanket of fur. She cried with him. She did not speak, none of those gathered did. This was Hemoth's moment. They were there for him. Quietly, each of the elders took a place surrounding the young Bear forming a circle, each with their head held high, antlers pointing to the sky. Adamir, with the fawns still at his heels, was the last elder to take position.

"Why is he crying Grandfather?" The fawns were very upset. "Is he hurt?"

"Yes, he is hurt." Adamir clearly stated for all to hear. "He is hurt. He will continue to release his feelings. We will stand here in this circle at his side until the last tear rolls down his face. That is what we do. He is ours now. He has nowhere else to go, nowhere else to turn. That will be enough talking."

Anessa looked up for a short fleeting glance. She took in the wisdom and hurt in each of the elder's eyes. She was always amazed at the character these creatures presented. They accepted Hemoth as one of their own with no questions asked. There was not a dry eye in the clearing. Every member of the herd was in attendance or on their way. She adored each of them. Bellon stood proudly in front of his new son. He couldn't be more in love with the cub's adopted mother.

The poor Grizzly cried himself to sleep protected in the circle. The young Deer lay down where they stood and slept. The mothers each made plans to gather food for Hemoth the following day. The stags and elders never once made any attempt to do anything but stand attentively in respect for Hemoth. The crying eventually subsided only to be replaced with what the Fallow believed to be sleeping mind dangers which caused more agony inside the thoughts of Hemoth. That too eventually faded away. Hemoth awoke emotionally and physically drained at the next sunrise. When he opened his puffy eyelids, he saw each and every member of the Fallow herd standing guard over him, Anessa still nuzzling his neck. The Fallow remained silent. If Hemoth wanted to talk then he would begin the conversation when he felt the need. The silence was loud in the clearing that morning. Hemoth was forever changed by the emotional blood letting and even more so by the unerring faithfulness of his new family. Dry tears began rolling down his cheeks again.

\*\*\*

Hugoth ate as much as the two Ellyphants combined. For a short time the two larger creatures rested from eating just to watch the Grizzly cub gorge himself. They figured at one point he would have enough. Much to their amazement the cub ate and ate and ate some more. Just when it seemed he was slowing down he got a second, third and fourth wind. He ate until he could reach no higher in the tree. He looked to both sides, only to see more trees heavily weighed down by the tantalizing fruits.

"Hugoth, do you think maybe you have had enough to eat, at least until we walk further down the path?" Bastone felt he needed to slow down the cub's ravenous proceeding. What they had not mentioned to Hugoth would be clear very soon. If a creature eats too many of the persimmons, one's stomach could quite possibly rebel against the eater. The Ellyphants ate the persimmons as part of varied diet. The next course waited a short walk further down the path. Hugoth had not known that. Very soon he would wish he did.

"Hugoth, there is more to eat yet. I think you are gonna explode!" No sooner than Bastony finished his warning, Hugoth felt a rumbling deep within, way down in his gut.

"Explode? What do you mean Basto, Baston..." That was as far as Hugoth got. Out of the blue, the rumbling in his stomach burst forth from below, seeking a way out of the Grizzly. Hugoth moved quickly behind some tall grass, the persimmons were attacking with the same gusto Hugoth showed them. It wasn't a pretty sight. The two Ellyphants were glad they had not witnessed the persimmons' retaliation. Hugoth emerged from the tall grass exhausted. He looked at Bastone, "Is there something else we can eat? I'm hungry all over again."

Bastone lifted his trunk. He pointed down the path. "Follow us, Hugoth. There is something down the path which will be easier on your belly; just don't eat as much."

Bastony blew a loud honk out of his trunk. "This way young creature!"

Bastony followed closely behind Poppa. He laughed all the way down the path. Hugoth followed Bastony. He was curious. Had he liked the persimmons too much or had the persimmons not liked him? "Maybe on another day, fruit. Maybe on another day, I will beat you and you will stay in my belly. I only hope that day does not come too soon. Bastony, what are we eating next?"

"You will soon see, Hugoth. These are my favorite!" Bastony could not wait.

Very soon Hugoth noticed a large area of tall thick stalks of a strange grass growing as far as his eyes could see. As they moved closer to the stalks, Hugoth noticed how tall each stalk actually was. "Wow! That grass is tall!" Hugoth was excited to see new things. He had never seen grass like this before.

Bastony trotted into the tall stalks and ripped a few of them up with his trunk. "Hey Hugoth come over here! You have to try these!"

Hugoth was feeling a little better, but not good enough to run to Bastony's side. When he finally arrived, the young Ellyphant tossed some grass stalks to him. The curious Bear swatted them down with his paws. "How do I eat these?" he asked.

Immediately, Bastone answered that question. "You eat these very slowly, cub, very slowly. They taste very sweet so you may want to eat them as fast as you ate the persimmons, but you know how that turned out. Do you understand what I am trying to say, Hugoth?"

"Yes sir, I do. I will eat slowly. I will not stuff myself like I did last time. I will never get full before sun time if the food doesn't stay in my belly."

"Good, you have learned a valuable lesson. If you want to grow up strong, you have to eat your food in moderation. You can eat a lot, just not all at the same time. I will teach you all that I know. Look at Bastony, he is getting big and he eats less than you at one time, but he eats all day long!" He proudly turned to give his son a pat on the head. "Right, Ellyphant?"

"Yes Poppa, all day long!"

Hugoth broke a few of the stalks. Carefully nudging them around with his nose, he made sure they were not going to try to eat him back after he ate them. He took a bite. To his surprise, the stalks tasted even better than the fruit. "I like these more than the fruit! What do you call them?"

Bastony answered between bites. "Sweet stalks."

"Sweet stalks? That's it?"

"Yep. Sweet stalks."

"Hmm, sweet stalks it is." Hugoth took a seat amid the uprooted stalks to continue eating. He ate each stalk slowly, chewing them until the last drop of sweetness was coaxed from each one. This time, much to Bastone's satisfaction, Hugoth failed to fill his belly completely to the top.

"Are you little ones ready to move on?" Bastone was ready to head back to their dwelling. Dark was arriving soon. He disliked the darkness. The darkness is when Bastony's mother left. Somehow he couldn't let go of that.

## 23

**M**ystic smiled, "Hemoth, your brother seems a lot like you. He has the same gentle manner and fierce loyalty. You both seem to have a heart for others nearly as big as your chests. The fact that you are mirror images of each other is only part of it."

Lightning commented, "He favors his left paw if that makes any difference."

Hemoth raised his right paw, "This is my dominant side."

"Until we get to know you better, that's about all we can say. We have to get you two back together, although you each have fared very well by yourselves."

The questions and answer session went on for quite a while. It only stopped when Madaliene made her reappearance among them. This time she was Madaliene again. The gown, the tiara, the fancy shoes and the styled hair were missing. She was a stunningly beautiful girl. She now wore flat soled riding boots, dark purple riding pants and a loose comfortable shirt. Her mane of curls flowed freely around her shoulders.

"Hey, I'm back. I hope my wardrobe is not too casual for all of you."

Hemoth quickly answered, "Now you look like the girl I know."

"I think I like this look better. But you know, once a princess...always a princess. I don't understand why Gamma did not hide it from any of you."

Hemoth smiled at her, "Madaliene my dear, had any of these creatures tried any deplorable acts like kidnapping or if they attempted to kill you or the old ones, they would have never made it out of this mountain. It was not a needed secret in here. Now you don't need to go prancing down the lane looking like you did. That might draw some unwanted attention."

"I suppose you're right Hemoth."

Gamma re-entered the room wearing attire much the same as Madaliene except her riding boots were brown, pants dark blue. "I see we have dressed alike again. Something on your mind young Princess?"

"I need to get out of here!"

"I think that will be taken care of very soon, or as soon as your grandfather awakens."

She turned to Mystic, "Can you take Madaliene back to Nuorg with you? I feel she needs to begin there if she wants to find Evaliene. There is some connection, but since I have never been, I have no way of knowing for sure."

Mystic pondered the question for a moment. "I think I can do that. We shouldn't all go. What else is on your mind, if I may ask?"

Gamma took a seat again, only this time in Gann's chair. "Where do I start? The letter from Evaliene was written under duress. Gann and I need to know how severe. Is she still alive? How did whoever made her write it find out about her? How did they track her down when we don't even know where she is! What do they want from her? Are they coming after us next? You see Mystic there is a lot on my mind. I can only tackle one thing at a time. Our story is complex. We have alienated a lot of people for a lot of different reasons. The main reason is that we don't play favorites. There is no gray area in our decision making. If it's right, it's right and if it's wrong, well...it's wrong. Those we served were well taken care of. Royalty has its place. We foresaw serious problems ahead. We disappeared in order to return to prominence once the wrongdoers had run their course. We assumed the people would revolt, hence our cue to return. That never happened with most of the world. The people were swallowed up by snake oil salesmen masquerading as great leaders."

"Where was your kingdom if I may ask?"

"Everywhere, we ruled everywhere. Every small corner of this earth was under our dominion. I know it sounds very boastful and it may be, however, our family was in total control. We had our assistants, our aides if you will, to govern different places, but our family was the main ruling authority. Maybe the world got too big for us, who knows for sure? There came a time when we met more opposition from more areas than we could tolerate. Death threats were the least of our problems. Now, here we are. The Terrible Years have come and gone just as we thought. Now it seems they are coming around again and there is no need for that to happen. The evil must be found and rooted out. That is what we plan to have your group help us with. It's our time to shine once again." As she spoke, Frederick could not help but be drawn back to her wrists and her shiny bracelets.

Silently, without much emotion, Frederick jotted in his notes. "Dominion? That sounds somewhat out of character."

The Cheetah listened closely to every word spoken so passionately by Gamma. "I know what you are saying, but when you say "the evil must be rooted out"? How and by what means do you think that could actually occur? Evil has been around since this world started to spin. Can you not qualify that statement where it would be more realistic?"

Lightning was listening to every word, "Excuse me, the world spins?"

"Yes Lightning, it spins." Mystic sometimes wondered if Lightning ever really listened. Vincen had been over the phenomenon with them long ago.

"I hear the reservation in your voice, Bubba. However, you did hear me correctly. Now I'm not saying it will ever happen, but should that small detail prevent us from trying?"

Mystic cleared his throat, "Ahem, Gamma how can your saying that explain why you and Gann have been holed up in this mountain? Wouldn't it have been a better plan to be out in the world eradicating evil intentions wherever they lie and whenever they began?"

"My, I have never met such a uniquely gifted group of four-leggers as you. You think more deeply and speak more intelligently than I can imagine most of my old friends comprehending. You must have wonderful teachers!"

"Yes we have," Mystic said with pride gleaming. "I only hope you will meet Vincen. He was my teacher of record. My parents were taken very early in my life. Bubba's mother and father were intellectually gifted as well. He comes from a very different world than either Lightning or me."

Gamma continued with a growing admiration for her guests. "Yes, I would imagine he does. One thing you can't deny is teaching from wonderfully talented teachers. But, you need to be aware, some intelligence can be misdirected. Sometimes intelligence has a way of skewing every truth any way it wants. Too much intelligence is sometimes a bad thing. It can make you start questioning your innate feelings, even questioning your beliefs in certain things you believe but can't see."

"Oh yes, Bubba can talk about that for days." Mystic threw an inquisitive glance at the Cat.

Frederick stirred, "Gamma, I think you are onto something here. I must admit I was drifting off a bit, but I think we may be on to something. Bubba, what did the winger say to you as she approached you the final time?"

"Beware of the intelligents. Why?"

Frederick peered at his notes. "Perrie, you were dropped here by a large winger. Am I correct?"

Perrie became active. She swooped into the circle of Talkers. "Yes sir, you are correct. It was a gigantic winger with white patches under enormous wings. Quite frightening and calming, if there can be both in one creature."

"What did it say? Can you remember word for word?"

"No, I don't remember much. I do remember that nothing was said for the longest period of time. It told me to stay where I was dropped." She twitched her eyes, "They would find me...and...and...yes! It said beware of the intelligents."

"That is very coincidental is it not?" Frederick looked directly to Gamma. "Both of these attackees were told the very same, very short sentence. I consider it to be a warning of some nature, do you?"

"I suppose it could be, Frederick. But then again, everything can be a warning if taken the wrong way. I must check on Gann, he has been out for some time now." She excused herself, leaving the rest to talk amongst themselves. She stole a glance over her shoulder as she made her way to Gann's side. She found him as she left him, out cold or at least she thought.

"What have you found out, lovely wife?" Gann moved no noticeable muscles apart from those required to speak.

Gamma whispered back, "Lots. They are a wise group, more intelligent than we thought. We should have never given up studying the creatures. Whoever said that people would dominate the world was badly mistaken. And Frederick, I think he is getting curious."

"What about Hemoth or Madaliene? Do they suspect anything?"

"No, I don't think so. What about the Staff? Is it one of the four?"

"Look at me, woman! I just barely brushed the edge of one page and it nearly killed me."

"Do you think that gave anything away?"

"Who knows? No one ever told us that would happen."

"How come it doesn't affect Frederick just as it did you?"

"Maybe because he is not like us. If I remember correctly he is a Mounte or did he say? All I know for sure is we can't even think about touching the innards of that thing again. It will kill me for sure next time."

"Fine, we won't try it again. That means we have to keep them alive longer. Until we get some help, Frederick will stay among the living."

"What about the rest of them?

Gamma smiled at her husband lying stretched out on the scattered cushions, "This is a very big mountain. I'm absolutely sure each of them will find their way into a room they may not get out of."

"Even Hemoth? We know nothing of him."

"Even Hemoth."

Frederick watched Gann and Gamma openly. He was not worried about getting caught. He could not help but wonder why the Staff papers had reacted so violently with Gann. He had not been affected with the same intensity. He noticed the one-sided conversation taking place. If he was correct, Gann was conversing with Gamma and was not concealing it very well. Frederick motioned for Mystic's attention. He slid all of the papers back into the Staff and sealed it tightly. Mystic eyed him with interest.

"Mystic, do not let this out of your possession again. Do you understand?"

The Great Wolf gazed back at the two-legger, "What is going on here Frederick?"

"That my friend will be revealed soon enough. Get ready to roll the globe on my cue."

"What? It's not even glowing."

"Trust me, it will be."

"I can't see it."

Frederick bent down to look Mystic in the eye. "Again, trust me Mystic, on my cue. No more questions…got it?"

Mystic nodded. "I'll watch you closely."

"Good. Things are about to get interesting."

Frederick peeked as Gamma helped Gann to his feet, continuing their conversation. She carefully steadied him as they limped back to the group.

Bubba was nearly asleep at Lightning's side. "So you survived, did you? You gave us all quite a scare."

Madaliene rushed to Gann's weak side to help Gamma. "If you ever do anything that insane again, sir, you will have me to deal with directly. Gamma may be too old to discipline you accordingly, but I still can." She grinned.

Frederick watched the play with concern.

Gamma sat Gann down in his chair then stood behind him. "Well, now that all of the drama is over, I need each or your unwavering attention. We have a small detail to share with you that we may have omitted in our earlier discussions. When we were talking about who we were, Gann and I, none of you caught on, which will make our next move easier for us. We are not who you think we are..."

Frederick instantly jumped to their side, raised rapier in one hand, the other hand thrust into his bag now slung over his back. "I know who you are and I have been waiting for this opportunity since I first met you. Enough with these four-leggers! I am tired of them second guessing my every move." He rushed first to Mystic, who stood stunned at the sudden change of demeanor in the older two-leggers. "You first Wolf, Prince of the Great Forest. Come to terms with this!" Frederick jumped in front of the Great Wolf with his back to Gamma and Gann. With both hands, he thrust the blade into Mystic's side, once, twice and a third time for good measure. A steady flow of thick red liquid covered the blade. Before another creature could react, Frederick had pierced Bubba and Lightning multiple times with more red liquid dripping from the blade to the cavern floor. All of them went down in silent heaps. The darkness of the room cast a morbid pall on the inert bodies lying at Frederick's feet. He raised the blade in victory. "My, that felt good. Gamma, should I do away with the Grizzly and the girl as well? I am at your service."

Hemoth immediately got between Madaliene and Frederick. "I will cut you in half with one swipe of my paw, Frederick. I suggest you make your final run for the door. You will never take this child as long as I am breathing."

Madaliene cowered behind the Bear's massive flank, tears pulsing from her eyes. "No, this can't be happening..."

Gamma and Gann smiled grins of triumph. The role they played all of these years was reaching another milestone. Gamma pulled a bow and arrow from the back of Gann's chair. "That won't be necessary, Frederick. I will take care of Hemoth with my own arrow. The girl will have to be dealt with later. We still need her." Gamma fitted her arrow. She pulled hard on the bow string. It was aimed at a soft spot between Hemoth's wide shoulders.

Frederick made a huge production of walking around the bodies, positioning himself in the arrow's flight path as he gestured madly about. "Now we will finally have the Staff and the globe to ourselves. We will return the rightful Hewitt's to power all across this world. The weak have had their time. It has amounted to nothing but sniveling and cowardice for years. The Hewitt name must again take its rightful place. We must make our move now! It is our time!"

A screeching, etching sound followed a rolling, eerily transparent ball as it made its way into the center of the crowd, halting the rantings of Frederick and the gloating of Gamma and Gann. All in attendance watched in silence as the globe rolled to a perfect stop. Gamma and Gann looked in complete surprise at each other, mouths agape. A brilliant flash of light exploded from the ball, blinding all seeing eyes. A complete hush fell on the mountain. In the midst of the silence, very faint echoes of short, mournful screams floated into nothing. The mountain relaxed. Every creature in the chamber remained flat on the floor, remnants of the light melting from their bodies and still clinging to the walls. A calming iridescent glimmer sat quietly by, enveloping the shadows, adding a sparkling afterthought to each inanimate object. As each body began to slowly rise from the floor, all eyes searched for Frederick. He was found with his back propped against the over stuffed-chair where Gann had once been sitting.

"So you knew?" Mystic asked.

"When did you know?" Bubba followed.

"How did you know?" Lightning quizzed.

"What was that?" Hemoth begged.

"What just happened? Where are my grandparents?" Madaliene asked.

Frederick twirled the rapier around in one hand while he wiped the gooey, dark fruit juice from the blade. "I don't really know, Mystic. Some things you sense more than you know. Bubba, Gamma dropped a few words here and there...they were spoken from jealously not devotion to her granddaughter. Lightning, Gamma talked like a scorned, spoiled lover, not a doting queen or devoted grandmother. Gann was her side-kick. Hemoth, who were those people? Madaliene, how long have they been here?"

Madaliene answered now through mysteriously tearless eyes. "As long as I have been here, they have been my grandparents. Were they imposters? If so, I don't guess I ever knew my real Gann and Gamma. I'm only 16 years old, they say. I have no idea when the switch was made."

"How about you, Hemoth? You know anything about this? I hope you know you were set up to die along with the rest of us."

Hemoth sighed, "It all seems too well-planned to be fake. My concern now is why was this fortress built? Is it to aid the good fight or the bad fight? Should we soon expect others coming to populate Gamma and Gann's position? What now?"

Frederick rose to his feet. He walked around the room, rubbing his hands around his face, searching the floor for something in particular. He saw it. "We need Sig's opinion on this matter. He has been here the entire time. What have you to say, Falcon?" Frederick bent to the floor and picked up a jeweled bracelet, the same bracelet previously worn by Gamma. He reached into his pocket and pulled out a necklace to match. "Princess, I believe these are yours."

"They are?" Madaliene took the necklace and bracelet from Frederick. "Where did you find this?" She held the necklace in front of her.

"That, I found with your real grandmother."

Perrie sat cowering in a harbored nook. She was having trouble comprehending the previous event. "Uh Frederick, Sig is not here. He was close beside me just before the explosion of light. He must have flown off."

The tears welled in Madaliene's eyes and she heaved sincerely. "Not Sig. Please tell me he was not involved with this deception. My entire life has been role play for others." She fell back to the floor.

Lightning was at her side immediately with Hemoth. She was dwarfed by the size of the two Grizzlies. Her small proud frame looked tiny and hopeless between the two large four-leggers. The Bears sat silently at her side, looking to Frederick for some wise words.

He had none. This experience was becoming more intriguing with each passing moment. "Madaliene, I hate to do this to you. I hate to ask you these questions now but I must. What all do you know of this mountain fortress? Do you know if there are any documents detailing any of the rooms, armaments or mazes? I can't believe that those two had anything to do with its construction. This is much bigger than either of them."

"I know everything there is to know about this place. There are places they forbade me to go, but I went anyway. Gamma steered me one way while Gann would steer me another. Who were they and where are my true grandparents?"

A pall came over Frederick's face that was even noticeable in the dim light. "I think I have seen them before, in the cellar. I can't say for sure, it was horrible. I can't and won't explain it or describe what I saw to anyone...ever. Just know that the end of their lives was horrific." He sat down as the sickening memory weakened him.

"What do we do now?" Hemoth asked. "It is hard to believe Sig was in on this."

Mystic gathered the globe and placed it back on the Staff with an adept use of his snout combined with both front paws. He managed to slide it back in the holster which garnered much admiration from the group. "Nuorg?"

Frederick nodded in agreement. "Nuorg."

Hemoth was visibly giddy at this news. "Who besides me is going?" His inclusion in the trip to Nuorg was not open for debate. He was going!

Frederick leaned over, put his elbows on his knees and twiddled his thumbs. He took a few deep breaths. "Mystic, we need you and the Staff here. Perrie, you are so young, but you are the only winger we have at our service. You must stay with me and Mystic. Bubba, you must stay with us as well. Lightning, I think you and Hemoth should escort our young princess to Nuorg. Your ax-pike should be able to get you to a window with no trouble or extra work on your part."

A fluttering noise came from the pantry. "What was that?" Bubba asked.

"What do you mean the only winger you have left?" Sig flew in, carrying a thick, rolled up scroll containing several pages of documents. He lit on the arm of Frederick's chair. "Frederick, I believe you asked for this?"

Perrie was elated. "Sig! I thought you were gone! When did you leave the room?"

"I flew to the lowers as soon as I could. That is not the first time I have seen that globe roll. Go ahead, Frederick. Run me through with the rapier to prove it." The others looked at Sig with equal doubt and belief. Sig couldn't help but notice the look in their eyes. "Frederick! I demand you run me through with the rapier! Don't let me sit here in shame."

"Fine!" Frederick turned to the Falcon and with one smooth move, handled the rapier and stuck it all the way through the winger's body.

Sig never twitched a feather. He perched satisfied. "Now, is all doubt erased?"

"Well I'll be." Madaliene was overjoyed. "Did you know of the impersonations?"

Sig nodded, "Yes, I did. It was hard not to."

"Really? Then, I think I will kill you myself." She reached out to strangle the surprised Falcon. "I can't believe you hid that from me all of these years! Did you not trust me?"

"Please, could someone restrain her? She seems a bit perturbed!"

"Perturbed? I will show you how perturbed a young princess can get!" She lunged at him again.

Sig sidled closer to Frederick. "Uh Frederick, Hemoth? Someone get a hold of her. I have seen this streak in her before."

"Why did you not tell me Sig?"

"I was told not to. Please control yourself!"

"By who?"

"By me." Hemoth laid a huge paw on her shoulder. "I told him not to tell you."

"Oh mercy." Lightning sank to the ground.

"And the riddles just keep on coming." Bubba sank to the ground with Lightning.

Frederick tapped Hemoth on the flank with the rapier, pushing it well past the Grizzly's thick fur. "You did? Hmmph."

Mystic flopped onto his back legs. "Okay, story time..."

Hemoth roared a huge laugh. "Story time? I guess it is. Understand there is much of your story I need to hear also."

Sig seemed to have his feelings hurt. "What about these documents I just delivered? Is that not worthy of a thank you very much or something?"

"Sig, I told you to get those," Hemoth stated.

"But you told me that years ago. I thought it pretty self-starting to take it on my own to do it when I did."

"Yes Sig, it was. Very self-starting. An exhibition of brains and cunning unknown to any winger, I might add."

"Okay, now you are pushing it, Bear."

"Maybe." Hemoth shrugged.

"Years ago?" asked Madaliene.

Hemoth nodded, "Many, many years ago. I was a late secret-sharer with many of the original group who conceived this fortress. I am the Keeper of this place. I know almost all there is to know here. I vacated it when the switch was made. The real Gamma and Gann were ambushed and taken prisoner at the lake before Madaliene was born. I found out about it too late to do anything. They were tortured, forced to reveal the entrance and many other secrets, then taken away. There was nothing I could do to stop it. I was following another directive at the time. I had to leave."

Frederick was, again, resting his elbows on his knees. This time his head was cradled in his hands as he slowly rocked back and forth. "Okay, stop talking for a minute. I must start taking notes. Geesh, this is getting very complicated. Anyone hungry? I'm sure it is dark outside and we need to eat. What do you say Hemoth? Can we gather at the big table, set out a nice meal and eat while you entertain us with your story?"

"That sounds like an excellent idea, Frederick."

"I'll second that," Lightning added.

"Sig, if you would be so kind, please take your scroll to the table. Perrie, help Madaliene prepare some platters of food." Frederick gathered his notes together.

"Are you saying that just because we are the only females here?" Madaliene stood her ground.

"No, not really. Let's see a show of hands everyone." The creatures looked at him curiously. "Hmmph, it looks to me, Madaliene, that you and I are the only ones with hands here and mine are full and ignorant of your stores. What do you suggest?"

"Oh...whatever...come on Perrie." The Princess and the Falcon did as Frederick suggested.

Before long, the dining table was over-loaded with every type of edible in the pantry. Pitchers and basins were filled to the brims with juices, water and well-aged honey ales. Piles of nuts, fruits, dried berries and vegetables were placed neatly on the table. Lightning sat on the floor at one end while Hemoth took up the other. Madaliene and Frederick used two chairs while the remaining ones were moved away to allow space for Bubba and Mystic. The smaller four-leggers rounded up stools to sit on as Hemoth began his story.

"There are four staffs. There is the Staff of Hewitt, which Mystic has been chosen to bear. There is the Staff of O'shay, which Evaliene had in her possession the last we knew of her. There is the Staff of Polinetti, location unknown, and the Staff of Equakembo, whose location is also unknown. These staffs were made and sent to the four corners of the world. We know today that was metaphorically speaking, of course. Within each staff are the instructions on its use, various information, secrets and many other notes compiled throughout years and years of life."

Mystic raised a paw, "So, Hemoth, if there exists three more staffs, what power does each one have?"

Frederick was furiously attempting to keep up with his notes.

"I'm afraid we don't know the answer to that question, Mystic. That is why my association is struggling so much to contain all of the craziness going on out there right now. We don't know what to prepare for. I heard stories of your Staff, never believed them until today. Sig actually witnessed its magnificent workings a long, long time ago. He knew it was the one he saw those many years ago the minute he laid eyes on it. How it came to you is yet another mystery we don't need the answer for. The staffs choose who they want, our task is not to reason why. The odd part is the story tells us all of the staffs are not necessarily staffs. They are collectively called staffs, though they do not all resemble Mystic's. The others could be anything."

"Hemoth, do they all have the abilities this one does?"

"No Mystic, they do not. The one in your possession is the first one crafted. It is also the most powerful, the most complicated and the hardest one to figure out. As you know, the rapier and the ax-pike, Frederick's bag...they all benefitted from being in the presence of the globe when it went off. It is safe to say that everything in this chamber is now affected in some way. We may never know how, or they may make themselves known as needed. It is by far the most uncanny item I have ever seen."

Bubba spoke up, "So my point is, why do we keep waiting for trouble before we use it? Why don't we just walk into a place and unleash it? Just roll the thing out in front of us? Seems to me that would save a lot of time and maybe our lives."

"Though that may sound like the wisest move, it won't work, will it, Frederick?"

"No, Bubba, it won't. It is not a catchall, foolproof method for ridding ourselves of problems. Just like in here; it wasn't glowing. Why? Because no evil had manifested itself. There had been no threat to the globe. Gamma and Gann's posers did not threaten the globe, they threatened us. Charlie threatened the globe in Nuorg. He had demanded to take possession of the globe. That was an immediate threat. In here, the threat was made to us. I don't know for sure. There is so much in these notes to discern. It will be a long process I may not live to complete."

"What of your background Hemoth," asked Bubba. "When did you become involved in your association and who comprises it?"

"My history is a complex story, one I can tell you. The other, I cannot, for your own well being. Suffice it to say, the association has been around a very long time. Sig doesn't even know what it is and will never know."

Mystic was curious, "Why all of the secrecy, Grizzly?"

"Why not? Look what these two imposters found out in the last several years. Far too much for my sake or yours."

"I can understand that."

Frederick unrolled Sig's scroll. He perused through page after page, his jaw dropping a little more with each new tidbit of information. "The content in these papers is astounding. This mountain is far more than a fortress. It is a complete history of those who built it. There is nothing one would ever need that this mountain doesn't already contain. Let's get the mission to Nuorg started. Hemoth, Lightning, Madaliene and Perrie, you four will proceed without delay to Nuorg. The ax-pike should take you to one of the windows. When you arrive in Nuorg, find Hugoth. We need help here if we are to locate Evaliene. If she has her staff with her, I fear for her life. I pray it is not too late. Madaliene, you will carry my bag. There is enough of everything you could ever need in it. It may take you a while to find it, but there is food, clothing, water, fire starters…you name it."

"Can I lift it?"

"Give it a go, you might be surprised."

He handed the bag to her. She was surprised to find it now had no weight at all. It practically floated beside her. She ran to her room. After rummaging around, she returned with one completely full crate of arrows. After setting the crate on the floor, she opened the lid. Hundreds of hand crafted arrows with multi-colored shafts and feathers, each arrow meticulously weighted and balanced. To her amazement, the entire contents of the crate fit inside the bag. She was very happy. "I can only hope I will never need all of these, but if I do…we have them." She patted the bag lovingly.

"I hope you don't need any of them!" Lightning was hesitant at best with the thought of Madaliene having to use even one arrow.

"Madaliene, can you shoot to kill if the need arises?" Hemoth asked his charge with no emotion.

"Yes, Hemoth, I can. If it is a matter of our life or death, rest assured we will survive."

"That's what I needed to hear."

Lightning swallowed hard. He looked at his ax-pike for comfort. It said nothing.

"What are we waiting for? Lightning, hold that tool of yours out here and let's move!" Madaliene was invigorated. Her youthful enthusiasm bubbled around her.

"Be safe, all of you." Frederick backed away from the traveling group. "Perrie, there is someone you need to meet in Hugoth's Burg, her name is Karri. She is wise past her years."

"Karri?"

"Yes, she and her brother Rakki are Hawks, very good friends of Hugoth's."

"Yes sir."

"Perrie, are you sure you want to do this?" Sig asked very father-like.

"Sig, I have no choice. I have my own agenda to avenge. Of course I will go."

"Very well."

Hemoth, Lightning, Madaliene with Perrie on her shoulder moved very close together while the others backed away. Lightning held the ax-pike in front of him. "Frederick, should I tell it where we want to go?"

"No Lightning, it will take you where you need to go. I only hope that will be Nuorg."

Without further delay, Lightning professed his willingness to go where the ax-pike willed. It happened without warning. Instantaneously the exiting group was no longer in the mountain. There was no lingering residue of anything; four stayed, four were gone.

"That phenomenon looks much different from this side of things," Bubba stated.

"Indeed," added Mystic.

Frederick nodded. "Come on you two, Sig, take us to the library."

"Which one? There are several of them here. One for armaments, one for history, one for science, one for agriculture, one for governing, one for lineage, you name it."

"My goodness, take us to history first. I think we need to research who built this fortress. Maybe there is something we can learn there regarding the families."

"Very well, follow me." Sig was off.

Mystic looked at Frederick inquisitively, "How can we follow a winger that fast in these caves?"

No sooner had Mystic completed his question when Sig came flying back through the entrance to the den, "Sorry about that." He perched on Frederick's shoulder. "This way, please." Off they went, Frederick and Sig followed by Mystic and Bubba.

## 24

J ahnise stepped off the wooden ramp onto the soft grass. He smiled as he stared up at the hill and at his stick. "So I go again. Where shall you take me now, staff?" The tall lanky man took strong steps. His long strides carried him quickly up the hill. At the rise, he stopped, as if waiting for something. His staff began to vibrate. "So soon?" He asked aloud. The vibration continued for a brief moment and dissipated as quickly as it began. He heard a low commotion to his far left. He turned to look and grinned. "Only four I see? Well then, four it is." He walked in their direction.

*** 

"Whoa," Madaliene shouted.

"Shhh! We don't know where we are. You can't talk that loud!" Lightning tried to keep his voice to a whisper, but failed.

"Sorry."

"Where are we, Lightning?" Hemoth was staring down a hill looking at a crystal clear river in the distance. "My, that river is magnificent."

Lightning raised his snout high into the air. "Something is very familiar about the smell here." He sniffed some more.

Perrie was caught ogling the river in much the same way as Hemoth. "Fantastic."

"Wait a minute. We are in, and I can't believe I'm saying this, we must be in…"

"Nuorg! You are in the Land of Nuorg. Welcome my brothers."

The newcomers slowly spun around to face the voice. They all looked up at the dark handsome face of the very tall two-legger.

"One can only assume each of you is here with a purpose?"

Madaliene stepped closer to Jahnise. "Who are you?" She had never seen a person this tall or this dark.

"I am First King Jahnise Kotumanrunda Equakembo, King of the Great Plains. And who are you my lovely lady?"

"I am Madaliene O'shay."

"It is a pleasure to meet you Madaliene O'shay. Who are your friends?"

She pointed to Hemoth first, "This is Hemoth, a Grizzly Bear from the far north, Perrie a Peregrine Falcon from not so far up north and Lightning also a Grizzly Bear..."

Lightning cleared his throat, "Ahem, excuse me?"

"I mean Lightning, the Irregular Badger, Duke of the Great Meadow or something like that."

"Odd, he looks like a Grizzly Bear to me."

Madaliene tossed her hands and threw an intense glare at Lightning, "See! You are a Grizzly Bear!"

"No I'm not."

"Yes, you are!"

"No, I am not!"

"Yes, indeed you are!" She turned back to Jahnise smiling a very forced ear to ear smile.

"Now, now, I don't care what you are or say you are. You are here to help or you are lost, which will it be?"

Hemoth spoke next. "Please excuse Madaliene, she is extremely spirited. Did you say your last name is Equakembo?"

"I can see that Hemoth and yes, why do you ask?"

"So your walking stick should be...I'm sorry, our story is complex. Let me shorten it to this. We are on a journey to find Madaliene's sister Evaliene. The last message from her mentioned Nuorg. We arrived here much quicker than we planned, so we are a little shocked. Evaliene may be in dire trouble. She may have been taken prisoner by those who want to steal the Staff of O'shay from her."

Madaliene calmly stated, "Sir, I cannot let that happen."

Lightning continued to sniff the air as he listened. "You wouldn't happen to have a pot of Sweet Gulley mud with you?"

"What? No, no, I am a visitor here as well. I arrived a few days ago...I think. It's difficult to tell time here with no sunset or moonrise."

Lightning interjected a bit of wisdom. "In this land, they close the dwelling shutters to simulate night so the inhabitants can get the sleep they need." He began to wander around following his nose.

"What do you know of this land, Jahnise?" Hemoth wanted to find his brother.

"Not as much as your wandering friend over there. I have had my time away. Let us head back to the Burg. I am sure you will find your answers there." He turned to lead them in, "And maybe more." He recognized the striking resemblance Hemoth had to the Grizzly Hugoth and he smiled. "Follow me."

Madaliene quickly found it difficult to keep up with Jahnise's long strides. "You are quite a walker, Jahnise. You take one step for three of mine!"

"I am sorry, Madaliene. Shall I take smaller steps just for you?"

"Don't bother. Hemoth, come here please."

"As you wish, Princess." He hurried to Madaliene and stuck out a paw to help her climb aboard his back. She rode the rest of the way on the back of Hemoth with Perrie perched on her shoulder.

"This is so nice of you, Hemoth."

"Would you have it any other way my lady?"

"Now that you mention it...hmmm...nope, I'd have it no other way. Follow that King faithful steed!"

Lightning trailed behind, sniffing the air furiously for Sweet Gulley.

*** 

There was quite a commotion high in the trees above the entrance ramps. There was no warning of more visitors. No window watchers had reported an intrusion, so why were there now five creatures coming back to the gate when only one had left? The wingers were beside themselves. Many flew off to check with the watchers. One of the Goldens was summoned earlier to fly an errand for Hugoth, but now it looked like Hugoth was a member of the group coming in with Jahnise. How could that be? The Golden could clearly see Jahnise, a small two-legger, at least compared with Jahnise, one very attractive winger and two Bears. One of the Bears looked just like Hugoth. Where was Hugoth now? He wanted a closer look. He took wing.

Jahnise noticed the activity at the Burg's entrance. "Looks like we have company coming to take a look at you. They must be wondering how you arrived at their doorstep with no forewarning from a watcher."

Madaliene whispered in Hemoth's ear, "Should I draw my bow?"

267

"No! Are you out of your mind?" Hemoth shook his head, "Definitely not!"

"Is there a problem, Hemoth?" Jahnise asked as he kept his eye on the incoming winger.

"Nothing a fine willow switch couldn't fix Jahnise."

Madaliene reared back and popped Hemoth solidly on his muscular flank. He barley noticed. "Oww! That happens every time!" She shook her wrist to ease the stinging pain.

"As my mothers would say, Madaliene, it serves you right." Hemoth turned his eyes to the winger as well.

Perrie winked at Madaliene, "I wish there was someone still alive who cared for me as this Great Grizzly cares for you. You are so lucky."

Madaliene grinned, "Yes I am very thankful that this overgrown behemoth loves me!" She kicked his side for good measure.

Hemoth chuckled again, "Hey now, I almost felt that one!"

Lightning finally accepted the fact that Sweet Gulley was nowhere in their vicinity. "That Burg doesn't look familiar to me at all. A river ran past the front gate of the Burg we visited earlier."

The Golden Eagle dove on the group. He thought out loud, "That looks a lot like Hugoth from here." He pulled up into a braking position directly in front of Hemoth. "Hugoth? How did you get out here without us seeing you leave the gate?"

Jahnise answered for the Grizzly, "Winged friend, this is not Hugoth. This Bear is called Hemoth."

"Are you sure?" The Golden was not.

"Ride in with us. You will see."

"I will do that. At least they will have no reason to draw the bridge as long as I am breathing."

"Good point," added Madaliene.

Perrie could not take her eyes off of the Golden Eagle. She tried not to be obvious, but Madaliene caught her. "Perrie, your eyes are about to pop out of your head. You want to settle down a little?"

"What did you say Madaliene?"

"You heard me."

"Was it that obvious?"

"Uh huh, it was to me."

"Dreadful."

"Smitten."

"Really?"

"Listen. Try to be a little less male crazy if you can. I'm sure there are plenty of them here."

"I'll try, but you know it might be difficult." Her eyes sparkled.

Madaliene feigned a swoon and sighed.

The Golden was not one to see double. "Grizzly, if you are not Hugoth, you sure resemble him. Even your eyes are the same."

"When I see him face-to-face, everything will become very clear." Hemoth's voice welled with excitement.

"Do you want me to announce your presence?"

"No, unless you must. I would rather it be a surprise."

Jahnise joined in, "Let us surprise Hugoth. I need a jovial reunion to clear my thinking."

"Reunion?"

"Yes, I believe a tear-filled, joyous reunion is only a few steps away."

The commotion at the bridge was in full swing. All sizes of four-leggers and wingers were assembling at the entrance.

"Are they all here for us?" asked Perrie.

"No little Falcon, they are here to see Hemoth." Jahnise smiled as he held them at the foot of the first ramp. "Bongi, may we enter?"

Bongi tromped halfway down the upper ramp. He squinted his eyes and glared at Hemoth. "Are you not already here, Hugoth?"

"Bongi this is not Hugoth, this is Hemoth. We are also welcoming to our land his friends, Lightning, Perrie and Princess Madaliene O'shay." He waved the stick at each creature as he announced their names. He was secretly blessing each one with the unnoticed ceremony and a silent prayer. "May we enter Bongi?"

"Of course you may enter. Come with me." He asked the crowd for room. "There is no need to pile on us now. Everybody will get a chance to see our guests."

An Eagle dove on Lightning. Just as he steadied for landing, Lightning saw him. "Mystic!" He reared up on his back legs and caught the winger with his paw. "It is so good to see you again. How long has it been? Three or four day-rounds?"

"Three or four day-rounds? Lightning, you have been gone for months. Every creature here was concerned for all of you. We were not sure if you made it back to the Great Forest safely or got side-tracked."

269

Lightning looked confused, "Months? Mystic, that can't be true. It was maybe a few day-rounds ago at most when we followed my ax-pike out of here. Now you say months?"

"How is everyone? Are they okay? Are they well?"

"Why yes, of course they are." Lightning's thoughts were mixed.

"That is wonderful. Any news on your exploits?"

"Oh yes, there is a lot to tell you. Who else is here?"

"I came along with Donkhorse, Rakki, Karri and Hugoth, who, by the way, looks a lot like your friend over there."

"Yes, so we have been told."

Two other wingers burst from above. "Lightning! How are you?" Karri was firing questions as fast as she could.

"Hey Badger!" Rakki lit to one side of Mystic, Karri on the other. All three wingers balanced on Lightning's front leg.

At the top of the second ramp stood Donkhorse waiting patiently, "Hurry up will you, Badger!"

"Hey, Donkhorse! I'll get there!"

Hemoth, Madaliene and Perrie all smiled at the throng. Jahnise continued to lead them up the final ramp. The Golden took wing. He headed directly for the Keeper's dwelling. He smiled as he flew low past a galloping Okapi. "Don't wear yourself out Bongi. I'll let them know we have more guests."

Bongi slowed his pace gradually. "Sometimes...what I would give to have a set of wings." He continued walking at a normal pace to catch his breath.

The Golden had no idea who Hemoth was. When he lit on the sill of the largest window in the Keeper's meeting room, he just announced it like this, "Hugoth, Stewig, we have more guests. We have accompanying Jahnise a young girl, a young Falcon, and two Grizzly Bears although one seems to think himself a Badger."

Hugoth let a loud laugh escape his belly. "Hah! That must be Lightning. What is the other Grizzly called?"

"He is called Hemoth and he is the spitting image of you."

"What did you say he was called?"

"Hemoth, sir and he looks just like you."

"This can't be! Hemoth, they call him Hemoth?"

"Yes sir."

"I thought...I thought I would never see him again. Hemoth is my twin brother. Take me to him now!" It was fortunate that the door to the dwelling was open because Hugoth would have never felt it smashing behind him as he exited the dwelling.

# 25

Hemoth spent the following years of his life growing into a handsome example of Grizzliness. The Fallow herd grew with the births of fawns and diminished as the elders succumbed to old age. New elders took the place of departed ones, young does became mothers, and young stags became fathers. Life cycled on as the Grizzly grew into maturity, his early adult years directly ahead of him. An adventurous calling tugged at him every day, a calling to find others like himself, a calling which his adopted mother would not try to silence.

Anessa stepped lightly behind the group of Deer following the Grizzly. Her steps were slower than those ahead of her. Four pairs of her fawns walked proudly in the wake of the Bear. Directly after Hemoth came Deakin and Darley, then came three pairs of newer fawns, each dreading this day with equal heartbreak. Sadly missing from the parade was Bellon. Not long after the birth of the youngest set of fawns, he had sacrificed his life protecting Anessa from a large Cat--the same kind of Cat Hemoth had seen many years earlier. Hemoth was running with the fawns that day. He had regretted his decision ever since. Acting rather impulsively, he hunted the Cats for days, finally finding them boasting over a recent kill. Needless to say, a menacing Bear overtook Hemoth's jovial personality. The Cats never had a chance. Hemoth broke three of them in half before tossing their mangled bodies on piles of sharp rocks. The last Cat escaped with his life and a severely mangled tail, never to be seen again. The Grizzly never felt any remorse for what he did. In his mind, he was the Fallows' protector. He did what he did to save the remaining herd from Bellon's end. The elders each took time with Hemoth to counsel him for many days after the incident. It was during that time when Hemoth began to learn there were more than two sides of life. His innocence wasn't swept away with one broad stroke of a death experience, but rather it was eroded away by a gentle river of growing up. Everything changed for him after that.

At the break of the woods Hemoth stopped. He pivoted around on his hind legs to face the Deer behind him. Anessa walked up to him first as the others parted, clearing the way for her. "Hemoth, my adopted son, I will always be here for you. Bellon would say the same if he were here, as well as every Fallow that has passed before you. You are not one of us, but you are one of us. You are not a Fallow yet you are at the same time. We have taught you all we can teach you. I only wish we could teach you more of being a great Grizzly Bear. I do not want to change your mind, nor do I wish to prolong your departure. Maybe one day, our paths will cross again, but now go. Go with all of the love you can imagine from each of us."

With that short speech, Hemoth moved from the world of the Fallow Deer once again into the land of the Grizzly Bear. Each of the assembled stags lowered their antlered heads to Hemoth and the does batted tear-filled eyes before silently retracing their sorrowful path. Hemoth reverently nodded at each display of admiration. Once Anessa finished her good-bye, her great Grizzly Bear cub turned his massive body away from the herd's ground and stepped into his world again. A world of which he knew nothing of but was better prepared for than he could ever imagine.

***

Hugoth spent several years with the two Ellyphants, Bastone growing almost as large as his father and Hugoth keeping up as best he could. As time would have it, the day came when Hugoth decided he needed to see what the life of a Grizzly Bear was like outside the safe confines provided him by Bastone. Bastony was torn between following his brother or staying with and becoming the protector of his father. A deal had been made earlier that provided methods for Bastony to follow Hugoth had Bastone not been alive when Hugoth decided his time had come to leave the Ellyphants. The youngsters only recently found out how long even ancient Ellyphants live. It was then when Hugoth made his plans to venture out once again, this time voluntarily. Hugoth walked with Bastone and Bastony along the trails of his youth once again for the last time. The parting of the worlds was tearful and silent as if fate knew the role each of the players would play in the future of the combined worlds. The two

Ellyphants watched as the Grizzly Bear cub slowly made his way out of the thicket into the wide grassy glen Hugoth had run through so many years before. Hugoth turned one last time to the magnificent pair of behemoths, stood on his back legs and waved good-bye. The wave was answered with simultaneous trumpet blasts from the Ellyphant's raised trunks.

\*\*\*

The Golden flew down the main path with the Grizzly on his tail. "Make way!" He yelled to the passer-bys, "Crazed Grizzly coming through beneath me!"

Now the entry ramp was just ahead. The crowd parted as Hemoth led his group past the bridge supports. Hugoth rounded the last bend of the Burg's main path and slowed to a walk. The twins spied each other as the gathered crowd fell silent. Each huge Grizzly sized the other up, tears in every creature's eyes. The scene was touching and dreamlike. What is said at a reunion such as this? Are there accurate words to speak? Are there enough words? All that was said between the two Bears was this.

Hemoth began, "Hugoth, when the river parted...

Hugoth answered, "So did we."

## 26

"Sig, did you know of the imposters the entire time?" Frederick spoke as he walked the corridors of the mountain fortress, admiring the craftsmanship, imagining all of the many hours of labor put into each section. Not rough hammer and pick work but countless, painstaking years of delicate mallet and chisel work. Every door opening was designed and constructed to have no visible seams. The doors were built from splendid hardwoods such as walnut, cherry and maple. There was an absence of oak wood within the caverns. He wondered why.

Sig sat comfortably on the two-legger's shoulder guiding the team. "Yes, Frederick, I noticed a drastic change one day when they returned from the lake. Their clothes didn't fit the same as before. It was as if Gann had gotten shorter and Gamma taller and slightly thicker. The dress she wore to greet you looked flawless on the real Gamma. On the poser, it looked tight and out of place. The Gann poser always rolled up his pant legs. The real Gann never had to do that. It's funny how much you two-leggers think we don't see. Anyway, I was not in any position to make trouble, so I bided my time as well as I could. Before you knew it, all of these years had passed. When Madaliene came to the mountain, the both of them lived with renewed vigor. I can only imagine why. I did miss Gamma and Gann badly for years, but you know...what are you going to do? On several occasions I told Hemoth of the strangeness, he instructed me to go along with it. The end, I was told, was bigger than me or my feelings for Gamma and Gann. If they were no more, I hoped them a quick end."

"Well said, Falcon. If what I saw in the cellar was any indication of their end, it was horrid. That's all I'm saying on that. Are we getting closer to the libraries?"

"Yes, we are. They are just ahead to your right and left. They are lined with more books than the four of us can read in ten lifetimes."

"Is there anything to eat?" asked Bubba.

"Of course there is. Whatever you want, I can get for you."

"Fredrick, what could beware of the intelligents mean?" Mystic could not get that phrase out of his head.

"That is most random, Prince." Frederick shrugged. "I wish I knew. Hopefully we can find something about it in here."

Sig tapped Frederick on the neck with his wing. "Here we are. This door should start you on your quest for more answers."

Frederick unlatched the door and pushed it slightly open. Sig left his perch and squeezed through the opening. "I'll set your table."

Frederick pushed the door a little further. Boom! A crashing, thunderous roar rocked the entire mountain. Beyond the door, a bombastic ball of flame enveloped the entire room. Pages were ripped from books and entire shelves full of priceless tomes were vaporized. The door was slammed back at Frederick, sending him tumbling across the floor. Mystic and Bubba were lifted off the ground and thrown wickedly across the main corridor. They slammed into the far wall and melted to the ground. Smoke began to boil from around the partially open door.

Mystic struggled for breath. "Sig!" He called out. "Sig..." He collapsed to the hard floor.

Inside the room, an inferno blazed, fueled by thousands of pages of flaming history. Frederick reached for his bag, but it was not there. He took off his jacket and wrapped it around his head and face. He looked for his friends. They were laying unconscious, sprawled out on the floor. Turning back to the crackling door, he pushed it open. He was met with a heated blast of wind that scalded the skin on his face through his jacket. Backing out, he fought to un-wrap the jacket from his head. He frantically searched the many pockets, praying he would find it. He valiantly prodded and poked through every one of the pockets. As luck would have it, in the last pocket he found it; the rag he had held over his mouth when he first entered the stink hovering over the remnants of the barn. He closed the door as best he could fighting against the vacuum the flames created on the opposite side, holding it shut with his feet as he sat on the floor. He tossed aside his jacket and unfolded the rag. Kneading it back and forth in his hands, he sought for one tiny speck of dampness. It wasn't to be found. He raised his head to the ceiling, screaming out to anyone who could hear him. Again, he kneaded the rag, beginning to cry. He felt his heart ripping apart inside his chest.

"No, no, no, no! This can't be happening. No!" His guard was down. Tears, welling up in his caring brown eyes, slowly rolled down his cheeks, dropping on the dry rag. When the obvious happens, sometimes it appears as though one is being watched over by a higher power. The obvious happened. Steadily, the rag became wet. Soon it was dripping with water. Streams of clear water ran down Frederick's arms. He splashed it on his face, in his eyes. The scalded red skin returned to normal, pliable flesh. He rolled over on his stomach and crawled to Mystic, squeezing the life-giving liquid into the Wolf's mouth. Once Mystic began breathing steadily, Frederick crawled to Bubba and did the same. The Cheetah woke with a startle. Bubba was immediately on his feet pacing.

"Get back here, Bubba. You have some singed spots on your coat. I'll tell you when you are ready." Bubba reluctantly came back to Frederick's side. "That's better. Just a little more."

"What happened, Frederick?"

"We'll get to that later. Stay with Mystic. He was hurt badly."

"What are you doing?"

"I'm going in. Sig is still inside. I have to try and save him, then as many books as I can."

Frederick soaked his clothing, hair and all exposed skin with the wet rag. He ran into the door, forcing it back on its hinges. It swung wide into the raging blaze. The fire did not deter him. The flames wrapped themselves tightly around his extremities like muscular serpents finding nothing to latch on to. They swirled around him in anger. They wanted this two-legger. Nothing could match their intensity or so they thought. The stubborn legger was not cowering as most of them did. This one fought back with dogged determination. He wrung the small rag out over and over again on the fire. The blazes came at him continuously. Little by little, the two-legger and the rag were making progress. Starting with the books still on the shelves Frederick ran up and down the rows, shaking water off the rag onto anything solid that could catch it. The rag kept dripping water, no matter how much he shook it. Around the room he whirled like a madman, dousing a book or a piece of furniture. The smoke began to give way. He could see. More wringing and shaking of the rag, less and less of the fire to stop him. Frederick was squeezing the rag so tightly now that a steady sheet of water extinguished every flame or hot spot it touched. The fire receded at a rapid rate. Frederick did not stop. The floor was flooded with water. As he watched, the water began chasing flames up the massive bookcases, extinguishing the retreating inferno on contact. Satisfied that the water was working with him, he began a search for Sig. He called out desperately only to be met with a lonely nothing in return. Along the side of the wall lay a smoldering, unnatural looking pile. The water formed a perfect circle around the lifeless body. Frederick stepped over it, bent down and lifted it up. As the water hunted down the last of the fire, the two-legger stepped reverently out of the library with Sig delicately cradled in his arms. He gently shut the remains of the door behind him, leaving the mysterious water alone with its quarry.

Frederick crossed the threshold, walked a few paces and sat down on one of many ornately carved benches. He held Sig softly, slowly rocking as if the Falcon were a tiny baby. "I'm sorry, Sig. I am so sorry. You died a hero."

Bubba and Mystic stepped in front of him. Mystic nuzzled the warm clump of feathers, "The water couldn't help him?"

"No," Frederick answered, "It must have been his time. It left him alone. He has done his part in our journey. It's time for him to begin another journey of his own."

Bubba hopped onto the bench beside Frederick to lay a paw on Sig's body. "We have been giving the last rites to many a winger lately."

"Yes we have, Bubba, too many by my account."

"It's all well with Sig now," Mystic said solemnly. "He is flying free now, no more worries for him. I dread breaking the news to Madaliene."

"I had so much to ask him about this place. He must have been over one-hundred years old. I don't know how he lived so long." Frederick continued to cradle the dead Falcon.

Bubba whispered to the three of them, "I'm sure he lived a long time for living's sake, but then he lived the rest of his life on love."

Mystic agreed. "Very well said. What caused that thunder, Frederick?"

"The best I can tell, the library was set as a trap. Whoever set the trap, namely the posers, intended to kill us with it. If not for the Nuorg water, it would have succeeded."

"Do you think every room in this place is set as a trap?" Mystic eyed the long corridor lined with hundreds of doors.

"Yes I do, Mystic. We have to figure a way to foil each and every trap set for us."

Bubba agreed, "How? That alone could take thousands of clicks. What if each trap is different?"

"They are all the same. We weren't supposed to make it…remember? They built them all the same. The trick will be finding out how to defeat the trigger. Then we have to learn, in our short time here, everything Sig could have told us."

"Won't that be dangerous?" Mystic asked.

"I'll do it and pray for the best." Frederick turned his eyes to look down the long corridor also. "Pray indeed."

They sat mourning the loss of the brave Falcon for a long time. Their minds dealt with their loss, the callousness of the traps, how to deal with them individually and still protect the wealth of knowledge contained within each of the massive rooms.

"First we have to lay Sig to rest somewhere. Bubba, find me a cloth to cover him. Mystic, locate a marker worthy of his service. I am going back in to survey the damage. Surely all was not lost." Frederick stood up and placed Sig respectfully on the bench. Bubba jumped from the bench to find a suitable burial covering. Mystic headed down the corridor in search of a special ornament for his friend.

Frederick studied the charred door with a patient eye. He felt every edge, every seam, every chink in the wood grain for a hint to the trigger device. Then he inspected the hinges. The perfect craftsmanship made the hastily rigged lever easy to spot. It wasn't even hidden. Why should it be? The hinge pin had been pulled and replaced. At the top of the bottom hinge a crudely fashioned device made from a dinner fork was wedged between the pin's shoulder and the hinge plate. A silvery cord ran to its frayed end about an arm's length away. A black outline revealed the profile once of a short stack of crates. What had these crates been filled with? Frederick assumed a highly volatile explosive material. These types of materials were not widely available. Then, he thought of the armaments Sig had spoken of. Of course! The cord must have been used to activate some kind of short fuse. When he pushed the door open, the fuse was set in motion. When he did not enter the door behind Sig, he availed himself the time needed to survive the blast. Had all of them been in the room, their fates would have been sealed along with Sig's. He silently thanked his brave friend for saving their lives and forwarding his cause.

Frederick stood and began to gaze around the room at the haphazard piles of books in all conditions, from completely ruined to very salvageable. He turned a chair on its feet and pulled it up to a large, intact but sooty table. He wiped the table and several nearby books off with his still wet rag. The pages within the burned covers remained legible. He began to read.

# 27

The gigantic twin Grizzlies made a huge scene. Onlookers could have easily been disturbed by the violence shown from Bear to Bear, but it was all in play. They returned back to their cub days, rolling on the ground and slapping each other silly with fully grown paws. Leggers scattered out of fear as the Bears reunited.

"I thought this day would never come Hemoth!"

"Hugoth, I held out hope that someday it would!"

The playfulness restored a frivolity to the Burg that had been missing since many days before. Jahnise looked on joyfully as did every other friend and stranger to the twins. Madaliene cried big tears. She was soon joined by Donkhorse, Rakki, Karri, Perrie and other creatures who knew of the separation story. Truthfully spoken, there were those in the crowd who did not fully understand the entire tear-jerking moment. They would know soon enough, but now they chose to let the meeting play out.

Behind Madaliene, one of the two-leggers was approaching her with a determined attitude. Although Hemoth was enjoying the long-awaited reunion with his brother he was keeping an eye glued to his charge. Ian politely begged the pardon of those in his path then thanked them for letting him through. Hemoth cast his full attention toward Madaliene.

"Excuse me Brother, who is that and what would he want with my charge?"

Hugoth caught a glance of Ian making his way to Madaliene. "No bother Brother. Ian is safe, eccentric but safe."

"I can take your word on that can I?"

Hugoth smiled a big toothy grin, "Welcome to Nuorg my Brother!"

***

"Excuse me lass, the name is Ian. You must me Madaliene O'shay. I know so much about you."

"Hello, it must be nice to meet you as well then I'm sure."

"Um...yes," Ian was running through the correct syntax to use here and opted to skip over all of it. "Yes it is nice to see you. Welcome to Nuorg Princess."

"How do you know I'm a Princess?"

"Oh...everyone here knows and most of us have been expecting you."

"Your speak is just a little weird don't you think?"

"No, I don't think so. Is it?"

"You seem to know much more than you are letting on. I can see behind your eyes. You are planning your words too deliberately. It is like you are afraid to say something wrong for fear of some retribution on my part. Is this not so?"

Ian was impressed by the lass' gift of perspicacity. "You may be more than we expected Princess Madaliene. Excuse me will you? I must speak with my fellow Keeper Hugoth if you please."

"Certainly, I have nowhere else to be."

"Thank you."

Perrie still perched on Madaliene's shoulder listening as Ian made his way through the crowd to Hugoth. "That was weird."

"I'll agree with that. Where is Lightning?"

"He's over there with those two Hawks and the Mule. He's got his snout deep into a pail full of something. He seems to like it, whatever it is."

"Don't you think we should join him?"

"Why yes I do...Princess."

***

Lightning's head popped out of the pail. "This goo is better than I ever remember. Another pail, please?"

"There is none left Badger. You just ate all there is in this area of the Burg. Maybe the Hawks can go replenish our supply." Donkhorse raised his head to them as they sat above him on the bridge controls.

"No, I don't think so. Of us three, I believe only you have the capacity for such a task. Do you agree Rakki?"

"Indeed I do Karri. Shouldn't we catch up with the old Eagle now or maybe Hugoth? I'm sure they have some lighter workloads for us to manage."

"I agree, Rakki. Lightning, do not make yourself a stranger. We would so love to catch up with you. It's been a very long time."

Lightning's face could not hide his confusion even through the strands of Sweet Gulley goo clinging to his facial fur. "See, that perplexes me to no end. Will one of you please tell me how long we have been gone?" He lapped as much goo from his face as his tongue could reach. "I can promise you it has been no more than..." He began to count in his head, "Eight...nine day-rounds at the very most."

Donkhorse laughed out loud. "Dear Badger, the shutters have been closed so many times the hinges have been replaced!"

"There is no way that could be right!"

"He is telling you the truth." Karri agreed with Donkhorse.

"Time passes at different speeds, Lightning. Just as the days of our many moods. When we are happy, time flies by. When we are sad or lonely, the days seem to never end. Too bad those cannot be reversed." Rakki solemnly reflected.

"Enough of this, Rakki, let us fly to Hugoth. Shall we?"

"Wonderful idea, Karri." Off they flew.

Donkhorse watched them briefly then turned to Lightning. "Someone is coming for you."

Lightning saw Madaliene coming his way. He wiped the remnants of the goo from his face and snout with both front paws. As he was cleaning off the last little bit Madaliene and Perrie arrived. "So, I take it you are finding Nuorg to your liking?"

Madaliene smiled at him, "Maybe you can say that."

Perrie chirped in, "And maybe you can't."

"Lightning, what are you cleaning from your snout? Looks to me like honey." She changed her look to a befuddled frown, "But it also looks like mud. Why are you eating mud?"

"Madaliene, believe me when I tell you, you would be amazed at this goo."

"Really? Then let me try it."

"Okay..." Lightning began tossing through the emptied pails. "Let me see...ah, here is some I must have missed." He handed a wooden pail to her.

"Yuck! You have had your Bear snout all in this."

"That would be Badger snout little Princess." Donkhorse snickered at the thought.

"You too?" She sighed. "What is it with four-leggers? He is obviously a Grizzly Bear just like Hemoth and Hugoth. Can you not see the unmistakable resemblance?"

Donkhorse and Lightning looked hurt.

"Oh please! Enough of the sad eyes. He's a Bear and I don't care what you say. Now, Lightning, yes or no? Did you have your Bear snout..."

Donkhorse shook his head miserably.

Madaliene began to think this argument could never be won. "Fair enough, your Badger snout all in this pail?"

"I did not."

Madaliene gave him a pert nod of her head then stuck her hand in and scraped up a handful of the thick goo. She put it to her mouth and tasted it with her tongue. "Oh my, this is very good."

Lightning grinned slyly at her. "That was Donkhorse's pail."

Madaliene gagged and wiped her hand on her riding pants. "What? A Mule snout is just as bad as a Bear snout." She coughed.

"Excuse me?" Donkhorse tried to keep the laugh inside him. It did not work.

Perrie was chuckling pretty hard also.

"Is there a non-tainted batch of this anywhere? I want to shoot you both with arrows where it will hurt, not kill you, just hurt...a lot!" Madaliene dropped the pail on Lightning's foot.

"Oww! You have some very serious issues, Princess." Lightning doubled over laughing.

Donkhorse stepped through a gate behind him, returning quickly with another untouched pail of goo, the handle clutched in his teeth. He swung it to Madaliene and she took it from him. "I just happened to save this one and maybe a few more from the devouring appetite of this Badger, Princess. Shall I scribble your name on it?"

"Well thank you, Mule." She dipped her finger in the muddy colored goo and tasted it out right. Her eyes opened wide. "I have to agree with Lightning, this is a delectable concoction. It's no wonder he was craving it since we arrived. I believe even I could eat this entire pail empty."

Lightning glared at Donkhorse. "You kept a pail from me? What kind of host are you?"

"You ate five of them. I had to save at least one for the rest of us." He glanced at Madaliene, "The name is Donkhorse, Princess."

\*\*\*

Mystic the Eagle looked down on the happenings with a bittersweet eye. The introduction of Jahnise to the tribunal gathering followed by a heartfelt speech, the reunion of the two great Grizzly Bears, Ian's introduction to Madaliene and now the ease with which the Princess made friends in this wonderful land, all of these were more or less planned out long ago. His lingering thought, where was Vincen? Why had he not been in the group with Lightning? Where were the others from his group? He decided he needed to find out. There was a correct way with things and an incorrect way with things. This time through he was instructed to make sure the incorrect things were not allowed to happen. He was, at this exact moment, not sure he could do that. Some things, even on a second, third or fourth time through couldn't be predicted. He needed to call the meeting to order soon. Time was, after all, backing up. He flew for Hugoth first.

"Hugoth," Mystic paused, "I beg your pardon, Hemoth. I am Mystic. I am the oldest and greatest of the Great Eagles. I implore you both to attend the meeting which was about to start in the Keeper's dwelling until your unannounced reunion took place. Hugoth, did you have any idea this was coming?"

"If you mean, did I know? No, I did not."

"Hmmph, that's odd. I really want to know why you didn't. Something must already be amiss and that is troubling."

Hemoth picked up on the underlying meaning in Mystic's questioning. "How would you have known?"

"Oh dear, I forgot you are Hugoth's twin and as his twin you are more than likely to be living in the same thought process he is, although you are completely unaware of it."

"What?"

"Simply stated, I or anyone for that matter can talk to you as a single entity whether you are two individuals or not. Should Hugoth pick up on what I am saying, you will also if you are in the same proximity of the questioning. It is, in reality, a very simple phenomenon."

"And you explained that to me why...?"

"Hemoth, you understood what I was asking Hugoth. You read between the lines. You want to know how we could have possibly known you were coming. One word my boy; Nuorg. This is a land of evolving mystery, interlaced backwards and forwards with time and variations of it."

"Okay..."

Hugoth brought both of them back to the now of the conversation. "Shall we proceed to the Keepers' dwelling then?"

"Yes, please do. I will meet you there. I must gather the attendees not already awaiting us." The Eagle flew off to invite Madaliene, Jahnise and several others.

As the Eagle took wing, Hemoth turned to Hugoth, "Can you tell me what exactly he was telling me?"

Hugoth shrugged. "Honestly? No. I'm in a daze when those ancients start talking like that trying to explain to me what is going on here. I'm sure the picture is much larger that the frame I stuck it in."

"Okay, sounds good to me. Where is the Keeper's dwelling?"

"It's up the path here, the largest Dwelling in this Burg. As a rule, we usually have the biggest dwelling because of the need for meeting space and so on."

"We usually have? Does that mean you are a Keeper also?"

"Yes it does. Can you believe it? I don't have the slightest clue. Who knows, you might be in line for the next Keeper opening...like the one here. Eekay just flew the coop. She was getting very irritable in her last days. She never wanted the job. I didn't understand her plight and she never wanted to talk about it."

The brothers made their way to the meeting. As they walked side-by-side, they nearly took over the whole path. There was a sliver left to slide by if necessary.

"Who is the dark two-legger? What is his story?"

"Jahnise Equakembo. He came to us from the Plains. Very important King in his land. Wonderful legger. Very wise, but he can be hard to deal with if you intend on wrong doing. This very morning he cut our population by a score of creatures."

"How did he do that?

"With that stick he carries. Jahnise is known to the ancients as Key number 3." "Key number 1 is the leader of Lightning's group."

"Yes, I know him. The Wolf, Mystic. How was he chosen?"

"I can't answer that. The Staff chose him."

"The Staff? How?"

"Again Brother, I don't know."

"That Staff is pretty potent. It sent an old pair of leggers posing as my friends on a journey."

"So he has learned to use it as needed I see."

"Obviously."

"There is the dwelling. I see we have several awaiting us already."

There were two lines of guests lining the walkway leading from the main path.

Every creature marveled at the likeness of the new Grizzly to the old one. Hugoth was the thicker of the two, Hemoth slightly taller. Either way, they were both huge for Grizzly Bears.

Bongi met them at the entrance. "Is Jahnise with you? There are several here requesting his presence. Everyone is very interested in that stick of his."

"He will be along. The old Eagle is rounding a few stragglers up as we speak."

"Eekay left this place in a mess. I have been doing my best to make it presentable, but you know how difficult it is for those of us with hooves. No dexterity at all."

"I'm sure it will be fine." Hugoth stepped inside followed by Hemoth. "Brother, you mentioned a pair of imposters. If you don't mind, would you please elaborate on that for me?"

"I don't mind at all. Wait, is Madaliene attending this meeting? She is my charge and I'm afraid I've walked off without her."

"Yes she will be coming shortly with Lightning and Donkhorse."

"Donkhorse? What kind of name is that for a Mule?"

"It's one he gave himself. His given name, hah! Let's just say it doesn't sound as nice."

***

Mystic the Eagle lit on Donkhorse's back. "What say you Lightning? Have you emptied our stores of Sweet Gulley goo? It looks as if you have half a pail smeared on your fur." He spoke to Donkhorse. "We must get back to Eekay's dwelling. We need to get a decision made and get everyone back to their own Burgs. I don't like leaving them Keeperless very long."

Donkhorse agreed. "Shall I bring these along?"

"Absolutely!" Mystic bowed to Madaliene. "The Princess will be a welcome addition to our group. Her Badger is already known to several of us."

"And me?" Perrie fluttered off Madaliene's shoulder to perch next to the Eagle.

Madaliene snickered at Mystic. "You too? You also think this Bear is a Badger? Have any of you ever seen a real Badger?" She bent over with her hands on the side of her head and shook her full head of curls loose. When she stood, her tresses commanded attention from all. "They are nothing at all like a Grizzly Bear I assure you." She noticed the stares immediately. "Is there something wrong?"

Perrie stared as well. "Madaliene, your hair...it is shining as if it were spun of gold. I don't remember it looking that way in the mountain."

A transformation was taking place. The little girl who grew up in the mountain under the watchful eyes of the posers was becoming who she was born to be. On the inside, she felt no difference. She had always known from her earliest understanding that she was born a princess. But, on the outside, her radiance was beginning to blossom. Inside the fortress, she was aesthetically trapped as a captive. Nuorg released all trappings. In Nuorg, she would be a celebrated princess with all of the respect and loyalty that honor deserved. Let it be known here as well...she was not just an ordinary princess.

***

Bongi led Hugoth and Hemoth to the meeting room. Several invitees were situated comfortably around the room. Most of the chairs were pushed to the walls since none of the four-leggers could use them. The chairs were much too small and visibly designed for two-legger use only. The three big Cats grouped together beside Ian and his family. Several wingers, including Rakki and Karri, perched on the back of the unused chairs. Kohlyn and Grendl waited patiently on the common table, writing utensils close at hand. Bongi offered the two Grizzlies a spot at the head of the table. Jahnise had a chair awaiting him to their left. Madaliene's spot was to the right of Hemoth with Lightning filling the void left over.

Mystic flew in the window. He announced the soon arrival of Jahnise and Stewig. "I apologize for the untimely delays today's events might have caused any of you. I urge you to return to your Burgs as quickly as possible once this meeting is adjourned." He stuck his head out the window. "Here they come now."

Jahnise and Stewig entered the room and took the places Bongi reserved for them.

Bongi took the floor. I witnessed today a feat I never thought I would ever see. My first question was why were those creatures purged from Nuorg? My second question was how did they get here? I realize Burg one had an incident similar to this a while back, but I also thought that may have been an isolated incident. Was it? I don't know. I don't think any of us do."

Hugoth stood. "I think my concern is this; if Nuorg is populated right now by creatures such as Charlie and these who have left us today, we need to have a cleansing if you will. I suggest Jahnise visit each of the other Burgs and perform the same deed as today. We cannot succeed with our goal as long as we have those among us willing to dismantle us from within. Are there any of you here who disagree with me? Cirrus, I want to hear what you have to say."

"I agree with you Hugoth. Many of you think I am the most head-strong and mean-spirited creature in our land. Many of you go out of your way to avoid me. I am a confident Tigress. I fear nothing except that which I do not know. I don't fear evil because I know evil. I don't fear good because I know good. I do fear secrecy for I am not secretive. I fear distrust because I am trusting. Me, Duister, Luiperd? We all want the best for our land and the lands above. We came here willingly as did most of you. I say let us get this meeting over with. Let us vote in Jahnise then have him purge each of our Burgs so we can move to the next phase of our plan." The intense Tigress turned to Hugoth. "Hugoth, what is our next phase? We are ready."

"Thank you, Ciruss. The times are nearing above. Hemoth has been walking up there for years, listening and seeing. He just experienced the phenomenon there that we witnessed in our Burg and just a short while ago here in your Burg. If we could only know the end first, I think our tasks would be much easier. I know from what I have heard that the wrongdoers, the evil sides, or whatever you want to call them are making loud noises. Again, I am not sure what our part to play in this is. Mystic, do you have more details?"

"Yes I do, Hugoth." Mystic the Eagle flew to Hemoth's shoulder to speak. "During his visit, Mystic, the Gray Wolf was able to unlock the original Staff. With the help of Frederick Mounte, they were able to open the compartments never before known to the rest of our history. The two-legger is very curious. He made notation after notation regarding every detail within the Staff. He compiled several volumes of his own gatherings. He must be brought back here once the two other keys are located. Princess Madaliene's sister was reported missing. She has the staff to be wielded by key number four, which is this girl." He acknowledged Madaliene with a nod of his head. "Evaliene is only the bearer of the staff in her possession and it must remain in her possession! She is vaguely aware of its...eh... possibilities, but her manner of wielding it is known to be reckless and temper-driven. The staff must be held by her until all of them are brought together. In short, that is our task. We Nuorgians are responsible for uniting all four staffs and the four proper keys. Two have been dropped on our door step, but the others are in peril, partly because we have no exact knowledge of their whereabouts."

Ciruss rose and led the big Cats to Jahnise's side. "We vow ourselves to Jahnise and the protection of his staff. You know he can't stay sequestered here. He cannot become a Keeper. We must accompany him back up there to prepare his lands. Hugoth, Mystic, you know as well as I do that new Keepers must be named for this Burg and mine."

Hugoth answered, "Yes, I know that, Ciruss. But as you also know, I could make no appointments unless you volunteered yourselves as you just did. I will now appoint replacements for you as you wish."

Jahnise stared unwavering into something not in the room. "I know my journey here was fate. I know my life until now was lived to learn. I too am ready to sacrifice all I have to bring to a close this incredible journey. I accept my responsibilities with great gratitude for being chosen by the Staff. One day I may even learn why." He stood towering over the other creatures. "I will wait for your instructions, Hugoth, as will my pride." He patted each of the big Cats on their shoulders.

Hugoth answered, "I am elated to hear that, Jahnise. Nuorg could have used you here but destiny needs you to return to the lands above."

Mystic turned to Hugoth, "Well? What is next?"

As Hugoth pondered his next word a loud ruckus became obvious to all inside the Keeper's dwelling. Outside Bongi was becoming irritated with two odd looking wingers standing on the ground, nearly looking him in the eye.

Mystic flew back to the window sill. "What is going on out there? Did anyone see Bongi leave this room?"

***

"You cannot enter the dwelling. Who are you?" The Okapi's protective side was apparent. "Were you invited here or not?"

"Eekay sent us. We have a very urgent message to deliver. Please we must speak with Jahnise."

"Jahnise? How did you know?"

Mystic was perched on Bongi's shoulder before the wingers finished saying Jahnise's name. Mystic has never seen this type of winger before. He tried to hide his dismay with their appearance. "What is this all about Bongi?"

"It seems these two Storks have an urgent message from Eekay."

"Did you think it might actually be urgent?"

"Not likely from a pair of these wingers."

Mystic glared at the newcomers. "What message do you have from Eekay?"

The tallest of the two raised his eyes at something behind Bongi. The pair at once bowed their heads in an evident show of respect. "Greetings First King."

Jahnise stood behind Bongi with his protectors at his side. Several of the other attendees wandered out behind him including Hugoth and Hemoth. Hugoth stepped around Bongi. "What is this message you have for Jahnise?"

"I apologize to you large creature, but Eekay instructed us to tell no creature other than the First King Jahnise."

Jahnise conceded to Hugoth's authority. "In our land I would accept that reasoning, but here? This is Hugoth's land. He is the leader here. Please tell him as you would tell me."

"As you ask, King." The shorter Stork began, "We witnessed the Lioness emerge from a cloud near the edge of our river. No sooner was she visible than she was stricken by a barrage of projectiles. A group of your kind..." He pointed his long beak at Jahnise, "...rushed to her. They beat her with clubs until she could no longer move. Then they vanished into the same cloud she came out of. We got to her as soon as we saw she could do us no harm. She was in a bad way. She instructed us to also race into the cloud. We don't know why, but we did. She told us to find Jahnise and tell him she was sorry. She told us to tell him she let them in. That was the last thing she said."

The taller Stork added, "She died right in front if us. We barely made it through the cloud. We had no idea where we were going or why. We were thrown into this place and rudely greeted by these tiny creatures who then sent us to you."

"Eekay is dead?" Bongi tried to remain stoic. "Why are those tiny creatures not with you?"

"They told us to come straight here."

The short Stork added, "They had to follow the group of leggers who dropped in before us. Can we go now?"

Hugoth looked at Mystic. "It's cracking. We must get this started." He addressed the group surrounding him. "I feel a terrible loss for Eekay. However, in her state, she has made a series of disastrous decisions that is affecting Nuorg right now. Send the wingers out. We must find the intruders and make sure they don't locate anymore cracks. Jahnise, I must beg you to loan us your protectors."

The look on Jahnise's face was solemn. "Hugoth, of course."

"Ciruss, you know what to do. Be careful. You must get them before they get you."

"Yes, Hugoth. Lend me the fastest wingers you have."

"Of course. Rakki, Karri? You two are in charge. Get the Goldens. You have to find the intruders. Turn their position over to Ciruss as soon as you have it. Understand?"

Rakki hopped to Hugoth's shoulder. "Yes, Hugoth, at once."

Rakki and Karri took wing with one Golden trailing. Shortly, a group was assembled and scattered to every Burg. The messages were sent to close all gates. No creature was allowed to enter or exit. The two-leggers were told to immediately prepare all measures for security concerns.

North of where Jahnise made his entrance, a well-armed band of two-leggers traveled haphazardly toward the mountains outside of Burg one. It was there they would find their safe havens from where they would run their operations. The scout marked the mountain for them on a hurriedly drawn map. They would be responsible for

292

finding their own entrance in. That the entrance was hidden did not seem to bother the leader. After all, Nuorg was only inhabited by a bunch of stupid animals and some cast-offs from their society above. How much trouble would they possibly find? In just a few clicks of an Eagle's eye, they would find out.

## 28

B ubba trotted down the corridor. Soon he found a royal looking cloth draped over a wooden chest beneath a portal carved to the outside. Illuminated by rays of light from the sky, the fabric cast a peculiar glow. With second and third glances, Bubba noticed several of these throughout the corridor. He gripped the drape with his teeth and pulled it off. It covered a gilded chest about as high as he stood and nearly as long. Once the drape slid off the chest, Bubba noticed how heavy it was. The drape felt more like a floor rug than a table cloth. It was so thin, but it nearly pulled him to the ground. The curious Cat moved back to the chest. This object required more inspection at another time. He left the drape where it lay and hurried back to Frederick.

Mystic, under the circumstances, was enjoying his hunt. The more attention he paid to his surroundings, the more he became aware of their simple elegance. The designs resembled several motifs used in his dwelling. He noticed something out of place when his paw accidentally sent a group of eating utensils scattering across the floor. As he turned to follow the skidding noise, he bumped into a few carelessly stacked small wooden boxes. On top of the stack sat several loops of a thin gray cording. The closest door was still ajar.

Back in the library, Frederick closed the first book. "My goodness, what a story. And that is only one book." He glanced around at the thousands still scattered about him. "This could take eons." Outside the door, he heard the pads of Bubba's paws as the Cheetah hurried toward him.

"Frederick, are you in there? Is it safe?"

"Please enter, Bubba. It is dirty in here, smells a lot of smoke, but otherwise safe unless you are scared of books. There are a lot of those in here."

Bubba stepped through the door, his eyes open in astonishment. "What is it with this place? Do the mysteries ever cease?" He timidly walked the perimeter of the room, basking in the incredible fortune of knowledge. "Frederick, you could never read through these books in your lifetime. This is just one of how many libraries?"

Mystic entered the door, the clicking of his claws giving away his position. "Frederick, I think you need to come with me quickly. I have found something I think is out of place. It may aid your thinking here."

Bubba turned his entire body to face Mystic. "What is it?"

"Oh, you are here as well. Then, both of you come with me. Quickly."

Frederick rose from his chair and joined Bubba as he slipped out the door. "What have you found, Mystic?"

"I don't know what, exactly. I do know whatever it is…is entirely out of place. I can say that with confidence." He led the way past several more doors. He finally stopped when he sent a fork sliding across the floor again."

"I see what you mean, Mystic. Why was that there?" Bubba kicked the fork further down the corridor.

Frederick eyed the strewn silverware as it sat glistening on the floor. "What else do you have for me, Prince?"

"These crates and the cording atop them. What does this mean? Is it helpful?"

Frederick knelt close the stack, running his fingers lightly over the inscribed lettering. He picked a loop of cord from the stack, rubbing it between the fingers of his left hand. "This is without a doubt very high quality, some of the best I have ever seen."

"What is it?" Mystic pleaded.

"The two-leggers call this fire cord. It's used to make fuses for explosives and this looks to be very powerful. I've never seen any of this texture or this flexible. The wrong kind of people would pay great sums for one roll of this."

"You two-leggers, I admire you but one day I hope we can live separately again. I wish to leave your kind to their own demise. I can't see the day when four-leggers would resort to this kind of fiendishness. It actually makes my heart sick."

"I understand Bubba. It is sometimes a twisted world we two-leggers live in."

"That's great. I love hearing that, but right now we have bigger contemplations. What do you think it's for, Frederick?" Mystic did not find it the time for speculation and pity.

"The posers used this and what's in these crates to rig the rooms to explode. What we need to figure out is if the room we just entered is the only one they booby-trapped or if it was one of several they completed before we arrived and threw their schedule off. Any suggestions?"

"How much time will you need?" Mystic inspected the cord for himself. "I just don't get it."

"I don't know how much time I'll need. Maybe one day someone will be able to assemble a crew together, tear the place apart, take it to another place, reassemble it, test it with every conceivable piece of equipment and draw a unanimous and fool proof conclusion within an hour's time."

"We don't use hours, Frederick." Bubba shook his head slightly.

"Yes, I'm sorry...something just came to my mind. Anyway, it could take years!"

"We don't have that long." Mystic accidentally bit into a length of fire cord tangled in his teeth. He swatted it with both paws. "Whoa! Is this stuff burning?" He gagged and spat. "Frederick! Get this out of my mouth!"

Frederick ripped the smoking cord from Mystic's stinging jaws. "What are you doing? Have you lost your mind? I said fire cord! It will burn!"

Mystic licked his snout and patted it with his paws. "The burning is not stopping!"

Frederick tossed Mystic his damp rag. "Chew on this."

Instantly, Mystic's mouth was back to normal. "That Nuorg water is life-saving," the Wolf understated.

Bubba closed his eyes and shook his head bewildered. "Never thought that would happen..."

"Mystic, again I think you have stumbled onto something. Hurry, I have an idea." Frederick snatched a coil of the fire cord and ran to the next door. He pressed it against the face of the door and to his delight, it stuck. From the very middle of the top, he ran a line continuously down the door to the very middle of the bottom, leaving no more than a Rat's tail at extending out on the floor. "You two, step way back. I hope this works." He stomped hard on the cord then dove at the feet of the four-leggers. "Cover your ears!"

A sound popped from the cord but it wasn't a bang or a boom. It was more of a puff. The four leggers watched anxiously. Frederick

296

disappointedly made his way to the door. It appeared completely intact. Not even a small splinter was out of place. "Sorry friends, I thought it might work. He turned away from the door, pressing against it as he slid to the floor. A high pitched hissing sound followed him down the door's length.

Bubba and Mystic looked at each other curiously then back to the door. "What was that for?" Bubba asked.

Frederick feared the worst. "Run for cover!" He shouted. He threw his hands up to his ears. Snap. He jerked around. "That's it? That is the best you can do?" He yelled at the door. He bumped the door jamb with open palms. "Come on! Do something!" Nothing happened.

Bubba out of curiosity, suggested to Frederick, "Try the handle."

"Okay, what can it hurt?" Frederick took hold of the door handle with both hands before pressing the lever down. As he pushed it down, he added, "This might be bad." As the lever reached the limit of its arc, Frederick applied more pressure. As he did, a barely noticeable line developed down the middle of the door, mimicking the line of the fire cord. One half of the door teetered, balancing precariously on the bottom. "Well, that's strange." Frederick fought to hold the door upright, it was very heavy. It fell away from him. It landed inside the room with a loud bang of its own. Fortunately for the group, that was the only bang.

Frederick breathed a heavy sigh of relief and stepped inside. Turning to the inside hinged side of the door he noticed a stack of 3 crates attached to the bottom door hinge with a length of fire cord and a fork. "I have to give them a passing grade for effort and a failing grade for creativity." He wasted no time disarming the trap. "Mystic, Bubba, try to find out what room we have here. I need to go open some more doors."

The Wolf and the Cheetah leaped into the room and began taking mental notes of the contents. Aside from the hard to believe craftsmanship in everything they saw, the leggers were astounded with the meticulous attention to detail paid to every item in the room, from the furniture and fixtures to the actual walls and ceilings. This was not a library, the lack of books made it obvious. They had no conceivable idea of what two-leggers would do in a room like this. There were a few high tables, a raised floor to one side, several chairs and not much else. To the back was a large flat object standing on thin legs.

"I don't see anything in here worth mentioning, do you?" Mystic was bored with the room.

"I really don't either. Let's catch up with Frederick. Maybe the next room will strike our fancy." Bubba followed behind Mystic as they exited the room.

Frederick was getting better at opening the doors. He was on his third when the four-leggers caught up to him. "Was there anything of note in the first room?"

"Nope," replied Mystic. "Not much of anything at all."

"I agree," said Bubba. "Maybe your kind would find someway to occupy time in there, but not us."

"Check out the second room. I think every room in this place was armed to kill whoever came in, friend or foe. I've found the same mechanism to the side of every door. I'm beginning to think the posers were not that ingenious.

"Let's check it out Mystic."

"Right behind you Bubba."

Frederick noticed as he disarmed the rooms that the fire cord extended just beyond the reach of the fully open door. He also noticed the edge of the door would almost touch the wall, everywhere that is, except at the bottom of the wall where a piece of wood about shin high interrupted its swing. The cord on every door, so far, was stuck halfway up the wood trim. He had an idea that might work; at least it would not involve splitting anymore doors if it worked. At his next stop he didn't use the fire cord. Instead he braced as if a coming explosion would slam the door against him again. With both hands on the door jamb, he pushed the door lever all the way down with his foot and held it there for a split second. He took a deep breath and prayed there was nothing inside this room that he may be sacrificing for a gut decision. Satisfied that it had to be done, he kicked the door open with as much force as he could muster. The door swung violently to its stop...there was no explosion. He waited, still no explosion. Convinced that his new method might have worked, he peeked inside the room, his eyes falling learnedly to the stack of dangerous crates. He spotted the fire cord and to his excitement saw that the edge of the door had cleaved it sharply in half. The door edge was so finely made it turned into a knife blade. The cord had no chance of survival. He used this method repeatedly down one side of the corridor and began to disarm the doors on the other side when he heard Mystic's call.

"Frederick! You need to see this!" Mystic called.

Bubba stood inside the room, transfixed at the contents. He was shocked by the numbers of what he witnessed. He was stunned with what comprised the bulk of it. As he and Mystic entered the room, they were met by hundreds of pairs of lifeless eyes staring back at them. They cautiously walked the nearest aisles, waiting for Frederick's arrival. Maybe he could explain the reason for a room such as this.

"What do you make of this, Bubba?" Mystic asked as they cautiously began to eye each individual. "More secrets of the two-leggers?"

"Your guess is as good as mine." Bubba hoped Frederick could explain this in terms they might understand.

"I'd be telling a tale if I told you this was not creepy to a yet unimagined level for me."

"I concur." Bubba could not help but cringe as blank stares followed their every move.

"How many do you think are in here?"

"No idea." They walked on, leery of what they may see next.

Frederick arrived at the open door and glanced around the door frame for a room description or signage. Finding none, he stepped inside. What he saw, he could handle, although he knew the four-leggers would not be coping as well. "Mystic, Bubba?"

At the sound of Frederick's voice the pair abruptly turned and came running for him. "What is this place?" "Can you believe all of this?" "What is it with you two-leggers?" "Is anything sacred to your kind?" "How many years does this represent?" "Reasons, please?" "Is this how two-leggers entertain themselves?"

The questions were flying from the four-leggers in rapid succession. Frederick said nothing. He inspected the first item he came to. A medium sized thing about half his height with antlers sprouting from the top of its head, a gold collar around its neck. To its side, a winger hung frozen in full flight, wings stretched wide, a shiny golden band wrapped around one leg. "My initial thought is that this is a trophy room."

Bubba looked at Frederick like he was crazy. "A trophy room? What did these creatures win? I don't want to play that game!"

"No, some two-leggers hunt four-leggers as sport."

"Yeah, I know the type, my family calls them poachers." The Cheetah continued his observations with disgust rising in his throat. "I'd like to call them meals."

Mystic noticed a large plaque near the middle of one wall. "Come over here. This may explain more." He stared up at the wooden shield with its gold embossed lettering. "I can't make out the small letters Frederick. If you please, will you read it for us?"

"I will try but it is so dark in here. There must be some kind of light source we haven't discovered yet."

Bubba became more disgusted with each creature he passed. "Trophy room? Try looking above you for a handle or a lever of some kind, two-legger. I'm sure whoever created this place made full arrangements for lighting. I'm sure they gloated over these poor leggers."

Frederick tried to overlook the acidic tone in Bubba's voice. He did as the Cheetah suggested. Searching the walls, he did find a lever near the door opposite of the hinge side. Cautiously he pushed the lever down. It did not budge. He pushed it up with no sign of movement. He tried pulling it to him. It moved effortlessly as he swung it in a smooth arc. The room grew brighter the farther the lever traveled. He shoved it flat against the wall. The room was swallowed up with bright light. "I need to discover how that works. This room has come alive."

"That would not be my first choice of words. All of these creatures, for some reason, seem to have remained dead. This room is certainly not alive!" Bubba was drifting away.

"It's a figure of speech, Bubba. Snap out of it. It's not Frederick's fault!" Mystic was searching for a good ending to this story.

"Yeah, whatever. The two-leggers are never at fault..."

"Mystic, don't bother with him right now. He can vent. This is creepy." Frederick read the plaque. It was lengthy to say the least.

Mystic read what he could make out. "Bubba, you might find this interesting."

"Probably not."

"Would you please come over here? I don't appreciate your attitude. I am a four-legger, remember!"

"You better have evidence to back that up."

As Frederick and Mystic read line after line, the meaning for the room became clear. This was not a trophy room. It was built as a shrine. All of the creatures were once loyal friends of the original builders of the fortress, each one with their own story. Over the years, as fate would have it, they succumbed to different causes. In order not to give away the project, the dead were prepared and entombed in this memorial chamber. Digging burial pits was time consuming and visible to prying eyes from the outside. Whether it made a difference to Bubba or not, there were also two-leggers entombed in the room according to the list. Each creature was fitted with a gold collar, band or tag engraved with their complete history and record of service. There was no distinction in groupings or rankings. Two-leggers were shown no preference over the four-leggers or wingers. The first to die were the first listed and so on. Each entry included a date of death, initials or names and a location.

"Bubba does this change your attitude at all?" Frederick asked.

"Yes it does. But I still loathe the thought of poachers."

"And you should. See if either of you can recognize any names from your past. I'm coming up empty; no Hewitts, no Mountes." Frederick stepped away from the plaque. He walked the wide, well illuminated aisles with great admiration for the lives represented. He occasionally read with interest the collar tags or leg bands.

"Frederick," Mystic barked, "There doesn't seem to be any complete names or titles here. These folk were very uninterested with status. Do the collars and tags contain more information?"

"Yes." A voice from far down the room answered back. "Some of these tags are very interesting. Come find me."

Bubba's attitude slowly returned to normal as he studied the plaque. Still not completely comfortable with the current explanation, he decided to muddle a bit longer in his puddle of contempt. He did not tag along with Mystic to the back of the room to meet up with Frederick. Instead he opted to walk the aisles alone, lost in his own reoccurring thoughts of years past, both good and bad.

## 29

"**I**an! Will somebody bring Ian here to me at once!" Hugoth was not worried about the intruders. Instead he was very concerned about the cracks appearing around the windows. "Where is he?"

Rakki came in fast. "Hugoth, we found them."

"Already?"

"At the rate they are traveling, you could have run them down on foot. They are heading toward our Burg, I assume to take shelter in the mountain."

"Let Ciruss know. They cannot be allowed in the mountain! Divert them to the river if possible. The river can protect itself. How many are there?"

"I will and I know. I will try. There are no more that 11 of them."

"Eleven? That's it?"

"I thought about that. Some of them may have gotten stuck in the crack."

"Well that would serve them right. I can't say I pity those unlucky scoundrels."

Hemoth was listening with great interest as this conversation unfolded. "What do you need from me, Brother?"

Hugoth looked him in the eye. "Hemoth, you and Lightning have but one deed to perform. You two are to guard Madaliene with your lives. She goes nowhere without you, understand?"

"Yes, Brother. Even down here in Nuorg some things never change."

"Thank you, Hemoth."

"Rakki, can we get to the mountain ahead of them?"

"I don't think so. Not at this late hour."

Hugoth turned to Mystic, the Eagle. "Mystic, can you keep them out of the mountain?"

"I don't see that as a problem Hugoth. I want to know how they know about it in the first place."

"As do I, sir."

Lightning stepped up with a determined look never before seen on his face. "Hugoth, how many of us would you like to place in the mountain?"

Hugoth was surprised. "Is there something about you I have overlooked there Badger?"

"It's not me you have overlooked, Hugoth, it's this." Lightning held the ax-pike in front of him. "Trust me, Hugoth, if you want in the mountain, I can get us in the mountain."

Lightning smiled a sly smile. A definite twinkle peeked from his eyes.

"If you say so, I believe you, Badger. What shall we do?"

"Place your group as near to me as possible. I don't know how many can make the skip but I feel we need to give it a try."

Madaliene positioned herself securely between Hemoth and Lightning.

"And where do you think you are going, Princess?" Hugoth asked.

"Perrie and I will go wherever these two Grizzlies go. There will be no discussion. I have enough supplies in my bag for a small squadron of creatures, as well as 'other' goodies."

"Hemoth, is this true?"

"Yes, Brother, I will have to agree with her."

"In that little bag?"

"This is Frederick's bag, Hugoth. Here, look inside." Madaliene tossed the bag to Hugoth as if she was tossing a small stick. "Catch!"

Hugoth stepped up to catch the bag. It was a mistake. The bag knocked him sideways, nearly rolling him over. "My mother, Madaliene! What is in that?"

"No more than I told you and lots more than you think." She laughed out loud as she stooped over and picked it up, slinging it back on her shoulder. "I think next time you should just take my word for it, huh?"

"I will never doubt you again, Princess." Hugoth gave Hemoth a look of utter disbelief. Hemoth smiled back.

"If I can offer my services, Hugoth, what shall I do?" Jahnise stood proudly at attention awaiting further instructions.

303

"Jahnise, I want you and your stick here. Stand near the gate. If you see anyone approaching for any reason and they are not us, then let your light shine. I want to question our visitors if possible, but if they come here before we get to them, then light them up."

Jahnise grinned, "It will be my pleasure, Keeper."

"Alright, Hugoth, who is going with us?" Lightning was enjoying his leadership role.

Hugoth glanced up to see Ciruss coming his way with Duister and Luiperd at here side. The three big Cats made for a very intimidating sight. The path parted in front of them as they neared Hugoth. "I hear you have the intruder's location. We returned as fast as we could."

"They are headed for the mountains of Burg one."

"We will never make it there ahead of them. What is your second plan?"

"We have another method of getting you there. It is...it's a little different."

Ciruss looked pleased. "Hugoth, we are in Nuorg. How much different could it be?"

"Fair enough Ciruss, you will be traveling with Hemoth, Lightning and the Princess."

The trio of big Cats eyed the Bears and the two-legger suspiciously.

"With them?" She asked.

"Yes."

"I'll agree with you, Hugoth. That is different."

Lightning took center stage, "If I may, Ciruss, move in closer. We don't want you to be left behind."

She shrugged, "Sure, I can't see how it would hurt our chances." The big Cats moved in tight to the Grizzlies.

Ciruss turned stone-cold for a moment. "Hugoth, to what means do we protect the mountain?"

Hugoth returned her determined look. "If possible, Ciruss, I would like to question them. If that is not possible...then...they must be killed. It's not simply them or us. It is either them or everything Nuorg was created for."

Ciruss sighed a heavy, labored sigh. "If all else fails, Hugoth, we will make it happen. Can the Princess and her companions do the same?"

"If you are asking what I think you are asking, Ciruss, I can and will do what I have to do in order to survive. I have a feeling there is a lot at stake if I don't survive this wild adventure." Madaliene stood firm in her resolve, her hair wild, her persona glistening with confidence.

"Princess," Ciruss replied, "I will hold you to that."

"Don't worry about me, Ciruss. I might surprise you."

"Very well." She looked at Lightning, "Now how are we traveling?"

Lightning held his ax-pike aloft and spoke to those around him, "Please, if you do not wish to go with us, step away." He focused on the ax-pike, "Take us to the mountain to repel the intruders and please let it be the mountain near Burg one…"

They vanished. Hugoth was left standing in front of the group once behind Lightning. They were speechless. "Was it me or did that Badger sound a bit unsure?"

Rakki added, "I do hope they are headed to the correct mountain. Hugoth, shall I?"

"Yes please. You, Karri and Mystic keep me posted. Take the Golden with you. Have him fly the gap."

"Absolutely." Rakki hurried away to catch the other wingers.

Hugoth placed a huge front paw on Jahnise's shoulder. "Please stay alert. Position yourself at the gate. I must try and make it to my Burg. There may be a way I can help there."

"But, Hugoth," Bongi seemed disheveled, "You told everyone to stay put. All of the gates are now closed."

"I'm not going through the front gate." He winked at Bongi and bid a wave to Stewig. "I am not a happy Grizzly right now. Where is Ian? Has no one found him yet?" The Bear was losing his pleasant nature. "Stewig, go round him up him and tell him to find what is causing the cracks and fix them immediately. He has free reign. Give him whatever he wants." With that, the mad Grizzly Bear strode to the gate followed by Jahnise and several others. He sent word ahead that he would be leaving the Burg. The bridge was down when he arrived and drawn the moment he stepped off the ramps. With a wave of his paw and a nod to Donkhorse, a very determined and angry Grizzly made his way to "Sweet Gulley" by way of "The Path to Where I Am Going".

Donkhorse watched as Hugoth steadily increased his speed before disappearing over the rise. To no creature in particular he stated, "I hope the best for you my friend."

Bongi, standing close by, agreed.

\*\*\*

Inside the mountains of Burg one, a small disturbance registered near a solid rock wall dotted with dark portals, one glowing like the sun. Out of thin air, a group of three big Cats, one two-legger, a Grizzly Bear, an irregular Badger and a Falcon materialized each a tad out of sorts. Lightning stepped away from the group to get his bearings.

"Wonderful," He said out loud. "I have been here before." He summoned his group. "There, on the second level. We will enter that portal and it will lead us where we need to go." He got no reaction from those with him that would lead him to think otherwise. "Let's go. Ciruss, when we get as far as we can go, you are in charge. Let us know what we need to do."

Ciruss, like the other Cats, was trying her best to shake the confusion from her head. "Uh…okay…sure."

Lightning took charge again. "Follow me. We have made excellent time getting here. I'm not sure if it's really good or really bad time. We need to get moving." He led the way up a ramp to the second level and trotted head long through the only lit portal in the wall.

Madaliene, with Perrie still clinging to her shoulder, was the slowest of the group. Duister felt bad as she tried to keep up with the four-leggers pace. "Princess, climb on my back. You are slowing us down."

Madaliene had never heard his voice before. "Thank you sir, I will gladly oblige you. Perrie, go ride with Hemoth."

"Yes, Princess."

"Duister what kind of cat are you?"

"I am Siberian, Princess. A Siberian Tiger."

"Are you that much different from Ciruss?"

"No, Princess, we are both Tigers, we are simply from different parts of the world. Hang on tight?"

Madaliene griped the Tiger's neck firmly. "Ready."

306

Duister, a large, quiet Siberian, was up to speed with a few powerful strides, catching the others before they noticed his absence. Unknown to most creatures, Grizzlies were capable of matching the big Cats' speed, so no member of the group needled Lightning's lack of drive as he thundered ahead. The group followed the portal as it led them capably through the mountain's innards.

Hemoth raced side-by-side with Lightning when the twisting, winding passageway allowed. "So, I take it you've been here before?"

"Yes, in a way. I haven't been exactly here in this particular tunnel, but I have been all through this mountain. Quite a journey it was too."

"You have never been in this tunnel before? How do you know where it is leading us?"

"Nope and I don't. I am proceeding on faith, Hemoth. Just because you've never seen it doesn't mean it's not worth believing in."

"Oh I know that to be true, Lightning. It's just...well, maybe a map or sketch of this mountain might be good to have?"

"Why? Then we wouldn't need faith to see it through. If we knew where it was going, faith would not be necessary. Anyway there are no maps known to exist of these tunnels." They kept speeding on.

Ciruss and Luiperd brought up the rear. "Luiperd, I am thankful it is not any darker in here. I don't think I would ever see you if that were so."

"Humor, no doubt." Luiperd did not have an abundant sense of frivolity, but then, neither did Ciruss.

"Yes, and a poor attempt at that. Sorry."

"Don't bother. What is your plan, Ciruss? Hugoth was adamant that we do whatever it takes to rid Nuorg of these intruders. Do we know they are for the bad?"

"Luiperd, they killed Eekay when she had no chance of protecting herself. I would say they were for the bad. I am very certain of it."

"I thought I left those days behind when I came here. Now am I to revert back for the sake of Nuorg? I'll tell you, Ciruss, sometimes I wish I'd just stayed in my tree."

"Luiperd, I don't enjoy killing either, but it is part of us. I think there is a slight chance this whole plan might actually work."

"Maybe, Ciruss, but have you ever met a two-legger you could trust with your life? They are so finicky. They have too many thoughts in their heads."

Madaliene listened to the conversation behind her. "Luiperd, you can trust me. I will never waiver on you. If I have the mind to say it, I will stick by it. Odd as it may seem to a four-legger, I was raised that way."

"You most certainly had a unique set of parents then Princess." Luiperd made the statement with no emotion.

"I had no parents that I remember. I was raised by a set of posers. They're gone now...banished to somewhere I never want to go. But in fact, the one who taught me my core beliefs was that huge Grizzly up there. He has been my protector along with my Falcon and me their wretched charge. I wish Sig had come with us. He would certainly have enjoyed this."

Hemoth chuckled. "I heard that, Mad. There is no way Sig would have enjoyed this. The old winger is much happier in your mountain. I can assure you of that."

"Whatever, Hemoth." She whispered to the Cats, "He thinks he knows everything."

"We are coming to the end of this tunnel." Lightning rushed ahead in order to get a fix on their position. He called the others. "I don't know where we are, but we have an excellent view of Burg one and a few others from here."

Beyond the Badger lay Nuorg. They were positioned high on the mountain; too high to be of any threat to the intruders.

"I am very tired Hemoth, does the sun ever set here?" Madaliene asked.

Luiperd answered, "That is not the sun Princess. But no, it does not."

Lightning spotted movement below. "Quiet, each of you take a look below. What is that ...I don't know, we are too high to tell."

"Not completely true Lightning." Perrie hopped to the edge of the tunnel's end. The opening was concealed from below by a natural knee wall in the rock formation. They would not be seen. "I clearly see them and I can count only nine. The other two must be hidden lookouts, possibly on the perimeter. Do you want me to fly down and scout?"

The group was impressed with the young winger. "Where did you come from, Perrie?" Madaliene did not hide her curiosity.

"I never told you the entire story Madaliene. I stopped telling you my history when you found out I came from a flesh-eating land. Remember?"

"You too?" Ciruss asked.

"Yes I did, Ma'am. Please don't hold it against me. It is the way of my kind."

"I won't if you will do the same."

"You need to add me to that list as well, Princess," Duister said.

Luiperd confessed, "Me too, Princess. In another place and time, you might have been a tasty meal for any of us. But personally, I hated the taste of two-leggers; too much salt."

Duister added, "And far too fatty. I think I'd rather have Bear." He eyed Lightning.

"I beg your pardon? You'd rather have Bear?" Lightning ignored the rest of the conversation. "As Madaliene would say...whatever."

Perrie was excitedly hopping around the knee wall. "Can I go, Hemoth? Can I?"

"By all means, Perrie. I think you have a lot to teach us. Fly Falcon!"

Perrie rocketed skyward up and behind the mountain.

"Where did she go, Hemoth?" Ciruss lifted up on the knee wall, looking about to catch a glimpse of the fleet Falcon. "My, that winger is fast."

Luiperd and Duister pulled themselves up beside Ciruss. Hemoth stared down over the top of them. "You know, Cats, if I get too hungry I think each of you might be tasty in your own right."

Lightning stood nearby. He merely shook his head.

"What is the plan, Ciruss? We can't attack from here. We'd likely be killed ourselves."

"Until we hear from Perrie I can't decide any action. We need to take out the lookouts first. They can't be too far away."

Lightning was beginning to have second thoughts about this whole hunting and attacking scenario. "How do we know these leggers mean us harm?"

Ciruss answered. "They killed Eekay with no provocation. That is how we know."

"They broke into Nuorg through a crack." Duister added as he scanned far to the left.

"And that is why I am ready to remove them from life as they know it." There was a sinister side of Luiperd, but he meant well.

Hemoth nodded, "If it must be so, I am here to protect my charge. I will do anything necessary to assure her safety. If it means ripping those leggers limb from limb, then so be it. I've done it before."

Now the others were afraid of Hemoth. He did not appear as menacing as the big Cats, but he was and besides that, he weighed nearly four times as much as Duister, who was a very big Tiger.

Madaliene saw a winger come in from the far side, behind the intruders. Unfortunately, he was low enough to be noticed. "Who is that? He is too big to be Perrie."

"It looks like the Golden who flew to us earlier." Ciruss strained her eyes for a better look. "What is he doing that low?"

It was a tragic mistake. An arrow was unleashed from the side of the intruders. Its target was the Golden. The Eagle never saw it coming. A darting object appeared from another angle. It arrived just as the arrow began to penetrate the chest feathers of the Eagle. It was Perrie. Somehow, she snatched the arrow out of the air with a magnificent display of acrobatic flying before it bore through the first layer of the Golden's feathers. She continued on at full pursuit beat, speeding out of the intruder's range.

"Eagles are so ridiculously thickheaded!" She screamed to herself knowing the Eagle would hear her now that he was flying in her wake. On they flew around the mountain. She knew better than head straight up the side. If the Falcon did that, it would without a doubt give away her friends' vantage point. Perrie flew to the edge of Nuorg's unique horizon then turned back when she was out of sight.

The Cats watched in awe as the Falcon schooled the larger Eagle. "That is one Falcon I would not mess with." Luiperd spoke sincerely as he praised the young winger.

Lightning agreed, "Especially when you know she might eat you. Hemoth, where is Madaliene?"

"Don't worry about me you overgrown bunch of four-leggers." She had climbed above them and settled on a tree limb with her bow outstretched and a fully loaded quiver easily within reach. "Which one do you want me shoot first?"

"Madaliene!" Hemoth shouted in a coarse whisper. "What are you doing?"

"They shot first. They will soon be wishing they hadn't. I'll take them all out." She pulled the bowstring taut.

Perrie dove past Hemoth straight into the cave opening. After dropping the arrow at Hemoth's feet, she disappeared, the Eagle close behind her. Soon, an argument deep inside the cave was heard by all.

Ciruss smiled, "I'd hate to be that Golden Eagle about now."

Hemoth picked up the arrow, scanned it, then, handed it to Madaliene. "Mad, have you ever seen anything like this before?"

Madaliene took the arrow and inspected its make-up. "I'd never shoot anything like this. This is worse than any arrow I've ever thrown away. Garbage, pretty much. Won't fly from here to there with any accuracy." She tossed it back to Hemoth. "Now, which one gets it first?"

The Cats exchanged glances while Lightning continued to shake his head. He raised his ax-pike to scratch his neck. That was all it took. A bolt of scraggly light shot to their position. Now, the yellow ball knew where they were as well as the intruders. Far below, several of them looked to see where the bolt of light struck. They were frightened until they barely recognized a series of heads ducking behind the rock knee wall. Suddenly, their fear vanished. It was instantly replaced by duty to their mission. A volley of arrows fell way short of their intended targets. Madaliene sat calmly in the tree while the four-leggers ran for cover in the cave. She drew the bow string to her cheek and searched for a target. She found it. The two-legger with the fanciest clothes showed too much of his jester-like uniform. She let her arrow fly. It found its mark deep inside the intruder's chest. Before he crumpled to the ground, Madaliene had targeted a second and a third intruder. Both of them received exquisitely made arrows exquisitely placed in the exact center of their chests. They fell to the ground with their leader.

Around their fallen comrades, the intruders scattered for cover. Wild orders were bandied back and forth as the surviving eight two-leggers pulled their fellows to cover too late. They were not prepared for a counter attack, especially an attack from a bunch of four-leggers.

"Who taught animals to shoot bows?" One cried.

"We will be wiped out if we stay here!"

Another arrow nocked, another arrow released. In rapid succession, intruders number four, five, six and seven were removed from the land of the living. That left four.

Madaliene shouted to Hemoth, "If you want any of them left to question, you had better get down there. I will cover you."

Hemoth poked his head out of the cave. "What are you doing?"

"I'm protecting myself and the rest of you!" She loosed another arrow. Number eight went down in a heap. "You need to hurry, Hemoth. There are only three of them left and I have a bead on number nine!"

"What do you want me to do?"

"Have Lightning's ax-pike take the rest of you down there. I'll hit the next one in the leg." And...she did. Number nine hollered out in pain as the arrow passed cleanly through his knee, giving him no chance to run away. "Number nine is down! Two more standing."

From where she sat in the tree, her view was unobstructed. She so badly wanted to loose another arrow, but she knew better. She couldn't take them all. Before she blinked to clear her eyes for the next shot, the surviving pair of two-leggers found themselves surrounded by an angry mob of four-leggers, one very ticked off Falcon and a pouting Golden Eagle. She smiled to herself, "Not bad Lightning, not bad at all."

The intruders were terrified. The taller of the two was very cooperative. The shorter one was livid. He drew a sword from his side and thrust it at the least aggressive looking Grizzly. Lightning was pulled backward as the shiny blade sliced off a patch of fur from his shoulder. Hemoth tossed him to the side and charged the intruder. He was too late. Duister dashed by Hemoth before the Grizzly could react. The Tiger leaped past the irate two-legger and, with one swat of his powerful paw, knocked him senseless.

Hemoth was elated when he saw no blood. Had Duister extended his claws, the two-legger could very well be in pieces all over the ground instead of being one complete, unconscious legger. "Duister, that was amazing. Thank you."

The last intruder gave up his weapons with no further struggle. He was smart enough to realize he had no other chance of survival. The wounded intruder cried out in pain. "Is there anyone here to help me with my leg? Surely these stupid animals are not the brains behind this ambush. There are more of us coming, count on it!"

"Would you shut your mouth, you sniveling coward?" The other conscious intruder outranked the wounded one. "Don't tell these inept animals anything. You know we have been told some of them can understand everything we say."

"Yes and that is impossible to believe. I would think even you would be smart enough to know a lie when you hear one! Where are you, humans? Come out and show yourselves to us. Let us see our adversaries and bring your archers. Bring them all. They must know they will soon be outmatched and outnumbered."

Madaliene made her way down mountain side with grace and equally abundant amounts of skill. She emerged none-the-less for wear from an entanglement of low trees walking straight for the wounded, boastful and ignorant two-legger. Her face was even more radiant than before, her hair, well...a lovely mess. "I have heard enough of your mouth coward!" She stormed the final few steps. "What business 'ave ye here in our land?"

The four-leggers surrounded the breathing two-leggers much like a thick, thorny hedge except this hedge was armed with razor sharp claws, teeth and very bad attitudes. When Madaliene stormed in and took charge, each and every one of her companions gained an even greater admiration for her.

"I'll be killing the next one that utters a word unless it's in answer to a question I'll be asking." She turned to her audience and winked. "Which one of ye be calling me friends here stupid? Was that you?" She walked into the taller legger's chest and pushed him to the ground. "Do yourself a favor and 'ave a seat when I talk to ye." She drew her bow and nocked yet another arrow. She did this with an ease not seen before by the intruders. "And who might this one be? Did he die from fright?" She drew the bow string and readied for a close range shot. She kicked the unconscious legger awake. When he came to the first thing he saw was the business end of the arrow a mere hand's width away from his rapidly beating heart. "So ye pile of rubbish, might you be the leader of this ill-fated huntin' partee?" She placed her foot on his fat stomach and applied enough pressure to make him gag. "Well? What you be sayin'? I don't have much time here. If this brilliant one over here says there are more of ye comin', don you think I should be preparing meself for it?" She turned to the four-leggers who were doing their best to hold in great amounts of laughter. "It's kind of a bad thing when eleven of ye cuss's come into my land and only three of ye are left standing, I mean alive, seems like only one of you are standing."

A defiant voice came from the one previously knocked unconscious. "Where are your archers, girl? Where is your leader? We demand to see him. He might be able to get himself out of this before it's too late."

Madaliene whirled around and loosed an arrow at the mouthy intruder. It stuck in the ground a fraction away from the man's neck, dead center between his chin and his shoulder. "Looks like I should be the one askin' questions 'round here, don it? What does your mother call ye? I'm not sure I want me four-legger friends hearing what I want to be callin' ye."

"You are as stupid as they are. Where is your father? He should be beaten for raising one such as you!"

Another arrow sliced the ground on the other side of the legger's neck. "One more word from ye and I won't miss." She turned to the wounded intruder still squirming on the ground. "Stop your sniveling, ye be a grown mahn." Madaliene bent over and yanked the arrow out of the man's leg. "Now, do ye feel a wee bit better lad?" The poor man cried out again in pain. "I'll take that as a no."

"Have you no feelings for the wounded?" The tall legger was frightened, very, very frightened. He had never seen a display such as this.

Madaliene turned to him, her eyes searing holes in his pale skin. "The answer to that question is a no. Ye are correct. I 'ave no feelings for the wounded or the unwounded for that matter. If you would like to stay unwounded, I suggest you give me your names right away."

He caved. "I am Lawrence. You pulled the arrow from Willem's leg and missed August's neck by inches."

"You fool, shut your mouth. Don't say another word. Her leader is watching us right now. He wants to know everything you are telling her. If you don't silence yourself, I will do it for you!"

Madaliene walked back to August and grinned as she stood over him. "I think your eyes might be uh lyin' to ye Lawrence." She knelt down beside August and tried to place a feather between shaft and his neck. "From here it looks much closer than inches."

314

August gritted his teeth before he made his last living move. As Madaliene rose to question Willem, August sprung to his feet. As he was making a move to shove a tiny blade into Madaliene's back, Luiperd swatted a black paw across August's back. Not as forward thinking as Duister, Luiperd's claws were fully extended. August slumped to the ground, the blade falling harmlessly to his side. Madaliene nonchalantly bent over to pick it up and placed it in her belt. "Princess, I was getting the feeling that he was a nasty two-legger." Luiperd did not apologize.

Willem and Lawrence began begging Madaliene for protection. She wrapped a torn piece of overshirt around Willem's leg to stem the bleeding. "Perrie, would you send the Golden for a wagon? I believe Hugoth wants to have a word with these two."

"Yes, Princess."

"Ciruss, can I ask you, Luiperd and Duister to watch these two until the wagon arrives? I want to take Luiperd with me, but he needs to stay here. I think he may be too hungry to simply watch after these two."

"As you wish, Princess. I will do anything you ask. You are quite a two-legged lady. May I ask a question of you?"

"What is it?"

"I just witnessed an amazing and disturbing display of your prowess with the bow from what can only be considered a staggering distance. I watched in awe as you harangued the surviving two-leggers to their breaking point. That troubled me for one your age should not have the kind of skill and emotionless insistence to deal with issues such as that. Your act was convincing beyond measure. How?"

Madaliene smiled a very sincere smile back. "Thank you Ciruss. They shot first. I was protecting my friends. I will protect my friends at any cost. Do not underestimate me. I will do what I have to do. You have made my good list. The time may come when you fall under my protective ways, if it does, rest assured you are my friend. As far as my skill with the bow?" She laughed. "You have seen nothing yet."

"I see, Princess. I have taken your words to heart. You have my admiration and respect. I would ask to be your second if I had not already vowed to protect Jahnise."

"Don't think of it, Ciruss. Jahnise needs you. I have Hemoth. If I find I require your assistance I will call for you and you will come."

Lawrence and Willem knew they had finally lost hope and maybe their senses. Each of them could have sworn on their own lives the animals were conversing with the girl. They were still waiting to see the rest of the archers emerge from the thickets and, finally, the leader of the whole rag-tag bunch.

Duister walked up to Madaliene and whispered something. She feigned a startled look. "No, please don't eat them!" She shouted that loud enough for Willem and Lawrence to hear clearly. "Eat the dead ones if you wish, but don't eat the live ones!" She turned to Hemoth, "That should do the trick, don't ye think?"

"Yes, Princess, it should. Do we walk back or use that thing of Lightning's?"

"I feel like walking." They proceeded back to the Burg. Lightning walked a few steps behind. He was still trying to grasp what had happened. He had never before seen anything like Madaliene.

Perrie lit on Madaliene's shoulder. "The Golden is on his way to his Burg. Anything else?"

Madaliene stopped in her tracks. "Lightning, can you take us to Burg One? I have a feeling we need to be there."

"I would love to, Princess. By the way, just who were you pretending to be back there?"

A cunning grin crawled across the young heroine's face. "I was an Irish pirate, Lightning. I'm hurt you had to ask!" She rested her head on Hemoth's flank. "Perrie, Rakki and Karri are over us now. Tell them where we are going. I am really tired." She climbed on Hemoth's back. "Hemoth, wake me when we arrive."

"Yes Princess."

Mystic, the Great Eagle, perched atop the rock wall guarding the cave opening, not sure he believed everything he had just seen. This Princess, this Madaliene...she was the real thing. The young maiden single-handedly and without remorse removed from Nuorg eight troublesome intruders before they had a chance to perform the vile bidding of those who sent them. She cowed two more into telling everything they knew and set another up for his demise. Madaliene was more than the Nuorgians could have hoped for. Young, intelligent, brave, loyal to a fault, she was without any doubt the Staffs' rightful facilitator. His plans changed permanently and for the better. He flew to find Hugoth.

\*\*\*

Jahnise kneeled behind the gate with no intention of abandoning his post, the stick in his grasp awaiting orders. He remained in this position, motionless since Hemoth's party left, eyes closed, praying for guidance and protection. With Stewig standing at his side, he occasionally drifted back to the plains where animals like the Rhinoceros and the others roamed freely. He never thought then what he was thinking now. Had the animals known the whole time? What caused the differences between them to widen so? He remembered several times throughout his life when he felt the animals actually staring through his eyes into his soul. Odd.

Jahnise turned to his other protected side, "So, Donkhorse, my new friend, what have you to tell me of Nuorg? Has this looming battle been brewing for some time now? Did my arrival hasten this intrusion by those meaning you harm? Why now?"

Donkhorse spoke to Jahnise without looking at him directly. "Those questions should be directed to Hugoth and the other Keepers. I am here to do as they ask. I have asked for no responsibilities and, in truth, I wish for none. I don't consider myself to be of the intellectual type. I have no confidence in making those kinds of decisions. I can take care of myself and my friends, but I would rather not do the thinking. I hope that does not offend you."

"It does not, friend. Once, I felt the same way about my decision making. I thought it should be someone else's burden until that legger ceased to exist. Decision making was thrust upon me as a very troublesome load, an unwanted gift to bear. Not a pleasant gift but a gift either way. A gift I had to open. Donkhorse, you may never have to make a decision the rest of your life, but if you do, be prepared for the consequences and trust your inner mind."

Donkhorse pondered Jahnise's advice. He looked even further away from the safe confines of the Burg's walls. He said nothing.

"What else is troubling you, friend?" As Jahnise spoke, the sincerity of his words was undeniable.

Donkhorse did not answer. His thoughts drifted to Hugoth. What did that Grizzly have in mind? Why had he left for Burg One alone?

\*\*\*

The Golden swiftly did as instructed. He flew satisfied that all of the talk would soon be dying down concerning the staffs and so forth. The truth was he missed his family and they did not live in Nuorg. Once within the Burg, he quickly sought out Bongi, finding him attempting to restore order after the little ado at the gates.

"Bongi, may I have a word with you?"

Bongi was startled by the Golden's sudden appearance. "Why are you here? Were you not following along with the Princess and her entourage?"

"Well, the Princess is the one who sent me back. Strangely enough, that youngster has very mature hunting skills."

"I'm sorry. I don't understand."

"The Princess has requested a cart for the two surviving members of the intruding party. The others were taken care of with an incredible show of marksmanship and wit."

"Okay, I am still not following you."

"Fine, I will spell it out for you. Madaliene just removed from the living eight intruders with her bow and arrows. She tricked another into getting killed by the big Cats. So you tell me. Anyway, she sent me after a cart to bring the survivors to Hugoth for questioning. Cirrus is in charge of watching them until the cart gets there and she is very likely to eat them first. So, what will it be?"

Bongi's face wore an unmistakable look of surprise. Unable to comprehend the huge implications of what he heard, Bongi dismissed a lengthy discussion. Instead he summoned a Horse, a cart and a couple of two-leggers to retrieve the two surviving intruders. He begged the Golden to take the cart tenders back to Cirrus. "Would you be so kind?"

"Of course I will, Bongi." The Golden simply said, "Follow me."

The gate was dropped, sending the cart on its way. Jahnise walked up to Bongi as the cart clattered down the lower ramp.

"What was all of that?" Jahnise asked.

"It seems the Princess has taken out the majority of the intruders with her bow. Two were left alive. She sent word for a cart to bring them back. I believe Hugoth intends to question them on what they know."

"Could this have been a rogue group?" Jahnise asked hoping for an answer very similar to yes.

"Highly doubtful, King."

Jahnise lifted the high end of his stick to his chin and pressed it into flesh. "My good friend, I was hoping for another answer which would not sound as foreboding."

"Yes, King, me too. I'm afraid it is too late for that."

"It seems to be the case, Bongi. What do we do now? If the intruders are taken care of...what now?" Jahnise's dark, caring eyes looked intensely at Bongi.

"I don't know, King. I don't know. I assume we need to seek Hugoth's opinion on that matter."

## 30

"Frederick, where are you?" Mystic padded to the back of the room very aware that his claws made an irritating noise on the polished rock floor. For obvious reasons, this room commanded a high degree of reverence.

"Follow the first aisle all the way to the back of the room then look up!"

Mystic did as he was told. He spotted Frederick higher up on a wide ladder with small cart wheels on the bottom, set so the ladder could be pushed parallel with the wall. "What have you found up there?"

"This wall has what I think have to be burial slots cut in to it. There are hundreds of them and most of them are sealed and there are tags. These tags say no more than the collars and leg bands. On every one of them you will find the full given name of the creature, a brief description of their life and how they died."

Bubba walked around the corner. "I found the same thing. Most of the tags I've read say died in service or lost in service or sacrificed in service."

"Sacrificed in service? What does that mean?" Mystic's curiosity jumped a level.

"No idea," replied Bubba as he turned another corner heading back to the front of the room. "Where did they put all of the rock they carved out of this place? Did they dig a gigantic hole in the lower levels to put it in?"

"I don't know. Maybe they did." Mystic found Frederick moving above him again. "Frederick." He turned back to Bubba, "Wait what? You can't dig a big hole in a mountain and then fill it with rock from another big hole in the mountain!" He shook that one off. "Sometimes that Cheetah says the most random things."

"Hey," Bubba called back, "They had to put it somewhere."

"Oh mercy. Frederick have you found any familiar names yet?"

"No, still looking. There is no order here except the one in which they died. There are more abbreviations. I think they might have something to do with the individual's rank and file or social standing. Who knows?" Frederick kept reading and rolling. "Mystic, there are a lot of aisles here. Pick a few and do some reading of your own. The more we know of these souls, the better."

Bubba was heading back in their direction. "There are no souls here, Frederick. There are only bodies. The souls have moved on. Souls inhabit bodies, bodies do not inhabit souls." The Cheetah kept searching for something he had no idea of.

"Another figure of speech Bubba, I apologize."

"Still wrong." The Cheetah was going one way with his feet and another way with his mind.

Frederick swung around to watch Bubba. There was something peculiar in the way he was acting. He flagged down Mystic as he made his way down another aisle. He waved him to the bottom of the ladder. "I wish you would stay a little closer to Bubba. He's acting strange. Something may be bothering him. Something is definitely on his mind."

"Where is he?"

Frederick pointed down the last aisle Bubba wandered into. Mystic nodded and hurried off to find him. Frederick returned to his research.

Mystic caught up with Bubba and followed him from an adjacent aisle. He watched quietly as Bubba read every tag on every creature. Then, for no reason known to the Wolf, Bubba stopped in his tracks and sat down staring directly at the next creature. A smile appeared on the Cheetah's face as he slowly contemplated what he saw.

Mystic kept his pace consistent as he accidentally turned down Bubba's row. When he caught up to him, the Cheetah was still staring at the same spot. Mystic said nothing as he sat at Bubba's side. He, too, was caught up in the sight holding the Cheetah's attention. They both sat there gawking in silence.

Frederick climbed down the ladder. The silence was beginning to bother him. He walked Bubba's aisle and soon found the four-leggers mesmerized with the creatures in front of them. "What have you found, Bubba?" Then Frederick saw it too.

"What do you think two-legger?" asked Bubba.

"Oh my," Frederick replied.

"I was beginning to expect this." Bubba cut his eyes, "How about you?"

"Uh uh, not at all," replied Frederick.

Mystic continued to stare at the sight blankly, "Now what?"

# 31

Hugoth ducked into the entrance of "The Path to Where I Was". He covered the distance from the Burg in short time. He wasn't Cheetah fast, but he could hold his own and his stamina was remarkable. As he entered the thick hedge hiding the path's entrance, a loud voice called to him.

"Hugoth, wait for me, son." It was Mystic the Great Eagle. After witnessing the earlier events, he flew high and spotted Hugoth's travels, giving him time to read the Grizzly's intentions. "What have you in mind?"

"Mystic, thank you for finding me. The events are coming together too quickly for me. I needed some space. I need some time to think."

"As only you should, Hugoth, as only you should. I came to find you after witnessing Princess Madaliene's…uh…I don't know how to say this nicely. Her…she…uh…Hugoth…with her bow and arrow, she decimated the group of intruders. She put eight of them down from halfway up the mountain. She wounded two more. The last one, well…she let him bring on his end with his inconsiderate ways. One of the Cats took him out."

"What are you telling me, Mystic? Did she give them no chance to show themselves and surrender to her?"

"No, Hugoth, she did not. It was apparent to me that the intruders shot first and Madaliene ended it soon after that. It was a frightening show of marksmanship. She is not to be messed with."

"From the sound of it, you are correct." The look on Hugoth's face was not readily describable. "Did she leave any survivors to question?"

"She absolutely did. She wounded one of them so he could not escape. The remaining breathing one gave up wisely. The big Cats were instructed to guard the captives until a cart arrived to carry them back to the Burg for you to question."

"I'm afraid I can't do that right now. I must get back to my Burg. Where is Hemoth? He could...?"

"Unfortunately not. He is with the Princess. They are headed, like you, to your Burg. Lightning is showing them the way."

"So you are telling me that Ciruss, Luiperd and Duister are guarding the captives?"

"I guess I am, yes."

"What if they get hungry?"

"Yes, I thought about that, too. The Princess did give them specific instructions not to eat the captives. Strangely enough, she said they could eat the others if they liked."

"You are kidding, right?"

"No, that is what she said."

"I hope she was not serious. Those Cats don't need to taste legger blood any time soon. It's been difficult enough to wean them off of it as it is."

"So what do we do then, Hugoth? What do you want me to do? Shall I fly for the princess?"

"She really told the Cats they could eat the dead ones? Oh my. That girl is going to be trouble."

Mystic agreed, "Understatement for the ages, Hugoth."

"Did anyone find Ian? He must secure all of the windows. We can't let anymore cracks develop. Until further word from me, all windows are sealed. Under no circumstances will anyone be called in or allowed out of Nuorg. Take care of it, Mystic. We are spread to thin too be a viable defense right now. I must do what I need in the tunnels. Please bring Madaliene, Hemoth and Lightning to me immediately after you give my instructions to Ian."

"Do you think it may be time?"

"Yes, I do. And tell Jahnise to get that stick of his ready."

"I am on my way, Hugoth."

"Mystic, sir?"

The old Eagle turned back to face Hugoth. "Yes?"

"Please be safe and fly fast before it is too late."

"No worries, Hugoth. I have lived my life for moments like these."

With a final twitch of his wings, Mystic was off to locate Ian. His tasks were not as daunting as they were critical to the next stage of the plan, a plan that was not yet set in stone or finalized in any fashion. Hugoth needed to formulate that plan immediately.

***

Luiperd stared maliciously at Willem, licking his lips to add another dimension of terror to the frightened intruder's experience. Ciruss eyed Lawrence with the same type of glare. Duister circled behind the two-leggers with a low, horrifyingly treacherous growl emanating from his throat.

Lawrence shook uncontrollably. Willem spent the trying times holding his eyes shut tightly for short periods of time. Thousands of perspiration beads made his scrawny facial features glisten.

"Lawrence, will they eat us as the girl mentioned? If they are going to, let them do it quickly."

"No Willem, please stop carrying on like that. She gave them permission to eat the dead ones and we are not dead yet."

"Yet is a key word there, Lawrence." Had Willem opened his eyes he would have seen the sinister smile and bright white fangs Luiperd so proudly bared. Fortunately for the intruders, the Cats had already eaten their Nuorg-mandated meals for the day. Their stomachs were full, but their playfulness was never quenched.

Duister passed behind Ciruss. "Can you believe these two? They have not yet discussed anything between themselves of any importance to us. May I provoke them a tiny bit? They must know something."

"I can't believe it either, cousin. What do you have in mind?"

"I was thinking…maybe we could scare them into talking. What if they know something that can help Hugoth decide what we should do? What if they know where the next intrusion will take place?"

"What if the next intrusion has already taken place?" Luiperd rose to his feet and began sniffing around Lawrence's neck, the Cat's heavy breath falling mercilessly about the two-legger's senses. "Oh, I don't know, Duister, why can't we eat one of them? The remaining one should tell all after that don't you think?" The Black Leopard continued tormenting the profusely perspiring intruder.

"We don't eat leggers here, Luiperd. You know that." Ciruss had trouble reading the Leopard on occasions and this was fast becoming exactly one of those times. "Remember? They taste fatty? Too much salt?"

"Yes, I did say something like that Ciruss, but I am more concerned about preserving our way of life above. I mean this plan, so far, is very complicated. Now that the princess has shown herself, things may get easier, however...that is not promised." Luiperd sniffed Lawrence's ears. "This legger needs a bath in the river."

Duister's ears perked up. "Ciruss, we should have thought of that sooner. Luiperd...wonderful idea!"

Ciruss was confused. "What is going on with you two?"

Duister answered, "Isn't it obvious? We take these two down to the river for a swim of sorts."

"We can't do that. We were instructed to wait on the cart."

"Very well, when the cart arrives, we will take them to the river first and then to the Burg."

"Charming idea, Duister." Luiperd continued to terrify the captives with hungry looks. "Who knows, after a swim in the river, they might even taste good." With that said, Luiperd roared ferociously into the ears of both two-leggers.

"Lawrence! They are going to eat us! I know it. They are not even sniffing after our fellow crusaders. They are only interested in us, in eating us."

"Willem, what did our leader tell us? Did he not say we were just the first of several infiltrations? Others will come for us. Don't let these Cats get the best of you."

"I can't believe you are saying that. That dark one there has you sized up for his next meal and the big Tiger is eying me like a dessert. I don't have a clue what the other one is thinking. If you ask me, she is the weak and stupid one...just sits there while the other two size us up."

Willem said the wrong thing. Had he known he was understood by all of the Cats, he would have chosen his words more appropriately. Ciruss was on him before he could shut his eyes again. A shrill cry escaped from his mouth as Ciruss walloped him with a pulverizing slap of her paw across the side of his head. The intruder fell back silently to the ground. Ciruss immediately was in Lawrence's face yelling at him as if he were a Talker. All Lawrence heard before he fainted were bone-chilling roars.

"If I had not made my promise all those years ago, you infinitesimal waste of two-legger flesh, I would rip you to pieces and feed you to the carrion! How dare you?" She raised a paw to flatten Lawrence. Fortunately for the two-legger, Luiperd barely managed to subdue the fury of the swat by catching Ciruss' front leg in his jaws.

Duister joined in to get Ciruss back under control. The two Cats muscled the irate Tigress away from Lawrence. He was now shaking uncontrollably.

"Ciruss! What was that for? You nearly killed him the first time you bashed him and your claws were sprung for the second time. What did you intend to do?" Duister pleaded with her to calm down.

Ciruss was livid. "I fully intended to cut that sniveling garbage in half!"

Luiperd spoke with a very calming demeanor. "Ciruss, Ciruss...you know why we are here. You know our mission. Please do not let your temper ruin what we...what every creature here wants to accomplish."

Duister raised his brow. "That sounds very unlike you, Luiperd. Are you alright?"

Luiperd rolled his eyes. "Please, Duister. Do you really think I am as vile as I act?"

"Well one never knows. It's hard to read you."

"And that is just how I like it." He focused again on Ciruss. "Now, Ciruss, are we to expect anymore of those outbursts from you?"

"That poor excuse for a human called me weak and stupid. I am not weak and stupid. Now if you don't mind, you can both release me now."

Lawrence watched in terror. From his point of view the Leopard and large Tiger just saved his life. He struggled to locate Willem laying flat on the ground behind him, with a huge, growing welt covering nearly his whole plump face. Blood trickled from his nose. He watched as the Cats appeared to converse with each other. A change of heart had not entered his mind. He spoke loudly, "If you only knew what was coming, you would release me and run fast for your life. Those that follow me will not be as unprepared as my group was. They will deal with your army of archers and make rugs out of each of your hides!"

That could have easily been the last thing he ever said. Instead, Duister retracted his claws at the last second, just before his paw made contact with Lawrence's shoulder. The two-legger was not killed. He was, however, knocked unconscious and to his right approximately two paces. He landed with a thud, struggling for his next breath. His future breaths would become more and more painful as his entire rib cage began to heal.

"Whoa, Duister, that was efficient." Luiperd snickered.

"You know, you can only take so much."

Ciruss shook her head. "So, it wasn't just me then?"

"I apologize, Ciruss. Some of these two-leggers are more than I can tolerate. How can they be so condescending, yet so small and fragile at the same time?"

Luiperd nodded, "What would change in their world if they knew we could understand them?"

"My thought as well." Ciruss huffed, "Why can't they understand we have feelings too? We have our families, our friends, our way of life. Who said the world belongs only to them?"

Duister leaned over Willem with disgust. "What do you know, fat little legger? What does your friend over there know? It would be wise of you to tell us."

***

Lightning led Hemoth and Perrie as best he could remember towards "The Path to Where I am Going". Madaliene clung tight to Hemoth's neck, sound asleep. Mystic, the Great Eagle, spotted them shortly after rising to his comfortable soaring altitude, winging along with full pursuit beats. "There they are. Bless Lightning, he is doing a splendid job leading the way." The old Eagle smiled.

"Lightning, how much further do we have to go?" Hemoth was in a hurry to meet back up with a Nuorgian. There were too many questions forming in his mind.

"Once we get to the path, it will lead us there straightaway."

"Fine, how far from here is the path?" Hemoth was antsy.

"Not so sure about that, Hemoth. If we keep traveling in this direction, it will find us. We should be coming up on Sweet Gulley pretty soon. We can take a break there."

"Break? We don't need a break. We need to get where we are going!"

"Why can't the ax-pike take us there?" Perrie felt anxious to get somewhere too.

"The ax-pike, Perrie, takes us where we need to be, not necessarily where we want to be." Lightning sounded sure of himself.

"Then," the Falcon continued, "Why should we not go where we need to be then?"

"The young winger asks a decent question, Lightning." Hemoth agreed with Perrie's assessment.

"You will get no argument from me. I am following Madaliene's instructions to the letter. You saw what she did back there. I don't want on the ugly side of that one, I'll tell you!"

Hemoth pondered the moment. "Perrie, can you nudge Princess awake? Don't startle her, but I think we need to use Lightning's ax-pike to take us where we need to be."

"Okay, Hemoth, I'll give it a try." She hopped next to the sleeping princess and began softly prodding her from sleep. "Madaliene, Madaliene, we need to speak with you. Can you wake for us?"

After several pleas, Madaliene managed to rouse from her deep and needed sleep. "Yes sweet Falcon, how can I help you?"

"Hemoth, Lightning, she is awake. You may ask your question." Perrie stood proudly beside the brave youngster.

"Princess, it has come to our attention that we may be needed somewhere other than where we are headed. We are asking your permission to use Lightning's device to take us to that very place. What say you? Can we proceed with that plan?" Hemoth continued a steady pace as Madaliene tossed the questions around in her mind.

"Do you feel like another adventure, Lightning?" Madaliene was coming around, her body a little groggy, but her mind sharp.

"I'm beginning to feel up for anything. What do you have in mind?"

"Hemoth, let's see where that ax thingy of Lightning's thinks we should be. Are you in?"

Hemoth slowed his steady pace to a stop. "Do I really have any choice, Princess?"

Madaliene jumped down from Hemoth's back and pounced in front of him, her face dwarfed by the Grizzly's mammoth head. She reached up to the sides of his face and grabbed two fists full of fur, pulling his eyes down to her level. "In a word...no!" Madaliene laughed out loud. "No. None of us have a choice. Lightning, tell that thing to take us wherever we need to be!"

Perrie looked on as Madaliene joyfully bounced around the Bears.

"Madaliene, are you sure about this?"

"No Perrie, I'm not sure about this. I'm not sure about anything anymore. I am feeling I was born for this type of thing!"

Perrie was not completely satisfied. "But Madaliene, eight two-leggers are no longer alive because of your bow and arrows. Has that not affected you at all?"

"Perrie, they shot first. Had they not shot first, I would not have reacted as I did. It was either them or us, was it not?"

"I can see your point...I think."

"Come now, Perrie, what if they had shot Hemoth or Lightning or me? How would you have felt then? We are past the point of weighing our options. I feel this entire land of Nuorg is my responsibility, is it not? They have been expecting me and now I am their princess. Is it not the duty of a princess to protect those loyal to her? I certainly won't take a threat on your life lightly, nor one to either of our two large friends here. Enough of this talk. Lightning, where do we need to be?"

Lightning bowed his head slightly to Madaliene. "One moment, Princess. Gather tightly." He held his ax-pike in front of him and asked the simple question. "Where should we be?"

***

The Golden Eagle flew as slow as possible as he led the cart to the captives. The two-leggers pushed the team of Horses as hard as possible. It wasn't long before the Golden began his descent to the side of the mountain. The driver noticed the change and begged the Horses for a little more speed. They obliged. Soon the clanking and creaking of the cart was heard by the Cats.

"Ciruss," Luiperd called, "I think we have company."

Duister loped down the path to lead the cart and company in. Ciruss quietly made her way to the still unconscious Lawrence. She gently slapped his face around a few times to wake him. She was hoping he would awake with stabbing pains in his sides.

The two-legger came around shortly. His eyes no longer bore the fire of disdain, they were foggy and swollen. One entire side of his chest was swelling; no doubt the result of several broken ribs.

"What do you want from me now?" The question dribbled from his lips. "Why don't you just kill me?" He knew the Tiger could not understand him. "You will be the first one to go if I have my..."

Ciruss put her paw over Lawrence's mouth to keep him quiet. If he didn't talk to her, then she wouldn't get angry. "Luiperd, can you try to wake the other one?"

Luiperd nonchalantly stepped to the side of Willem. A roar of gigantic proportions shocked Willem conscious. The intruder lay still and silent looking up at Luiperd with a mixture of hate and anguish. The Leopard laughed, "Ciruss, he is awake now." The black Leopard looked at Willem's bruised face with disgust. "It would so please me, two-legger, if you were dead." He turned to the oncoming cart. "You might want to load this one first. He may not make it all the way back alive. He gave us more trouble than the other one over there."

The lead Horse saw the bodies of the other intruders past Ciruss. "What happened here? Were any of you hurt? Where's the girl and her Bears?"

"All of that carnage was caused by that girl. She taught us a lesson none of us are soon to forget."

The second Horse snorted, "I count eight dead over there. You say the Princess took them all? How is that possible?

The two-leggers with the cart were not Talkers. They began to gently load Willem and Lawrence on the back of the cart. Lawrence mumbled something to one of them. "Why are you helping those vile animals? Where are you taking us?"

"We are taking you in for questioning and I suggest you tell us all we want to know or it won't be a pleasant end for either of you."

"What about my wounds? What about his face? How can we talk to you when we are so close to death?"

"From the looks of it, lad, you are not that close to death's mighty door. Louis, does this lad look near death to you?"

"Why no, Nathan, he looks like a perfectly fine bloke to me."

"See there, you, we think you look more than healthy." Lawrence was taken aback by the cart handler's apathy. "I don't believe this! You two are cohorts with these creatures! How can you possibly turn your back on your kind? Why…"

Nathan pressed a calloused, strong hand over Lawrence's mouth. "Listen to me, intruder, if I had found you first, you'd be like your friends over there. I have no tolerance for the likes of you. We are here, minding our business and you come creeping into our land like some kind of killer disease. You and your others, what would they have done to us if you had found us first? Huh? Would you have shown us any mercy? I don't think so. Best for you if you answer our questions and stop asking your own." He took a strong rope and wrapped it tightly, too tightly around Lawrence's hands then tied him to Willem and the both of them to the side of the cart.

"Nathan, it would be a terrible oversight on our part if one of these fell off the cart? Seems to me if one fell off, the other would follow and we would not be able to hear them cry for help since both of their mouths will be gagged." Louis immediately stuffed a wet rag into both of the captives mouth then secured it with a large brightly colored towel. "There, that should hold them for most of the ride back."

"Indeed it should, Louis." Nathan climbed up to the seat and politely asked the Horses to head back.

Willem and Lawrence looked at each other, terrified.

The lead Horse winked at Ciruss on the way out. "Tigress, when you get back to our Burg, if you come that way, will you please explain to me how the Princess did that?" He threw his head toward the eight unfortunate intruders.

Ciruss smiled back at him, "I will certainly try, sir." She called to Luiperd and Duister, "Shall we head back as well?"

"I think so, Ciruss. I didn't like what I was hearing about more intruders. We need to plan a strategy to protect Nuorg against those on the way."

Luiperd walked slowly between the dead intruders, sniffing each as he went. "For the breath in me, I don't know why two-leggers think we actually like to eat them…they stink so badly." He took a last sniff, "Just awful," before running to catch the cart.

*** 

As was the case in the earlier events, nothing of any spectacular note happened after Lightning asked his question. With a very orderly process, the ax-pike transported the group to their next location. They emerged out in the open, next to a well-used road leading to or from what seemed to be some kind of camp. The sun was setting in the west, not a cloud in the sky, a full orange moon floating lonely in the east.

"We are not in Nuorg anymore, are we?" Madaliene was the first to notice.

Hemoth was disturbed. "Madaliene, we are out in plain sight! What if someone saw us appear? We have to find cover quickly."

332

Madaliene looked around frantically. "There is no cover here, Hemoth! There is no place to go. Perrie, fly high. See what is around here and who or what may have seen us!"

Perrie said nothing, she was off.

"Lightning, I wish you had some control of that device of yours."

Hemoth was not afraid, he was wary.

"Madaliene instructed me to use it. You two know, as well as I, we have no control over this, none at all." He took in their new surroundings. This looks nothing like Nuorg or the Great Forest. It looks like a place soon to be full of two-leggers."

Perrie floated high above. She saw a gathering of two-leggers far off to the west, nothing closer. There was a high stand of reeds to the east. It could possibly provide a temporary place to hide and plan. But plan for what? She flew back to Madaliene.

"How far is it from here?" Hemoth began to head off.

"Wait, Hemoth! We are here for a purpose and hiding is not that purpose." Madaliene was determined to do what needed to be done here and move on.

"Well? What do you plan on doing, Princess?" Hemoth knew she was correct.

Madaliene twisted her bow in her hands. "Okay, this is what I'm going to do." She kneeled to the ground and opened up Frederick's bag. "Here is some food to tide you two giants over until Perrie and I get back. Get off this path so you won't be seen. We are heading toward the two-leggers."

Lightning's face turned hard. "You will not go anywhere without me!"

Hemoth concurred. "He is speaking only a half-truth, Madaliene. You will not be going without me either. Not on your young life. Am I making myself blatantly clear to you?"

"Great, Hemoth, thank you very much for your concern. However, I will be going only with Perrie."

"No, you won't."

"Yes, I will!"

"No, you will not!"

"I will too!"

"Not a ..."

Perrie noticed movement behind the arguing pair. "Excuse me, Princess. We have visitors approaching from behind you."

333

"Yes, I most certainly will and you can't...what, Perrie?" Madaliene stopped arguing long enough to answer.

"That's right. We have visitors...behind you."

Madaliene whirled around. "I don't see anything."

"Believe me, they are coming. I can see much farther than you can, Princess."

"Oh fine then. Hemoth, can you and Lightning move farther over there?" She placed the food back in the bag and stood up. She made a gesture to her left. "If we need you, you will know it. If we do, don't waste time getting back here."

"Are you sure?" asked Lightning.

"Yes. Now go quickly."

The Grizzlies hurried away. They struggled to blend in with the surroundings. Perrie watched as they attempted to lay their huge bodies tight to the ground. "Princess, that is funny." From where they stood, the two Bears appeared as two large furry rocks in the distance.

Madaliene walked towards the oncoming visitors. "Nothing like facing a problem head-on, is there, Perrie?"

"Nothing at all, Princess, nothing at all."

"Why are you calling me Princess now?"

"It seems to fit."

"Okay, but not in front of these visitors...right?"

"Right."

Madaliene walked to meet the crowd coming her way with her usual athletic grace, a stunning grin spread across her face. She shook her wild mane of hair and the sunlight enhanced its radiance to an eye-popping extent. She exuded confidence and tenacity. As the visitors neared, her grin faded slightly. Soon, she was standing directly in front of a large group of bedraggled people. She noticed most of them were children, her age or younger. A few weary adults were interspersed among them. Her face became stern and void of any cheerful hints. The crowd split around her and kept walking. No one said even a word. The state of their clothes combined with the look on their faces suggested a long period of defeat.

"Wait! All of you stop where you are!" She called to the Bears, "Hemoth, Lightning, come here quickly. Stop this group!"

There quickly seemed to be no leader of the group. They fearfully looked to each other for understanding, everyone fidgeting nervously.

"Now! Someone speak to me!" Princess Madaliene intended to get immediate answers.

A meek lone voice came from the group. "What would you expect us to say to you, girl? What do you want from us?"

Madaliene stepped up to the young boy. "I would expect answers to my questions for starters. I mean really, is that asking too much?"

"We have no answers for you or anybody else."

"How can you not have answers? My questions are simple enough." Madaliene was worried. She reached into Frederick's bag and pulled out a large apple and handed it to the boy. "Will this persuade you to talk?"

Before he could accept the apple, a larger boy ripped it from Madaliene's grasp. He began devouring it. "Excuse me?" Madaliene wrestled the apple from the larger boy's arm, nearly breaking it. "Did I offer this to you?" She defiantly handed the apple back to the young boy. "Eat this. If anyone else wants to take something from me, I would seriously advise against it."

One of the older leggers spoke. "Don't blame him Miss, we are all famished. The sight of anything to eat may very well send us all into a fit of chaos. What else do you have in that bag?"

The crowd pressed in, making Madaliene uneasy. Afraid to lash out at any particular person, she grabbed the large boy and separated him from the crowd. She cut her eyes to the lone adult brave enough to speak. "You need to persuade your friends here to take a few steps back and we can discuss this. I do not want anyone taking anything from anybody again. Is that understood?"

The boy had no energy to fight back. He was completely under Madaliene's control. Begrudgingly, the crowd fell back.

"She must be one of them!" Someone cried.

Another shouted, "We must run again!"

Behind the crowd a thunderous chorus of roars blasted through the assembled distrust and fear. Hemoth and Lightning stood on their hind legs, towering over the weak two-leggers.

"Save us, girl! Take your bow and kill these Bears before they kill us all!"

Madaliene shouted, "All of you get on the ground immediately! Now!"

Like a herd of beaten Dogs, the entire group of visitors fell shivering to the ground. Moans and crying erupted. Madaliene looked at Hemoth, then to Lightning. "Can some creature please tell me what is happening here?" The Princess was beside herself. "I don't think I can handle this."

The young boy, holding the apple stood up. "Are you a Ta...Tal...Talker? Are you speaking to those Bears? Do they want to kill us?" The fallen crowd hushed.

"What did you say, boy? Am I a Talker?" Madaliene raised her head to Hemoth. She shrugged her shoulders. Again she spoke to the boy, "Yes, I am a Talker. Are there others like me around here?"

An older man stood up, "No little lady, there are no Talkers around here anymore. They were all rounded up and punished years ago. Hardly a one survived. Those that did died soon after from their wounds. The boy's grandfather was the last one to die. Most of our townsfolk were taken prisoner. We are the only ones left. I guess you should say we were the weaker ones. I guess the enemy didn't need us. We have barely survived since they destroyed our lives."

Madaliene's face registered shock. "You will have to tell me more, sir, but wait..." She reached into Frederick's bag and began tossing edibles to all. Again, she turned inquisitive eyes to Hemoth. She didn't have to say anything. It suddenly dawned on them why they were here.

***

Bongi stood next to Jahnise as Stewig and Donkhorse approached them from different directions. Rakki and Karri dropped in momentarily. There were looks of concern on each face.

"It looks like I walked up on a funeral here." Donkhorse was the least melancholy of the bunch. "Why all of the gloom?"

Bongi searched the skies for any sign of an Eagle. "I can't really say right now. I need to speak with Mystic soon. That, my friends, is a definite."

"Bongi, would you like for us to track him down?" Karri read the concern in Bongi's voice.

"If you would be so kind, yes. Please find him. I don't have a good feeling about any of this. How was a herd of assorted four-leggers, wingers and cast-offs from the world up there supposed to fend this off? Can anybody answer that question?" Bongi's simple question held enormous implications.

As the group solemnly stood staring off into the distance, a commotion arose behind them. A young girl, crying hysterically, somehow managed to keep her dignity as she made her way quickly through the sparse crowd. "Bongi! Bongi! Come quickly. It's Father. He is hurt badly. Mother stayed with him. Please follow me! My brother is...is, my brother was taken. Hurry!" Before Bongi could answer her, Ian's daughter raced back to her father. She stopped and turned back to Bongi, "Are you coming or not?"

"Go Karri, find him. Rakki come with us."

Bongi, Stewig and Donkhorse followed Ian's distraught daughter through the Burg. Jahnise trailed behind for obvious reasons.

"Donkhorse, new friend, please...may I ride your back?"

Donkhorse pulled to a stop. "Certainly, King." Jahnise climbed aboard.

Bongi soon caught the distraught youngster. "Oliviia, Oliviia! Where are we headed?"

"To the tunnels."

"What tunnels? I know of no tunnels! Get on my back and hold tight. We can get there quicker if you are riding."

Olivia struggled up on Bongi's tall, sloping back. She wrapped her arms tightly around his smooth neck. "Please hurry, Bongi. Please hurry!"

***

Ian tried to keep his breathing normal. With each breath, droplets of blood intermingled with saliva, forming nauseating pink spittle. "We tried, dear. We tried."

Colleen Mecanelly cradled her husband's head in her lap. She sat slumped on the cold hard floor with crumpled folds of her dress cushioning him, a pool of blood seeping across the floor. "Don't you talk such as that, Ian. We have tried, aye and we will continue to try. There is not enough evil afore us to give up anything now."

"Where are the children?" He wanted only to focus on his mission, still his mind drifted where it was meant to be. "Are they well?"

"Livvy went for help, Ian. Patrick did not fare as well. I'm afraid he was taken back through the crack. Emiliia went after Patrick. They care for each other so much, dear, we have done well by them. They will succeed even if we don't."

"What do you mean by that, love?"

"Ian, this blood we are resting in…it's not only yours. I am of the mind that I'm right there with you."

"You too?"

"Afraid so. I was able to get a good stab in the last one through, but the one in front of him got me. I'm afraid that I won't be making it either."

"What of the children?"

"Like I said, dear Husband, we have done right by them. We have given them all we can. It's time to let them go." Tears streamed unabashedly down Colleen's beautiful face. The years had been kind to her. She was a magnificent woman. Slowly her bright, blue eyes hazed over.

"I agree with you, love, we need to let them go. Do you still have the ledger?"

"Yes Ian, I have it. Seems even the vilest of thieves has a modicum of modesty." She pulled a small book from beneath her vest and laid it on Ian's chest. "Here it is, like I said."

Ian somehow managed to place his index finger on the book's cover. He felt the embossed letters across its top. "One, two, three, four, five." He steadied his finger atop the fifth letter. "Love, do you think this will do it?"

"I can only hope it does, dear. And if you didn't know already, I have loved you since I first set me blue eyes upon you." She gently kissed his ashen forehead.

"Oh Colleen, you have been more than I could have asked for. God knew exactly what I needed in a woman. I have loved you from the first moment I saw you. Let us both pray we did the right thing."

"I think we did, Ian. It's time to let this life go, shall we?"

"Indeed…"

Ian squeezed Colleen's hand as tightly as he could as they breathed their last breaths together. The world kept spinning as they made their exit.

***

"We are almost there Bongi! Keep running." Oliviia urged the four-leggers on.

A clump of strange trees amid a grove of strange trees awaited them as they neared the southern wall. At the base of the wall one stone was left unturned. Oliviia jumped from Bongi's back, ran to the stone and turned it. Mechanizations began to labor. Bongi and Stewig looked at each other, very confused.

"Did you know of this?" Stewig asked.

"No I did not. I never heard a thing about it."

"The mysteries of Nuorg abound, Bongi. When will we know them all?"

"Aha my friends, mysteries are everywhere." Jahnise sat atop Donkhorse watching as the events unfolded. "The world above is a mystery to me. This place is a mystery to me. Mysteries are life, each with a mystery of their own."

"Come on!" The opening was now clear to all. Oliviia beckoned to the large four-leggers. "It's plenty big for each of you to enter. Please hurry!"

Jahnise entered first, after Oliviia. Next came Bongi, Donkhorse, Rakki and Stewig. Oliviia pushed hard on a large stone near the floor, the opening closed once again.

"Please, young one, promise me one day you will tell me more about this place." Jahnise rested his large, caring hand on her shoulder.

"Yes sir, one day. They are down here." She lit a small torch with a flint and led them down the single corridor. "Please, please... please."

None of the leggers bothered with the surroundings. There was one way in and one way out, or at least that is what they thought.

Ahead a soft light illuminated Ian and Colleen. They looked the same as when Oliviia left earlier. Jahnise took the lead. "Girl, please stay here with Bongi. If any intruders returned, let them take me and not you. Stewig, come running if you see trouble."

"No. I will not. I am coming with you right now!"

"No, girl, you will not. Stewig, keep her here until it is safe."

"Yes, King." Stewig blocked Oliviia's path. "Oliviia, you will stay here. Do you understand?"

Reluctantly Oliviia agreed. "Yes, Stewig."

As Jahnise approached the couple, his insides troubled him. Everything was too quiet. There were no moans of pain or whispers of life. He came to their side. It was obvious they had taken their last breaths gently and in love. He placed his hands over each face, sliding down his caring fingers and closing two pairs of lifeless eyes.

Kneeling by them, he uttered a silent prayer, then, he noticed Ian's finger pointing at the fifth letter in the title of his journal. "Well done Mister Ian. Well done."

Oliviia saw it all too clearly. She burst past Stewig, running at full speed. "No!"

Her mournful wail reverberated hauntingly through every crevice and every fissure in every rock in every tunnel beneath the Land of Nuorg.

## The end

# Glossary

**(Bird)let** -- (bird' let) Any bird older than a hatchling and younger than a tweenst.

**Bark kake**--(kak) Small muffin-like snacks of the Great Forest made from any favorite ingredient. When dry these delicacies resemble tree bark in look and texture, thus the name.

**Charge**--Any creature who has been assigned a protector.

**Four-legger**--(4' leg gar), The animals' word for all creatures that travel on four legs.

**Kaki**--(ka' ke), A sweet confection of Nuorg, eaten separately or with meals. Made with generous amounts of Sweet Gulley goo.

**Protectors**--Creatures of any kind assigned charges.

**Secret sharer**--One of a group of elders in a pack burdened by experience and wisdom.

**Sky-traveler / Winger** --A winged creature that does not depend on its feet for anything other than standing.

**Two-legger** --(too' leg gar), The animals' word for a human being, male or female.

**Twos**--A term used condescendingly by the four-leggers of the Far North to describe two-leggers.

**Water-livver / Swimmer**--Any of a number of creatures who live their entire life below the water's surface. A high source of protein when eaten by leggers. They have absolutely no personality.

**Watcher**--A sentinel or guard

# About the Author

Chris McCollum lives with his wife of 24 years, Jeanne Coffman McCollum, and their 2 children, Christopher and Madilynn, in Franklin, Tennessee. A longtime fan of J.R.R. Tolkien, C.S. Lewis, Clive Cussler, McCartney/Lennon and many more varied wordsmiths, he has spent the better part of his life crafting words into some form or another whether it be short stories, bedtime stories, anecdotes, poems or songs. Fortunately for him, his parents allowed lots of room for creativity in his early years. Originally from West Tennessee, He has made his home in Franklin, Tennessee for the last 32 years.

Please visit the website: www.landofnuorg.com or follow "The Land of Nuorg" on Facebook.

CPSIA information can be obtained at www.ICGtesting.com
Printed in the USA
LVOW06*1624041215

464652LV00003B/7/P